THE THIN LINES BETWEEN PAST, PRESENT,
AND FUTURE VANISH WHEN YOU LOSE...

CONTROL

"Reading *Control* . . . one cannot afford to miss a
word. Do so and you're traveling through a maze without
a string around your finger. . . . Those of us who love
thrillers have bottomless appetites for blind seers with
Seeing Eye dogs, killers with hands like hams, and women
to whom something terrible happens at Bloomingdale's."
—Mary Cantwell, *The New York Times*

"Dazzling. . . . The wit and dash of the style, the virtuosity
of the plotting, the absorbing quirkiness of the characters,
and the boldness of its raid upon the bizarre make Gold-
man's latest psychological thriller a dazzling entertain-
ment." —*Publisher's Weekly*

"Vivid . . . highly complex. . . . Reads as though composed
with nerves jangling and emotions at high pitch."
—*John Barkham Reviews*

"Filled with psychological menace and shocking plot
twists. . . . The reader will be left breathless."
—*B. Dalton Merchandise Bulletin*

WILLIAM GOLDMAN

CONTROL

A DELL BOOK

Published by
Dell Publishing Co., Inc.
1 Dag Hammarskjold Plaza
New York, New York 10017

For information address Delacorte Press,
New York, New York.

Dell ® TM 681510, Dell Publishing Co., Inc.

ISBN: 0-440-11464-0

Reprinted by arrangement with Delacorte Press
Printed in the United States of America
First Dell printing—April 1983

FOR DAVID SHABER

*. . . Many puzzling observations
have turned up in medicine,
psychology, and anthropology.
In all these areas, effects
have been reported that would
seem possibly to be the result
of some sort of psychic causation,
although at this stage it is
impossible, of course, to say
what the explanation is.*

J. B. RHINE
New World of the Mind

PART I

VICTIMS

PART II

TRACKERS

PART III

CONFRONTATIONS

VICTIMS

EDITH

If there was one place in this world Edith never expected trouble, it was Bloomingdale's.

For two reasons, one minor, one major. The minor reason was familiarity: Edith had shopped the store since childhood. The family duplex was at 65th and Park, so when her mother needed to buy her overalls or Mary Janes, logic dictated Bloomingdale's.

Edith's mother never much liked the place. And with good enough reason, since it's difficult for people today to remember that not so long ago, the giant department store at 59th and Lex wasn't much above Macy's in quality, and certainly ranked far below Altman's or Bergdorf's or Saks.

Mrs. Mazursky, a sweet tub, naturally could have afforded cabs anywhere she wanted, but something in her rebelled at the financial waste. She was wealthy now, very, but she had been born middle-class Brooklyn, and even though her body presently inhabited Manhattan's Upper East Side, her soul would never budge from Flatbush Avenue.

By the time Edith was ten, she was allowed to go off to the store alone, on the proviso that she had been good the day before, which Edith generally managed to be only on days ending in *y*. So she would bathe carefully and don her best party dress and take a small purse and skip on over.

And spend, literally, hours. Riding the escalators, and lingering in the toy department, and staring at the foods from all over the world, and sitting in the furniture floor samples while imagining adventures that often involved her having to step in for Nancy Drew when Nancy was mysteriously taken ill, and studying the paintings on the walls in the decorator showrooms, carefully noting how the painting would have altered if she had been dealing with the canvas.

Country children often fantasize on hilltops or in treehouses; Edith's magic place was Bloomingdale's and it kept its hold on her while she grew. No better proof need be given than the simple recounting of the furor Edith caused when she was thirty-two and attending one of Sally Levinson's *very* formal dinner parties.

Sally had been Edith's roommate at Radcliffe, and was her dearest dearest friend. (She was also an anglophile of maddening proportions. A Chicago girl, her English accent would have shamed Alistair Cooke.) Upon graduation, with part of her inheritance, she opened an art gallery on 57th Street. She was aggressive and tasteful and willing to gamble on unknown talent, and soon she had one of the best galleries on 57th Street. Once that fact was established, Sally said "screw" to all the fancies and moved to the Village, and when that became too chic, to SoHo. Eventually she bought a building in TriBeCa before anyone could even spell it, and today people come from this country and abroad to see just what it is that Sally Levinson is up to *now*. Few things still give Sally more pleasure than standing by her windows and watching the rich, with that panicked look in their eyes—ye Gods, where *are* we?—moving along TriBeCa's streets frantically trying to find the sanctuary of the Levinson Gallery.

Sally was born rich but she never thought much about it. She wasn't sure if she'd been born a Lesbian or not, but she knew she was one. She hid it, of course, kept her hair long, wore lots of makeup, dated every weekend at Francis Parker in her teens. She was popular at Radcliffe, probably more than Edith, who became her roommate junior year. They had both wanted singles, the administration had erred, they decided what the hell, let's try it and see.

By Christmas of that year, Sally was terribly, and as it turned out, permanently in love with Edith. Oh, not physically. She would have cut off her hand before it tried to touch.

It was just that if you were Sally, Sally the dyke from Chicago, if you had her demons inside you, dawn and night inside you, you had to love Edith Mazursky, she was just that tranquil, that decent, that nonjudgmental. Edith was simply, in other words, so fucking *good*.

By spring vacation, the time had come to decide on senior year roommates. Edith, one morning over coffee, suggested they continue on. Sally, of course thrilled, simply blew hard into her steaming cup and said that well, she'd have to think about it. Edith, certainly surprised, perhaps hurt, said that well, that was probably a wise thing to do.

Edith took her books and went off to classes. Sally cut her classes and lay alone on her bed, chain smoking. She had always suspected it would be hard the first time she told someone. She never guessed it would be immobilizing. It seemed fair to her that before she accepted Edith's suggestion, Edith know her truth. But more than that, Edith was the first straight person Sally had met who she felt might not just not scorn her, but might even understand.

How to tell, though; how to tell?

That night, late, when Sally came in from "Having a few at the local" as she always put it, Edith was getting ready for sleep, face scrubbed, sitting on the edge of her bed, brushing her thick reddish hair. Sally suspected that if Edith had ego about anything, it was that, her hair; on an Irisher like Maureen O'Hara it was nice enough; on a Jewish girl from Manhattan it was gold.

Sally flopped in the overstuffed chair across the room. "Phillip again?" she asked. Edith had been seeing Phillip Holtzman for several months now and they were obviously in love.

Edith nodded, went on brushing her reddish hair. A hundred strokes, no matter what.

"Ya get in?" Sally wondered.

Edith didn't honor the remark with a reply.

"Well how 'bout bare tit?"

Edith gave Sally a look.

"That's how men talk, isn't it? I mean, tell me that's not the way they go on about us? Gonna marry Phillip?"

Edith put her brush down, sat there in silence, just staring at her roommate. Waiting.

"Me, I wonder if I'll ever marry," Sally said finally. "Where is it fucking written that marriage is ice cream? Sure, if it's kids you're after, I wouldn't want some bastard, that's shitty to the kid, but maybe I'll just"—and now the words came faster—"you wanna screw, you live with some guy, you're bored, it's on to the next, no papers, no contract—or living alone, who's to say that's so terrible—you get horny, you hit your local, pick up some jerk, bring him back, let him plug away for a while, or maybe, or maybe if that's not the answer, then—"

Suddenly from Edith now: "Shh."

Sally quieted.

"I know." And it was clear from her tone that she did know. Everything. And that she didn't much care. Sally got out the vodka, poured herself a double. Edith went back to brushing her hair . . .

So they roomed together senior year, becoming like sisters, spatting like sisters too, often about Sally's anger that Edith pissed away her talent, because it was evident to Sally even then that Edith had the hands *and* the eye, that Edith could paint. Though she rarely did.

On graduation, Edith married Phillip and Sally got terribly angry that Edith was so hidebound by tradition that she wouldn't let Sally be best man at the ceremony.

And when Edith got quickly and happily pregnant Sally went to England where she studied art for two years and came back with that accent that only Edith was allowed to tease her about. And she opened her gallery and began giving parties at her "digs," a large, terraced Fifth Avenue apartment just up from the Pierre, that she bought with another part of her inheritance. The view of the city was startling and different, depending on the time of year.

The parties were more or less the same. A dozen guests. Talented painters, some of them known; endless English, some of them titled. Art critics and art buyers, and Edith and Phillip whenever they wanted to come. The main courses were always fancy French—even Sally couldn't bring herself to inflict shepherd's pie on the unsuspecting. But the wine was always "claret," the appetizer smoked salmon from Fortnum and Mason's.

The Bloomingdale's furor that Edith created happened all very fast. Lady somebody or other, who was seated to Edith's left, had never been to America before and quietly inquired as to where it might be best to shop.

Edith's answer was obvious.

"Bite your tongue," Sally said to Edith, and then to Lady somebody or other, "Edith's a bit of a wag, ignore the child. Bendel's or Bergdorf's would more than suit your needs."

"I prefer Bloomingdale's," Edith replied.

"Ticky-tacky," Sally said.

Edith turned to Lady whatever. "You'll thank me."

"Edith," Sally warned, with just enough of a shift in tone to bring all other conversations to a halt. Phillip, seated between the ladies, had heard and loved these spats for years. He sat there, arms folded, the only one at the table smiling.

"Let her try it and see, Sally . . ."

"—why don't you send our visitors to Lane Bryant, Edith?— no—*no*—I've got it—they can feel really ritzy and visit S. Fucking Klein's—"

"—you're a silly child, Sally Levinson, because I think Bloomingdale's happens to be the greatest department store in the world—"

And now the battle was fully joined. *"Greater than Harrods, you twit?"*

"Far! Yes!! *Now and forever!"*

"Stop her, Phillip," Sally said, reaching for his hand. "Stop her or you'll find me in an early grave."

Alas, it was Edith who found one . . .

The major reason Edith never expected trouble around 59th and Lex was simply this: Edith *never* expected trouble, period. And with good reason. She rarely experienced any. Oh, she broke her arm badly one year at camp. And Kate, her firstborn, came complete with asthma, serious asthma, but again, that was a disease of youth, more often than not, something you outgrew. Her many friends, when they talked about it, considered Edith just an extraordinarily lucky human being.

Not true, not true. She worked at her luck. Relentlessly. From the time she was ten. It was, perhaps, Edith's chief inheritance from her father.

"Who is she?" Mrs. Mazursky screamed. She had to be screaming because Edith, eight and a half, could hear her mother from three rooms away. It was night and past her bedtime, lights had long since gone out, but just the same she left her bed and padded down the hall. Her parents were not screamers. Clearly an Event was taking place, and Events were meant to be Attended.

"Oh Jesus, Myrtle, close it up," Sol Mazursky said. If Edith's mother was a tub, the only word for Sol was "blimp." Even if you adored him, as Edith did, the word had to come to mind. At five three and one ninety-five, svelte he wasn't. And his shape had nothing to do with glands. He ate everything; he was constantly hungry.

"I'll kill her," Myrtle Mazursky went on, louder, her voice just beginning to crack.

"Myrtle, there's no 'her.' I got a nose like Durante and I'm eighty pounds over, who's gonna fall for me?"

"You're rich," Myrtle said.

I didn't know that, Edith thought, just by the open doorway now. And until then, she never had. She just more or less assumed that everybody lived in fifteen-room duplexes on Park Avenue. Or could if they wanted.

"Some riches I got—my wife could get employment shouting at the Fulton Fish Market easy."

"Women will do anything for money. There are plenty of such people."

"Baby, I'm gonna tell you again—I'm going out for a business appointment."

"Don't call me 'baby'—and who has business at ten o'clock at night except monkey business?" And now came a wail. "She's probably a *shiksa.*"

"There's no one else—"

"—liar—"

"—on my *honor,* for Chrissakes—"

"—you're going to see a woman, I can tell it, it's ten o'clock at night and you just put on your best suit and you were *humming* while you knotted your tie, *a wife notices such things—*"

Then a long pause. And after that, softly: "I *am* going to see a woman, a *shiksa,* her name is Kristin with a *K* and she is blond—"

"—I don't want to hear, Sol—"

"—you want to know who the enemy is, don't you? Just shut up and let me tell you. She's just turned twenty-four and she's almost five eight, she *towers* over me, we laugh about it. We laugh about a lot of things. *She* thinks I'm funny, the way my wife once did."

Deep intakes of breath from Myrtle now.

"Kristin lives on 55th Street, just off Third, and when I walk through the door she's gonna give me a big hug, and then she's gonna rumple my hair and lead me to the sofa and offer me a Scotch. I'm gonna say, 'a weak one, maybe,' and she'll make it, like an expert, just the way I like my Chivas. A splash of soda, no ice. And then she's gonna stir it and bring it to me and bend down and hand it over and she'll be wearing a silk blouse but no bra, she doesn't like bras, she doesn't need them, and I'll sit there all smiles and just look up at her and then it'll be *her* turn to sit and guess where she's gonna rest that perfect *tush* of hers."

Pause. Silence.

Now Sol, roaring: "*Right in the lap of Mister Howard K. Kassel- baum of Chicago who keeps her and is who I'm having my goddam business meeting with!*"

"Who is this Kasselbaum?"

"Precisely a question Mrs. Kasselbaum is asking these days. She thought she married a plodder, it turns out he's Errol Flynn. He is also one of the rising stars in the Loop real estate market."

"How could you put me through this?"

"How could you think I was having an affair?"

"Why an appointment this late? Why didn't you have dinner with him?"

"Because I like to eat with my wife, a blossoming shrew. And my daughter. Who I love more even than food. And who at this very moment is up several hours past her bedtime."

Darn, Edith thought, I must have moved my shadow. She hesitated, then entered the huge bedroom rubbing her eyes, yawn- ing, going quickly to her father, giving him a hug.

"No good," her father said. "Ship her back to acting school."

Edith went and hugged her mother.

"How much did you hear?" her father asked.

"Not anything much at all, Daddy."

"How much did you hear?" her father asked. He was not a man who repeated himself frivolously.

"Just from 'Who is she' on."

"Well, ignore it, it was nonsense, just a little show I put on to torment your mother." Now he picked her up. She was quick and bright and pretty and already blessed with her wonderful reddish hair. "Come," Mr. Mazursky said, and he beckoned to his wife, and they all walked downstairs in silence.

And into the living room where Edith never went, because even if you just looked at something, it broke. The living room meant this was going to be special.

"Do you think your parents love each other?"

Edith nodded. No reason not to. Not only did she think it, it was true.

"What all that up there was about, at least this is my opinion" —he looked at his wife now—"Tell me if I'm right."

Myrtle nodded.

"What all that was about was not some nonexistent creature but just this: I work too hard. Who goes out at night for business? Ridiculous. Yes?"

Mrs. Mazursky gestured around the antique-filled room. "We don't need any more."

"Don't bring money into this—money is *nothing.*" He turned Edith in his lap to face him. "Do you know what I do, Edith?"

Edith giggled. "Of course I know. You go to the office."

Sol looked at Myrtle and smiled. "The kid understands everything." He played with Edith's hair gently. "My old man—"

"—you mean Grandpa?—"

"—same guy. Okay. He owned some buildings in Brooklyn. Not schlock, but not major league. *I* was the one convinced him to expand into Manhattan. Give it a shot."

"And who your age has done better? Thirty-seven years old, just barely."

Sol looked at his wife. "But I'm still not major league, baby. Can I call you 'baby' again?"

Myrtle nodded.

"They sit around there, those guys, and if my name is mentioned, the most they might say is, 'Mazursky? Good man. Word means something. Got a wife going through what looks like preliminary menopause, got a daughter gonna be a great painter; nice solid club fighter. But not a champion.' "

"What's so terrible about that?" Myrtle said.

"Nothing. Who said 'terrible'? Except for one thing: all I want to be in my heart is the most important real estate man in town." He was rocking Edith now. "Honey, I want there to be a Mazursky Towers on Fifth Avenue that shines like gold. I want a Mazursky Plaza. I see Mazursky Fountains spouting all over the city. None of this comes easy, y'understand." He looked at his wife now. "I'm gonna have to start busting my chops."

"*Start?* Jesus, Sol, what do you think you've been doing?"

"I'm going into business with this Chicago guy. And I'm opening an office in L.A. The core's gonna stay right here, naturally, but I want to keep 'em guessing, all those guys at all the clubs. All kind of a game, y'understand?"

Edith wasn't sure she did but she nodded anyway.

"Well, if you want to excel in games, tell me how you do that."

"You beat."

"Right, honey, but how? I'll tell you. You try with *everything.* What do you try with?"

"Everything?"

"Right again. Tonight's the night the business starts expanding, baby. Daddy's gonna be traveling a lot and working a lot and no matter where he is, he'll call you."

Myrtle began now to sharply shake her head.

Sol looked at his daughter. "I'm going to tell you the family motto now, Edith—*my* daddy told me and I'm telling you. I'll say it and then *we'll* say it together. Okay?"

Edith waited.

" 'When you're not practicing, remember, someone somewhere is practicing, and when you meet him he will win.' Okay? Both together?"

"When you're not practicing—"

"—practicing—"

"—remember someone somewhere is practicing—"

"—is practicing—"

"Good. Now say the last alone for Daddy."

"And when you meet him he will win," Edith said. It was easy to remember. And she loved her father's kiss. She just wished her mother's head would stop shaking . . .

The last of the ninth came and went for Sol not much more than a year later, and though he tried like hell to force it into extra innings, it was no go, and on the way back in the limo, Edith, in the jump seat, was the only one with the least sense of control.

Control.

She had no notion then of the importance that word's meaning would come to have for her, but as she sat in the jump seat staring at the driver's neck, she could hear she was the only one in the vicinity who was silent—both her mother and Sol's dad had totally lost it.

Lost control.

Myrtle holed up in the duplex those next months, keening,

usually in black. Edith, in her standard Brearley uniform—navy
blue jumper and pleated skirt—went straight on back to school.
The school authorities kept close tabs on her at first, traumas
being no fun for anybody, especially ten-year-olds whose fathers
die, but Edith gave them no cause for worry. Oh, her grades
slipped slightly—she was no longer first in her class but closer to
tenth—but that was still an excellent achievement.

For Edith it was a lot more than that; when you were tenth, you
were in control.

She breezed through Brearley, her only close call coming junior
year when she did the painted backdrops for a ghastly production
of *The Cherry Orchard.* It was such a sad play, it moved her so,
the faded grandeur of the characters, that she spent long hours
after school fiddling with her work. You don't paint sadness, of
course, you feel sadness, and somehow transmit that feeling to the
art work and when she was done, she was exhausted. Not an
unpleasant fatigue.

The next day, though, when she got to school, there was un-
pleasantness enough for everybody. Because the head of the drama
department had seen her work and brought in the head of the art
department who brought in the head of the school, and they
summoned her, all three of them to the room where her backdrops
were.

"Edith I just love these," the drama head said. The Headmistress nodded. They both then looked at the art department.

Edith's eyes flicked for the door.

The Art head, a painter herself, studied the main object, an
enormous panorama of the cherry orchard itself. The colors were
autumn colors. And the overall feeling was one of such sadness.
"I didn't know you could paint like this, Edith."

"I didn't *paint* that," Edith said quickly. "I just *copied* it."

"Copied?"

"Well, I don't mean I traced it or anything, but I didn't make
it up either. I mean, it was just an illustration I found in a book
about other productions of *The Cherry Orchard* and I just enlarged it. 'Enlarged' I should have said, not 'copied.' "

"From *our* library?" the drama head asked.

"Actually no, it was my father's book, he loved Chekhov, his
father was from Russia originally."

"This is all getting beside the point," the Headmistress said.
"What matters is the work. It's gifted work, Edith."

"Just an enlargement," Edith replied. "But thank you."

"You must paint more," the art department told her.

"Oh I will, I will," Edith said, smiling at them all. Naturally, it was the last time at Brearley she ever picked up a brush.

Radcliffe was unavoidable. Sol had wanted a son, a Harvard son, so what could Edith do? She maintained an easy A-minus average, did a number of helpful extracurricular activities and was, for someone naturally quiet, popular. No surprise there really. By her late teens, Edith stood five six, with a good lithe figure and a good warm face. Not pretty in a cheerleading way, but the features were strong, she was obviously kind, and her reddish hair by now tumbled wonderfully down her shoulders.

Sally Levinson was her first close friend, and Sally *was* pretty in a cheerleading way. Small and blond, pert and bouncy. At least in appearance. She had as foul a mouth and good a mind as any man at Harvard and said she didn't give a shit who knew it. She and Edith made a team more formidable than most men wanted to tangle with.

Phillip Holtzman seemed the least afraid. He was older than they, he had been in service and was in the Graduate Business School at Harvard while Edith was still a junior. He was tall and thin and people said he looked like Abraham Lincoln, which drove Phillip slightly crazy, since as he patiently explained— Phillip did *everything* with great patience—he didn't resemble Lincoln at all. Who he looked like was Raymond Massey who had played Abraham Lincoln, both on the stage and in the movies, and Massey didn't look like Lincoln either. All of Phillip's reasoning came to naught: his nickname at the B School was, then and forever, Honest Abe.

"You gonna marry him now or after graduation?" Sally asked after Edith came in from a date one evening. Sally was in bed reading Berenson, her God.

"Oh stop it," Edith said.

"Well it's so *obvious,* you ass. You never fight, you never argue. You're both so *decent.* It makes me sick, Edith, it really does. You probably compete with each other to see which of you feels more guilty after you fuck." Pleased with her tirade, she went back to Berenson.

Actually, Edith and Phillip fucked happily and well. And they did, in point of fact, argue. An increasing amount as senior year was coming to a close, Phillip's Business School graduation too.

Always about the same thing: Edith wanted Phillip to take over the family business; Phillip wanted to strike out on his own. He'd always been a scholarship student and Edith's money had never been much of a plus in his eyes. But more than that, as he told her again and again, if he assumed an ongoing enterprise, how would he ever know if he had what it took, whatever "it" was. Edith countered that he was just being stubborn, that Sol had always planned for the Mazursky company to be a family company, that Sol had taken over from *his* father and she, Edith, was surely not going into the real estate business, so if he wanted her, Phillip had no choice.

Well I want to marry you, Phillip said. But I'm my own man.

Then maybe we ought to think about it for a month or so, Edith said.

It was during that month she met Doyle.

Doyle. Doyle Ackerman. A Yalie. A swimmer. A star. Not all that bright. Or all that kind. And he was the first man that obviously was after her because of her money. But he had the best body Edith had ever seen. And he moved with instinctive grace. And he seemed always to be back-lit, he was that beautiful.

Edith was almost ashamed of the way he made her feel. So she kept it all quite secret. Phillip never knew about Doyle. Even Sally, who did know, kept her mouth shut. Edith would say she was going to New York on weekends, but instead head for New Haven where Doyle would take her to his roommate's parents' summer place on the water near Mystic. It was still out of season. No one was around. Not a lot to do. But bed.

She made her deal with Phillip before the month was out. He was studying for a major final but she tracked him to his carrel and suggested that they be original and get married in June, six weeks away. And that he work three years for Mazursky's. He could start in the mailroom for all she cared.

Phillip doubted Mazursky's had a mailroom. It was a real estate concern, not the U.S. Post Office.

Edith said she thought everybody started in the mailroom.

Phillip said go on.

After three years he could quit and no arguments.

Promise?

All she wanted was for him to be a millionaire, why was that so terrible.

Phillip smiled, said June was fine and now please shoo so he could study. She left him to his labors, but then a few moments later, she tiptoed back and took a quiet peek. He looked a lot in profile like Lincoln . . .

Phillip did not become a millionaire immediately; it was well over five years before the deed was done, and busy years they were. Whatever his needs were, Edith filled them. At first he would come home at night, silent and tight, because after all his college study what did he turn out to be but a son-in-law.

That was all they thought of him in the Mazursky offices. Some Harvard hotshot who had managed to snooker the heiress into marriage because he wasn't smart enough to make it on his own.

So untrue, Edith soothed. False, all false. And she buoyed him and boosted him, pushed when he needed pushing, shoved when he had to be shoved. Within a year, the bosses at Mazursky knew that someone Special had come in to roost. Because Phillip was that—inexperienced, sure, but brilliant. And tenacious. You told him something once and he had it. He was there before you in the morning, hours after you at night.

Edith never felt remotely alone, because that first year, happily, Kate came along, asthma and all, quickly followed by Abigail and Caroline—no Robin or Pamby for Edith, thank you very much.

And if she was attentive to Phillip's needs, she was at least that with the girls. Being who she was, she could have afforded whatever help she deemed necessary, but except for a wonderful Colombian named Alicia, Edith did it all. The cooking, the diapering, the walking in the park. (Carl Schurz. They lived on East End then. It wasn't till Edith turned thirty that they made the move to the house on Beekman.)

When it came time to find schools, the easy thing was just ship the three to Brearley; except something nagged at Edith, she wasn't sure it was right for all. So she thought and fretted before deciding that Kate, the most studious, might follow in her footsteps, but that Abby, the most artistic, ought to give a try to Dalton while wild Caroline could best thrive in the rough-and-tumble of Ethical.

It was more work for Edith, all the trips to the various institutions, but worth it, since the girls did wonderfully. As did Phillip.

And Edith most of all.

When she was thirty-three, and the girls were ten, eleven, and twelve and Phillip was starting to get famous in the business community, she said to him, one night, after their lovemaking, "I'd like to paint."

"Paint?"

"Yes. I'm alone all day now and the back maid's room is just used for laundry. It could make a studio. I don't need much room."

"Do it. Wonderful."

"I'll stop as soon as they come home. Or if you want to take me with you on a trip. Or—"

Phillip kissed her on the mouth, then stroked her reddish hair. "You've been so selfish all these years, there's just no end to it." They fell asleep in each other's arms. They still did that.

So Edith took the back maid's room and cleared it out and cleaned it up and bought the basics and set to work. She stopped each day whenever the first child got home, and she never started until the last had left in the morning. And if one of them was ill, she didn't paint at all.

But except for those times, she put a lot of effort into her work. It was understood the room was off-limits to the family. When she was ready for things to be seen, they would, of course, be available to one and all. But until then, the maid's-room door stayed shut.

It was months and months later before she opened it for Phillip. There was a canvas resting on her easel, a large canvas, perhaps six feet by four. Covered by a dropcloth. "The truth now," Edith said.

Phillip gave his Boy Scout sign.

Edith pulled the dropcloth clear and waited while he looked. (He was staring at the first of what were to be eventually referred to as the "Mazursky Madonnas," but no one knew that then.) What he was staring at was a meticulously brushed work of a woman standing by an endless clothesline that snaked around the entire canvas. The line ran clear off the top right of the work, going to eternity as it were. And the clothes got progressively larger as the unseen child grew. And on the face of the mother, the washerwoman, the female faced with this seemingly Sisyphean labor of a lifetime, was a dazed, perhaps imbecilic smile.

"I'm terribly proud of you," Phillip said.

"Oh boy," Edith said. "Am I in trouble."

"Well, you said the truth."

Edith made a laugh. "And I meant it, but when I said the truth, I didn't mean you couldn't lie a little."

"I am proud of you. That's a tremendous amount of work. I think it's fabulous you did it."

"But?"

"I don't know anything about painting, you know damn well I don't."

"But?"

Phillip sighed. "It's not exactly what you'd call a happy painting, is it, Edith?"

"I suppose not."

"Aren't you happy, Edith?"

She was and said so.

"I guess I just like happy pictures, that's all."

Edith made a nod . . .

The instant Sally knocked the next morning Edith was at the door with, "I hadn't meant to show you anything yet, I'm not ready for you yet, but I need an opinion and—"

"—oh dawling," Sally interrupted, her accent almost too thick to understand. "I'm sure if you've done little cutesy-wootsy girls with big eyes I'll just adore it."

"You can cut the English shit, Sally!"

Sally knew a Moment when one was at hand. She said no more, simply gestured for Edith to lead on. They went to the maid's room, removed the dropcloth, looked at the thing in silence.

Sally broke it finally. "Do me a dozen, I'll give you a show."

Not the kind of statement that could be mistaken for bad news.

Edith increased her work hours from then on. Not that she burst into a wild creative frenzy. She was still a mother. And she was still a wife. But her painting became an integral part of her. And within a year, she'd done a dozen paintings. And Sally gave the show.

It was neither critically, nor financially, triumphant.

No one came close to buying a painting, and when that fact became unassailable, just before the show closed, Sally set about, in secret, buying them all herself. She phoned various clients and had some buy one, most two, and she swore them to silence; they

sent her checks, so Sally could exuberantly show Edith, and Sally
sent her own checks to them back by return mail.

And there were pitifully few reviews.

But they were murderous.

SIC TRANSIT ETC.

One must mourn the passing of the Levinson
Gallery. Not that it's closed, understand. The
doors, alas, are still open. But any pretense toward quality must now solely remain in what
remains of the mind of Mistress Levinson.

This fall is by no means sudden. These reflec-
tions are merely the result of seeing the latest
Levinson offering, entitled "The Mazursky
Madonnas."

Conceivably Mazursky has talent, but so do
many graduates of the Art Students League.
She may actually understand line and color and
if she works very hard for a decade or two, could
be deserving of a show. But now it is amateur-
ism run rampant on a field of blue.

The Madonnas, by the way, are basically house-
wives in various states of despair. It is not our
province to discuss what is and is not proper
subject matter for artists to undertake. Crane
did *The Red Badge of Courage* and never saw
battle. But when a New York real estate heiress
chooses to throw her lot with the plight of poor
wedded women, one has to wonder—they did,
after all, *choose* to get married, didn't they?

"He's a rotten little turd," Sally cried, trying to rip the copy of
the *Voice* from Edith's hand. Sally had read the review that morning, had rushed up to Edith's to head off any possibility of Edith
seeing the notice, but when she got there, it was too late. Edith
had taken to buying the *Voice* since she'd begun painting—no one
did a better job of covering the offbeat, at least not to Edith's
thinking.

Edith put the paper down. "Phillip invested in a play once. I

remember, after the reviews came out, we all got very busy trying
to find quotes we could use for an ad in the *Times*. If galleries did
that, we could say 'deserving'—"

"—He's been out to get me for years—ever since I told him his
boyfriend had bad breath—he's not reviewing you, he's reviewing
me. He's an ass and he knows nothing—Jesus Christ, you sold
every goddam painting, doesn't that prove he's a fool?"

Edith rewarded this outburst with a hug. She held tiny Sally
with great gentleness and said, "You, my dumpling, are the fool.
You poor dear dumb sweet thing, sneaking around, buying those
paintings yourself, pretending you weren't."

"Who told—I'll kill 'em—"

"—Edith was not born yesterday," Edith said. "Not where
Sally is concerned. And I'm not upset, my darling—I never expected to have a show, I had a show. How many thousands of
people out there who would die for one. I am not yet El Greco,
I am not Van Gogh, and I plan to continue because it gives me
such pleasure. And I would like to talk to you now about that. I
would like to talk about 'The Blues.' "

"What, you evil bitch, are 'The Blues'?"

Edith moved across the living room and stared out at the East
River. "I liked it when you gave my show a title—'Madonnas'
focused things for me. I'd like to do another series and I want to
call it 'The Blues.' "

"Tell me."

"Well you know, Hopper for example, when he paints, it's not
that the people are derelicts or broken, but there's often something
in the coloring that makes it all so ineffably moving."

"Yes."

"Well, I thought what I wanted to do was paint just people I
love dearly—large, bigger-than-life canvases—and I want them to
be accurate and flattering and all that—but somehow, if I can
color them properly, I want them to be sad. Because really, life
is people you love and sadness, and I wanted to try to get that
down. I would paint Phillip."

And me, Sally thought.

"And my parents—I can do my father from photographs."

And me, Sally thought.

"And of course, the three girls." Edith paused then; a wind
feathered the river and she watched it.

Shit, Sally thought.

"Just the seven of you," Edith said then.

"I haven't the patience to pose," Sally said quickly; "just the family is best."

"Please," Edith said. "I really need you to be the seventh and last."

"Oh shit, I hate it when you whine, all right, I'll pose for you, just quit that sheep-dog look, I've got a weak stomach and it's early in the day."

So Edith began to concentrate her thoughts on "The Blues." She studied all the great portraitists, and she read and reread Chekhov to see how he did it with words, and she began a series of pencil sketches and it was clear, even from them, that she was on to something, she was working very close to her subconscious, and the emotions showed through. She kept at it and at it, working long after the girls came home now.

Still, when they needed items—leotards, book bags, anything at all—Edith did the doing. Trying to compress these labors into one shopping trip per week. As she did on a Thursday, the first week in February, late on a biting afternoon, when she put aside her sketches, changed, made out a shopping list, brushed her reddish hair, threw on her navy blue coat, and set out on what was to be, astonishingly, her final trip to Bloomingdale's.

2

BILLY BOY

—and now the nigger on the right began to fade, shouting "can't, can't make it"—but Billy Boy kept up the pace across the yard, increased it even, because nothing tired him, nothing stopped him, even the gunfire that was aimed down at them from the towers. There was less gunfire now than a minute before, as more and more prisoners broke, more and more guards panicked and began looking toward their own safety, and that was good, that was good.

Only the sirens, the sirens were louder, screaming like they were monsters on their own and that was bad, and then one of the niggers on the left caught one in the knee and did a flip, landed hard, tried to crawl, but you don't crawl with a kneecap gone, you don't crawl far, but he tried, because up ahead was the laundry gate and it was open which was good, no, better than good, because it wasn't just open, no, it was open and there wasn't any guard—

Except now there was. Billy Boy led the half-dozen niggers and it all seemed so perfect, the early February evening warm, so you wouldn't freeze if you had to run awhile, and not many stars so it would be really dark when you wanted it that way—except now, as they rounded the last corner and headed toward the gate from the shadows, now there was the outline of a guard, one hero guard, armed, one hero guard with one mother of a rifle and Billy Boy led the charge toward him and Billy Boy was the farthest ahead and Billy Boy was in the center so the first shot should have gone dead at Billy Boy but the guard was white, so he went for a nigger and one shot, one hit, then he tried a second nigger but no go, Billy Boy was close enough by then, close enough to make a fist of his right hand, a club of his arm, and one swing later and the guard was out on the ground and while another of the niggers grabbed the rifle Billy Boy was through the gate and into the street and running, running, it didn't matter which direction, there was the prison wall on one side, small houses on the other, and up the street now a car was coming toward them, but the driver saw what he was in for, and the brakes shrieked, and the car tried making reverse but no go, the motor died, and the driver threw the door open and ran toward the nearest small house while Billy Boy led the niggers into the car and shit, it was one of those foreign bugs, no power, no size, and while the niggers piled in around him, Billy Boy turned the key and the wounded nigger said, "start you motherfucker," and you could tell the panic but Billy Boy felt none of it, his hands were made for keys, keys and motors and anything else you wanted, his hands were magic so naturally the car started right up and he spun into a driveway, *vrroom*ed off back the way the car had come.

So it was a go, all systems were go like on the way to the moon, except Billy Boy didn't know this part of Illinois, who the hell knew shit about downstate Illinois, unless you were born there and if you were born there you didn't know shit about anything, that's how dumb the hayseeds were, and he turned left at the first corner he came to, just because it was a corner and it led away from the walls, and then the first chance he had for a right, he took that and from the back came a nigger's voice going "Hey where the fuck you fuckin' goin'?" and Billy Boy made his voice big, big and deep when he said, "You got a problem?" and you could hear the nigger shitting in his britches as he quick said, "You're doin' it, just keep doin' it, you're doin' it good," and Billy Boy nodded, felt the time coming for another turn, a left, and first chance he grabbed it and this was a straight stretch of road now, houses, sure, but not many people, and he gunned the mother, foot to the floor all out gunned it and all the niggers, you could tell they were really excited now, really up now, the prison was long long gone—

—then Billy Boy stopped the car.

He got out fast and they just looked at him, their questions falling over each other, "Whass up?—where the fuck you goin'? —you crazy—?"

He didn't answer. No way he could answer. He had an answer,

sure, a great answer, but it wasn't the kind of thing you could say—

—Billy Boy *sensed* things, that was all there was to it. He didn't know how, he didn't know why, he just knew that he sensed things, and he was sensing something now, sensing that it was time to get out, time to keep moving but not in the car, and without a look back he began to run toward a field and when the car roared down the road leaving him in the darkness, he didn't feel alone or bad, no, he felt that things were right, solid, the car was fast but it wasn't solid, not anymore.

He got to the field fast and made his way to the far side and the first thing coming along was a girl, a girl on a bike and she was really barreling and he thought that maybe what he should do was just go out and grab the handlebars and shake her off and ride away and then he thought that maybe he ought to shake her off and then slip it to her, love her up good and fast, no one was in his class when it came to quick loving, they never forgot it after Billy Boy got off them, and what if this one was pretty, what if this one was—

—no. Not now. He *sensed* it was wrong. Not a girl. Not a bike. Not now. Wrong. Wrong. Run. That was the thing now. Just run.

He just ran.

He didn't need a bike. Not now. He didn't need a girl. Not now. He needed a girl, but *not now*—what he needed now was this: a stop sign and a tree. Up ahead he saw a tree. But no stop sign. The next corner was nothing. It was a shit corner, a nothing corner.

He ran on.

The next corner had a stop sign. It was a great fucking stop sign. But no tree.

Shit.

The next corner had them both, a stop sign and a tree—except the tree wasn't a tree, it was like a twig more, nothing you could use.

More corners.

Then he was there.

Waiting.

A car came up to the stop sign. Paused. Billy Boy didn't budge —another bug, another goddam foreign job—they were bad luck tonight—not always, sometimes you could do okay with a foreign

job, but he'd already left one tonight, there was no point to getting
in another. Not when he sensed what he needed was a Cadillac.

Next up was a Chevy. No go. He waited. Next up was a Buick.
It was big but it wasn't a Caddie and he was about to let it go when
he sensed he was being picky, too picky, nothing wrong with a
Buick, he'd made it plenty of times in a Buick, so as the car halted
by the sign he burst out from the tree and the driver was on the
other side but who cared, Billy Boy just ripped open the near door,
and the driver was a big guy but who cared, Billy Boy just ripped
him loose from the wheel, pulled him across the car and out, made
a fist of his right hand, made a club of his arm, and one swing later
the Buick guy was wiggling on the ground as Billy Boy slid in and
vrrooom, gone.

Gone but not safe, not with these clothes, not with these clothes
and no money and those were items that needed fast taking care
of, so if it was an open place first, he'd go for the money, if a
clothing store, the other, he didn't care which order, he needed
both.

The clothing store was dark. He pulled in the back, parked with
the motor on, wondered what he would find he could use, comfort
was important in clothes and comfortable clothes weren't all that
easy, at least not for him, but beggars couldn't be anything else
but, until they had clothes and bread, so he shouldered the back
door open and the alarm was so quick and loud it shocked even
him—goddam two-bit store, what the hell did it need to have an
alarm that big for?—but he was inside, no time to waste with
questions, and first he found some raincoats, got one that seemed
maybe like it might be okay, then a pile of work shirts was no
good, kid stuff, but another pile two counters down was better and
he grabbed one of those and finally some jeans, it was hard to see
sizes, so he took half a dozen and headed back out the door—

—right into a cop, a cop with a pistol, but before there were
words he threw the clothes dead at the mouth of the gun and the
cop was surprised long enough for Billy Boy to reach him and
once he reached a cop, it was *over,* man, and when this cop was
groggy on the ground Billy Boy took his pistol and aimed it at the
cop's nuts and the cop cried *"Jesus, please"* and as Billy Boy
picked up his clothes he aimed it at the cop's eyes and the crying
was louder now, "Don't—Christ—gimme a—*donnnn't*—" this
last and loudest coming as Billy Boy began to fire—

—KA-BLAMM—
—KA-BLAMM—
—and now moving in close, three in succession.
You had to laugh. The fucking cop passed out. You had to really laugh at a thing like that. Because all the shots missed; close, sure, but misses. And still he passed out.
Chickenshit cops these days.
He aimed his final bullet at a police car tire, tossed the pistol away, back in the Buick and *Vrrooooooom*! A few miles on he saw a dark garage, pulled in, motor running, quick changed clothes. They weren't good but not so terrible either. They'd do. They'd have to.
And he'd have to leave the Buick, he didn't sense it, he *knew* it, because the cop would be awake about now and he'd seen the Buick so the Buick was about to become another portion of his past.
He pulled into the first shopping center he came to, got out, waited in darkness. An old guy came along pushing a cart full of food. He loaded the food into his car, took out his keys, and Billy didn't even bother making a fist of his hand, a club of his arm, not for an old guy—for an old guy a swipe was enough, a backhander, and as the old guy folded up Billy Boy grabbed his wallet and car keys, took off again on the road, counting the bread as he went along—
—shit, six bucks, he should have made a club after all, teach the old guy about coming out at night with an empty wallet. He reached back for the food, rummaged around, felt what should have been an apple but it was an onion, reached again, snagged an orange this time, peeled it as he drove, ate it down fast—
—the car slowed. Billy Boy gave a glance at the gas gauge. Empty. He *really* should have clubbed that old guy. The car coasted to a stop and he started running again, not on the road but across a huge barren stretch of Illinois land, because in the distance there were streaks, streaks of light, and as he kept on running the streaks turned into headlights and once he saw the turnpike clear, Billy Boy knew his next stop would be one of those service areas and now ahead he saw the streaks turning off and he picked up his pace as the service area assumed shape in the February darkness, and when he finally reached it he almost went inside because he had the six bucks and you could buy burgers with that,

only more important than eating was moving, and he went to where the cars were and right away along came this Shrimp and if a swipe was enough to handle the old guy, this one coming now, this Shrimp with the pale blue eyes, you could take care of with a finger snap—

—only Billy Boy sensed that was wrong. Big wrong. As the Shrimp came toward him what Billy Boy sensed was . . . was . . .

. . . fear?

"Ex—excuse me, sir, but I could sure use a lift."

The little guy looked at him quietly; nothing showed in the pale blue eyes.

"Swear to God I won't be no trouble."

"You drive?"

"Yessir. I do. I drive good."

Again, the little guy looked at him quietly.

"Please."

"Wouldn't mind some company," the little guy said. And he gestured toward his car.

Toward a Cadillac!

Billy Boy waited while the car was unlocked. Carefully so as not to upset anything, he got in. His hands stroked the leather.

"I'm driving all night."

"Yessir. No problem. I'd like that. Fine with me."

"You want to use the facilities, use them now."

"Huh?"

"Do you want to piss or not?"

He did. "Oh no sir. Just fine, thank you." What the hell, no point in getting people mad at you.

The wondercar began to glide.

So smooth. So smooth. Billy Boy just sat there. Everything was good now. He sensed that.

"You didn't ask where we were going."

"I didn't?"

"No."

"Well, where are we going?"

"New York City."

So smooth. So smooth. Billy Boy just sat still. Everything was great now. Because even though he had never been there, Billy Boy had always sensed that the Apple was going to be the end of the line . . .

3

THEO AND CHARLOTTE

They undressed in silence.

They stood across the small bed from each other, their backs to each other, concentrating on their clothing. He had always been aware of the plainness of his room, but never so much as now, with Charlotte, for the first time, inside—she was, for him, that beautiful.

Correction.

Not *just* for him. He had seen, these past months, too many male heads turn whenever Charlotte had made an entrance. He had noted, these past months, the following flick in the eyes of their wives—from their men, to this woman, to their men again. With her black hair framing her pale skin, with the straight nose, the wide mouth, the wide violet eyes, she was clearly not a creature to be competed with, not by others of her sex. And just as clearly, she was meant to be surrounded by luxurious things.

His room was hardly luxurious. When he had fantasized their lovemaking, he had imagined much. Musicians somewhere, out of sight of course, floating perhaps, surrounding them with sound, string quartets, piano trios, Mozart, Chopin, Liszt. And perfumed air. And silken sheets (black? Did he dare black?). And their bodies miraculously tinted gold. And— And—

He finally managed to unbutton his shirt, but before he took it off he turned, glanced at the lone candle illuminating this square, dreary, plain, barren room. "Too harsh for us," he managed. Then to be sure she understood, he added, "Candlelight."

The perfect face turned toward him.

He blew out the candle, lifted the shade. "We deserve to be lit by the moon, Charlotte," and he made a quick gesture toward the February night.

In the dark silence now, the perfect smile.

He turned away and was startled at the amount of courage required to drop his shirt to the floor. For the moment, he was not nearly that brave. It was not the fact that he was so completely inexperienced that blocked him. He had confessed to her that he was still, ye Gods, a virgin. That he had managed to go through four years at Oberlin without once coming close to a naked female form.

Two truths had to be faced. One was that his body, his naked body, humiliated him. He was that frail, that sickly in appearance. He had never in his life weighed one hundred twenty pounds or stood more than five feet six. Not only did he not look strong, he had little skill at resisting epidemics. When a sickness was around, he would catch it. And he always seemed to have a cough.

But he had a wonderfully aesthetic face, much older seeming than his twenty-two years. His eyes were pale blue, he was subject to headaches and minor pain, so he had with him always the look of someone brilliant, someone special, someone deeply haunted.

In other words, he resembled nothing so much as precisely what he was: a young, sensitive, unknown, but unquestionably gifted Romantic poet.

And he loathed being a cliché.

"Theo," Charlotte whispered then.

Startled: "What?"

Calm: "It's just I like saying your name. Theo. I can say it all I want. Tell me you don't mind."

"I love you so," he told her, which was, of course, true, and saved him from lying to her.

Because he *hated* his name. He had been born Theodore Duncan and except for his long-dead mother who used to call him first "The Bairn" and then just "Bairn" alone, a word from her past, from what was left of her Scottish girlhood, the world had always called him Theo.

"Ted" was his heart's desire.

Whenever he met a stranger and they exchanged names, he would refer to himself as Ted. "Ted Duncan's the name." Because Ted could be a hero, Ted could be a captain, Ted could smile at girls confident that they'd smile back.

In school, he would sign tests and papers, "Ted Duncan." Sometimes he would underline the "Ted." When things were desperate, he would even draw arrows pointing directly at the name.

But he looked like a Theo.

He behaved like a Theo.

He had a Theo's mind.

And sadly, a Theo's body.

So "Ted" never took. To that small portion of the civilized world with which he had come in contact, he was then and now and forever, "Theo."

"Theo is my genius," Charlotte whispered then.

He believed that she believed it. "Morphy pales," he said.

"Who?"

"Paul Morphy. The chess player. No matter what anyone says about the ones today, no one was as brilliant as Paul Morphy. Before he was ten he could beat the world. Before he was twenty-five, he went mad."

"What a tutor my children have. What a blessing for them."

He looked at her. She was no closer to total nudity than he. He understood how terrifying this must be for her. Just as he was a virgin, she had never before begun an affair. But there was something in her tone that indicated to him she was holding something from him. He asked her what it was. She replied he was imagining. He insisted.

"I just wanted to say," Charlotte began; "I just wanted you to know that even if Mr. Stewart were to burst in on us now—" He had never heard her refer to her husband as anything other than that: Mr. Stewart. Did she, he wondered, in the bedroom? 'Oh that was lovely, Mr. Stewart, we just fit, thank you ever so much.' "—even if he entered roaring and condemned me to a life of permanent humiliation, I would not regret an instant of our time together. Or what we're about to do."

It was certainly a confidence-building speech and it enabled him quickly to undress entirely and slip naked into the narrow bed with the rough sheets and wait for her to do the same. And while he waited, he faced the second truth which was this: Was there a reason he was untested when it came to feminine companionship? Why did he sometimes look at men with powerful shoulders? Was it simple envy or the never simple fact that he was *different*? That he, in other words, deviated from the norm. Should he have been born in ancient Greece when they didn't mind that sort of thing? He lay in the narrow bed looking at her. She was half undressed now, her blouse off, and half turned away. But she was as glorious as he had prayed. And now he prayed again. Because he did love her. And if love meant, occasionally, penetration, he suspected the toughest test of his career might be soon upon him, and he would have traded all his college A's for a simple C-plus now. Theo closed his eyes. Please, he prayed, spare me this humiliation. Then he reached down and touched himself.

God clearly existed—he was already hard.

Charlotte heard him sink onto the mattress, so she knew that the time for this childlike dawdling was just about over. Still, she could not yet bring herself to take off her skirt.

Because it had to be perfect. Because Theo was a poet. Who saw the world with a poet's eye. And there was nothing very poetic about the sight of her stomach. Doctor Willcox, though reputed to be the best at New York Hospital, had butchered the first Caesarean, and even though she shifted physicians, when she had her second child that same way, the damage was permanently done. Not so much the scar, bad as it was, long and ugly; discolored. Worse was that her stomach muscles never regained their tone. She was, and had been for ten years now, pot-bellied. Not in clothes. Dressed, she was today exactly what she had always been: the most coveted woman in any room she cared to enter.

She never had an awkward age as a child. By nature lazy, she had somehow been born into a bewilderingly bright family. Her father, Thomas Bridgeman, had been first in his class at Harvard Law and, relatively unusual for a person in that position, had gone into the practice of law. Often, the very top students stay on and teach. Precisely what her older brother had done; he was today professor of law at Harvard. Her younger brother, always the rebel, had all but unhinged the Bridgemans by shunning jurisprudence and was already, at twenty-seven, on his way to a first-class career in medicine. Even her mother had been, for a time, headmistress of a fine private school.

Charlotte was only beautiful.

And her size only made the beauty more startling. No porcelain child, this; she reached her final height, over five feet nine, before she was fifteen. Her weight, then as now, was always within a pound or two of one hundred thirty. She was naturally athletic, graceful, and terribly strong.

Since everything external had come so easily, had always been present, she took it for granted. She had little ego about her appearance. It was just there. The laziness, which would have gnawed at her parents in a son, presented no problem in such a daughter. They seemed proud and pampered her unmercifully. At the age of eighteen, Charlotte was done with school. It bored her, she had no particular aptitude for it. College would have been an overpowering waste. The idea of work bored her too, and though doubtless she could have gotten a job through her father's contacts, keeping one was not a test anyone seemed anxious to put her to.

In total then, she was, at the age of eighteen, in all ways, a perfectly beautiful and perfectly useless ornament. Which was, in all ways, precisely what Mr. W. Nelson Stewart was in the market for.

"I want you to pay attention now," her father said. "Sit down, Charlotte. This is going to be fairly important."

Charlotte sat in the chair across from his desk. She already knew it was going to be important. Her father rarely asked her to come down to his Wall Street office. She looked at him now. He was slightly taller than she was, and his hair was going fast. But he had a tiny dark mustache that twitched when he was excited, and his eyes were always bright, and she adored him.

"I would like you to consider marrying Nelson Stewart," her father said.

"Why isn't Mr. Stewart asking me?"

"Mr. Stewart is not keen, at this stage of his life, to face rejection."

"Can I reject him? Do I have a choice?"

"Every choice. But I do want you, as I said, to *consider*. There are positives and there are negatives. May I list some of them for you?"

"You do what you want, Daddy."

"Charlotte, for the duration of this crucifyingly important discussion, please stop calling me 'Daddy.' "

Charlotte promised to do her best.

"I know this must strike you as being horrendously old-fashioned, a talk like this. And I urged Nelson to have it with you himself. But he's simply too shy. That is one of his positives, Charlotte. He is shy around you because, to be frank, he is smitten with you. Since I am his lawyer and have been for twenty years,

I think I can vouch for his character. This is a decent man, my darling; a bit of a violent temper, true, but only in matters of business and only when he has been lied to. Or in other ways cheated. He has never raised his voice to me and will never, I'm sure, be anything but a gentleman with you."

"But he's so old."

"I'm still dealing with the positives, darling, now don't interrupt again. As you know he's involved in the stock market, which is not unlike my saying the Rockefellers are involved in the oil business. I exaggerate, of course, but you get my point."

"But we're not poor or anything."

"No, dear, but we're not rich or anything either. Not rich in the sense that I'm talking rich. All right: he can support you, he reveres you, his character is for all intents and purposes flawless, plus he's known you all your life. When you were a baby, he used to play on the floor with you. He's watched you grow, has a month ever gone by that you haven't spent time with Nelson?"

"I don't know, is that important? The negatives are what I want to hear, if you don't mind."

"All right. You mentioned age, and with reason. Nelson isn't 'old' but he certainly is not exactly of your generation—"

"—he's fifty—"

"—darling he's forty-four—"

"—he *looks* fifty—"

"—Nelson is more than aware that he isn't a matinee idol—"

"—and I hate those rimless glasses—"

"—Charlotte, we're not talking about *his* rimless glasses, we're talking about *your* life!"

She could tell by his tone they were nearing the end.

"He's never married, he wants to marry now, he wants a lot of children, you'll make a splendid mother." He smiled.

"What?"

"I was just thinking: if your children have just half of your looks and half of Nelson's brains, they'll own the world."

Was that a compliment? Charlotte wondered. She decided it was.

"There are all those positives and but three negatives: he is not beautiful, he is not young, and you don't love him."

Wasn't that last alone a good enough reason to say no? Charlotte wondered. (Her father's bright eyes burned.) Charlotte decided it wasn't.

The courtship was perfunctory but totally civilized. He wanted nothing physical from her. At least now. He talked of the children he wanted, his visions for them. Occasionally, when he took her hand she wondered if it was preparatory to a more serious maneuver but it never was. Had it been, she would have been dutiful. Charlotte suspected that Nelson Stewart was never going to be inflamed with passion. Well, the same could be said for her. So far, at any rate. Sex was a duty and she knew when the time came she would prove competent.

He lived on Fifth, in what Charlotte thought a perfect place to begin married life, but he felt it was far too small. So he bought an enormous house on Gramercy Park, with an added small place in the back that would be fine for staff. The house had many bedrooms, each child would obviously have *his* own. (He wasn't crazy to teach daughters the ways of the Market.) And the private park across the street would make life easy for Charlotte when pram time came each day.

During this period, she realized certain things her father had told her were true. Nelson Stewart was indeed shy. Remarkably so for a man of his power. The Market was everything, and he did all that he could to keep distractions to a minimum. Example: his clothes. He bought them only from Brooks Brothers. (He put great faith in brand names. Brooks was impeccable, you could trust the place. And at the start, he insisted Charlotte frequent Lord & Taylor for the same reason: trust.) And when he shopped at Brooks, he had his own salesman whom he would contact before his visit and outline his needs. So as he reached the store, all was in readiness, shoes, shirts, suits, whatever else. Laid out in one special area, his salesman hovering. Nelson would enter, always exactly on time, enter, pick, and be gone. He had a fine wardrobe but it was doubtful if he ever spent more than ten minutes in the store at any one time.

Their wedding was dutifully covered by the *Times*. A city the size of New York is obviously too large to have such a thing as a Most Eligible Bachelor. But on any list of five, W. Nelson Stewart would have properly belonged. So there was publicity, even though he shunned it when he could.

They honeymooned in Europe for almost a month, during which time they had sex weekly. Charlotte did her best to pleasure him, but she was always slow to moisten while he was always quick to come, something of a problem.

Life in the ensuing months was almost entirely quiet. Nelson Stewart liked his home life that way. He was a Bostonian and never really enjoyed the pace of Manhattan, but if you were in the Market, Boston simply wasn't good enough, not if you had skills such as his. So they rarely went out. The only restaurant he frequented was Sweet's, the great old place on Fulton near the river. He went there because he felt it was easily the finest fish house in town. And also because, he said, it somehow reminded him of home.

Before their first year was out, Charlotte gave birth to W. Nelson Jr., the event damaged only by the hack work of the surgeon. Charlotte never realized, until months later when she had done her best to get her stomach flat again, the extent of her vanity. She exercised relentlessly after her firstborn.

But alas.

The next year Burgess (named after the father's father) came along but after that there would be no further children. It was simply not medically sound. That news obviously saddened Nelson—he would never have his brood now—and he turned more than ever toward his empire.

Charlotte mothered the boys.

Or tried to.

Wanted to.

But there were always so many servants in the way. There was never the least question in Nelson Stewart's mind that his children would be outstanding. He insisted on it. They were, after all, Stewarts.

It came as something of a shock to him when he perceived that they had inherited *his* beauty and his *wife's* brains. They were pudgy little things, sweet enough natured, but dreadful at sports and always behind in their studies at Columbia Grammar. At first he did nothing. Then, when the boys were seven and eight, the tutors began. And the basement of the great home was turned into a gymnasium.

Charlotte watched it happen. That was all she did really, all she could do. Watch. Oh, at first, she tried reasoning with him. Too much pressure on the boys too soon. That kind of thinking.

He would have none of it. He had waited so long for children that when they disappointed, there was no remedy other than immediate action. And in truth, by the time the boys were eight

and nine, there was evident improvement. They were still prone
to heaviness, true, but they could box now, and no one their age
mocked them anymore. And not most but all of their Columbia
Grammar teachers saw the change in their academics. Their
grades were better than good, edging toward excellence.

Charlotte began to drift.

She had no real interests. Oh she tried. She mentioned one
evening that she'd always wanted piano lessons as a child and the
next week what should be in the library awaiting her but a Stein-
way grand. She read the Sunday *Times* dutifully, occasionally
visited the natives in Central Park and Washington Square. And
she fought her way as often as she could through the Metropolitan
Museum.

But she had no true passion for any of it. It was as if somewhere
along the line she had checked her heart and forgotten to pick it
up.

When she was twenty-nine, when the boys were nine and ten,
when she was still as big and beautiful as a dozen years before,
except for the stomach scars, Charlotte had, for her, a rare moment of insight. The dead-leaves road that was to be the rest of
her life momentarily illuminated itself to her and, much to the
astonishment of the children, who were finishing their roast beef,
and Mr. Stewart, who had already finished his, she broke at the
dinner table. Facing as quickly as she could away, she fled the
table and raced all but blind toward her bedroom.

After allowing a proper composure time, W. Nelson Stewart
entered and observed that it couldn't have been anything he'd said
since he hadn't said anything. Charlotte was abjectly apologetic.
How could he dream it was anything of his doing? He was a
superb provider, and kind. What, then, he wondered? You know
how I get this time of the month, she tried. Ahh, he said; ahh, of
course. He asked then when she was due and she replied perhaps
the next day, perhaps the day after.

That night he returned, naked under his robe. She was surprised, feigned pleasure at his mounting. She was dry and he came
too quickly, but they knew their roles so well by then that they
got through it without much pain.

He was, he told her, proud of her. As she was of him, she said,
and in truth, was. I'll let you rest, you must be tired, he said, and
with his robe on, left.

Charlotte stared the night away.

Soon after, the boys turned ten and eleven. And Charlotte turned thirty. And the new tutor arrived from Oberlin . . .

Before she was prone, before she had a chance to do or say a thing, he had turned his body toward her and she could feel he was hard while she was dry and for a moment she wanted to push him away so they might begin again, but now his mouth was on hers, his hands were firm on her big shoulders and he jabbed his tongue at her with such force she knew he was panicked, was acting out of lack of knowledge, was so in need of her tenderness because that was the true meaning of manhood, the ability to forgo force as a path that led nowhere, so Charlotte made a sound she hoped indicated pleasure, because the last thing she wanted was to crush him now, and then she broke the kiss and immediately began another, and this time it was her tongue doing the probing, only soft, gentle, and she made the sound again, hoping it indicated now increased pleasure and it must have, because when his tongue came back it was without the previous almost anger. But the fear was still with him, she could tell as he went next for her wondrous breasts, too too hard he went, kneading them as if they were somehow not connected with the rest of her body, like mounds of dough on a marble table, and she made another sound, and kissed his mouth again, managing to break his hold on her bosom, and when she'd tongued his mouth gently, she lowered her head slightly, tongued, again gently, his tiny male nipples, and they became hard quickly; he was a quick learner, this blessed Theo of hers, he had to be, poets understood, for now he was sucking her nipples and it was their turn to be hard. He was trying to penetrate her now but she wasn't yet moist and if there was ever an ultimate rebuff that was it, to be a man, pulsing and anxious only to find the entrance shut, so she touched him there briefly, briefly kissed his breasts again, tongued his mouth, made her sounds, praying there was nothing wrong with her—she was in bed with that person in the world she most wanted to be in bed with yet how could he know that except by words, and bed is not a place for words except words after. "Such a bad boy," she whispered, but he kept trying to force himself on her, so she said, "Bad boys must be punished," and she began to roll him off from his position on top of her and of course he resisted but that didn't make her stop and in a moment they were tussling there in the small bed, and Charlotte was bigger and heavier and as it began to turn out, stronger; he resisted, tried to, did his best, but slowly, she got the better of it; they were side by side for a moment but only briefly, before she forced his hands down and got astride of him. She held his hands to the mattress and he resisted more than before until suddenly he stopped, pushed up his head, for there waiting for him was a breast, and he suckled it almost as if he had a fever, and the only reason he released it was to wrap his mouth around her other breast, and Charlotte was losing control now, and her legs widened for him and in and up he moved, and minutes later they were still like that, still like that, and she had read of such things, had heard of such things in the schoolyard when girls told stories, it was possible, they said, it was truly possible if there was love that a man and a woman might, a man and a woman might, if there was genuine love between them they might actually climax, climax both of them as one and Charlotte could hear his time was near and Jesus, dear sweet Jesus, so was hers, and his arms went around her and his eyes shut tight and he cried out as did she cry out, her eyes shut tight, and their bodies rhythmed, first with spasms almost violent, then, slower, then slower still, and when it was done, when they were done rather, Charlotte kissed his eyes and worried that her weight might tire him, and rolled alongside her Theo, telling him only that she loved him, and she didn't expect more in return than the fact that he felt the same, but when what she got was silence she glanced at him and saw he was looking at the ceiling, and frightened suddenly that the experience she had just been through was not a shared one, she repeated that she loved him, a bit louder.

Then his eyelids began to flutter.

More frightened, Charlotte stretched out, took his hand, made as if to touch it with her lips.

Theo ripped free of her.

And on his face now: pain.

And the eyelids going faster.

"Not afraid," Theo whispered.

"Of course not," Charlotte whispered back. "Why should you be?"

"Not afraid!" Theo repeated. And then a third time, loudest of all: *"NOT . . . A . . . FRAID!"* And as Charlotte, stunned, rolled up on one elbow she had never seen eyelids move like Theo's were moving now, because you could not force them to flutter that quickly, no one could bid them to.

"Theo, Theo listen," Charlotte said.

But he was clearly not in a listening mood. His mouth began to work, and finally he was saying *"Burr"* or *"Bear"* or was it *"Burden"* he was repeating over and over?

Charlotte at last understood. Or at least had a good idea, because when he'd read her his poems, many of them were simply meant to be love lyrics, the outpourings of a delicate creature with too much emotion to know quite where to store it all. But many others had a deeper ambition, they dealt with Him and behavior, and most of all, morality, and torment, and the word he was saying now, that word was *"Burn."* "Burn" repeated, but softer until it was a whispered litany, ". . . burn . . . burn . . ." Charlotte knew about his headaches, he had told her, and his black moods were no secret from her either, but this now was undeserved, because *he* hadn't done anything, she'd done it all: *"I seduced you"* she wanted to say, though she didn't because he was not in a mood to believe it, because, as she watched, and she couldn't be totally sure but as she watched he rubbed his eyes, or she thought he was doing that, rubbing them, except he was rubbing too hard, and as she saw that rubbing them was probably less what he had in mind than tearing them from his sockets she grabbed his small hands and he ripped free but she was back again instantly, tearing his fingers away and he ripped free again and slapped her, slapped her again, and in an instant they were where they had been not all that many minutes before, battling, physically testing one another except before it was a preamble to as close as she could ever come to anything ecstatic, whereas now it was turning into something quite different, a fight for life, for dear life, *her* dear's.

HAGGERTY'S KID

Haggerty knew before he was fifteen that he was going to marry the Rafferty girl down the block. She was Irish, she was Catholic, her father and grandfather had been cops too, she understood.

She wasn't a genius, but she was smarter than he was; she wasn't a beauty, but he never forgot her fifteenth summer when her breasts arrived along with strange thoughts in his head. They held hands and necked and went to Coney Island and she swatted his thick fingers when he got fresh. She was saving it, Helen Rafferty said. For what, *for what Jesus?* Haggerty said. For when it's legal, she told him. Helen that could be years. *Years.* She ran her hands along her body. Worth the wait, she assured him.

They married while Haggerty was at the Police Academy and their first night she *demanded* to know, after, if it was or not worth the wait and he hurriedly answered yes, absolutely, but inside he was momentarily troubled because it turned out she was more sexually adventurous than he was. That trouble soon gloriously disappeared. He loved her a great deal, as much as he thought was safe. More even.

But her true value didn't come till later. The first time he was badly mugged walking a tour, she didn't ask about it, didn't weep. She tended him, got him going, no questions at all. She understood not to ask. And the first time he was shot—no, the first time he was badly shot—again her eyes did not moisten. Forthright, let's improve this, let's get that working again, on with the next. She understood.

If their marriage was serene, so was their daughter, Elaine, pretty enough, but not too pretty to cause conceit, quick enough in school but not too quick to cause envy. Helen called her their pink child. Pink skin, favorite color, pink; personality the same. Never a problem at all.

Frank Jr. more than made up for her. Angry, feisty, raw. He cried when a baby, simmered as he grew. But it was not till he reached his teens that he began to steal. Haggerty strapped him the first time he was caught. Did no good. Strapped him the second time too. Results the same.

Haggerty, a detective now, used to take long walks alone on lunch hour to the East River, smoking and staring, the container of coffee his only company. His son was a thief. Frank Jr. stole. A cop for a father—not only that, an honest one—and he stole. His grandfathers both in the force and he stole.

Bad situation.

News began to get out. Frank Jr. was caught a few times, caught at dime stores and candy counters and clothing outfits. And Haggerty couldn't keep it quiet. It was too juicy. Around the precinct it became common knowledge: Haggerty's kid was a whacko.

Bad situation, getting worse.

Being a cop anywhere is a bitch, but trying to cut it in the Apple squares the tensions. Though there are, occasionally, some strange compensations. Like the plastic surgeon on lower Park Avenue who charges a ton for lifts and tucks but who does kneecaps—policemen's kneecaps—free. You tear up a knee on duty, you go to lower Park to the surgeon. And in, would you believe, Staten Island, there's a brilliant dentist who does jaw reconstructions. For cops. As a sideline.

And then there's the Lorber Foundation.

Ike Lorber wrote books, taught, traveled, lectured, and was generally considered to be just about the most successful, or at least the highest priced shrink in the city. The Foundation—it was really a clinic, but for legal reasons Ike's lawyers wanted it called a foundation—was a large limestone house on Fifth just below Sinai. There was a receptionist, several other shrinks, several other apprentice shrinks, not to mention Lorber's wife, Essy, an analyst of distinction on her own.

Haggerty was just the least intimidated. He mumbled to the receptionist—the elderly prune type—that he had an appointment to see Doctor Lorber and she quick came back with, *Which?* and he managed that it was Doctor Isaac he wanted and she told him to sit so he sat. Then, a while later, she told him to stand. He stood.

She beckoned for him to follow so he did that too. Finally, she opened a large door and there, seated at an enormous desk, was the Man himself.

Haggerty hadn't known what to expect. Witch doctors weren't his province and more than that, they frightened him. But you couldn't be frightened by this guy.

Placid. That was the word for Ike Lorber. You got the feeling from his expression that he had heard it all, every terror, and no matter what you did, you couldn't shock him and he wouldn't think bad of you. Middle-aged, middle-sized, quick-eyed.

And calm.

Sit down, Frank; thanks for coming over.

Haggerty nodded.

Talking to Captain Hoffman. Said you were into sort of a situation.

The boy steals.

And gets caught.

Yessir. That too.

Which is worse I wonder.

Pause. The stealing.

I took stuff when I was young. Don't most kids?

I can't say. I know that . . .

Yes, Frank?

I know I never took a thing in all my life. Don't think bad of me, but I never broke the law.

What a world we live in, Frank, when a man has to say don't think bad of me about being honest.

Everybody's cutting corners nowadays, sir. I was brought up not to. Probably sounds stuffy to you but there it is.

And the boy's how old?

Almost sixteen.

And this is hard for you, isn't it, Frank? Being here now, talking about it?

Pause.

Take your time, Frank—nothing but time here.

Pause. Tightness in the throat. Finally: it just fucking kills me, Doctor Lorber.

Nod. His name?

Pause.

Easy, now; really.

Again the tightness. Finally: His name is Frank Jr.

A glance at the thick appointment book. A scratching out of something. Could you bring Frank Jr. here tomorrow do you think? After dinner I'm free. Eight tomorrow night, that fit with your schedule?

Nod.

Writing in something beside where the scratching was.

He may not want to come, you're sure you can be here?

I don't know that the sun will rise, Doctor Lorber—but I promise you this: the boy will most definitely be here . . .

The next evening, in front of the large house, Frank Jr. said, "I'm not gonna talk to no kike."

Haggerty hit him hard across the side of the head. "You don't call me a mick, you don't call me a spud, you don't call him a kike."

"A hebe then."

Haggerty raised his hand to strike again.

"Well he's a Jew, I can't be talking to one of them."

Haggerty dropped his hand. "Oh, are you wrong," he said, and, grabbing his son by the elbow, steered him to the door and rang. Doctor Lorber answered, the three of them talked briefly, then Frank Jr. followed the placid man into the office.

Haggerty waited the hour.

They came quietly out, and Frank Jr. asked if he could go outside. Doctor Lorber nodded. The boy left them. Tomorrow night might be beneficial, same time all right?

Haggerty hesitated. I did some checking.

Always get another opinion, Frank.

You cost.

I know. Outrageously. More than anyone, I hope. It helps my ego.

It'll have to be installments.

Hmm?

I haven't got a lot of money.

Well fortunately I have, Frank, so leave my finances to my accountant why don't you. Tomorrow night then?

Is he going to be all right?

Can't talk to you, Frank; medical ethics, you understand?

Frank didn't, but he said tomorrow night would be fine.

He brought the boy again the following evening, waited the hour. The third session, the next Tuesday, Frank thought for a moment, that as he waited he heard, ever so briefly, tears. But he wasn't sure. But on the fourth session, he was.

Analysis, if it's anything, is an inexact science, and supportive therapy is lucky when it reaches that level. And there were no Joan Crawford moments for Frank Jr., no epiphanies. But after the sixth session it wasn't necessary for his father to come along on the weekly meetings. And after four months, the meetings themselves stopped. Frank Jr. wore no halo—he was just an ordinary average run-of-the-mill fucked-up teen-ager now.

> Dear Doctor Lorber:
>
> Last night at dinner the boy talked about college. Not for long, and he was cautious, but the word did pass his lips.
>
> I don't know what someone with my skills could ever do for someone with yours. But I pray for the opportunity.
>
> Yours
Frank Haggerty, Sr.

Not much of a note but it took Haggerty three days to get the thoughts down. Not three solid days, he did other things. But his mind was always on what he wanted to write. He mailed it fully confident that he would never hear from the great Doctor Lorber again.

It took a number of years. But he heard.

"Detective Haggerty, please."

"Yes." It was the receptionist prune.

"Detective *Frank* Haggerty?"

"Speaking."

"Doctor Lorber was wondering if you could find some spare time to—"

"—just tell me when—"

"Tonight."

It was definitely not the prune who opened the door that evening. Haggerty stood outside the Foundation, perspiring heavily in the June night as this *vision* appeared in the doorway. Tall, nineteen maybe, athletic build, black hair, skin like Merle Oberon which only made more startling the sea-blue eyes. "You must be Mr. Haggerty," she said.

Haggerty never messed around with women, never even paid

attention to the young ones. If I was twenty now, he thought, I'd never have got close to you. He nodded at his name.

She gestured for him please to enter. "My name's Karen," she told him, closing the door. "I'm the daughter. You know where Father's office is?"

"I think."

"Is he ever waiting for you." She gave him a smile that was as good as the rest of her, turned and started upstairs.

Haggerty watched her body move. Special creature, he decided. A genuine stunner but didn't seem conceited. He tugged at his coat, doing what he could with the wrinkles, then headed toward the large office at the end of the hall.

The placid man was gone. The Ike Lorber waiting inside looked physically like the earlier version. But whereas the former occupant was quiet, reasoned, calm, this one now jumped around, talked nervously, as if there were dashes around everything.

"—Frank—Frank, Christ, good to see you, how's Frank Jr?"

"—fine sir. Lives out west now, Washington, good job with Boeing, doing well . . ." Haggerty stopped then when he realized the doctor wasn't paying the least attention. Ike walked around his desk, sometimes pausing briefly at the window, staring out at the small garden in the rear.

"—You met Karen?—"

"Yes. Lovely."

"—the inside is better than the outside, believe me—gonna make a great analyst—genuine feel for people—brilliant insights —popular at Bryn Mawr—not just a bookworm—adjusted, considerate, I'm crazy about her—"

"She sounds wonderful."

Now Ike Lorber whirled, stared at Haggerty. "—she's a twin, Frank—she's got a twin brother—and it's him, it's my son that's killing me—"

"Drugs?"

"—if only it was—" He stopped abruptly, sat heavily into his desk chair. "—Can you believe that?—a father saying such a thing about a son?—about a beloved son?—terrible—terrible—"

"What's the boy done?"

"—what has Eric done?—you catch their names?—Karen is Karen Horney Lorber, Eric's middle name is Fromm—great figures in our field—Frank, from the start this whole Foundation was theirs—God gave us these incredible children, these glories, these fraternal twins were handed down from on high—well adjusted, kind—I stress that because it ain't easy having shrinks for parents, most of our shrink friends, their kids are more fucked up than their patients—but as good as Karen's doing at Bryn Mawr, Eric's that way at Swarthmore—they'll be seniors next year and *already med schools want them*—"

"But he's changed his mind."

"—right—he told me—yesterday—man to man—I didn't sleep —how could a man sleep?—his mother will die—I'm calm in comparison—"

"What does he want to be?"

Ike Lorber shook and shook his head. "A gumshoe," he said finally. "A shoulder tapper. My glorious son has decided to be a policeman."

Haggerty thought it best to say nothing.

The doctor sat back in his chair, sighing.

"A passing fancy," Haggerty said.

"Eric doesn't have such things. He ruminates at length before decisions." He looked at Haggerty now. "Will you talk to the boy?"

"Of course."

"Explain things to him—explain what a horrible mistake it would be—"

"—but I love the life—I wouldn't be anything else—"

"—Frank—Frank Jesus—do I have to tell you the way I feel about the police? How many hundreds of hours do I donate each year? But this is a special kid."

"If he can be a great doctor, that's what he must be," Haggerty said. "I saw what you did for my son."

"Then you'll help me."

"Just tell me how."

"I've thought exactly how—some night when it's convenient, I want you to meet Eric, talk to him honestly, take him around with you, show him the reality."

"Done."

"Plus one more thing."

"Name it."

"I want you to scare the shit out of him . . . ."

* * * * *

"Will we really see a crime?" Eric asked.

Haggerty slowly piloted his car along Broadway; he saw a place up on 138th Street, so he pulled in to park. It was the first Saturday in July, three in the morning, steaming hot, and from a rooftop up ahead some guy was screaming as he threw bottles down onto the pavement.

"Fantastic," Eric said, staring out at the Harlem night. He could not hide his excitement any more than he could stop his ceaseless looking around.

Haggerty turned off the car motor, pocketed the keys, lit a Camel. So far he had done nothing right in the way of disabusing the kid of his notion. They'd started with a steak dinner at Gallagher's. There were a bunch of other detectives eating when they came in, and they all noted Haggerty and his companion. And they kept watching them. At first Haggerty thought it was because of the way the kid was dressed—neat dark gray dacron and cotton suit, blue button-down shirt, red rep tie. Haggerty wore his usual off-duty costume—an old baggy jacket just to hide his gun, faded pants, short-sleeve shirt, no tie.

Who was he kidding, that wasn't it. Eric was just as startling to look at in his way as his twin was in hers. Big, powerful, moved well. And the same olive complexion, the same sea-blue eyes.

Haggerty told him horror stories over dinner—when the junkie cracked his skull, when he took the cleaver shot in the stomach, and they thought he was dead from blood loss, when the loony he'd put away got out and shot him three times point-blank and God alone knew how he'd stayed alive. And on this last one he described the slow healing months, the pain, the pressure he'd put on his family, how his daughter almost cracked with worry; Haggerty piled it on. All the stories were true, of course, he never lied, not about anything, but usually if he talked about them at all it was only because someone else brought it up and he grazed over them, never going into detail. Now he went into detail. The fear, the hurt, the knowledge that some nut was going to any day blow you away tomorrow, the miserable way it ripped at any semblance of family fabric, if it was sad or gory, Haggerty let it out.

Eric just kept saying "Really." Or "Incredible." Or "God, I wish I could have been there."

Once, when Haggerty went to the men's room, Cooney followed

him. Cooney had the next desk over in the precinct house. "Who's the co-ed?" Cooney wondered.

"Would you believe, a recruit? I'm trying to talk him out of it."

"Play down the glamorous aspects then," Cooney advised. "Don't tell him about the free apples we get from fruit stands."

"Mum's the word," Haggerty promised and he went back to the table. After dinner, they walked through Times Square, Haggerty pointing out various points of sleaze. Then a long drive through the South Bronx, burned out and shameful.

And last, always last, Harlem.

"Now we're just going to sit quiet and watch," Haggerty said. He pointed out the newsstand a short distance away on the corner. The bar in the middle of the block, the dance hall beside it and across the street another dance hall, Earl's, big and very loud. "Earl's is a bad place, capital B."

"How so?"

"People get hurt in there. Frequently."

Eric stared across the street toward the large, lit place, the music surging out from the open doors. On the sidewalk in front of them, a number of drunks leaned on the buildings for support. Now a man left the bar, hesitated on the street a moment and a drunk left the support of the building, lost his balance, fell against the man who'd just left the bar. No harm though. The bar patron shoved the drunk away. The drunk staggered back to the safety of the building.

"If we see a crime, will you arrest the guy?"

"I'm off duty, Eric; I guarantee you I won't."

"You mean you'll just let it happen? A *crime*?"

"It's like rebounding in basketball—if you go after every one you'll get tired and pretty soon you'll start missing some that are your responsibility. You play basketball?"

"I'm not into team sports. But I know what you mean."

Haggerty lit another Camel.

Eric continued to stare around, trying to spot something. "I wonder, when will we see a crime?"

"We already saw one."

Eric looked at the older man.

"The drunk," Haggerty explained patiently, indicating the man leaning against the building. "He just picked the pocket of the man who left the bar."

"You're serious."

"Indeed."

"Damn, and I missed it." Eric said and he shook his head. "Boy, do I have a lot to learn."

Haggerty gestured toward the newsstand. The owner was old and small, and needed a cane to hobble around. What business he was doing was in the Sunday *Daily News*. "See the owner?"

"I do, yessir."

Now he gestured again. "Now, see those two playing with the spaldeen at the corner?"

"The little kids without the shirts you mean?"

"They are little but Hispanics tend to be. But I'd guess they were your age. Damn close anyway. And I'd also guess that when they feel so inclined, they will mug and rob the newsstand owner."

"He's a cripple."

"That shows how smart they are. Nobody in his right mind is going to mug Bronko Nagurski. Let me explain about muggers to you, Eric. Except for the fact that it's low in social prestige, it's not a bad occupation. Short hours, excellent wages, the taxes are very low. What muggers want to avoid is just what the rest of us want to avoid: trouble. Heaven for a mugger is an old woman alone on crutches."

"And you don't think we could stop them?"

"You can't stop crime, Eric—that's why the job is so draining —it flows on over you. And the tide is rising."

Eric was silent a moment and then began to laugh. "I was just thinking of a story—true story—about this famous legendary con man named Yellow Kid Weil. Wore yellow kid gloves. Immaculate gentleman. And he used to work the ocean liners. First class. Sail over, become friends with someone rich, and then cheat them in a card game the last night or get them to invest in something not so legal. And this one trip on the last night he had this old fat guy ripe and ready and they're starting a rummy game when Weil looks up and this other con man is signaling to him to come over. Weil tries to ignore him but this other con man comes right up to the table and says, 'I'm glad you two know each other'— *the old fat guy was a con man too.*" Eric laughed again, forced it, then went silent. "Now why did I tell that?"

Haggerty sat there smoking. Ahead of them, in the next block, a number of bottles crashed against the pavement.

"I guess I was thinking what if the other guy was a pickpocket too."

The two shirtless Puerto Ricans moved a few steps closer to the newsstand, playing expert catch with the spaldeen.

"I still don't get it."

"I was trying to make everything come out all right I guess. If they'd picked each other's pockets, no one would have lost."

More bottles shattered in the darkness up ahead.

"Eric, what the hell are you doing here?"

"You mean why did I decide to be a policeman? Well, there were a bunch of us at Swarthmore interested in the Peace Corps—after graduation, you understand—for the experience. And . . ." He stopped now, looking at a tall beautiful woman who exited the dance hall by the bar. "That black lady's a whore, obviously, right? Or a madam do you think?"

"Too young and pretty for a madam, and she's also a man." Haggerty pointed. "Transvestite bar."

Eric just stared at her.

"What's wrong with the Peace Corps?"

"Nothing—nothing at all—but the Philadelphia police—Swarthmore's not far from Philly—they've got a new recruiting program and they sent a guy to campus—not too warmly received. But he said, 'Why do you want to go across the world to help out in some jungle? Believe me, we've got plenty of jungles at home.' *Plenty of jungles at home*—I couldn't get that phrase to leave me. So I went in and talked to some police in Philadelphia—ground-breaking questions, that kind of thing. And it seemed logical. Not in Philly, I'm a local, I want to work here."

"You do well in school?"

"Well, I ought to, I put in the hours."

"A's?"

"Sure, but my dad expects it, my mom too, Karen does good work, no reason for me not to."

"Eric—I really like you—I don't know you well, but you seem very open, honest, and full of potential—so go to med school."

"Like a good boy, you mean? And spend the rest of my life listening to loonies? Sorry—I know it's old hat to you, but I can't think of much more exciting than bringing in a criminal, a guy who's caused pain, that's *something.*"

"*You don't bring them in!*—and if you do, their lawyers get them out—mostly you collar acidheads, dropouts, *dammit!*" and he stopped suddenly, rolled down his window.

Gunfire from across the street, from inside Earl's.

Haggerty sat there.

Now screams.

"Shit," Haggerty said as he got his gun out, whirled on Eric. *"You listen to me*—you lock this door when I'm out and you sit here. You don't move, got that? You sit right here until I'm back. *Don't do a fucking thing but sit!"*

Eric swallowed, made a nod.

Haggerty threw the car door open and took off across the street. Eric reached over, slammed the door shut, locked it.

Haggerty moved to the sidewalk, slowed, then made a quick move inside.

Gone.

Alone and white in Harlem, in the middle of an angry summer steamer, Eric was crushed to find—no question, no lying about it —panic building.

Ridiculous.

Now stop it!

In the first place, the car was locked. He was safe inside. Point two: Mr. Haggerty was just across the street. True he was out of sight and true again, perhaps even now he was engaged in a gunfight, but there was no disputing the fact that he was around, he was in the area, and he was not about to let anything happen to Eric.

And of course and most of all, Eric could take care of himself.

He was six one, almost two, and he weighed a solid one ninety-five. He was athletic. And he could box. His right was lethal and his left was well formed and the gym coach at Swarthmore had told him to try out for the Golden Gloves, that he had a real shot, if he put in the hours, at being champion.

So how could a locked-in potential Golden Glover with an armed protector feel anything but calm.

Ridiculous indeed.

Eric stared across the street toward Earl's, where the screams were building. A growing crowd filled the sidewalk sprawling into the street itself.

Tick tick tick—

—Eric whirled.

The transvestite stood outside the window tapping his long nail against the glass. Tick tick tick.

Eric ignored him.

Tick tick tick.

Eric turned his back to the window and concentrated on Earl's across the street.

One more tick tick tick and then silence.

Eric kept his attention on Earl's until it was safe. Then he kept it there a while longer. When he finally turned and faced front the two Spanish kids had moved in closer to the newsman with the cane. And the transvestite was sitting on the hood looking in at him through the windshield.

"Get off," Eric said.

The transvestite cupped his hand over one ear and shook his head.

"Off," Eric repeated, louder.

The black man still kept his hand by his ear. Now he pointed to the window and gestured for Eric to roll it down.

Eric hesitated, then rolled it down. Two inches. No more.

"Let's you and me boogie," the transvestite said, getting off the car, leaning by the window.

"I'm not really much in the mood for boogieing, sir," Eric said.

"*Sir!*" the transvestite exploded. "What you mean 'sir'?"

"Ma'am, I meant ma'am, I'm sorry," Eric said quickly.

The black man put his lips by the window opening. He whispered, "I'll take you places you never been."

"I can't leave the car just now," Eric said. "I'm meeting my wife and children here any minute."

"Roun' the worl'—over the falls—"

Eric made no reply, just watched the Spanish kids tossing their spaldeen. The news dealer with the cane was eyeing them now.

Eric felt the dark fingers now gently caressing his cheek. He cried out, felt foolish, but there it was.

"God sure been good to you," the black man said. Then he snaked his thin arm back through the window, looked at Eric for a long moment before turning, walking pridefully back into the bar.

The crowd at Earl's was even larger now. But the screaming had peaked, and there were no more gun sounds.

Why did you cry out like a baby? Jesus. A skinny sick guy and you with a right cross that can drop people. With a jab that sets them up and a cross that puts them down. And still you cry out like a jerk.

More action from Earl's now—people from Eric's side of the street began crossing over in larger numbers.

Which meant there were very few people left around the newsstand.

Eric watched.

The two kids were very close to the newsstand now.

I wish Mr. Haggerty were here, Eric thought.

The tiny old black newsstand owner glanced around. He busied himself straightening the stacks of papers. But one hand was very tight around his cane.

The two kids stopped playing catch. One of them tucked the spaldeen into his jeans pocket.

And now the sidewalk was empty.

Probably they won't do anything, Eric thought. Probably they're just two kids out for a night on the town. Probably they'll see all the action on the sidewalk across the street and go over and see what's going on. Probably . . . Probably . . .

I don't want to watch, Eric decided and he turned his body away and stared across the street.

The newsstand was not that far from the car, just up ahead at the corner and Eric had to concentrate very hard on the crowd across the street in order not to be upset by the cry that came, he assumed, from the old man with the cane.

Now another cry.

Eric studied the crowd across the street. No one paid any attention to what was happening at the newsstand; no one even turned.

He'd fought enough to know what punches sounded like, and he stared across, listening to the blows coming from the direction of the newsstand.

Please, Mr. Haggerty, Eric thought. You must hurry.

Now the sound of a body hitting hard against pavement.

Eric was burning up in the car, so he pulled his tie off hard and managed to get out of his suit coat. He unbuttoned his shirt at the neck and then when there was nothing more to do, he whirled in the seat and stared front.

The old man was trying to rise from the sidewalk. His cane was

beside him and they had him down and one of them was going
through his pockets and as Eric watched a handful of bills came
into view and then they were going for his other pockets but they
didn't produce much and one of them held him down while the
other grabbed some magazines and then they were done and ready
to go—

—but the old man held tight to one of their ankles.

"Leave him alone!" Eric shouted from the car.

The one with the magazines started off and the one with the
money wanted to—

—but the old man would not release his hold on the ankle.

The one with the magazines came back and the one who was
held tried to kick with his free leg—

—but the grip remained.

At least it did until the one with the magazines picked up the
cane and brought it down across the face of the old man, and Eric
said "aw shit" and threw the door open and took off and the kids
saw him and took off too, and they could fly and this was their
turf and in a blink they were around the corner and tearing up the
dark street but they were slow, compared to Eric they were molas-
ses and probably they sensed that because halfway up the block
they turned, racing into a deserted lot.

Eric trapped them easily. They were caught in the farthest
corner where the walls of the lot connected, and they were breathing heavily. Eric waited for his eyes to get better accustomed. He
kept ten feet away, watching them until one of them started
screaming, *"This got nothin' to do with you, get the fuck out of it."*

Eric felt he had to say something and he hoped he didn't blow
things now. It was important they realize they were in trouble,
they had no choices left, they were his to do with just what he
wanted—only he wasn't exactly sure how you got all that across.
His throat felt dry and he hoped it wouldn't squeak on him.
"Don't make me hurt you," he said easily in the night, and it
sounded—he had to admit it—it sounded so goddam authentic
and tough Cagney would have nodded in approval. No bluster.
Not yet. Just authority—"Don't make me hurt you" implied that
it was up to them, if they wanted pain, he could deliver it.

In the dark, the two kids looked at each other. "You're asking
for it, asshole," the one with the magazines said, but his tone was
already weaker than before.

"Give me what you stole," Eric said, again quietly.

Again they looked at each other and there were bricks scattered on the floor of the lot and suddenly the one with the money stooped and grabbed for one and Eric boomed *"I'll tear you fucking apart you give me trouble—"*

The brick might have been on fire he dropped it that quickly.

God *damn*, Eric thought, it worked.

"This ain't your business," the magazine kid said.

But there was whining in his voice now.

"I want it all, everything you took."

"Can we keep the *Playboys*—?"

"You keep nothing, I want it now!"

"Okay, shit, okay," the money kid said, and he nervously walked to Eric, held out the cash, and as Eric took it the magazine kid handed over the magazines and the money kid kicked Eric's testicles up toward his stomach and in the beat or two that exists between the blow and the pain, Eric began to say "Now get out of here" except the "nnnn" was all he had time to begin before his hands went to his genitals and he pitched forward onto the bricks, the world white now with pain. He was aware as they knelt and scrabbled for their belongings, and nothing he could do would stop them, and after they were standing he wasn't sure which of them began kicking his ribs in and which was the one stomping his face but he did what he feebly could, one arm trying to protect the body, the other the head, and did they enjoy it, Eric wondered, the world whiter, it seemed like they did, and would they stop, Eric wondered, the white shrouding him now and maybe they never would have if Haggerty hadn't come.

Haggerty knelt beside the body, letting the other two skitter away. Carefully he cradled Eric, lifted him, ran . . .

Karen, the twin, sat in silence in an uncomfortable chair in the hospital corridor. She said nothing, just stared down toward the end and a window that looked like it was coming up dawn. Haggerty paced. He never felt less in control of himself, never more failed. The parents were in the room with the victim and had been for a while.

I owed the man a favor, Haggerty thought. He saved my son and I owed him and look what I did. *Look what I did!* He glanced at the room, then moved to the end of the corridor and stepped into the exit stairwell so he could light a Camel.

And a great kid too. Sure naïve, sure insanely romantic, but he didn't dream about making it on Wall Street and he didn't dream about boffing everything that moved, no—he dreamed of bringing in the bad guys.

And look what you did, look what you did!

He stomped out the cigarette, looked back down toward the room—nothing. He lit another butt. How was he going to face Doctor Lorber. What could he say? Haggerty sat on the top step and smoked. Ten minutes without moving, maybe twenty, maybe he would have never moved if the hand hadn't rested on his shoulder and there was Doctor Lorber kneeling beside him.

"It just happened," Haggerty said, "I didn't mean for it, I was showing him around, we were parked, it was going okay, and then this gunfight started and I had to do something and I guess he left the car or I don't know, I only do know that my God, I never meant for it to happen." He looked at Eric's father now.

Who was almost smiling.

"He'll be coming to soon. No damage of a permanent type. The face will heal, the ribs are cracked and broken but that should be the worst thing that ever happens to him."

"I'll make it up to you, Doctor Lorber—I won't rest till I do. You've got my word on that." He stood then, and they left the stairwell, moving back into the corridor. Karen was sitting with an older woman now, the mother.

"You don't understand something, Frank—you did what I asked—young people today don't meet reality soon enough—I guarantee you, when Eric comes to, he'll have some brains." He lowered his voice. "It's a terrible thing to say, but the way things turned out—couldn't be better."

A nurse came out of Eric's room. "Is Karen here? He'd like to see Karen."

Karen stood, looked at her parents, started hesitantly toward the room. She reached the doorway. The nurse waited outside, gestured for Karen to enter. But it was hard. She and Eric were close, always—eerily close with their minds. They sometimes answered questions the other one hadn't asked. Not asked out loud.

In the room now she told herself she was going to be a doctor, she could look at a wounded patient, but she wasn't prepared. If he'd been a stranger she'd have recoiled, what with his eyes swollen totally shut and his mouth almost as bad and God knew what the rest of his body looked like beneath the sheet. He had tubes

all over and what skin there was was red and blue with bruisings
and she managed "Hey Little," her private name for him since he
came fifteen minutes after her arrival, which meant she was the
big one of the family.

". . . oh . . ."

"Easy." She took his hand.

". . . oh Kawen . . ." he whispered, his mouth too swollen to
make *r*'s.

She was afraid she was going to unravel then, so quickly she told
him, "You sound like Elmer Fudd."

That almost made him laugh but it also caused terrible pain.

"Oh Christ I'm sorry," Karen said. "I am, Little, please believe
me, no more jokes, it's all going to be fine, there's no damage,
you'll forget everything about this night."

". . . no . . ."

"Believe me, you will."

". . . Kawen . . . ?"

"What?"

". . . I wuved it . . ."

Karen said nothing.

". . . I did an' . . . an' you know what . . . ?"

"What, Little?"

". . . gonn be po-weese-munnn . . ."

There was not widespread joy in the Lorber household when
Eric's decision was announced. Ike and Essy berated themselves,
which is what parents do best, asking endlessly where they went
wrong, how did such a curse come to fall on them and not some
neighboring gentile. And they hoped, as Eric left for his senior
year at Swarthmore, for a return of sanity.

He did wonderfully that year, no surprise, and they received
more letters from him than ever, about his classes and his friends
and there was no mention of the law. They were pleased with him
and how his year was going, but then they didn't know that several
nights a week after his work was done, Eric took a bus into South
Philly to study the one subject he felt he had to learn before
graduation: night-fighting. Because yes he was quick and sure he
could drop you with his right, but not at night, not when there
were shadows. The beating in Harlem he tried to consider a blessing: mistakes were what you learned from. (Although he prayed

more than once to have a someday opportunity to meet those two
Spaniards again. And if that happened, he knew one thing: he
would be ready.)

From the beginning of his life, people always attributed brilliance to Eric but he wasn't buying. What he was willing to do was
outwork anybody. Whatever it took to get something done he was
more than willing to give. And now he moved through the South
Philly bars, the most dangerous ones he could find, and he nursed
beers and fights weren't hard to find and he watched them, learning not much at all, just waiting.

Then one dark night he saw an aging black bartender dispose
of three construction workers in less than two minutes, and he
knew he had his man. Eric approached the older man when the
bar closed and said excuse me sir and then made his pitch.

Jed Randolph, for that was the bartender's name, just stared
Eric down. "What are you, some Ivy League asshole on a scav-
enger hunt?"

Eric assured him that was not the case.

"And you want me to beat the shit out of you? *And you'll pay
me?*"

Eric admitted it wasn't your everyday request.

Randolph wanted no part of it until Eric suggested a fee of
fifteen dollars per session.

Class began the following Saturday.

Randolph had been a fighter and in the merchant marine and
he knew many things, how to hurt with your fingertips, how to
banish, momentarily, pain, how to make an ally of darkness. And
if in the beginning, he pulled his blows somewhat, that didn't
mean Eric wasn't badly whipped when he went back to school.
And after a month, the whippings became less severe and Mr.
Randolph was able to swing more freely and he was pleased,
because Eric was a quick study, and he intuitively almost picked
up when to run and when to fall, when to take pain and how, most
especially, to give it.

Eric invited Mr. Randolph to his graduation, introduced him
to his parents as his phys. ed. teacher where Mr. Randolph spoke
warmly of the boy even though he had to admit, he said, there
were some who might consider Eric to be *very very* strange.

* * * * *

"Your kid's in the Academy," Cooney said one autumn day. Cooney, at Gallagher's, had called Eric a "co-ed." He was Haggerty's partner at the 19th now, hanging on till retirement, and he knew how much the beating in Harlem had taken out of Haggerty.

Haggerty had his own contacts so he knew where Eric was and that he was doing exceptionally well. "How's he doing I wonder?" he asked.

"My word is 'fair,' " Cooney said.

Haggerty went back to reading Dick Young in the *News*. "Fair" was good coming from Cooney, who not only gave away ice in the winter, he also hated Jews . . .

"Your kid's heading for the 28th," Cooney said one morning when they were getting coffee.

"Harlem, huh; tough beat. Wonder why he picked it?"

"Obvious why—he's a kike, he's a pusher, he wants to make a record, get ahead, that's why they own the world, y'know, they push harder."

"He only did fair at the Academy."

"—who said that?—"

"—you said that—"

"—he didn't do fair, he did tops, but he's rich, he had a lot of contacts, his old man knows a lot of people in the Commissioner's office—"

"—it was pull got him to the top, that what you're saying?" Cooney nodded. "How else?" he said with total confidence . . .

"Your 'kid' lucked into a drug bust, first fucking week on patrol," Cooney said. He seemed sour. His stomach was off.

"His father probably set it up for him to score," Haggerty said. Cooney belched and looked at him. *"Whaaat?"*

"His old man's got a lot of contacts," Haggerty said. "I heard that someplace . . ."

"He stopped a bloodbath," Cooney said some weeks later.

"Who?" Haggerty said, sharpening a pencil. Eric had called to tell him as soon as he was off duty. They were meeting now irregularly, when their schedules permitted, for coffee and shoptalk. Eric always had a lot of questions.

"Your 'kid'—up at Earl's. Big rumble. Half a dozen people involved."

"Did he talk them into being reasonable? Jews are good at talking."

"He cold-cocked a couple, the rest got the message."

Haggerty was silent for a moment. "Couldn't have been his old man, helping him, do you think?"

"I'm tired hearing about his old man," Cooney said as he stormed off to the water cooler . . .

"I don't be-*lieve* this," Cooney said one spring morning.

Haggerty looked casually over from his desk. "Hmm?"

"He got a *murderer*. Your kid. I never got a fuckin' murderer in thirty years."

"Probably lucked into it," Haggerty consoled.

Cooney exploded—"It wasn't luck—*it wasn't luck*—he *deduced* it—" He looked at Haggerty now bewildered. "What's going *on* up there?"

It was becoming increasingly clear, even to the Cooneys, that a bomb had exploded at the 28th Precinct.

To move on up from patrolman, to get the detective's gold shield, takes time. Sometimes you can fall into it—if you collar Jack the Ripper they'll advance you on the spot—and it helps to have a rabbi in a position of import, a precinct captain or a headquarters man. But usually you advance only with time. Three years is fast.

Interest in Eric began before he was into his second year. But he stayed where he was. He liked the 28th, he explained, he didn't know enough to move on yet. And nothing would change his mind. And nothing did.

Till Cooney retired.

Then it helped to have a rabbi, especially one named Haggerty, and it took some maneuvering, sure, but what doesn't when you're dealing with the police department. Bottom line: he was just short of twenty-seven when he became Haggerty's partner. He achieved the same kind of record at the 19th as he'd had in Harlem, remarkable considering the opportunities are less when your precinct house is on East 67th Street than up north. He played things the way Haggerty always did, very low key. But one way or another, Eric's reputation grew. He wasn't famous like Popeye Doyle in fiction or Serpico in fact. But no one denied he was certainly a presence.

And when E. F. Lorber talked, people listened . . .

5

EDITH

Edith was tempted to take a cab, it was that February bitter. As she left the "Beekman Place place"—Sally insisted on referring to the house as that—a taxi cruised by and she went so far as to raise her hand, and when it stopped, she was suddenly embarrassed. "It's better for me if I walk," she explained. "*That's* what you hailed me for?—to tell me *that?*" He shook his head. "Even in Beekman Place they got *meshuganas.*" Edith broke out laughing and quickly got out a dollar bill, handed it over. The driver, gnarled and permanently suspicious, eyed the green paper a moment before pocketing it. "If that's what you tip for *not* riding, lady, I sure the hell wish you'd got in."

"You made me laugh," Edith told him. "I haven't done that enough lately." He waved, drove off; Edith began to walk, thinking about what she'd said. It was true—she hadn't been laughing enough lately. The painting had started to become obsessive. And probably the children were complaining to themselves about her inattentiveness, and perhaps Phillip was worrying that she was entering some kind of life *crise,* but it just wasn't so. She was painting better. Week by week. She could feel it in her fingers. And more than that, Sally told her it was true.

Pulling her navy blue coat tight around her, Edith set out for First Avenue and started uptown. It was after four so she didn't window-shop at all, but in an antique store she caught sight of herself in an old mirror and her reddish hair, long and loose, was much too schoolgirlish Edith decided. And more than that, with this weather, she was silly not to have worn a scarf. Maybe I'll buy myself one at Bloomingdale's, she thought. Something in cashmere perhaps. Extra long for extra cold days. She felt good about that actually; the idea of actually buying something for herself and not Phillip or the girls proved a pleasing novelty.

In the middle 50's she ran over the list in her mind. Phillip: a new red silk tie. The one he had was his favorite, and it was valiant, but nothing could survive the dollop of vinaigrette sauce Phillip accidentally fed it the evening earlier at Le Veau d'Or. "You poor dear," Edith said, looking at his suddenly stricken Lincolnesque face. "It's like you've lost an old friend."

So a new red silk tie was first on the agenda. And an extra long cashmere scarf, that came next. And then, oh then the girls.

Never terribly religious, Edith still believed that Up There Someone was on the lookout for those less fortunate. But when it came to the subject of Kate, Abigail, and Caroline, she was sometimes not all that sure. It wasn't their growth spurts, which rendered all new clothes instantly, it seemed, obsolete. If children stayed the same size, grownups wouldn't be able to say "my how you've grown" and then where would the art of intergenerational conversation be? And it wasn't their incessant competitiveness—being young, they all three naturally were subscribers to the "chocolate cake" theory of love, i.e., love was a cake, the more that were around to share the smaller each portion became. The idea of there being a cake for each was beyond them yet. So they competed over everything, and Edith didn't mind so much that the loser always wept, and she even survived the odd fact that the winner seemed also to be in tears.

What was truly hard to face was that she had three beloveds, aged fourteen, thirteen, and twelve, and *all three were hurtling into puberty at precisely the same time*. Kate, the fourteen-year-old, was a little late; Caroline, the baby, a bit precocious, Abby in the middle right on the button.

It was not easy.

A cross glance from either parent of course produced hysteria. Fine. What child likes cross looks? But a sweet look had the same effect. Or a puzzled one. *Everything* produced hysteria. "How was school today?" Hysteria. "What was the name of that cute boy from Collegiate?" Quick tears. "Shall we send out for Chinese food?" "Chinese food, when I'm *dieting*? Wahhh." And it did no good later to try and explain that the reason for the suggestion of Chinese food was because it was common knowledge that it was thinning. "*Common knowledge?* You mean you talk to everybody about how fat I am? *WAAAAHHHHHHHHHHHHHHHH!*"

As she cut across 57th to Second Avenue, Edith wondered could she, when she was Edith Mazursky, have been the same to her mother as her brood was tormenting her now? Doubtful. Not because her mother disallowed tears—on the contrary, weeping was always part of Myrtle's own arsenal. But she was also of the generation and temperament that didn't just ignore a thing like puberty, she absolutely *denied its existence*. It was at most, a rumor, like menopause, and no more a fit subject for serious conversation than flying saucers.

Edith moved quickly up Second Avenue now, wondering if she shouldn't have tried the same tack as Myrtle, total unswerving blind ignorance—her girls found her that way anyway, ignorant, unswerving, and blind—so probably it would have been worth the gamble. Curse Benjamin Spock anyway, Edith thought. Him and his "You know more than you think you know" approach to upbringing.

She was still moving uptown now, quickly in the increasing cold, when she saw a man running diagonally across Second in her direction, and instinctively she took a firmer grip on her purse, this in spite of the fact that the approaching figure might just have been —though it was hard to tell detail in this light—the handsomest man she had ever seen. He was running now, dead at her, and Edith looked quickly behind to see who his target was. But then he was on her, lifting her up in the air, trying to kiss her as she struggled. "Edith, Edith Mazursky Jesus son of a bitch."

When she at last realized it was Doyle Ackerman who held her in his arms, Edith stopped struggling.

He put her down, took her hand, led her quickly into the coffee shop on the corner, sat down across from her in the empty back booth. He was tanned, and wore a camel's hair topcoat. Or perhaps it was vicuña, Edith never was much on that kind of thing. But she knew enough to see it was expensive. As was the dark gray suit he wore beneath.

Edith kept her navy blue topcoat on as long as she could. The dress underneath had never been stylish, even when it was new, and it was certainly not that now. She looked across at him. In fifteen years, he hadn't gained a pound. Perhaps he was even trimmer now than when his perfect swimmer's body had addled her brains. "Doyle," she managed. "It's perfectly obvious you've let yourself go to seed. For shame."

Doyle smiled, said "Coffee?" She nodded, so he said to the waitress by their table, "One coffee, one tea. And the coffee . . ." He hesitated only a moment. "Cream, no sugar." He looked at Edith. "I remember right?"

How could you not be impressed? Edith said as much.

Doyle laughed. "Funny, y'know," Doyle said. "I knew back at Yale all those assholes could outgrind me, but I always was one hundred sure I'd end up ahead. On account of I remember reading an article about this top bartender once, and he said that the secret of success was remembering a customer's name because once you had their name they were yours for life."

"So you decided to remember how everyone liked their coffee, is that it?" Edith said. "Dale Carnegie insists there's more to it than that." She could not quite grab the name of the girl Doyle had married. It was hotel money though; that much she was sure.

"Okay, fifteen years in thirty seconds, you wanna go first or me?"

Their order came. Edith gestured for Doyle to begin.

"Well, I married Angie Florsheim and we live in Miami—*we* both still live there, but not together. *Pffffft.* I see the kids though. And I run the business."

"A hotel or something?" Edith said.

"Before *I* arrived it was 'a' hotel. It is now, believe me, many."

"That's wonderful, Doyle."

"*I* know things, Edith. I got a sense for the public pulse, you know what I mean?"

Edith indicated that she did.

"I decided to diversify. I knew one thing: Miami's a cycle town and the hotel's a cycle business. So, I went into an amusement park operation. I bought into a shopping center. I bought boats for chartering. I . . ."

Edith stirred her coffee, staring at the liquid now, listening to him. I and I and I and I and I . . . She took a sip, smiled at him, hoped the fact that her eyes were glazing over was reasonably well hidden. Dear God, what in the world would we have talked about for fifteen years?

"Me?" she said when he finally asked her resumé. "Just a housewife. Three girls. And I do a little painting when I can."

He reached across the table now, momentarily took her hand. "We had some fantastic times, remember?"

"Doyle, you broke my heart, remember?"

"I didn't and you know it."

"*I* most certainly do know it, and the only reason you might not is you weren't there when you did it. I came down to New Haven expecting you to meet me and there was your roommate with the news that you were going into the hotel business."

Doyle raised his right hand. "I always tried to let girls down easy," he said. "It was best the way I did it."

"It was chicken; I distinctly remember thinking that at the time."

"Well, it all worked out great. I'm in great shape and you're bearing up pretty good yourself from the looks of things. You married that tall guy on the rebound, huh?"

"Those things happen."

"And it's been great?"

Edith thought very carefully before she answered. She spoke then with some precision: "Not great, but never less than good. And getting better every year. Those things happen too."

"He never knew about us, did he?"

"Never."

"I always tried to keep my relationships quiet; it was best that way," Doyle said. And then he said, "Dinner?"

Edith hesitated, because it might be fun to let Phillip see what an idiot she'd been, but then, he probably would tease her unmercifully about Doyle for years to come. Imitate him even. It wouldn't be all that hard to imitate Doyle actually; all you'd need do was use the first person singular pronoun as often as possible and make believe you were Mortimer Snerd with two years of Andover behind you.

"Nothing glamorous," he said into the silence. "I'm into health a lot. Not a nut. I'm not a vegetarian or anything. But fish tends to be my mainstay."

"Phillip loves Gloucester House," Edith said. "I'll have to check, he may be working late though."

"I'm only interested *if* he's working late," Doyle said. "And Gloucester House is too well known, it's a crossroads, y'know? There's these two on Fulton Street. Sloppy Louie's and Sweet's. Great fish and you don't run into a lot of people, y'know?"

Edith could barely wait to get out and call Sally Levinson. To reject the boy who broke your silly heart—Christmas in February. "Oh Doyle," she said. "I have the children to think about."

"The children?"

"I don't think I could lose you again. I couldn't trust myself, Doyle. You're too beautiful."

"I'm a lot more than looks, Edith."

Edith almost asked what, but there was no point to stumping him, what did it prove. "We must remember each other as we were," she said. "I've got to get to my shopping, Doyle."

"You're turning me down?"

"For now. Perhaps the next time we meet you'll be into macrobiotics and then think of the music we'll make." She stood.

"Here, here," he said, scribbling on something. It was a business card and he handed it to her. "Put this in your purse. My private number's on the back."

"Bliss," Edith said, putting the card along with her charge cards and turning for the door. "Doyle," she said finally and with total seriousness. "You have absolutely made my day." And she practically floated back out into the night and across town to Third and perhaps, had she been in a less glowing mood, she might have noted that for whatever reason, the cold, the threat of snow, the flow of pedestrian traffic was altering. Sometimes the street from Third to Bloomingdale's was flooded, sometimes not.

This was one of the "not" times.

So conceivably Edith, a more down-to-earth Edith, might have noted that the dark street was, if not empty, certainly, at least for this moment, on the way to being more than half deserted. And those that did walk walked quickly, eyes on the ground, bodies tilted forward against the wind and cold.

As Edith began the block, she might even have been bothered by the dark stairway that led to the basement of a brownstone. Ordinarily those stairs are gated and locked. This was open. Forced perhaps. Or forgotten. But in either case, an enormous shadow moved slightly in that opening.

But probably Edith would have plunged on to her beloved Bloomingdale's anyway. My God, *what* could happen to a nice Jewish girl who had just experienced that most blessed of all emotions, revenge? Hot damn, thought Edith Mazursky Holtzman.

Her heels clicked, clicked, clicked on the sidewalk. What indeed . . . ?

6

BILLY BOY

"The bus station please," Billy Boy said when the Shrimp asked him where he wanted to be let off. He always went to them first whenever he hit a new town. There wasn't anyplace you could get the feel of things like you could in a bus station.

"You got it." Then no more talk till the Caddie pulled to a halt by Port Authority.

It had been that kind of trip. Fast driving, loud music, not a lot of chitchat. In the beginning it had been talky enough. The Shrimp —he had these pale blue eyes that looked through you sometimes —he'd gone to school in the Midwest someplace, Indiana or Ohio, and then he'd become an Angelino before deciding to make it in New York.

"What the fuck's an Angelino?" Billy Boy asked.

"Someone from Los Angeles."

"That makes me a Milwaukee-eeno then," Billy Boy said, and he roared his laughter, because it was so funny.

Only the Shrimp didn't think so. He didn't even smile. Just gunned the Caddie along the turnpike.

Billy Boy, frightened suddenly, told himself to Jesus watch it! So that was when their long silences began.

They got a flat on the Pennsy and the Shrimp was all hot and bothered but Billy Boy was so happy. If there was one thing he knew it was cars. No. He knew a lot about a helluva lot, but one of the things he knew *most* about was cars. He changed the Caddie's tire so fast the Shrimp couldn't goddam believe it. Then he asked if Billy Boy wanted the wheel a little and you don't say no to a Caddie, not ever, so he pushed it hard until they began getting into heavy traffic and up ahead in the late morning sun he saw it there.

New York!

It was one thing to be King in Milwaukee or Memphis or any of the other spots along his way. But shit.

New York!

"You better drive from here," he said, and they switched in the car, the Shrimp taking the wheel, Billy Boy lifting him across into position, then sliding the rest of the way to the passenger's spot again.

The tunnel was murder so it was close to one when the Caddie stopped at 41st and Eighth. "Hope your sister's surprised," the Shrimp said.

Billy Boy just stared. "Huh?"

"You told me you were surprising your sister."

"Oh, naturally." Pause. "But didn't I also tell you I wanted the bus station?"

"This is Port Authority."

Billy Boy stared at the huge building. "Isn't there a smaller one?"

"Nothing's smaller in New York."

Billy Boy nodded, got out, muttered "thanks." The air was suddenly so cold. He buttoned up his raincoat to the neck. It was still so cold.

"For the tire change," the Shrimp said, and he handed over ten. "Take it!"

Billy Boy grabbed the bread. He didn't know which was his bigger fear all of a sudden, the Shrimp or the City. "You're a good guy, you'll live a long time."

The Shrimp looked at him funny. "Yeah?"

"Believe me," Billy Boy said. "I can tell things like that." And then he walked into Port Authority.

It was all fucked up, construction everywhere, arrows and pillars and thousands of people and—

—and why were they looking at him? All of them looking. At him. Dead at him.

They weren't.

Not all. Shit, a lot weren't.

But a lot were.

A lot.

Too many.

It was his clothes. Here it was winter in the Apple and he had his prison shoes still and the jeans he'd taken and over the jeans the raincoat. In the winter in the Apple he was in a raincoat, no wonder they were looking. He quick went into a store where a nigger girl said, "May I help you find a book, sir?" and he said, "Why would I want a fucking book, for Chrissakes," and as she started glancing around—for help?—so did he, and there was every reason for him to want a book, it was a *book* store, and watch your mouth, you don't swear like that at niggers, not in the Apple, they treated niggers different than back in other places, better sometimes, so he muttered "excuse me," and hurried back out of the store.

And all the people were still looking at his clothes.

He went into a liquor store and asked to use the phone but the old Jew just pointed at a sign on the wall—"No Checks, No Phones"—and Billy Boy was back in the main corridor again, with all the people staring.

Ahead, at last, he saw some phone booths.

Two empty.

Good luck.

He sat in the first.

Bad luck.

Out of order.

Both.

He got in line to use one of the three working ones. Then he realized he needed the Yellow Pages. It meant maybe losing his place in line but he needed the Yellow Pages bad. So he left the line, opened the book, licked his thumb and forefinger, turned and turned until he found what he needed, then stood in line again.

"Hero's" he heard, when his time finally came.

"I'm new in town," Billy Boy said into the phone. "And I wondered how much things cost here."

"I can't give no prices over the phone, Mac, but I'll tell you this: we're cheaper than Primo's, we're cheaper than King Size. And our quality's tops. What do you need?"

"Maybe a sweater and maybe some pants and a shirt too or like that. Socks. Underwear. Y'know."

"The works, huh? Sounds like you got a heavy date." And he kind of laughed.

Billy Boy tried to laugh too. What the hell did clothes have to do with women? You wanted a woman, you slipped her some bread, what the fuck did clothes have to do with fucking? "That's right, the works. But it's gotta fit good."

"How big are you?"

"Big enough. And it's gotta fit good."

"We do half the wrestlers play the Garden, just come on in."

"How much though?"

"Top quality? Couple hundred'll see you fine. I'm interested in customer satisfaction, I never yet lost a sale over money, just come on over. We're open till seven."

Couple hundred. Two rich women ought to have that much. Maybe one. This was New York. "It'll be after dark before I can get there. Where are you; like I said I'm new in town."

"Just behind Bloomingdale's, can't miss us."

Billy Boy left the booth and found his way as quickly as he could to the men's room to check it out. It was big and not so bad as some. Couple queens off by the far sink, but who cared about a couple queens? He studied the place a long time and it really made him feel good. He could, if he had to, spend the night here. He didn't want that, naturally. A hotel room with a bed would be a ton better. What he wanted was to get the clothes and a couple top-class bottles of whiskey and see a broad for a few minutes and then sleep. But that would require pulling a job or two. If he pulled the job, fine, it was hotel time. If he didn't, not all that bad, he'd spend the night here.

Everything depended on one not-so-small point: Was this or wasn't it a lucky day?

"Is this my lucky day?"

The Spic lady looked up from doing her nails. There were two kids behind her in the doorway. Behind them, a TV was blaring and men laughed.

Billy Boy waited in the doorway on Eighth Avenue. "That's all I wanna know, how much?"

"You must come in and sit down," the Spic lady said. She pointed to the Fortune-teller sign in the window. "I know everything but not from a distance."

Billy Boy sat across from her, held out his hands palms up. "Is this my lucky day, yes or no, I wanna pull a job so you tell me."

She blinked. "What you mean 'pull a job'?"

"*Get* a job," Billy Boy said quickly. "I got to apply after employment and I wanna know should I or maybe it's best if I wait till tomorrow." He pushed his hands toward her.

"Two palms is ten, five each."

"Can you tell luck either way?"

"I could bullshit you with one. But a thing like luck I can only be positive with two."

"Both then." Her kids were out of the doorway now, looking up at him.

"Don't they bother you?"

"They help me—sometimes they can be very sensitive."

"So can I," Billy Boy said. "Sometimes."

"Take out the ten, hold it tight, make a wish."

Billy Boy did what she said and almost wished that he could fuck all Charlie's Angels one after the other. But then he quick decided that was dumb. The one with the hair was long gone and if he wanted three at once he could buy three at once. If this was a lucky day. I better wish this is my lucky day, he decided, and did.

She took the ten, put it under an ashtray on the table beside her. Then she took his palms, stared at them, began quickly to talk. ". . . through your palms I see this is a time of great decision for you . . . through your palms I see that next month will be lucky days for you . . . through—"

"Today, lady. I don't give a shit about next month, okay?"

"I'm closing in on the truth, you think that's so easy?"

"No. I'm just anxious. Go on."

". . . through your palms I see that though you don't cry on the outside, inside your heart has many tears . . . through your palms I see you are a good man, and many people love you, but you got trouble showing you love them back . . . your wife or your girl friend, she loves you because you are a good man . . ."

"And you are a phony fortune-teller," Billy Boy said, "Gimme my ten."

Suddenly she shouted very loud in Spanish.

Billy Boy just sat there.

There were footsteps and male voices.

Billy Boy blinked and waited.

Two Spics with knives came through the doorway. She shouted at them in Spanish. They both looked at Billy Boy. One of them was just in white underwear shorts. He was little with a big knife. The other one had a bigger knife and he had pants on. The kids moved to the wall and stared up at everything. The one with just underwear said, "Out, asshole," and he gestured toward the door with his thumb.

"She's a phony fortune-teller," Billy Boy explained. "I'm better than her and I want my ten dollars back."

The one with pants moved a step forward, his knife held in front of him, his body balanced. "What you *want* and what you *get* ain't necessarily the same, bimbo." On the word "get" he pushed his knife higher into the air, making his meaning very clear.

Billy Boy sat there blinking. This was New York and you had to be careful. But they were making a fool of him. She was a phony fortune-teller and that was a bad thing, because some of the greatest people he had ever met were fortune-tellers—no, more—some of the greatest people who ever lived were fortune-tellers. It was a job you didn't bullshit around with so even though it was New York and even though he knew he had to be careful, he quickly stood and turned his right hand into a fist and turned his right arm into a club and raised it high and took two steps toward the one with pants who started all of a sudden screaming "Give him the fucking money, Jesus Christ, you trying to get me killed?" and then he turned and ran back down the corridor and the one with just underwear grabbed the bill from under the ashtray and threw it to Billy Boy and then he turned and began beating up on the fortune-teller while he screamed at her in Spanish and the kids by the wall still watched in silence and they were the last things Billy Boy looked at as he left, shaking his head, wondering what kids like that were gonna turn out to be, living a life like that?

"Is this my lucky day or not and how much is it gonna cost me?" Billy Boy said to the next fortune-teller, a black one. She had her storefront between Eighth and Ninth, on forty-something street, right near the first, both of them right near the bus station. That was just one of the great things about stations, all the fortune-tellers. When you were at a station you weren't home and when you weren't home you weren't safe and when you weren't safe, that was when a fortune-teller really came in handy. A good one. And this black lady looked good. Sometimes the black ones *knew*.

"Not a penny. Come sit."

Billy Boy squinted at her. "How do you pay your rent then if you don't charge nothing?"

"Come sit."

Billy Boy looked around. Same storefront setup as before. A corridor leading back. The TV on. Now here came three little black kids, peeking out. "Okay," he said finally, taking the chair across from her, holding out his hands palms up. "But don't try bullshitting me about how I'm crying on the inside or my wife really loves me or I'll have a Merry Christmas. Is today a lucky day? Period. Yes or no?"

"Do you sleep?"

"Huh?"

"At night. Do you sleep?"

" 'Course."

"Well, not me. I sit up all night in my trances. That's when my candlevision comes."

"Your what comes?"

"And when I said no money, I meant no money. I don't want nothing from you till you can't stand but to give it to me. Till you are desperate to hand it over. Till you are so grateful you got to slip me bread or you'll die of a guilty conscience. *Then* you pay me all you want. I got no limits then. You get me?"

Billy Boy didn't.

"I don't take nothing in advance, that's all. I'm different from a lot of these honkys and Spics—there's a lot of phonies in this town, believe me."

Billy Boy did.

"Now you wanna know about a lucky day. Sheeeat. That's nothin' to wanna know. With candlevision, I can tell you a lucky *hour.* I can pin down the lucky goddam *minute.* And it costs spit. All the risk is mine. You interested? 'Cause if you are, fine, we set to it, if you're not, good-bye, there's others need me."

"I need you," Billy Boy said. "What do I have to do?"

"Sleep. Sleep and dream. Sleep and dream and leave the rest to me. 'Cause while you're sleeping, you're not alone."

"No?"

"One of my vision candles will be right alongside you. Nineteen vision candles are what you'll take away from here. One for nineteen nights. Nineteen is a special number for me. Each candle burns the night and while you sleep, I have my visions. And you come back each day and ask me anything and I'll tell you what the visions told me. And after nineteen days, if you want to give me a diamond bracelet, I'll let you. A fur, I'll let you. You want to come up here in a limousine and sign it over to me, I'll let you, *because I'll have earned it.* You will have found the right woman to make you happy. You will have found the right job to make you rich. And best of all, you will have found a person—*me*—who will take away all your troubles forever." She reached down into the table beside her chair and took out a bundle of long candles with strange symbols painted on them. "Nineteen for you," she said, indicating the candles. "And twenty-nine for me."

Billy Boy reached out for the candles gently, so as not to damage them.

"*And twenty-nine for me,*" the black lady said, holding out her hand now. "I import these fuckers from Tibet. Them's hand-painted magic symbols on each one. You know what magic paint costs nowadays?"

"I'm supposed to pay you twenty-nine dollars?" Billy Boy said. "Why not a hundred?"

" 'Cause fifty ain't a special number for me and twenty-nine is."

Billy Boy was starting to get angry now.

"Don't you lookit me like that—I'll tell you how bad a day this is for you, you look at me like that—"

"—you don't know for sure," Billy Boy said, but he was up now, backing for the door.

She closed her eyes and started shouting: "Today is shit for you —today is worse than shit, today is *pain for you*—"

Billy Boy ran out into the street, his hands over his ears. He knocked over a couple of people on his way back to Eighth Avenue. It was cold now. It was cold and after three and starting to get dark. And—and—*he still didn't know!*

The third place was different—different and better, he could tell that right away. Just off Ninth Avenue, directly behind the bus station. There were no kids hanging around. Just a dog. A gigantic Seeing Eye shepherd. And the lady was white, and old, and pale, and blind. "Is this my lucky day?" Billy Boy said quietly.

The shepherd growled.

"Shhhhhh," the ancient voice whispered.

"It's important," Billy Boy said. "Ten dollars is my limit and I'm in a hurry."

She gestured for him to sit alongside her on the tattered couch. Billy Boy did as he was told until the shepherd growled again, louder, and got up—it was a big mother and now the growl was worse and you could see the jagged teeth.

The old woman held out her hand and instantly the dog quieted.

She made another gesture and it quickly lay down at her feet. Billy Boy sat then, and she reached for his right hand, took it, held it tight, then loose, then tight again. Finally she ran the tips of her fingers over his rough palm. "You have done many bad things in your life," came the whisper now. She wore thick black glasses and her head was always tilted slightly left. "You have hurt many people with these hands, so why do you deserve luck?"

"Because I done many good things too."

"Not a strong enough reason. But I'll tell you what is. You deserve luck *because you are special.*"

"I only got ten dollars, don't bullshit me and try for more, there ain't more."

"I can prove you are special. You know things. The future sometimes, don't deny it. Sometimes the past. You've been here before, don't deny it."

"I don't like to talk about that."

"We must. Because I'm special. I sense a great deal. But my dog. My beast. He senses most. Did you hear him growl when you came in? Did you hear him growl louder when you came near? He doesn't growl, my beast. He is trained to silence. Except when the special ones come near. The ones who can sense things. Who can tell the future and the past."

"I said already I don't like talking about that. People don't understand. They think you're crazy."

"They think I'm crazy too. I know this is a lucky day for you. Money will come to you today. More money than you hope for. That is in the future and I can tell that. I traveled across the country once in a covered wagon. I was raped and scalped by two Apache braves. That was in the past and I can tell that too. Were you ever in a covered wagon?"

Billy Boy hesitated. "No," he said finally.

"But you admit you are special?"

Billy Boy hesitated again. He wanted so to talk about it, but sometimes when you did, they laughed at you.

"I won't laugh," the blind one said.

"I gotta get to a store," Billy Boy said.

"What do I call you?—I don't want your name, but I have to call you something. You can call me 'Duchess.' "

"Were you one once?"

The ancient blind face made a smile. "No. But I always wanted to be."

"Billy Boy." He stood then, headed for the door.

"You can pay me the ten when you come back later."

"How do you know I'm coming back later?"

From the giant shepherd now, a deep growl. The blind one reached down, stroked its fur. "We know many things, don't we, Beast?"

Again, from far inside the throat, the growl . . .

It was getting really cold when he hit the streets again, leaving the blind woman's place, turning one time, seeing her sitting there behind those glasses, stroking the giant dog.

Billy Boy pulled his raincoat tight around him and began to walk, stopping only once, to ask where this Bloomingdale's was and how long a walk were we talking about. He had money in his pocket. It was cold and he could have cabbed. But the thought never crossed his mind. No reason for it to.

He was good at streets.

And sure, he'd never navigated any with this kind of population, but he knew it wouldn't matter. He felt at home on streets. He wasn't much at memory, but he could tell you all the shops on a block after he'd walked it once. He could do that when he wasn't even trying to remember. He understood somehow the way each street had its own style, its own rhythm. And he could change his pace to fit. It was not possible, of course, for someone who looked the way Billy Boy looked to be unnoticeable. But all things considered, he came as close as anyone could.

They were selling all kinds of crap along the sidewalks on Broadway. Billy Boy bought a cap, black, and wool, and he pulled it down so his ears were covered. As he adjusted it, he looked around at Times Square. What a place. You wanted something, you could sure find it in Times Square. A black whore with good legs, a Chink one with tits—surprise—a blond one with a pretty face. He couldn't believe it. Pretty. White. Really blond. Doing it for money. What a place.

"Who's smokin'? Who's smokin'?" A little old guy scurried by. He held a bunch of joints in his hand. Billy Boy watched him and he was glad he did, because the next thing that happened was the guy with the joints bumped into a cop for Chrissakes, and never once quit with his spiel. "Who's smokin'? Who's smokin'—Sorry Mac—Who's smokin'?"

Billy Boy started walking again. What a place, Times Square. If you had the bread, you couldn't get closer to heaven.

He was gonna have the bread. Soon. More than he hoped for. The Duchess had told him. Three four hundred maybe? Blow half on clothes, then quick back here to ball his brains out, grass, booze, sleep. And the same tomorrow only tomorrow would be even better because tomorrow he'd wake up here, right in the center of the world, Newwwwww Yawwwwwwwwwwk.

He crossed over on 47th and the Jews made him nervous at first, till he realized from the storefronts this was the diamond market. Everything bought and sold. Top dollar for top quality. Jewels, watches, furs. There were signs all over. Too bad, but he wasn't anticipating being able to do business with these guys. Wouldn't that be something though, haggling with some old kike about how much was this mink worth and *outlasting* him, *beating* him, making him pay more than he wanted.

Now he walked up Fifth Avenue, his walk properly somber. All the stores. All the fancy windows. You had to be some kind of rich to do your shopping on Fifth Avenue.

On 58th, the stores stopped so he headed east again and at Lex, caught his first sight of Bloomingdale's. It was the whole effing block, like Field's in Chicago. Billy Boy walked around the place twice, getting the feel, getting the feel. Then he walked the blocks around the stores, getting the feel, looking for his spot.

He passed Hero's and checked their merchandise, pleased with what he saw. Always smart to have something to do in the area after you've pulled a job. All the cops think you run after a job. Only the dumb ones do. If you were smart, smart like Billy Boy, you lingered.

Now it must have been well after four and he needed to land. Fifty-ninth between Third and Lexington felt right. Close to dark now, but more than that—

—to hell with "more than that"—59th and Lexington was right because he *sensed* it was right, period.

Lots of small buildings. Up ahead was one with dark stairs leading down. A delivery entrance kind of. It had a gate across it, but the gate was in rotten shape, and Billy Boy moved next to it, tested it.

He could rip it open easy. So he did.

Now all he had to do was wait for the flow to be right. Everyone talks about traffic flow, about how there will be a bunch of cars, then fewer, then none, then a bunch again. Well, people flowed like that too. If you were patient, there were times when there was, for a moment, no one going by.

Well, Billy Boy was patient. Not in life. Not most of the time at all. He was the reverse most of the time. But on the streets, he was patient. When he had to be. He had to be now. It didn't bother him at all, the waiting.

He was good at streets.

Good at streets, good at waiting, good at making his hand a fist, his arm a club, it was amazing they ever caught him. No, not amazing. It only happened when he worked on an unlucky day and shit, anybody could catch him then, a kid could catch him then, a goddam little baby could—

—except this wasn't like that, not just because of what the Duchess said, he had more proof than that because here, right here right now the street was in a silent time and here she came, a woman alone, in a navy blue coat, not paying attention to where she was going, no, she was looking at something, a piece of paper, a list maybe, and . . . and . . .

And he let her go by. He could have grabbed her with the one hand, clubbed her with the other, but he let her go by. For no reason except she just looked so goddam happy about something and when you were lucky, like he was, you could be nice, you could afford to be, and this one in the dark blue coat, the one he let go on account of her smile, why spoil her day?

He waited.

The flow was heavy all of a sudden so he took a step farther down the dark cement stairs beside the building. He pulled his black wool cap snug. He could have followed the stairs to the bottom, made a stab at forcing the service door or whatever was supposed to keep people out. The street gate was shit, probably the service door was the same. He could have been inside fast, and then shouldered open a couple apartment doors, or knocked and said he was the asshole delivery man or something else like he used to do when he was a kid.

But inside was not a place for him anymore. Inside meant hallways and people shouting or bimbos with guns just in case.

Billy Boy didn't like inside work. He never understood people who did. Why take risks like that when there wasn't a city in the world that didn't have streets and there wasn't a street in the world that didn't get dark and when you were on a street in the dark—correction—when *he* was on a street in the dark, and his luck was running good, he was gold, he was king, he was Lombardi's Packers driving for a pressure touchdown, no way to stop the score, and Billy Boy had his score before she had a shot at even blinking, one second she was just this slob with a shopping bag ambling along the suddenly quiet street, the next she was struggling as he dragged her down the stairs, his left hand over her mouth his right arm clubbing down and then she wasn't struggling anymore and as she went unconscious, Billy Boy heard something that shocked him, the sound of broken glass—

—broken glass? Falling from between her now limp legs?—a lampshade was it? He couldn't see enough in the darkness to tell for sure, but son of a bitch shit he didn't have to see to know that what he'd done, what he'd gotten for his first time out in the Apple, on what was supposed to be a lucky day—what he had in his arms was a nothing, a lump, a fucking no-good bag lady, a shoplifter who stole garbage, who stole lampshades and—

—and now other crap was tumbling to the dark steps, more garbage, sure, that was all—and the Duchess said he'd be lucky! —well, she'd pay, she'd pay—

—it was crystal.

Not a lampshade. Billy Boy bent down and stared at the shattered remnants of the cut-glass crystal dish stolen from Bloomingdale's. And lying beside the crystal pieces was one of those watches with the numbers and another watch of gold and a thinner gold watch, a woman's watch, and gold bracelets and gold necklaces and this was no bag lady of a shoplifter, no, this was the queen of them all, and Billy Boy ripped open her purse and there were more gold bracelets in there and cash, cash, in twenties and fifties and "Police!" this woman was shouting, not the one he'd clubbed but a new one standing at the top of the stairs with reddish hair and a blue coat and screaming again and again "Police! Police, *somebody please get the police now*!" and God knows how long she'd have gone on if Billy Boy hadn't gotten one hand to her arm, yanked her into the darkness, made his fist, made his club and *smash, smash,* once in the face, once in the temple to make

sure and he could hear things tearing inside her, he'd given good
shots and right where he wanted—

—but she wouldn't shut up.

". . . helllppppp . . ." she went, soft, but loud enough if someone
was passing by and again, ". . . helpppppp . . ." so he made the
biggest fist he ever made and raised his club higher than ever
before and with all his weight balanced perfect he crashed home
against the side of her neck and that knocked the "helllppppps
. . ." out of her good, and quickly he grabbed the cash and the
watches and the gold, all the gold, and then he moved up the
stairs, stepping over the queen of the shoplifters who was starting
soft to moan, stepping over the other one too, but then he came
to a quick halt because she was at a crazy angle, this one, her head
was lying at an almost scary angle, and for just a second it crossed
his mind she might be dead, and if somehow this one here with
the reddish hair and the dark coat, if somehow her time had come,
well, it wasn't his fault, you couldn't blame Billy Boy, no way, no
way, because what was the line that funny nigger guy said, "I
didn't do it, it wasn't me, the devil made me buy this dress," well,
it was the same here, New York made him nervous, he didn't
know how things worked in New York, how hard to hit and it was
New York that made him hit so hard, New York was the devil,
his devil anyway . . .

7

CHARLOTTE AND THEO

Mr. Stewart was going to Boston, or so he informed the family at breakfast.

His treasured Aunt Beth, perhaps the one person left alive he truly cared for, or at least so it seemed more often than not, to Charlotte, had been taken suddenly ill. Nothing "of consequence" was the way he put it, meaning not terminal. But it might be "a friendly gesture of support," again the way he put it, to say a brief hello.

"I'll pack," Charlotte said.

"No need," he returned. "You stay with the children."

"Of course," Charlotte answered.

"Will you bring presents?" W. Nelson Jr. asked.

"Who is deserving?" his father asked back.

"I am, I am," Burgess chanted.

"Prove that last."

"Theo says my grammar is almost perfect now. And I got one hundred in arithmetic yesterday."

"Top in the class?" Mr. Stewart asked.

"Better," Burgess replied, sticking out his tongue at his one-year-older brother. "Top in the *family.*"

The rimless glasses came slightly down, eyed the oldest son. There was silence.

Mumbled from Nelson Jr: "I got a ninety. But my test was harder."

"Says who, says who?" Burgess chanted.

"Top in the class?" Mr. Stewart asked.

"There were three better," W. Nelson Jr. replied.

"And in the class how many?"

"Twelve."

Mr. Stewart took off his rimless glasses, carefully cleaned them. "Fourth out of twelve and you ask reward?" He shook his head. "You know where fourth out of twelve places you in the outside world? *Do you?*"

"Nossir."

"With the second-raters." And now his voice began to rise in agitation. *"I gave you my name, boy!* And no Stewart runs with the pack. That is forbidden behavior."

"Yessir."

"So, do you want me to bring you presents?"

Pause. It was hard. "Nossir."

"And why not?"

"I'm not deserving."

"Quite right."

"But *I* was perfect," Burgess said.

"No, you were not, you were monstrous, you were nasty and petty and spiteful. And with all that, you want me to bring you presents?"

Pause. Blinked-back tears. "I got a hundred though."

His father stared from behind the clean rimless glasses.

"But I behaved badly. I'm not deserving either."

W. Nelson Stewart, Sr. stood. The others followed. "I'll return midafternoon to pack. The children will be back from school, I'll say good-bye to you all then. But let me say one thing to you all now." They watched. "Theo is doing most excellent work on your studies. But he has let your manners slip. I will have no more of this bickering. I *hate* this bickering. I was never allowed to bicker when I was your age."

"But you were an only child," Charlotte said.

He glared at her, but only briefly. "Perhaps that did have something to do with it," he allowed, and then he led them all three out of the room.

After she had gotten her husband off to work and the boys to school, Charlotte proceeded to the basement, into the gymnasium and beyond it, to the tutor's study. Theo was, as always, hard at work. He assigned the boys' papers over the weekends and then spent many hours commenting on their efforts. His comments were invariably longer than their themes. He stood when she entered.

"Mr. Stewart is going to Boston," she said.

"Family matters?"

She nodded.

"Nothing wrong, I hope."

"No, and I can prove it: Mrs. Stewart is remaining here."

He nodded.

"Meaning," Charlotte said, before she paused and did a genuinely audacious thing: she grazed her fingertips across the tight front of his trousers. "Meaning your friend down there and I are going to have some rather long and hard and glorious hours together."

He tried not to, but he flushed whatever the color is just beyond crimson.

How could she not love him?

That bold move of hers, the reaching out and touching his trousers, was, in point of fact, their first moment of physical contact since the seduction. And his "headache" that followed. He had called it that the next morning when they talked quick and quiet in his office.

" 'Guilt-ache' you mean," Charlotte said, and she could tell from the brief flicker in his blue poet's eyes he liked her made-up word.

"Whatever. The point is, I don't want to talk about it."

"There's nothing to talk about, Theo," she answered. And truthfully, she felt, there wasn't. He had struggled wildly and she had proved stronger. Certainly that could have been an embarrassment. No man wants the woman of his dreams to be a better wrestler than he is. But was she still that, the woman of his dreams? She had been, she knew, the night before.

So they had fought and she had won and as his resistance crumpled, it crumpled quickly, and then his eyelids had fluttered wildly as they had when his "guilt-ache" began, and then he was asleep, exhausted, leaden. She waited until she was sure he was safe, until his breathing was very deep and even, before she quietly left.

Not to sleep that night.

"There is a great deal to talk about, Charlotte, and we must do it now and then never again is that clear?" Theo began. They sat in the living room, the first chance the next morning they had to be alone.

"I don't like that 'never.' "

"Here it comes, get ready: We must never meet again."

"For a genius, you are such a silly, Theo. How can we 'never meet again' "—she was purposely melodramatic on those words —"when we *live* in the same house?"

"When I said 'meet' I didn't mean 'meet.' "

"Ah. Well, you're a poet and you have a way with words. I'm just a poor housewife and I don't. So you must explain. If you didn't mean 'meet' when you said 'meet' what did you intend?"

Pause. "You know."

"Ah, but I don't."

He was getting embarrassed now. He pointed upward in the direction of his room.

"Ceiling?" Charlotte said. "Roof? I'm a dull girl and I hate word games. I lose at them."

Now the blue eyes blazed in frustration. "You know damn well what we're talking about."

"Yes my baby, I do—you mean, poor sweet thing, that you must never 'defile' me again, although how in the world you can 'defile' the mother of Nelson and Burgess I'm not quite sure. Perhaps 'enter' is the choicest word. You must never 'enter' me again. Have I got it now?"

"You have it." He nodded curtly, started out of the enormous room.

"How wrong I can be," Charlotte said to his back. "All night long I thought you'd enjoyed it."

"*Shit,*" he said, and for a moment she was frightened. He whirled on her. "When I woke up this morning I lay there not thinking about the bad part—"

"—the guilt-ache—"

"—yes, that, but what had gone before and I realized that nothing, no mother crooning and rocking me, no present as a child, no praise, no friend, no poem, nothing had ever made me quite that glad about myself." He reached into a trouser pocket. "I must read you something."

"A poem? I love your poems."

"You don't know a goddam thing about them."

"Not about poetry, no, I'm ignorant of poetry, but not yours. I can tell my Theo's verse from a million other poets. Test me sometime, if you dare."

He sat across from her in an overstuffed chair. "This is a copy of the letter I wrote your husband, my job application if you will. Remember this: I was a college graduate in Ohio who dreamed of coming to New York. I had no money, no skills, no chance. And desperate I wrote this." He began to read.

> Dear Mr. Stewart:
>
> My name is Theodore Duncan and no, you don't know me and yes, this is an application for a job. The only reason I dare write you is this: my middle name is Stewart and my late mother, on more than one occasion, pointed out your name in the Cleveland paper and said we were somehow related. Frankly, I'm not sure it's true.
>
> I want to be a poet and I want to be a poet in New York. Cleveland is not noted for an overactive literary life.
>
> I could claim all sorts of skills but I won't. I was good at school. I graduated top in my class at Oberlin. I've always been top in my class academically.
>
> I feel like a fool having written this much. I swear that if you can help me, I will never give you cause for regret.
>
> And please do not feel obliged to answer this letter.
>
> > Your conceivable cousin,
> > Ted Duncan

He stopped reading. "I don't think there's much need for us to continue this," he said.

"Wrong."

"I'm sorry then, but if that letter doesn't make clear why our behavior is just a little bit shabby, then I've no business thinking I can write. Charlotte, understand now—I've *met* other poets. I've *been* to readings. There are bookshops I can browse in. *I'm not alone anymore.* All because he gave me this chance."

"If I were just a frustrated housewife, and you were just a frustrated young man with a penis and no place to put it, we would be done as of now."

"That's all we are, my dear."

"Wrong. Special is what we are."

"I don't see it, sorry."

"I'll be brief—I've never met anyone as bright as you, or nearly as insecure. I'm the only chance you have to be the poet you dream of being. I'm the only one with confidence enough for both. And you know I'm right."

"As I said before, you don't know a goddam thing about my poetry."

"And as I said before, test me sometime."

Charlotte never expected there to be a test at all, much less one that began the following morning. She was set to go to Tiffany's when he met her by the front door and handed her some folded pages. "A few short poems," he said.

She unfolded the papers, looked at his elegant, almost feminine handwriting. Confused, she smiled. "Did you write all four last night?"

"The *hand*writing is clearly mine. The *creation* is for you to say, but of course, since you know all about my work, that will prove no problem."

"I don't understand." She began to read one, stopped, looked at him.

"I *might* have created all. Or none. Or one. Or two or three. Tell me this evening, why don't you, which, if any, are mine. Have a pleasant shop." He turned and left her there.

Charlotte decided Tiffany's would always have diamonds, so she hurried to the Society Library, settled herself off in a private corner, and looked carefully at the first of the four poems.

I met a traveler from an antique land
Who said: Two vast and trunkless legs of stone
Stand in the desert. Near them, on the sand,
Half sunk, a shattered visage lies, whose frown,
And wrinkled lip, and sneer of cold command,
Tell that its sculptor well those passions read
Which yet survive, stamped on these lifeless things,
The hand that mocked them and the heart that fed;
And on the pedestal these words appear:
"My name is Ozymandias, king of kings:
Look on my works, ye Mighty, and despair!"
Nothing beside remains. Round the decay

Of that colossal wreck, boundless and bare,
The lone and level sands stretch far away.

Now what in the world can *that* be about? Charlotte wondered.
She knew absolutely nothing about poetry from her schooling. It
was always beyond her and confusing her and more than any of
that, it was just so *dull. All* poetry was dull.

Except her Theo's.

But could he have written this, this weird *thing,* this totally
unromantic story of Ozy-whoozias alone in the desert?

Perhaps. If he was trying to trick her.

And this was, after all, a test. And not an unimportant one,
because she knew that if she passed, she had him. And if she failed,
she—

—pointless to pursue those thoughts, old girl; you're *not* going
to fail. She studied the second poem.

Much have I travell'd in the realms of gold,
And many goodly states and kingdoms seen;
Round many western islands have I been
Which bards in fealty to Apollo hold.

Oft of one wide expanse had I been told
That deep-browed Homer ruled as his demesne;
Yet did I never breathe its pure serene
Till I heard Chapman speak out loud and bold:

Then felt I like some watcher of the skies
When a new planet swims into his ken;
Or like stout Cortez when with eagle eyes
He star'd at the Pacific—and all his men
Look'd at each other with a wild surmise—
Silent, upon a peak in Darien.

Dear God, Charlotte thought, spirit sagging; bring back Ozy-
whoozias. Why the old-fashioned parts, the "ofts" and spelling
"stared" with an apostrophe?

Of course Theo worshipped the old-fashioned poets; his heroes
were never the current new rages. But still. Wait though!—it
ended with Darien and he knew that Mr. Stewart was contemplating buying an estate in Darien, Connecticut. So maybe the "peak

in Darien" was about the hill on the estate, and maybe "stout Cortez" referred to her husband, he was obviously stout. So maybe this was his, and it was about her moving to the country and leaving poor Theo behind.

Possible. Possible. But where was the romance? Charlotte rubbed her eyes, began the third poem.

> So, we'll go no more a-roving
>   So late into the night,
> Though the heart be still as loving
>   And the moon be still as bright.
>
> For the sword outwears its sheath,
>   And the soul wears out the breast,
> And the heart must pause to breathe,
>   And love itself have rest.
>
> Though the night was made for loving
>   And the day returns too soon,
> Yet we'll go no more a-roving
>   By the light of the moon.

Here was the romance and Charlotte felt despair. This was a poem she at least understood, much as she might wish not to. This was Theo saying good-bye. Good-bye big and pretty, and in ten years you'll still be big but you won't be pretty.

Still dumb, though.

Still big and dumb.

Not the kind of creature a poet keeps around for inspiration. Probably he had written them all, all four. He had certainly handed them to her in this order. The first to fool her, the second the hints got broader, this third said good-bye. What could the last be after? Insults perhaps? Jokes at her expense? I don't much want to read this last one, Charlotte thought. But I must. But I must.

> Now sleeps the crimson petal, now the white;
> Nor waves the cypress in the palace walk;
> Nor winks the gold fin in the porphyry font:
> The firefly wakens: waken thou with me. . . .
>
> Now folds the lily all her sweetness up,
> And slips into the bosom of the lake:

> So fold thyself, my dearest, thou, and slip
> Into my bosom and be lost in me. . . .

Brilliant original ideas were not an everyday occurrence in Charlotte's life, but as she sat transfixed by this final poem, this masterpiece of Theo's, this glorious framing of their feeling for each other, she remembered that he had three ultimate heroes, the three great romantic poets: Shelley, Byron, and Keats.

And she held four poems in her hands.

What courage it must have taken to put his talents in amongst theirs and pray that she would somehow know.

How could anyone not know? They were undeniably great, but her Theo was a genius. Charlotte read the final poem, the lily poem she immediately called it, one more time, then went to the desk of the New York Society Library and asked for the works of Mr. Keats, Mr. Shelley, Mr. Lord Byron. (Did you call him that, she wondered? Was "Lord" like a first name or did you just say "Byron"? Never mind. It mattered not at all.)

When the books came she took them back to her private corner and found in each the index of first lines.

She was only one hundred percent correct. The one about not going roving was called just that, "So, We'll Go No More A-Roving" and it was Byron's, Lord or otherwise. And the dopey one about the statue was Shelley's "Ozymandias." In the library now Charlotte had to giggle. The one she thought concerned real estate in Darien, Connecticut, was called "On First Looking into Chapman's Homer" and Mr. Keats claimed credit for that one. Still laughing, she returned the volumes, thanked the librarian, and decided that few mortals were more deserving of a little gift from Tiffany's. So folding the poems, her lily one on top, into her purse, she floated there.

The rest of that day and well into the evening, she totally ignored Theo whenever they passed in the halls and she knew he was looking for some reaction from her. She kept her face frozen enjoying every moment. Then, shortly before bed she sought him out briefly, looked at him as coldly as she could, which considering her feelings for him wasn't all that long. "The lily poem, obviously," she told him then, shoving the three other handwritten pages back to him. "And I'll keep it." Pause. "That is if you don't mind."

From the look of things, he didn't mind at all.

Alone in her bedroom, ready for sleep, Charlotte read the poem again and again, slowly committing it to memory, a skill at which she never much excelled.

> Now sleeps the crimson petal, now the white;
> Nor waves the cypress in the palace walk;
> Nor winks the gold fin in the porphyry font:
> The firefly wakens: waken thou with me. . . .
>
> Now folds the lily all her sweetness up,
> And slips into the bosom of the lake:
> So fold thyself, my dearest, thou, and slip
> Into my bosom and be lost in me. . . .

She lay naked and alone between her silken sheets, brow furrowed. Because the second verse came quite fast really, at least fast for her. But that damned first verse kept escaping her. It was that damned line about the gold fin in the porphyry font. What in the name of heaven could a porphyry font be? If she knew, it would clearly help the memorizing, but the dictionary was downstairs in the library and if she went down this late, what if Mr. Stewart came in suddenly, bothered by the noise and asked, alarmed, what in the world she was doing with that incriminating dictionary in her hand and she would say "Oh nothing, just checking the meaning of porphyry font, I'm forgetting the silliest things these days, one morning you wake up and porphyry font is right there along with nine times nine and the next morning, whoops, quite gone." "Unlikely," he would say. "No, true," she would say, perhaps beginning to fidget now beneath the glare behind those rimless glasses and he would say, "It could have waited till morning," and she would say, "Perhaps you're right, I'll look it up then" and he would say, "No, it was too important to wait, *why,* tell me *why,* 'porphyry font' sounds like a poetic image and there is only one person in this house who uses poetic images and that is Theo, and I've been on to you, I've been on to you Miss for quite some time, and tell me here and now what is happening between you and that boy—" "Man. Man, more man than you'll ever be, with all your money and power," and he was screaming at her then, "We'll see about that Miss, oh yes believe thee me, we shall see about that my lady," and "Why in the world are your eyes closed?"

"What?" Charlotte stared at her husband, standing by the foot of her bed, clad in his robe and, she knew, little else.

"And what is that paper in your hand?"

Quickly she said, "I didn't want to bother you about it but I've been in such a quandary."

"Tell me."

"I will," Charlotte said, and she touched the side of her bed. "Here."

He sat where she indicated.

"It's . . ." and then her words drained away.

"What?"

"Don't be upset with what I have to say." She dropped the paper on her bed table. "Please. We'll talk about it later. But not now." She threw the sheets back and showed her naked body. "I want you too much now."

He took off his robe and she reached for him and he mounted, ready, and then there came two surprises: she was moist and he did not come too quickly. She began to rock her hips and he did not seem upset with her because he kissed her, which there often hadn't been time for in the past, and when he did come, later, he cried out as he orgasmed, certainly a first. Then instead of putting on his robe and bidding her adieu, he lay alongside and stroked her body.

"Now your quandary."

"Quandary?"

He pointed to the handwritten paper on the bed table.

She handed it to him, suggested he read it.

"It's a poem."

"Read it and then we'll talk."

"I know nothing of poetry. I have no interest in poetry. I have never understood the gain involved in studying poetry."

"Well I'm certainly no expert, Nelson, besides the obvious ones, the romantic ones, Shelley and the others. Byron and Keats and you know."

"I've already told you I don't know."

"And I've already asked you please to give it your attention." He did that then.

"Here's my quandary, Nelson—"

"—why are you fidgeting?—why are you nervous?—"

"—if you'll *stop interrupting*—" She pulled the sheet over her. "Touch me as you just were doing. I liked that."

"If I'd known you liked it, I would have done it, I assure you, more frequently."

"Well, you know now and our future certainly lies ahead of us so we'll have lots of touching then, won't we?" She was talking too quickly, far too quickly, and she told herself to slow down. Everything depended on her slowing down. "Well, as I was on my way out the door earlier today, Theo practically pounced on me —he startled me, Nelson, he truly gave me *such* a surprise—"

"—why are you talking so fast? You *are* nervous."

"Perhaps I am, it's this quandary in which you find me."

"A very long quandary it seems. And getting longer and longer."

"I'm sorry. As I say, there Theo came pouncing with this paper in my hand. A poem he'd written, he said. I said how wonderful, we all knew of his poetic ambitions, but I had to get to Tiffany's. Take this with you and read it please, he said. I asked why and this is what Theo said: 'I'm teaching the boys poetry now, they have good minds and I thought that, instead of teaching them a dead poet, what if I taught them a few of mine? Because they couldn't very well ask Shelley what he meant in "Ozymandias" they could certainly ask *me* what *I* meant since *I* was right there in the room with them.' "

He read the poem again, reached for his robe.

"Anyway, to finish, Nelson—he didn't want to vary from the curriculum without *our* knowing it. In other words, he was paid to help them with their schoolwork and since this was not their schoolwork, he wanted my approval. Or *our* approval, I should say. He wanted us to say yes to the poem before he gave it to the boys."

Nelson Stewart put his feet on the floor, sat and rubbed his eyes. "It's one of the worst things I've ever read," he said finally.

"Isn't it, though," Charlotte agreed.

"One doesn't have to be a professional garbage man to know refuse when he sees it. My God, Charlotte, the thing doesn't even rhyme."

"Now you see my quandary. How do I tell Theodore we don't approve of his teaching this to the boys? How do I do it without offending him. Or what if he quits?"

"He'll be leaving soon enough, I suspect," W. Nelson Stewart said, standing now.

"Oh? Has he given his notice?"

"I had planned on his departure at the end of the school year. But after *this*"—he slapped the back of his fingers against the poem—"well, no need to pitch the lad on the street, he is possibly a cousin and all. And certainly brilliant—"

"—the boys like him," Charlotte said. "They've each said that to me. Independently of the other."

"He may not be all that beneficial to the boys, if you understand me."

Charlotte didn't.

"Well dear God look at these words: 'crimson petals' and 'fireflies' and sweet lilies folding up and do I have to go on?"

Charlotte asked that he please do.

"I would never accuse another without proof. I am not so constructed. But these are rather *feminine* words, don't you think? Not exactly bursting with rugged vitality, wouldn't you agree?"

Charlotte wished he would reach his conclusion and said so.

"I don't think Theo is liable to marry a woman," Nelson Stewart said, pausing ever so briefly after the word *marry*. "And I don't think I want him much around my boys." He left the room then and no action was taken immediately. Because the next morning came the news of the sudden indisposition of his beloved Aunt Beth, which meant, of course, he had to to to Boston . . .

It was a bitter February afternoon with winds that would scare a child. Charlotte stood in his bedroom, watching him pack. Nelson liked to pack himself. There was really precious little in this world Nelson didn't prefer doing for himself. And this was to be a quick journey, one night, perhaps two. He packed lightly. In the event of trouble, he still had clothes at Aunt Beth's place.

Closing the clasps, he picked up the leather bag, hurried down the stairs, Charlotte in pursuit. By the front door Theo waited, respectfully behind the boys. Nelson hugged his sons good-bye, only to discover they insisted on accompanying him outside to where his driver stood waiting.

Pleased with their decision, he opened the door, shooed them out, kissed Charlotte discreetly. "And don't let me hear any stories about you chasing after unattached ladies," he said suddenly to Theo, and before the tutor could reply, Nelson went on: "You've got to watch your reputation as a womanizer, Theo." With that and a laugh, he was out the door and gone.

Theo walked quietly up the stairs to the large window, watching the children accompany their father. The driver tried helping with the luggage, was quickly rebuffed, so he contented himself with opening the door. W. Nelson Stewart got inside. "What was that last about?" Theo wondered to Charlotte, as she moved close behind him.

"Who can be certain with him?" Charlotte said.

And standing framed in the large second-story window, she wrapped her arms tight around Theo, and he struggled, told her sharply that the boys might see (and they did, they did, they saw their mother's arms), but none of it mattered. Nothing he said mattered. Because they sent a message to each other quite past words. He told her she was worthy, she told him he was male, they were locked.

8

LIKE NO OTHER STORE
IN THE WORLD

No more than five minutes after triumphantly leaving Doyle Ackerman, smiling to herself but humming out loud, Edith entered Bloomingdale's. The beatific feeling of revenge that filled her when she bid farewell to Doyle in the coffee shop had been replaced now by an urge toward creativity: Edith was trying her hand at a limerick:

> There once was a Yalie named Ackerman
> Who lured lots of girls to the sack—erman.
> His eyes were quite bright.
> His teeth were quite white.
> But his brains were those of a Packer—man.

*Horr*ible, Edith decided as she wandered along the aisles. Not only did "sack—erman" stink, the word "Packer-man" wasn't what she meant at all—she meant one who played for the Green Bay Packers. A goon. A "duhhhhh" type. Still, she consoled herself, "Ackerman" wasn't the easiest word to limerick around with. Now if his name had been Doyle *Dane,* she could have made a last line out of Milne, a man of "Very Little *Brain"* or along those lines, which though hardly Shakespearean was at least a step up the literary ladder.

It was a bit warm in the store so she took off her navy blue coat. She was wearing a frumpy dress from her old Peck and Peck days, beige with a little frilled collar. She tossed her coat over an arm and consoled herself still further with the thought that she was, after all, not a writer but a painter. Maybe not yet very good but with a chance. More than a chance, Sally said, and Sally Levinson was as tough a critic as any of them any day. Very good was in the bag, Sally said. The jury was out on the next rung though, according to Sally.

God, Edith thought, what an incredible thing it must be to give pleasure. To sweat at a canvas, to feel so helpless most of the time, so invincible on rare occasions; but then, years later, to have a stranger say, perhaps, "Oh yes, that's a Mazursky, isn't she wonderful."

She always thought of herself, when she thought of herself as a painter at all, as "Mazursky." She hoped Phillip wouldn't mind. A bunch of art critics would be studying a room of Mazurskys now. In the Museum of Modern Art on 53rd. "I would rate her with Cassatt" one of them would say. "Above Cassatt, certainly, but below O'Keeffe," another would argue. "Ridiculous," a third would say, "Below Cassatt but above O'Keeffe." And then a fourth would say, "Does it matter? Must we rank greatness? Can't we just say how blessed we are that they were born, Mazursky, Cassatt, and O'Keeffe?"

Edith got out her list now, sighed at all the things the girls needed, then put the list quickly into her purse because there, *there* ahead of her Bloomingdale's was selling cashmere scarves. Long cashmere scarves. On *sale*. Edith stopped by the cashmere counter. Revenge and a sale on the same day, I must be on the cusp of something.

She fingered a green scarf, because Phillip loved green with her reddish hair, and in truth it was a good color for her. But because of that, she kept buying greenies and never experimented. "May I have the muted brown one there, please," Edith said to the shopgirl, and charged it, telling the girl not to bother wrapping it, she'd wear it home. Tossing the muted brown scarf loosely around her shoulders, she headed for the men's shop, more specifically, the necktie department.

The area was empty, which surprised her. In spite of her passion for the place, Edith well knew Bloomingdale's little tricks—all the big stores had them. Macy's, for instance, had a special crew that went out ahead of all furniture delivery trucks making sure no one was home so the furniture men could leave their "We were here, where were you?" notes. Well, Bloomingdale's made it hard for you to shop. If there were ninety shoppers in the dress department, the salespeople all slipped down the stairs to shoes. If there was a run on perfume, all those employees snuck to the buttons area.

"Yes?" the necktie salesman asked.

Edith liked him immediately. He was one of those bright attractive young men who went to one of those wonderful sort of unknown schools, Colby or Bowdoin or Middlebury, and was getting his doctorate eventually. "I need a glorious red necktie," Edith said, "but one with special properties."

"We are very long today on glorious," he assured her. "A truckload of glorious arrived from our Jersey plant. But you'll have to be specific on the special properties."

"It must be absolutely guaranteed one hundred percent gravy resistant."

He snapped his fingers. "Damn; sold the last one an hour ago."

They both laughed then until Edith got excited. "I've got it, I know what I'll do, I'll buy him a tie and then I'll hand him another box with a bib in it."

The salesman said, "Lady, that is *funny.*" He leaned on the glass countertop and really started laughing. Finally, he bent down, opened the side of the counter, and took out perhaps a dozen silk ties.

Edith began to spin.

The young salesman blinked.

Edith took her muted brown cashmere scarf and held it out at both ends, spinning slowly around, her arms rising to above shoulder level, an awkward Pavlova.

Across the men's shop, the suit buyer looked over.

Edith continued to spin, and her arms went higher, straight up now.

A woman from Scarsdale, who had been buying socks, began to scream.

The tie salesman began to run around the counter.

Edith's hands were clenched now. Still high, her body still spinning.

The suit buyer rushed to the security phone.

Edith smashed her fists straight down toward the glass counter, *through* the glass counter, and, of course instantly there was blood and then Edith jammed her arms together, forcing her wrists into the shards of glass, twisting her wrists back and forth in rhythm.

The buyer dropped the phone, the lady from Scarsdale cratered, the tie salesman could only stand and watch now.

As Edith raised her arms up high again, palms facing her, the inside of her wrists close to her eyes, and as the blood bubbled down, any onlooker would, of course, have been shocked, but if that onlooker could have forced his way past the shock, forced his concentration onto Edith's face, he might have wondered at the expression reflected there; was it possibly relief? Could it have been joy? Perhaps exultation . . . ?

PART II

TRACKERS

1

ROUTINE

Haggerty stared down into the dead eyes of the red-haired woman in the blue coat and waited for the light-headedness to come. There were times, especially when he allowed himself more than several shots of decent whiskey, when his whole life seemed to have been nothing but shoot-outs and stake-outs and blood-baths and pain, and still he could not rid himself of the light-headedness. Whenever he first looked at a new corpse it would unbidden come. Eric knew of his affliction, his wife had known. That was all. It wasn't anybody's business; besides, Haggerty didn't trust a whole lot of people.

Two once, one now.

And here it came, so he faked a yawn, covering his face with his big hands, and though he felt giddy, he knew it would pass. And it did. He could stare down at the woman now, without fear.

Without much fear, anyway.

Around him on the dark steps there was considerable activity: coming slowly to consciousness, another woman, bits of broken glass or crystal by her. And working with their quiet efficiency, members of the Crime Scene Unit were doing their job. Taking pictures, ferreting out whatever might be useful: hairs, prints, fibers, skin, blood.

Haggerty picked up the dead woman's purse, hesitated only a moment. It always seemed to him like what it was, an unseemly invasion. Sometimes with women it was like a zoo in there, but he could tell as he opened this plain object now, that the corpse had been, when previously allowed to breathe, neat if not fastidious.

Her name was Alice Oliver. Librarian. Scarsdale. Single.

American Express. Texaco. Thirty-eight dollars . . . twenty-six cents. And a single seat for tonight, the sixth of February, 1981, for *A Chorus Line*.

Alice my dear, Haggerty thought, it was a great musical, and I hope you've seen it already. What a shame it would be to wait all those years to see it and then *this* the evening of the show.

Haggerty had no interest in theatre, but he loved musicals. If he had a hobby it was that. He saw them all, not just the *Fair Lady*s. *Flahooley*—he'd been there for its expiration. And *Portofino. Buttrio Square. Thirteen Daughters. Kelly* even. One performance but he'd caught a preview. Not to mention his prize, *Breakfast at Tiffany's,* which closed in midweek before it opened.

"Oh," Haggerty muttered out loud, because he found then, at the bottom of her purse, a small white envelope and inside were the remnants—frayed and faded and broken—of what had clearly once been rose petals. Haggerty stared at them, feeling guilty. I hope he loved you, Haggerty thought, or at the very least, I hope he didn't break your heart. Usually, his mind didn't range so close to the sentimental—

—but there was something about this body that bothered him. The *angle.* The *angle* of the neck. Of the broken neck—he was no doctor but surely it had to have been broken. He'd never seen a neck quite like that before, God knew what the weapon was, what size club. And he wanted to talk about the angle, speculate on it with Eric.

Only Eric was late. Haggerty glanced at his watch, blew on his hands, knelt down by the red-haired woman and waited in the February cold.

It was several minutes before Haggerty heard the familiar footsteps coming toward him. He was shivering now as he stood, looked at the approaching younger man. "What the hell kept you?" he said.

"Your crap," Eric said, and he shoved a pint bottle of colorless liquid into Haggerty's big hands.

"Not here, Jesus," Haggerty said, looking around in an almost furtive way, quickly pocketing the bottle. It was DMSO and Haggerty practically lived on it now. He had bursitis in his right shoulder and arthritis in both hands and the DMSO had been his salvation, ever since he heard about the liquid one night on *60 Minutes.* It was a paint solvent, controversial, and illegal, at least in New York. Haggerty talked about it a good deal after he'd seen the program and he wondered aloud to Eric if it would help his problems and sometimes they would pass drugstores that sold it even though it wasn't legal and Haggerty would say again how curious he was as to whether it would help or not.

"Buy some you're driving me crazy," Eric would urge, only Haggerty wouldn't, and that was how things went until Eric realized the old man never would, because he'd been a cop for thirty-plus years now, immaculate, and what if he got caught?

So Eric bought it for him, scowling but dutiful, and Haggerty repaid him to the penny and what drove Eric almost round the bend was that stores never always had it—one week yes, then six months without—so he had to skulk around buying the liquid pints where he could find them.

Haggerty got instant relief and it kept his pain bearable. It was indeed a wondrous substance, DMSO, except for the garlic side effects. Not only did your breath smell of garlic, so did your body, and Haggerty took to concealing the former problem by becoming at his age a compulsive Dentyne man.

And he all but bathed in Aqua Velva. Not only did he rub it on his face after shaving, he kept some in the glove compartment of his car. And each morning he would soak his shirt in Aqua Velva, waiting for it to dry, enduring the odd looks that sometimes came his way . . .

He watched now as Eric knelt by the dead woman, studied the horrid angle of the neck. He looked up at Haggerty. "What do you think did it?" Haggerty said quietly.

Eric stood. "Pray it wasn't a fist," he replied, staring now at the fat lady surrounded by broken glass who was talking to the young patrolman who first reported the violence.

"Us decent citizens are the backbone of the city," the fat lady began. "How are we supposed to live here with the crime all around? Where were you when I needed help, giving a jaywalking ticket to a cripple?"

"We do the best we can, ma'am," the young patrolman said.

"All my hard-earned precious things, gone. *Gone,*" she said, then she said "ouch"—this last referred to a piece of crystal that jabbed into her as she changed into a different sitting position.

"An ambulance should be here real soon," the young patrolman said, consolingly. "We'll get you to a first-class hospital, they'll check you out right away, you'll feel a whole lot better ma'am, I can promise that."

And now there were tears in the fat lady's eyes. "*I had mementos,*" she said. "Family memories. Heirlooms I was carrying— I'm not going to feel better, I'll never feel better, they'll probably check me out and find I got cancer."

"Don't work yourself up, ma'am; please."

Now the tears were streaming down her face. "Lemme tell you something: you're young, you don't know this yet, I'm old so I do —life is a bummer."

"I understand why you're upset, you've got every reason to be upset, but—"

"—*a bummer, you get me?* I support my family, I work seven days out of seven, when's my reward?" Now she lifted her tear-stained face to the sky. "*I'm waiting, God.*" The young cop quickly handed her his handkerchief. The fat lady buried her face in it and made sobbing sounds.

Eric could not help applauding.

Her face snapped away from the kerchief, her eyes searching, bright with anger.

"It's me, Sophie," Eric said, moving toward her.

"Oh hey, Eric," the fat lady said, "you on this?"

"It's possible."

"Good. Cause this *putz*—" she jerked a thumb at the young patrolman—"he don't know shit."

"What's going on?" the young patrolman said.

"She was about to hit you for a loan of ten," Haggerty explained. "That's what the tears were building to."

"You win some, you lose some, it never hurts to try," Sophie said.

"There is a shaky black man who works 34th Street," Eric said.

Sophie cut in—"Jimmy the hat?"

Eric nodded. "He and Sophie here are royalty." He turned to the young patrolman. "The king and queen of shoplifters. The first time I ran Sophie in I was stunned—not by the amount—any *gonif* can steal a lot—but by the exquisite taste of what she'd acquired that day. But I never knew you to go in for crystal," Eric said, pointing to the broken bits of glass surrounding her.

"I'm innocent—I swear—I was mugged just like an ordinary person."

Haggerty looked at the young patrolman. "Maybe the ambulance is here." He pointed up toward the street.

The young patrolman hesitated, then left them.

"That's funny," Sophie said then. "I thought it was him."

"You thought what was him?"

"I smell Aqua Velva—figured it was the young guy."

"I don't smell any Aqua Velva," Haggerty said quickly. "Get on with your story."

"Somebody stinks of Aqua Velva," Sophie insisted. "I got a sensitive nose and it's gonna make me sneeze."

"There's no goddam Aqua Velva!" Haggerty said loud. "Now quit stalling."

Eric looked dead at her then. "We're dealing with a murder, so don't screw around."

"Okay, okay, just—" She sneezed then. Then she did it again. Then she started to talk. "I was done for the day and heading to meet my girl friend at this bar on First."

"Anything we can trace?"

Sophie shook her head. "Watches and bracelets mostly. Nothing real unusual."

"See the guy?"

"It happened so unexpected. I felt this pull when the hand went over my mouth and I tried fighting it but no way."

"Color?"

"Couldn't tell. He hit me and I went out except I heard—I think I did anyway, heard this woman yelling to stop it. Then I drifted. He murdered her?"

"She was gonna see *Chorus Line*," Haggerty said.

"Can I have her ticket?" Sophie asked.

"Your stock," Eric told her, "just went down."

The Assistant Medical Examiner hated his life. If he had been *Chief* Medical Examiner it would have been no rosebed since he had, from childhood, been an opera lover and more than anything wanted to be Richard Wagner. But being assistant and at the same time being four years *older* than his superior made for a lot of long nights. He sat in his office now and looked at the two detectives. "You want a shot?" he asked Eric, taking a bottle of rotgut from his desk. "Either of you?"

"We're on duty," Haggerty said. He tried not to rub his right shoulder.

"We're *all* on duty," the Assistant Medical Examiner said, taking a long swallow.

"Was it a hand?" Eric said.

"I would think."

"I've got big hands," Eric said, "but not half big enough to do that. Haggerty's got hams and he couldn't do it either. What are we dealing with? Why did he kill her? He could have just dazed her like he did Sophie."

The Assistant M.E. took another drink.

Eric looked at Haggerty. "I think it's someone new in town."

"You keep track of killers do you?" the Assistant M.E. said.

"Yeah, he does," Haggerty said.

"Shit," Eric said and he stood. "As if we didn't have enough already."

"You sure it was motiveless?" the Assistant M.E. asked.

"Just a lady librarian come to town for a spin," Haggerty said. He looked at his watch. It was after ten. "She was gonna see *Chorus Line* but it's too late now."

"Life's full of tragedy," the Assistant Medical Examiner replied. "I almost had a ticket to the Met." He finished the bottle, lobbed it toward his wastebasket, missed. It hit the hard floor and shattered. They left him picking up the pieces . . .

Outside, the February night was frosting up. "You go on home," Eric said. Haggerty had taken a small one-room place over near Yorkville between First and York. It wasn't much, but he hadn't needed much after Helen had died three years before.

"You?"

"I'm itchy," Eric said.

"Want company?"

Eric saw from the way Haggerty was favoring his right side that the bursitis was hitting him bad. He made a face, sniffed the air several times.

"Bullshit, you don't smell it, I put in a fresh piece of gum not ten minutes ago." Then he paused. "Do you smell it? Am I garlicky? Tell me goddamit."

"It's not as bad as sometimes," Eric said. He loved tormenting Haggerty about the DMSO. The truth was that since he'd started using the stuff, between the Dentyne and the Aqua Velva, he'd never smelled better. Eric told him so.

"Everyone's a critic," Haggerty said as he waved, walked away . . .

It was well after ten and Eric headed for Port Authority. When he hit Times Square he stopped in a liquor store and bought a pint of Jack Daniel's. Putting it in his pocket, he walked to the bus station and inside, hoping it wouldn't take him forever to locate Tillie.

A cop is as good as his contacts, "voices" Eric called them; he had fewer than many of his peers, but he valued them, treated them as well as he possibly could, none better than Tillie.

Because she was so frail.

Frail and ancient with no last name and her life had altered years before when she saw John Gielgud walking through the bus station, coming back to the city from Princeton. She had seen his Hamlet, Tillie told Eric once, and that man on that stage was the most beautiful creation of God, except for Liberace in his early days on television.

If a legend like Sir John could walk Port Authority, the possibilities were indeed endless and through the years Tillie had spotted Henry Fonda twice, the second time with Joshua Logan, and John Travolta before he got famous but she knew he would she said, from the walk he had and his eyes. If there was such a thing as perfect pitch, and there was, Tillie had as close to perfect face memory as anyone Eric had encountered and she had been helpful to him many times on runaways. She lived in the terminal now, alone with her plastic bags, and the police let her pretty much to herself once Eric passed the word. Usually she located herself on the front bench at the second floor where most of the people had to pass by. Occasionally she walked around the building and she was good friends with a pusher who shined shoes directly across on Eighth Avenue. Once a week she trudged to Grand Central for a shower.

Eric moved into the row of benches behind her now. He took off his topcoat, folded it beside him. Tillie was staring ahead at the stragglers hurrying for their late buses to wherever. Eric leaned forward, put his strong fingers to her neck, gently began massaging her old skin. "Don't ever stop," Tillie said.

"Very tense," Eric told her. Especially the right side. She carried her bags mostly with her right arm and the strain was apparent.

"Saw the saddest thing, Eric—around noon—two girls—thirteen at the most—one just a beauty, other all fat and pimply—they sat down at the end of this row and you knew they didn't know what to do now—come this far, got to the Apple, but then what? —and this slick fella, he descended, you gather me—big hat, slick clothes, white teeth—and he sat between 'em and offered butts and they all lit up an' then a joint an' they lit that too—now this slick guy he put his fingers on the beaut's arm—talkin' and rubbin' her skin—she listened and it was like he was the answer to all her prayers she had that kind of look when she left with him—just a beaut an' you know she'll be dead in three years."

"Sad all right," Eric said.

"*No,*" Tillie said, her tone almost reprimanding. "Just shut up till I get to the sad part, I'm not there to the sad part yet, Eric, what's the matter with you?"

"Sorry."

"The fat pimply one—they left her flat—she just stared after 'em and then she cried and cried—when you can't even give it away, *that's* sad."

Eric reached into his coat pocket for the Jack Daniel's.

"I didn't say you could stop massaging."

Eric handed her the bottle.

"That's a good enough reason." She opened it, took a drink. But very daintily. Everything Tillie did was like that—the movements graceful and small. She gestured now for him to sit beside her. He moved up a row. "Pretty as ever," Tillie said. Then: "What you after?"

Eric told her.

"Don't think so," she said after a moment. "No giants recently."

Eric shrugged; it was a long shot.

"Saw a *female* must have stood six eight. Slumped so I couldn't be positive—but six eight seemed about right."

A lot of newcomers to the city lingered around Port Authority. Eric asked her to call if anything happened.

"Six eight," Tillie mused, taking another dainty swallow. Then a third, then a fourth. She put the bottle into one of her plastic bags. She never slept really. But she napped a lot. "Six eight and a girl—even if you looked like Garbo, who'd care? Isn't that sad, six eight?"

"Not if she has a hook shot," Eric said. He got up, grabbed his coat.

Tillie lay down on the bench, muttering she'd outlived everyone she'd ever cared for.

Eric thought that might be the saddest thing of all . . .

He loved his apartment. Not the building—it was just another of the new-ugly-white brick-soon-to-be-slum jobs that dotted Manhattan, where even the hard of hearing knew when the neighbor upstairs flushed the john.

But the location was something else again. Eric lived on the thirty-fifth floor overlooking Lincoln Center. In the middle of the Met there were the Chagall tapestries. And always the great open plaza between the three theatres. Balanchine worked there, Bach was played; Sills sang, Perlman fiddled. It was nice to know that, to remember it each night you came home from dealing with the bruised citizens or the terrifying young who were coming up through the pavements like some vile new growth from the center of the earth—they had no consciences, these young.

Eric opened his refrigerator, took out two bottles of beer, careful not to check the labels. He opened them both, poured them into tall thin glasses, making sure there was half to three quarters of an inch of foam at the top. Then he carried the glasses to the large window that viewed the plaza. He swirled the glasses, one after the other, checking for cling; he carefully compared their bouquets and colors. The tasting moment was coming up now, and he smiled at how much he enjoyed the anticipation.

He had been, for half a dozen years now, into beer. He had always liked it, how could anyone not like it, but his interest had only become deep when he got involved in a case with a man who was an importer. All had ended well, they became distantly acquainted, and the man, to show his gratitude for his wife's safe return, began giving Eric bottles and packs and cases of beer, many of them not ordinarily available in America. Some of them were upchuck-making—probably you had to be a native Tanzanian to truly enjoy the subtleties of Kilimanjaro lager, of Tusker brewed in Kenya—but many, if not most, were stunning. St. Pauli Girl and Pilsner Urquell were famous, and thank God for that, but Schwechater was at least their peer and . . .

Eric tasted the first beer. Ahh. Excellent. German more than likely. Perhaps Bavarian in locale. Probably bottom fermented.

Now the second. *Ahhhh.* Lighter, yes, but a clarity of flavor that was quite remarkable.

Again the first. Excellent. High marks.

Again the second. The winner, no question.

Eric went back to where the bottles were, checked the first. Jever. Remember that name, an outstanding product: Jever. Now he put the Jever down, checked the second bottle.

Piels?

Eric stared at it. Piels for Chrissakes. I must really be tired. He laughed out loud, finished both bottles, and soon was sleeping.

He was up the next morning before dawn, exercised, showered, dressed, headed for the 19th, poured a mug of coffee, started working the phones. It took three hours before he lucked out.

"Yeah we had a break, two days ago," the voice said.

"I've been calling institutions where there's been trouble," Eric said. "Just where in Illinois are you?"

"You know Illinois?"

"I don't."

"Then what the fuck you care?"

"Hey asshole, we're on the same side, easy."

"Downstate. Not Chicago."

"And you had a break?"

"Forty-five sambos, two not. But that's over."

"You've got them all back?"

"Practically."

"Then you haven't got them all back."

"You a wise guy?"

"Nope—but when I ask someone if something's been done and they say, 'practically as good as done,' then I know it hasn't been done. How many still at large?"

"We've got one holed up now in Peoria. And Billy Boy's been sighted in Chicago. Nobody could miss him, so that takes care of the lot."

Eric could feel starting now a slight pressure at his temple.

"You still there?" the Illinois guy said.

"Why," Eric asked, "could nobody miss him?"

"On account of how he looks, obviously."

"Is he very big?"

"Depends what you mean. He's not all that tall, how tall are you?"

"Under six two."

"That's all he is, if that."

"Is he wide? Are his hands wide?"

"That's a funny question—"

"—just answer it please."

"Well, yeah. What he looks like, he's white and all, but what he looks like is one of those oriental guys, the sumo guys—shoulders out to here, broad in the beam—Billy Boy must weigh two eighty—one man can't bring him down."

"I think he's here," Eric said.

"Well you're wrong," the Illinois guy said. "Because first, like I said, we got a report he was spotted in Milwaukee, and B, he would never go to New York, never went near it yet—"

"—his name, please."

"William Winslow. But like I told you, Billy Boy's what he's called."

William Winslow, Eric wrote down. William "Billy Boy" Winslow.

"I'll tell you something—be glad he ain't there—count your blessings, from what I read you got enough troubles."

"Tell me."

"You know the expression that goes something like that if you can't say something good about somebody don't say anything at all? Well, you *can't* say anything good about Billy Boy. He's a shit sadist with a brain like a pea. Also he's fucking eerie."

Eric waited.

"He claims he's special—he 'senses' things, he 'knows' things, the past and the future and all that—lots of people are interested in that; hell, everybody's interested in it, my wife reads her horoscope every day in the papers—only Billy Boy *believes* it. I'm telling you, count your blessings he's not there."

"I will," Eric said, and he got off the phone as gracefully as he could, because if Billy Boy could "sense" things, well why should he have the monopoly on that ability.

He was here. No question in Eric's mind, he was here. An eerie shit sadist had come to town. An eerie shit sadist killer with the brain of a pea. Eric rubbed his eyes.

Good news for Rupert Murdoch and the tabloids, bad for the rest of the world . . .

2

HENRY THE K

Immaculate, fastidious, and desperately uncomfortable, Leo Trude made his way through Times Square. His custom-made Meledandri suit and tailored topcoat could not have been more out of place anywhere than here, in the midst of the porn parlors, derelicts, and drifters who somehow thrived on 42nd Street.

He resented having to walk, did Leo, but it was snowing lightly, traffic was totally snarled, and he was late for his meeting with the Duchess. Rarely did she ever contact him and on those occasions, it had been more than worth his while. Leo picked up his pace, contenting himself with the thought that he would not be with her long—he disliked the Duchess—he disliked all cripples and the Duchess certainly qualified. Blind with her head forever tilted left and old with black glasses and parchment skin and that giant killer dog she adored and—

—someone had recognized him. A drunk, leaning against the glass window of the fast food emporium. The drunk raised an arm as if to wave.

Trude turned his head and hurried even faster.

Up ahead now was the Port Authority building and just behind it, on Ninth, was the Duchess's tiny parlor. Trude crossed Eighth and continued walking quickly on the far side of the street from the bus terminal.

"God bless you," an old lady said to him.

Trude ignored her, or tried to ignore her, but he was aware that he was blushing just a bit. Not enough so anyone would notice.

Anyone except himself. Angry, Trude stormed on. Ahead he noticed a group of moronic Spanish youths in a doorway, probably wondering whom to mug next, whose lives to alter. Trude touched his inside coat pocket without really meaning to, but he didn't normally carry a thousand dollars in new bills in this part of town. The Duchess was expensive.

Value for money was always expensive.

He got to Ninth and crossed again, then moved down toward his destination. The snow was falling more heavily now, and he cursed himself for not wearing his homburg. His brown curly hair was wet and his glasses needed cleaning.

"Please, sir," a well-dressed woman said—a Jersey commuter most likely. She held out a piece of paper and a pencil stub.

Trude kept on walking.

She walked with him. "I know you must think I'm intruding—"

"—you are intruding," he assured her.

But she would not be denied. "It would just mean so much to my children." She was pleading now. "My son . . . you're a hero to my son. I mean that." She hurried in front of him now, blocking his way.

Trude sighed.

"Here. And bless you."

Trude scribbled quickly, handed it back to her. Then she excitedly ran across the street against traffic and entered the terminal. Trude watched, half hoping a cab might clip her. He was genuinely upset now, and he needed a moment before dealing with the Duchess, so he stepped under an awning, got out his Sulka kerchief, cleaned his glasses, mopped his hair, all the while contemplating his curse.

Was it his fault he looked like Henry Kissinger?

Ever since Nixon made the fat Jew (the Nixonian terminology) head of state, Trude's life had been intermittently annoying. Yesterday someone had confided to him on Fifth Avenue—a Wall Street type it was—that he had it on unimpeachable authority that Haig was on his way out and he, Henry the K, would soon be reannointed. When he had dined once at The Palace he had been asked three times where were his secret service men.

The outrage of course was that Trude didn't really resemble the other man that much. Trude was thinner, taller, younger, had no Strangelovian accent. In fact, when he and Kissinger both taught at Harvard, Trude disliked the other man intensely, thought him a second-rate thinker with no real talent save self-aggrandizement.

But to much of the general populace, they might as well have been Chang and Eng.

Composed finally, Trude took the last few steps, walked into the Duchess's parlor.

"You're late," she said.

Trude looked at the thick black glasses and wondered again if she was, in fact, blind. "I could have been anybody," he said, "I hadn't spoken."

"Your walk betrays you. You walk like an arrogant man."

Trude decided not to pursue that line of inquiry any further. "It's snowing, I had to walk."

"You don't have to tell *me* that it snows—I know such things, I hear the snow fall." Her voice had gotten louder.

Trude decided he didn't much want to pursue that one either. She sat alone on the couch, her head tilted. Behind her was a beaded curtain. From back there now: a growl.

"Come or stay as you wish," she said.

"I'm not sure I understand," Trude began.

"I was not speaking to you. He heard me raise my voice and he worried."

Trude watched the beaded curtains part and then the giant dog came toward him.

"Stand still, there'll be no harm."

Trude made very sure he stood very very still.

The animal sniffed him, then turned, curled up at her feet. But its eyes remained on Trude.

"To business," the Duchess said.

"You contacted me. I came."

"Did you bring money?"

"Some."

"Did you bring a thousand?"

"A thousand means an ultra," Trude said. No point in giving it to her without some prodding. "Are you sure? Have you proof?"

"Yes I am sure. But proof is your province."

"True."

She held out her hand for the money.

"What's his name?" Trude asked before paying.

She dropped her hand. The Beast began to make its sound. Trude gave her the envelope. She took out the bills, counted them, running her fingers over and over the green paper.

How does she know they're not singles, he wondered.

Evidently, she did. "Winslow," she answered finally.

"And where is he?"

"He comes here many times, but irregularly."

"Where does he stay?"

"Different places. He does not wish to be found. I can tell you with assurance he is not a member of the College of Cardinals."

Trude sat in a chair across from her, took out his pen and note pad. "Tell me everything you know."

"I will. But you must be careful this time."

"I'm always careful," Trude said.

The Duchess shook her head. "Remember the Mazursky business."

"Ah yes, well, that . . ."

3

WATER

Once the ambulance got Edith to the emergency room at New York Hospital, it became very soon apparent that she wasn't going to die. There was so much blood that the work was at first feverish but that phase passed and the interns functioned as they usually did, with quick and telling adroitness. By the time she was finally wheeled to a private room, there was no doubt in any attending physician's mind about her survival.

Not that she was about to go anywhere; she was in something, probably shock, and a tremendous number of stitches were needed to close up her arms, which took longer than wished because of the enormous number of glass slivers that were caught in and beneath her skin.

Sally and Phillip began their vigil immediately. They sat with the unconscious body, took occasional strolls down the corridor so Sally could smoke. Phillip had his theories, which he told Sally. Sally told him his theories were, frankly, horseshit. Phillip, his Lincolnian look getting a bit strained by events, wondered if Sally had any better reasons explaining why Edith Mazursky Holtzman should, one February afternoon, become suicidal in a department store.

Sally didn't.

Edith slept more than a day. Phillip had to leave eventually, not because of business but because he had three girls at home, three teen-age girls at home, and how did you explain to them that this odd event had happened that would probably cloud their lives, probably forever.

Sally thought there were times it wasn't so terrible being a daughter of Lesbos.

"Should I lie to them?" Phillip wondered.

"Of course," Sally said. "You must, since we don't know what the truth is."

Phillip nodded. He hugged Sally, got up to go. He looked so suddenly withered Sally could only think of the beautiful young girl who had left Shangri-la. He came back eventually, many hours later, stayed as long as he could, then left again, a pattern he continued.

Sally simply moved into the hospital. She kept her gallery closed for the duration, and when she needed toilet articles, she tipped an orderly an obscene amount to dash out to the drugstore. When the nurses tried pulling their official act it was no contest —although not as cute and perky as in her Radcliffe days, Sally was still more than presentable, and the combination of her June Allysonish appearance coupled with her sailor's use of language routed the opposition.

Which is why, when Edith finally opened her eyes the first time, Sally was there. Edith blinked, said nothing. Sally said nothing back. They simply touched fingertips till Edith drifted again. The second awakening was stronger—Edith managed to request food —broth—and got most of it down. The third time she roused herself. Color was returning to her face. Very softly Edith said, "You stayed."

"I should think you'd know me by now," Sally said. "When there's a major social event, *nothing* will drag me away." She tried a bright smile.

Edith watched her closely.

Then the brightness left Sally's face. "I tried," she managed, shaking her head. "I shouldn't tell you anything like this; the doctors said you're not ready."

"Tell me what? Is Phillip all right? Are the children?"

"Worse," Sally whispered.

"What could be worse?" Edith said.

Sally looked straight at her and said it: "Bloomingdale's canceled your charge card."

Even drugged and in pain, Edith began to laugh.

"I fought them, though, Edith—I tried so hard—went all the way to the top—but they said there were strict store rules: 'when a customer bleeds on the merchandise, that's it.' "

"You were always mean, Sally Levinson," Edith said. And then she drifted.

Later. Edith blinking.

Sally sitting as before.

"Still here?" from Edith.

Sally nodded. "They drop the price after six."

"I do care for you so."

"Love me so."

"Yes."

"And I love you and that's why, my dear Edith, you can rest assured of something."

"What?"

"That no matter what happens, that no matter how many thousands of hours we spend together as the years go by, that under no conditions will I ever bring up what happened in Bloomingdale's."

Edith nodded.

"Edith?"

"Yes?"

"What the fuck happened in Bloomingdale's?"

Edith made the saddest smile. And was silent for the longest time. She was tired and her voice was barely audible.

Sally leaned far forward.

". . . control . . ." Edith said. Then she was drifting again.

Night now. "What do you think happened?" Edith spoke the words with her eyes closed.

Sally hesitated. She knew Edith more than well enough to know that the question meant that Edith wanted to talk about it, felt strong enough to. Sally told the truth: "Not the foggiest."

"And Phillip?"

Careful. "What about him?"

"You must have talked with him."

Easy now. "In generalities, sure. 'Did she seem depressed? Was she upset about anything?' But since the answers to all those were 'no, not depressed, no, not upset' he's just as out to lunch as I am." Edith's eyes were open now, studying Sally. Sally put her palm up in the air and said what she always did when it was necessary to convince Edith of the truth: "My right hand to God."

Of course, she was lying.

Phillip had an entire scenario worked out, and Sally had told him he was being a goddam fool. But he was not to be shaken.

First of all, the crucifying reviews for her exhibit had rocked Edith much more terribly than she had ever let on.

And second was the business with Doyle Ackerman.

Sally asked who the hell that was.

Phillip reprimanded her for lying—the Yale man, the beautiful swimmer that Edith was in love with, had had the affair with, back in school.

Sally, stunned that Phillip knew a thing about Edith and the swimmer, was even more stunned to find that Phillip had discovered Doyle's business card and handwritten phone number right at the top of things in Edith's purse. They were clearly seeing each other, Phillip concluded. And my suspicion is that he discarded her. Being thrown aside by her lover after failing so miserably in her art, that had done the Bloomingdale's trick.

Sally flailed at him, told him he was full of shit and to shut up.

Phillip, easily the best man Sally had ever known, shook his head; he hadn't been enough for Edith. If only he'd been a better man somehow, it all might have been avoided.

Sally continued her attack, calling him fucking crazy.

He replied that he was not, but that what had transpired in the store, *that* was crazy.

Sally was forced to nod.

And it *did* happen.

Sally nodded again.

Phillip's peroration was brief and simple: if it happened, then there must be a reason, and he asked her to come up with a sounder scenario than his.

Sally couldn't. Only Edith could do that.

"I was going to buy Phillip a new red silk tie," Edith said then. "Among other chores. Items for the girls. So off I went."

Sally sat forward in the hospital chair, tucked her legs up under her. "You walked?"

Edith hesitated, then smiled. "That's right, I remember now, I had a silly moment with a cab. I hailed one and then decided I shouldn't but by that time he'd stopped and I said something to the effect that it would be better for me if I walked and he looked at me and in that wonderful New York tone the old ones still use, he said, 'For this she stops me?' Something like that, anyhow, and I laughed and tipped him and started on my way."

"This is sure interesting so far, Edith," Sally said. "Earthshaking stuff."

"Just wait. I was walking briskly, not doing much window-shopping—"

"—do me a favor and spare me the window-shopping details, huh?"

"Doyle Ackerman," Edith said then, and she looked at Sally, almost smiling.

Sally said, "That name supposed to mean something?"

"Just think about it."

Sally hesitated for what she considered a proper amount of time. "The pimple-brained swimmer!" Their voices were a notch higher now; it was as if they were back in school.

"The *beautiful* pimple-brained swimmer, if you don't mind. My single mad passionate affair—the one Phillip never knew about."

"You ran into him?"

"Indeed."

"Don't tell me—he's lost his hair and got a paunch."

"Wrong. More of a dish than ever."

"I'm getting horny," Sally said. "Get on with it."

"Well, we had coffee. You remember how he broke my heart."

"I was there, tootsie. Remember who nursed you. Now get on with it—you're having coffee and . . ."

"It was just so wonderful."

"*What* was so fucking wonderful?"

"He *wanted* me, Sally. Middle-aged mother of three, and this perfectly breathtaking specimen was on the prowl."

"So you went to his hotel and then what?"

Edith shook her head. "Sally, I know this is against all laws of physical science, but his brain has *shrunk.*"

Sally couldn't help laughing.

"It's true—I don't know how he makes it across the street without accident."

"You're telling me you shot him down."

"In flames. I played Anna Karenina for my farewell—wasn't it Anna Karenina?—those long-suffering women get all mixed up for me—'the children, Doyle, we must think of the children'—anyway, out I traipsed. It was glorious."

"I don't believe it," Sally said. "It's too perfect—have you got proof?"

"What kind of proof could I have?"

"Oh, I don't know, a picture of him—or his card, maybe, his business card with some kind of message—"

"He did give me his business card. I stuck it in my purse. He put his phone number on it. I think it's unlisted."

Sally looked at Edith, slowly shook her head. "That would convince me, I admit it."

"Oh dear," Edith said then.

Sally waited.

"Now I have to tell about the control part."

"Sweetie, you don't gotta tell nothing you don't wanna tell. You're probably tired anyway."

"I am tired," Edith said, her voice softening.

"Well, then."

"But I *want* to."

"Well, then."

"And if you're me, and there's something you have to tell somebody, who else can that somebody be but you?"

"Make it brief then, Edith. Just get to it and over with."

Edith shut her eyes for a moment. "You know how important it's always been to me—probably ever since my father died—to be in control, on top of things."

"I've heard tell."

"Well, I got to Bloomingdale's a few minutes after leaving Doyle, and I felt so fine I bought myself a present, a scarf, and then I went to the tie department . . ." Now a long pause.

Sally waited.

Edith quietly began to weep.

Sally reached out, took her hand.

Edith turned her head away.

Very sweetly Sally said, "Aw shit now, c'mon."

Edith lay there.

Sally waited.

". . . it was just the worst moment, Sally . . . it came so fast . . ." Now her voice trailed off.

"Can you describe it?"

"Maybe."

"Try."

"Something was in my brain besides my brain," Edith said. "All, all my carefully built-up defenses, gone. Invaded. In the middle of my brain. It was like a child was thinking inside me—a child that *knew* me—and hated me so—all my failings burst out, all the bad things I'd done in my life, all those scars and guilts were ripped free and loose inside and I spun around, tried to get to it, tried to make it stop, but it kept on getting worse, it was as if all your sins and evils were bursting free and tormenting you, and *enjoying tormenting you*—and I knew I had to do something because it was as if you were being tortured by a sadist, by an ultimate sadist, only that sadist was you, and whatever steps you have to take to make it stop"—now she looked at her bandaged arms—"you take them."

During the outburst Sally could see the cost in energy, and she said nothing when Edith was done, just leaned forward, smoothed Edith's lovely reddish hair. When Edith was asleep again, she kept on for a while, then contented herself holding Edith's hand.

Sally was exhausted too, and when the night nurse whispered the room across the hall was vacant and wouldn't she feel better with a decent night's rest, Sally felt genuinely grateful. She had more trouble getting to sleep than she thought, considering how whipped she was. Edith's phrase kept recurring, making her wonder. "Something was inside my brain besides my brain . . ." What the fuck could it be, Sally wondered.

Whatever it was, it returned in the hours before dawn.

Edith's long-time wish for cremation was, of course, honored. And she'd also wanted just the family to gather in the living room of the Beekman Place place for a really good glass of champagne and Phillip was unable to function much so Sally bought a magnum of Roederer Cristal from Sherry-Lehmann and maybe they would have gotten through it—it would have been awful but they might have made the moment work, if Edith's mother, old Mrs. Mazursky, hadn't chosen to invite the rabbi of her congregation.

She didn't tell anyone she'd done it, and until he arrived, she contented herself moving around the room, from Phillip to Sally to the daughters, Abigail, Caroline, and Kate, saying that Edith was a bubble of a child. "Your mother was a bubble of a child," she said to the children. "My daughter was a bubble of a child," she said to poor, dazed Phillip.

Sally, anxious to avoid her turn, went to the large picture window and stared out; ordinarily it was one of the premier views of the city, but since Edith had chosen to drown in that same East River that flowed so beautifully by, the view, at least for now, possessed sorrows.

Sally turned sharply from it, hoisted the magnum from the nearby table, filled her glass, put the bottle down, drained her glass, lifted the bottle back up, filled the glass again. It was while she was intent on this that she heard the words, "Oh thank God, come in, Rabbi."

Stunned, Sally looked as the chubby old woman went to the tall man in the doorway. He was impeccably coiffed, Sally watched as he smiled a perfect smile of sympathy, and as she watched she wondered did she hate him more for how he looked or that he was there.

"I've asked Rabbi Korngold to say a few words," Mrs. Mazursky said.

Sally watched as Phillip, dear thing that he was, tried to stop the festivities before they rolled. "I don't remember Edith having requested . . ." he began. "I hadn't intended . . ." he tried again.

I wish I was family, Sally thought. But she wasn't, she told herself. And her job was to shut up.

In a deep, controlled voice, Rabbi Korngold said something in Hebrew.

At least Sally assumed it was Hebrew. Probably a prayer. Getting her mind off the situation, she studied Phillip, washed up and slumping, Lincolnesque no more. And the three daughters: Kate, angry at her mother's betrayal, Abby, angry but still more stunned, Caroline, forlorn but fighting not to give in to tears.

"Edith Mazursky Holtzman," Rabbi Korngold said, his voice growing deeper as he repeated the name. "Edith . . . Mazursky . . . Holtzman . . . a flower plucked before her springtime."

Now Caroline had lost her fight, was weeping.

"What can we say of Edith Mazursky Holtzman . . . what can we capture in mere words of her joyous spirit; how can we encapsulate a spirit as wide as the horizon . . . ?" He looked at the girls now. "Who but you can know the greatness of your loss?"

There went Abby.

Kate was still fighting the good fight.

The rabbi turned toward Kate now. "You must not sorrow because you are alone. You are not alone. You have your memories and they are gold."

Kate began to sob. She ran to her weeping father, buried her head. Mrs. Mazursky had been in tears since the rabbi had cleared his throat.

He moved into the center of the room now, spread his long arms, his voice deeper and slower than ever. "Yes, they are gold, our memories of Edith Mazursky Holtzman . . . and gold shines . . . and our memories shine . . . they shine today . . . they will shine tomorrow . . . they will shine forever . . ." He pointed to Mrs. Mazursky ". . . daughter memories . . ." Now to the girls. ". . . mother memories . . ." Last to Phillip. ". . . and memories of wife . . . for she was fully all those things, a daughter, a mother, a wife—"

"—*and painter!*" Sally cut in. "Now you must stop this."

"What?—" He spun toward Sally.

"She was also a painter."

"A painter, of course."

"No, I don't think you knew that," Sally said. "But she was very good, really a remarkable gift and Lord knows where it would have taken her and I suppose it's sad we'll never find out, but lots of things are sad, aren't they, sir."

"Oh yes," Rabbi Korngold said. He looked around now, not quite certain as to what to do next.

Sally was more than certain. Yes she was small and pert and on occasion, demure, but she could also be, on occasion, a tank, and that was the role she played now, moving toward the rabbi, clasping his hand, starting him deftly toward the door. "We won't forget your appearance here," Sally told him, hoping it was ambiguous enough.

"Thank you," the rabbi answered.

"And if we need you, we'll feel free to contact you."

"My phone is always open," Rabbi Korngold said, which isn't quite what he meant to say, he had meant to say that it was his *door*, of course, that was open, and he wondered if he ought to clarify the thought, but a look at his escort made him decide not to.

Sally stayed in the doorway till he was gone. Then she faced the room. Phillip, still holding Kate, nodded a "thank you." Sally looked at them all. Then she said, "My beloveds: we are here because Edith chose to desert us. Maybe someday we'll know why . . ."

She crossed to the champagne, drank a glass empty, poured it back full, sat and stared out at the river. Behind her now, she could hear the tears subsiding.

Sally didn't cry. Ever. Sometimes she wished she could. She sat at a table that was placed by the window and put her chin in her hands, hoping Mrs. Mazursky wouldn't be angry at her for ending the peroration early.

Evidently she wasn't, since not too many minutes later, the old lady was standing beside Sally, saying that Edith was just a bubble of a child.

"I'm sure, Mrs. Mazursky."

"She was, she was. A bubble. Just a bubble of a child."

Sally nodded.

Now Mrs. Mazursky leaned close, whispered into Sally's ear. "And it was an accident. That." She pointed toward the water. "I'm positive. It was an accident. Believe me."

Sally tried very hard to nod again. But it wasn't easy.

An accident?

Forget it was the middle of the night when Edith drowned. Forget it was February. Forget it was freezing. Forget it was the East River. Forget she was wearing only a hospital gown.

She couldn't swim . . .

LA DOLCE VITA

—Billy Boy stood silently on the steps, took a last look at the two women lying below, and wondered what the hell to do now—

—he had meant to go to Hero's, to go to Hero's and get clothes, but that was before he got lucky with the queen of the shop-lifters—

—and before he hit the nosy bitch with the red hair—

—if he went to Hero's now he'd go without money, and maybe they were the kind of place that took gold watches and gold bracelets and all the other stuff he'd jammed in his pockets, but then again, maybe they weren't. This was in New York, and in Milwaukee there were places that did and in Waukegan there were plenty of places that did but New York you didn't want them laughing at you.

So what he had to do was barter, the gold for some bread, and what he also had to do, *right now,* was get the hell away. He climbed the steps and there were half a dozen people standing clustered so he said, "Get the cops, didja for Chrissakes call the cops?" and when they shook their heads he exploded, "What's wrong with you people, I gotta do *everything*?" and he pulled his black wool cap down tight around his head and bulled away, calling out "Police" a few times until he was safe out of sight around the corner which is when he started running—

—running? Are you crazy? You know what they do to guys in New York who run away from crimes? Book 'em and throw away the key.

He stopped and took a deep breath. He was—he had to admit it—flustered. *Flustered.* And they were looking at him. All the people were looking at him. They knew. People from the Apple knew when you'd done something, unless you were smart enough to fake 'em, and he was smart enough in Milwaukee and he was a whiz in Waukegan, but New York? He wished then what he always did after a job—

—lemme be invisible—I wanna be invisible, I wanna make 'em stop *staring*—

The Duchess. She said it was a lucky day, and hadn't it been lucky so far, hadn't she been on the money?

The money. If he gave her some, she'd protect him, make 'em stop staring, make him as good as invisible, make him safe . . .

The Beast growled as he entered. " 'Scuse," Billy Boy muttered, and he took a seat across the room, making no noise, because the Duchess was talking to a client, an old black lady.

"She misses you, of course she misses you, every day she misses you," the Duchess said. "But she's happy. And that's the main thing."

"Main thing," the old black lady repeated. "An' she don't doubt I love her?"

"Never. She loves you too. And when you cross over, she'll be there to take your hand."

The black lady nodded, took out some rumpled bills, handed them over. "I broke my health putting her through school. Two jobs every day of the worl'. Hardly seems worth it now."

"God works in mysterious ways," the Duchess said.

"See you again in a month," the black lady said, and she moved with pain to the door and was gone.

"I hate that 'God works in mysterious ways' garbage, but sometimes you just have to bullshit the people."

"But you weren't bullshitting me."

"How could I? You'd know."

"I would, wouldn't I." He fumbled into his pocket. "Here—this gold bracelet's for you—I found it in the street while I was applying for a job. The job went great so I thought you deserved this."

"You can't buy luck."

"I just thought you'd like it," Billy Boy said.

"I do. We both do, don't we?" The Beast, in reply, growled.

"Maybe I'll come back again."

"I'm always here."

"An' it's still my lucky day?"

She put the gold bracelet on her thin wrist. Then she said, softly, "Fear nothing, you're on fire."

That was almost as good as being invisible . . .

He tried several Eighth Avenue places before he found one that
was right. He sensed it as soon as he stepped from the darkness
of the street to the greater darkness of the bar. A ton of hookers
moving restless to the beat of the nigger music coming from the
juke. And in the rear, a bunch of well-dressed pimps, sitting like
they owned the world.

Billy Boy took a seat in the corner of the bar, ordered a seven
and seven. A couple of hookers hit on him right off but he brushed
them, they weren't right. The fourth or fifth was white and
scrawny, burned to pieces; anyone who'd work a chick that hard
had to have money. "I could learn to like you a lot," she said. "Bet
you're big all over."

"I want your pimp," Billy Boy said.

She looked shocked. "I got no one. Free-lance all the way."

"Too bad." He took out a ten, put it on the bar. "I'd of given
you that if you'd brought him over."

"I think maybe my agent's here," she answered. "In the back."

Billy Boy faced front, said nothing, nursed his seven and seven.
In a minute the burnout was back. "He'll be most glad to talk to
you," she said, pointing toward a large black man in a cowboy hat
who was moving toward them. Billy Boy pushed her the ten and
she left.

"What's doing, my man?" the black guy said.

"I'm a little short on cash," Billy Boy told him.

"So's half the civilized world."

Billy Boy took out a man's gold watch, flashed it briefly, put it
back in his pocket. "There's more. I'm selling, if you wanna buy.
But not here."

"A business venture, huh. Well, I shouldn't but I will—promise
you won't take advantage of me, my man; you look awful smart."
He was smiling all the time he talked and Billy Boy tried not to let
it bother him. They left the bar, went around the corner to a flop-
house, paid for a room on the second floor. Billy Boy followed the
other guy up. He was big, six four, and he moved like an athlete.

Inside the room, Billy Boy emptied his pockets on the bed,
dropping the gold bracelets and the earrings and the men's
watches and the women's watches. A ton of stuff.

"Relative die and leave you this?"

"Why you all the time smiling? You could piss people off smiling like that."

"It's a mean world, I try to spread happiness." He studied half a dozen bracelets, examined a watch. "Looks like quality stuff. But then, what do I know?"

"It's the best. Straight from Bloomington's."

Now the black guy started laughing. *"Dale's,* my man. Bloom-ing*dale's."*

Billy Boy could feel his hand starting to turn into a fist.

"Eighty bucks," the black guy said.

"You listen now—you listen now—I got a number inside my head—if you guess more than my number, you get all this—if you guess less than the number inside my head, deep shit is what you're into." He opened the bathroom door, tested it, made his arm a club, and blasted the door off its hinges.

"Thousand," the black guy said—"Jesus, it ain't worth more'n that—"

Billy Boy started toward him. The number in his head had been two fifty but he was on fire.

"Twelve hunnerd's all I got!"

Billy Boy held out his hand for the money, got it, watched as the pimp grabbed the merchandise, went to the door, opened it. "Don't never come back to that bar," he said, and he took off.

Billy Boy went right back to the bar, ordered another seven and seven, took it back to a chair near where the pimp was sitting with half a dozen others.

Not one of them even budged. And most of them looked afraid. Billy Boy liked that. He never felt fear. But scaring other people, that was more fun than anything.

He got up, left the bar. He was hungry. He spotted a McDonald's and went in. It wasn't too crowded and when it was his turn he ordered six Big Macs. "To go?" the girl asked. He shook his head, paid, went to a table, started to eat.

A little kid began to giggle.

Billy Boy glanced up. The little kid was pointing to another little kid—pointing at the six hamburgers. Now their folks were looking too. Billy Boy turned and stared around the other way. Same story. People were watching him.

Just lemme be invisible shit!

He finished the second sandwich, got up, left the rest uneaten. He couldn't help that he had a big appetite. It took a lot to fill him, so he went to a Burger King and ordered a couple of Whoppers.

He wanted a bunch but they'd start looking at him again if he did that. His next stop was the Colonel where he had four pieces of the crispy. Then he found an Arthur Treacher's and finished up with fish. Then he found a whore, made a deal, took her in the hallway of a tenement. Then he headed back down to Ninth Avenue where the Duchess was.

They went well into the morning talking about their lives . . .

He woke in some fleabag, checked to see his money was safe. It was, which was good, cause sometimes when he boozed it bad he did dumb things—there were two empties on the floor, two quarts before sleep, and usually that wasn't any big deal but he'd been inside so long he was out of practice. Booze was like anything else, you had to practice.

He got up and went to the sink, put some water on his face. His hangover was pretty bad but you didn't get them when you were locked inside, so don't bitch he told himself. Now he studied himself in the mirror.

Brown eyes, brown hair, average features—except they spotted him because he was so wide. The shoulders belonged on a bigger man. When you were built like he was built you carried your own spotlight. Sometimes he tried slumping, tried being five eleven instead of over six one. And sometimes it didn't work. Wishing again for invisibility, he opened the door, walked down to the lobby. He'd paid in advance and there was no way he'd come back here again—different places each night, you had to keep moving —so when the rummy room clerk said good day he just grunted and kept on going.

First thing he saw on the street was a Chink hooker staring at the sun. Dainty, black-haired. He paid her, trailed her into a room she had, got his money's worth, left. What a great city. Whores in the morning. What a sweet life.

Hero's looked better in the daylight than when he'd checked it out the afternoon before. Great-looking threads. That was what the niggers called them back inside: "heavy threads, man." Been in America all these years and the assholes still couldn't speak English.

"Yessir?" the salesman said. Big guy. Six six. Slim build. Average hands.

Billy Boy looked around the place. He was it as far as customers went. Still he felt nervous—how long had it been since he'd bought clothes? Years and years. Inside they gave you what to wear, outside he took. He tried to smile and said, "Some heavy threads."

"We've got the best," the salesman said. "I'm Nick, you're . . . ?"

"Will. An' I want the works. I wanna suit. I wanna shirt. I want it should all fit perfect."

Nick raised his right hand. "The day something leaves this place that doesn't fit perfect is the day I close." He took a step back, studied Billy Boy. "What's your neck?"

"Don't know."

"Wonderful—cause I'm a great guesser and I'd put you at . . ." He studied Billy again. "Eighteen and a half neck, thirty-six sleeve." He got a tape measure, expertly applied it, showed it to Billy Boy. "On the button. For a suit, maybe you ought to try a fifty long, athletic cut. That sound okay?"

"Just so they're heavy threads is all I care."

"Now color." He led the way to the suit area. "Young man like you, I wouldn't want to see you in old colors. Dark gray, navy blue, that's drab."

"You pick, okay? I just want it now."

"We're a one-day store, Will. I'll do the measuring, tailor comes in this afternoon, you can have the shebang before we close. Seven all right?"

"An' them—an' them!" Billy Boy pointed to the salesman's boots. He was talking too loud, much too loud, but he couldn't help it. *"I want them too!"*

"Not for sale I'm afraid. Those are mine. Custom-made special. Cost me three hundred."

Billy Boy put his foot beside the salesman's. They were about the same size. "I'll pay five hundred for what you got on."

Nick smiled. "Can't Will—I need them for my job—people like a big salesman in a shop like this—Adler's only gives you two, these give me four plus."

"Six hundred," Billy Boy said.

"Just not for sale," Nick told him.

Billy Boy said he understood, paid cash in advance for the clothes, promised he'd be back by seven.

It was closer to quarter after when he knocked at the dark store. There was a pause before Nick appeared from the back, nodded when he saw who it was, opened up. "I was about to lock up and leave," he said.

"Sorry," from Billy Boy.

"No harm. All's done." He indicated a hanger of clothes and a box of shirts. "Come back real soon."

"Don't I get to try 'em on? What if the pants aren't right?"

Nick looked at his watch. "The wife's waiting."

"I'll hurry. Promise."

Nick pointed the way in the back to a curtained-off area. Billy Boy disappeared. Nick paced. Billy Boy called out then, "You better come look at this." Nick went behind the curtained area. The last thing he saw was a club coming down . . .

The police arrived before eight and by then the crowds had already begun and by nine there were mobs of people standing in a semicircle around the lit clothing store. It was cold but more and more of them kept coming, watching the police go in and out of the store and the blond giant didn't arrive until nine thirty when he went up to a group of black kids and said, pointing to the store, "Trouble?" and the black kids looked at him, studied him, then looked away and said, "Murder," and the blond giant moved on down to another group of people, young couples, and he said, "Is it true, a murder?" and the couples looked at him awhile then said, "Broke the guy's neck," and the blond giant moved away, down to some businessmen, and said, "Murdered I hear, neck broke and all," and the oldest businessman said, "Murdered and robbed, money, clothes, everything, they found him naked and dead," and the blond giant shook his head, moved on, and as he continued to mingle, continued to move from group to group, Billy Boy wanted to whoop out loud like a kid when he gets his first two-wheeler. Because that's what it was like—his slumping days were over, he stood six foot six now because he was wearing the boots, the special four-inch elevator boots, and the brand new three hundred dollar long-haired blond wig fit perfect, *perfect,* and as he moved along he knew people were looking at him and he loved it, because they were looking at him, sure, but they weren't *seeing* him, he wasn't there.

Two detectives came out of the clothing store and walked right past him. The older one smelled of aftershave and the younger one was big with eyes so blue and Billy Boy tapped the old one on the shoulder and said, "Excuse me, sir, but someone down the way said the poor man was naked with his neck broke, and I wondered, what's the city coming to?" They were deep in conversation and neither of them answered, just shrugged, moved away. Billy Boy stared after them. The old one kept on walking.

The blue-eyed one stopped, slowly turned, stared back. Enormous, unconquered, invisible at last, Billy Boy made a smile . . .

5

THE LAST TO KNOW

Feeling very much a fool—no, worse—feeling very much an *old* fool, W. Nelson Stewart silently unlocked the great front door of his mansion and stepped inside. It was midnight of the day of his supposed Boston trip, and bitter. He had been hesitating outside for more than a few minutes, and now as he stood there in the darkness, he shivered, shivered with the cold.

At least that was one reason.

Probably a greater contributor was simply fear, fear of what he suspected might be going on between Charlotte and Theo—no, worse—fear of what he *knew* to be going on between them.

He crept now toward the staircase.

Crept. That was the right word. Here he was, a decent fellow, a decent somber admittedly humorless businessman, mid-fifties, worth a million and more for every year, reduced to skulking.

To skulk was lower in dignity than to creep.

I have never committed an immoral act in my life, Nelson Stewart thought, never knowingly wronged another, and here I am, stealthily slinking *into my own house,* prowling up *my own stairs,* intent on lurking in the dark to catch *my own wife* in the arms of another.

Part of his mind said "get out, stop this, it doesn't matter, this is not what you do well, you don't belong here" and for a moment he paused on the stairs and glanced back at the door.

But he did belong here. It was, after all, his home.

And of course, it did, it did matter.

He had cared for Charlotte Bridgeman since she was born, had watched her become perhaps the one genuine beauty it had ever been his great pleasure to know, had married her, babied her, fathered children with her.

Only to be betrayed.

The act of betrayal was not in itself so surprising. Nelson remembered the looks Charlotte got when they entered rooms together. And he knew he was, to her, old, and he knew he had more stomach than necessary and his rimless glasses were not the sort a hero might wear. And there were always so many younger men in the world—as you got older, he realized, their number increased; thirty was now a younger man to him, thirty-five even.

But in his mind, if he was to lose Charlotte, it was also to an athlete, someone who matched her beauty. A man who played tennis or golf and of course had money and the graces and darting eyes; that sort of figure might replace him.

Not a Theo.

Not an undernourished less than manly trashy poet. At the top of the stairs now, Nelson wondered again at the incredible choice Charlotte had made. And though he was yet short of tangible proof, he had caught the looks between them, seen the flushes of cheek, caught the occasional stammer.

As he crossed silently toward his bedroom, he allowed for the possibility that he was wrong. That she had not betrayed. That his jealousy was simply getting brewed stronger with age. Fifty-five. He was fifty-five, she was just past thirty.

But Theo was young and that must be the greater part of it. Plus: he was though dreary to Nelson, undoubtedly soulful to her. Probably he read her poetry aloud. Probably he spoke in metaphor.

But surely there could not be much physical between them.

Nelson entered his bedroom, crossed it, carefully unlocked and turned the terrace door. Their rooms were close, his and Charlotte's, and the terrace went the entire length of the house. He slipped outside now, walking very slowly. A step at a time. Pause. Another. Pause. Breath. No sound. Step. Pause. Step. Pause. As he approached her bedroom, he slowed even more. There was a splash of light where the curtains parted. Not much. But more than sufficient for his needs.

W. Nelson Stewart moved to where the bed was entirely within his view. He stepped back, taking no chance of being seen from within. Then he waited.

Theo was seated on her bed, his hands clasped in his lap, a tatty robe tight around his ridiculous body. He wore old slippers, torn. One of his toes protruded.

W. Nelson Stewart shook his head. For such a creature, betrayal. For such a forlorn wet kitten of a man, a life thrown away. No sense, no sense at all.

Charlotte entered the room now from her dressing room area. Her black hair framed her pale face; her violet eyes had never been brighter. She wore a long elegant robe her husband had lovingly bought her in Paris on their honeymoon.

Theo stood.

Charlotte gestured sharply, gestured down.

Theo sat.

Charlotte approached the bed.

Nelson approached the window.

She knelt, reached out, took off one of his slippers, then the other. Then she stood, reached out, took his hands. And kissed them. And kissed them. She brought him to his feet their hands still clasped.

Nelson moved back a quiet step.

She put her fingers to the sash around his robe, untied it. The robe parted. Theo was naked. She put her hands beneath the robe, moved it back until it fell from his shoulders. It fell to the floor. She bent, picked it up, touched it gently with her strong fingers, stroked the robe smooth, lay it carefully at the foot of the bed. Then she stood in front of him and leaning forward, put her tongue to his nipple. Theo reached for her. She took his hands, replaced them at his sides. She kissed his other nipple, then knelt in front of him briefly and kissed him again.

It was somewhere in there that Nelson knew he had to kill them.

Break the little bastard's back, rip out her offending tongue, storm in, surprise them, destroy them but let them live enough to suffer for their sins, beat them, slash them, crush them—

—with what?

He looked at his hands—they were small, unused to violence, soft, useless when it came to feats of strength. And even though Charlotte was a woman she was strong, and Theo though small, was young and—and—

—with the pistol.

He turned, walked along the terrace, reentered his room, moved swiftly to the door and to the stairs beyond. Down the stairs and then he turned toward the library. He went immediately to the large desk, took his keys, unlocked the central drawer. Then he reached inside toward the deep right corner, pulled the pistol out.

It had never been fired. Certainly never by him. He had bought it years before when two robberies had taken place on Gramercy Park within a week. He opened it now just long enough to see the bullets were in place.

Then back up the stairs, to his room, to the terrace door, to outside. He was amazed at the clarity of his mind. While he had waited outside the house before entering, he had imagined all kinds of wild scenes, all kinds of rage bursting from him. But he felt no rage now. Just a desire for order, for justice, for sins to be repaid.

The night air was no longer cold to him. He walked along the terrace steadily, steadily without fear approached the light. The gun was at his side. He stared into the room.

Theo was pursuing his wife.

He was still naked, emaciated, worthless. She was still beautiful in her Paris robe. He pursued her slowly around her bed. She retreated, he advanced. Then he leapt forward, grabbed her, brought her to him, kissed her.

Charlotte turned her head away. He tried again to kiss her. Again she would have none of it. He tried to hold her tight but she broke free and stepped away. She pointed sharply to the bed. He made for her again but she gestured to the bed a second time, more sharply. She meant it—*sit—down.*

Theo sat.

Charlotte moved in front of him. Slowly her hands went to her own sash. She was about to disrobe.

The pistol was level now, level and aimed at Theo—Nelson wanted her to be the first to see her loved one's pain.

And it was then that Charlotte began to dance. Not like a waltz, not really steps at all. But it was some kind of dance movement, her shoulders dipped and her hips undulated and—

—and as Nelson watched he realized she was vamping him. She was Cleopatra now, she was flirting with Antony. Charlotte's eyes flashed and gradually the robe came off one shoulder and her hips kept moving—

—and as Nelson watched what had so recently been passion now became, to his eyes, ridiculous and sad. Charlotte was never graceful and she was always big and her eyes narrowed as she dropped the robe to the floor and now she was naked too, except naked her breasts were soft and sagging and her poor stomach bulged from the scars of giving birth.

Nelson stared at his wife, then at his pistol. Dear God, he had actually contemplated using the thing. Had considered stamping "scandal" beside his family name forever. Inside now, Charlotte raised her long arms and continued her slow movements. Theo sat as before, pale and implausible on the bed. What a terrible thing almost happened, Nelson thought, watching his aging beauty of a wife, scarred and simple, at most with half a mind. Not an item to go berserk over. Hardly that. She was snapping her fingers now as her dance of passion continued. Feigned passion, Nelson thought. He doubted the real thing had ever happened to her. Not even doubted; he knew.

Whenever they had sex, she was always dry . . .

6

THE CAPTURE OF BILLY BOY

It was their day off, Eric was in a foul mood, so Haggerty decided they could do with the double sirloin at Wally's.

Haggerty treasured his days off now. When he was first alone, they were a bitch. Crazy-making. But once he finally admitted Helen was not going to pull a Lazarus, he realized what he had to do was block out his time, not leave himself unattended spaces. So he always slept late, no problem, he was good at sleeping, even better when he was allowed to doze. He loved dropping off again, coming to half an hour later, stretching, getting the pillow back smooth, then snoozing another twenty, thirty minutes; he was a great dozer.

Then up and coffee and a bagel bought the night before, the bagel toasted and sometimes with peanut butter, sometimes cream cheese. Then a long letter to Frank Jr., in middle management now at Boeing, and how are the grandkids, that sort of breezy note.

Then, since his days off were generally Saturday, dress up, the good suit and a fresh ironed shirt and a bow tie for pizzazz, and off to theatre. If there was a new musical in town, he'd head straight for it, buy a ticket or, if they were sold out, a standing room. If there wasn't a new musical, which was the case today, instead of seeing one, he'd catch maybe four or five.

But you had to time it just right, and of course, the theatres had to be reasonably close to each other. You could handle *Annie* and *Evita* since one was on 52nd Street, the other just around the corner. *Sugar Babies* was up there too, so that could fit nicely. But if you wanted to add in *A Chorus Line* you needed track shoes, since the Shubert Theatre was eight crowded blocks away, down on 44th.

Haggerty felt like *A Chorus Line* today—he loved the opening. All the dancers going "five-six-seven-eight" and their bodies trying to get the steps right—if "Rose's Turn" gave *Gypsy* the best ending to any musical, Haggerty felt *A Chorus Line* laid claim to the greatest start.

It was almost two and most of the crowd was already in when he walked up to the man taking tickets, flashed the gold badge, and muttered, "just checking," as he hurried inside. The ticket taker knew his face, but even if he didn't, no one gave cops or firemen trouble when it came to standing in the back on Broadway.

Haggerty knew that strictly speaking, what he was doing wasn't honest—screw "strictly speaking," it was *dis*honest. But he tried to tell himself he'd paid seven times full price to see the whole show, and if something odd broke out in the audience, well, a detective was already there, ready to quell the disturbance.

Now there went the houselights.

Haggerty stood in the back corner; a child again. Of course, he'd never been to Broadway when he was a child, but if he had been so blessed, he knew what he'd have felt then was what he was feeling now.

Half an hour later he left, stood on the sidewalk, checked the time. It was tricky, doing this kind of thing, because it had to be perfect or it was nothing. You paid to see Babe Ruth hit a home run, not to see the teams run into their dugouts at the end of an inning.

Hmmm. Although *Deathtrap* wasn't strictly speaking a musical —screw "strictly speaking," what's the matter with you today, it's a *play*. In any case, Haggerty liked the shocker at the first act curtain and the way the audience buzz-buzzed as they made their way up the aisle. But he also was a great fan of the title number from *They're Playing Our Song*. The problem was they could run very close to each other in time. And if one show started a few minutes late, you could be in trouble.

Risk it, Haggerty told himself, and he did, catching them both scooting from the Music Box to the Imperial with ease. "Just checking" he told the old lady at the Imperial flashing the gold badge. "Go with God, Haggerty," she said, opening the door for him, letting him bathe in the magic. Haggerty applauded loudly with his big hands, letting the kids up on stage know his appreciation, then went back to the sidewalk, checked his watch, and pleased, walked slowly to the Belasco for the great "Black and Blue" number that summed up *Ain't Misbehavin'*.

Then he went home, poured himself a shot of whiskey, ran the tub. He had been on his feet a good while today, and his legs ached because, strictly speaking, he was no cookie anymore. You must stop with this "strictly speaking" bullshit, he told himself then. You're *old*. So he rested in the tub and sipped his drink and then napped, first setting the alarm, and then, rested and cheery, he began to think about dinner.

That was what Haggerty did on his days off.

Eric didn't believe in them.

Oh, every so often he'd get in his car and just drive, up to New England when the leaves were turning, that kind of thing. Or just pack up and grab some girl or other and hotfoot it down to the Caribbean, leave your mind at home, let your body do the talking. But as a rule, especially when things were going badly, he stayed close to home.

And things were going very badly now.

He had spent much of the day at his desk at the 19th, working the phones. But he had gone out several times, once to aid in bringing to justice two adorable-looking eleven-year-old boys who had put a heated iron on the face of a six-year-old girl who lived in the same apartment house. The girl was scarred permanently; the boys thought it was funny.

Another incident involved a merchant on Third who objected to a pushcart vendor selling belts on the sidewalk when he, the merchant, happened to also sell belts *and* pay taxes. They had argued, the merchant had pushed the vendor, they argued some more, louder; another push. Then screams, a shove, and the vendor, a young man, had dropped dead of an apparent stroke making the merchant, an honest and decent murderer, but a murderer nonetheless. Eric got little pleasure out of booking him.

But in many ways the high point of his day concerned Mrs. Atherton. Close to eighty, she lived in a town house on 70th off Park. Her maid, Cleo, had been with her for five years when Cleo told Mrs. Atherton she had to leave because her son O.J. was getting in trouble and she had to return to the islands. Mrs. Atherton insisted O.J. come live with his mother, they fixed up the spare room beside the kitchen, and everything went fine for a

week, until today in point of fact, when O.J. raped the old woman.
Cleo was the one who called the 19th about it and Eric was the
one who got to accompany the old woman to Lenox Hill. The last
thing she said to Eric, touching his hand with her broken fingers
was, "I don't want to lose Cleo, I don't want my Cleo to leave me."

All of which led to words with Captain Haig. Captain Haig ran
the 19th and was well thought of at Headquarters. He was a
ruddy, handsome man, a good drinker, and possessed a wondrous
memory for names. Eric felt he was a bigot and genuinely detested
him. But quietly. Captain Haig wasn't crazy about Eric either.

"He fucked her?" Captain Haig said to Eric. "Eighty years old
and he *fucked* her?"

Eric suggested the Captain read the report.

"Was there sodomy?" the Captain asked.

Eric looked up from his desk. "Do you really care?"

"What's that supposed to mean?"

"I just wondered if it would make your day or not— it strikes
me as sort of an imbecilic question."

"Watch your mouth."

Eric waited for his superior to leave.

Captain Haig moved in close. "The question had a meaning,
because there's a war going on in the streets, and when Goldwater
talked about it all you liberals thought he was a nut, but now you
know he was right, and the reason the war's not going to get any
better is because there are facts that can't be said. They're different
from the rest of us—that's a fact—no fifteen-year-old white kid
would have raped her." He stalked off.

Idiot, Eric told himself. He's an asshole and *you* know he's an
asshole and *he* knows you know he's an asshole so why do you
have to *call* him an asshole? Not smart. Not your basic smooth
move.

Well, blame it on Billy Boy.

Or rather, on the absence of same.

That, coupled with any number of other facts. Like no one other
than Eric was at all convinced that this William "Billy Boy"
Winslow was the killer. He had been spotted only yesterday, or
someone like him had been spotted, in South Florida. And there
was no connection between the Oliver woman and the clothing
salesman other than that both of their necks had been broken.
Lots of people got their necks broken, check the files. Also the

clothing salesman had a brother-in-law whom he was on the outs with and who had disappeared over the last few days which made him a more than likely suspect. Plus Captain Haig was convinced the killers were young, not so gifted, and black. Only Eric knew. Or thought he knew. Except no one could find him. None of Eric's "voices" gave a cry. No sound, nothing. Billy Boy had simply disappeared.

"I booked us at Wally's at nine," Haggerty said, walking in, sitting on the edge of Eric's desk. "It's almost that now, get your coat on."

"I guess I'm not so hungry," Eric said.

Haggerty got Eric's coat, tossed it into Eric's lap. "We'll have the double sirloin."

Eric was very serious about steaks. Whenever a new steak house opened, he was always among the first to give it a shot. But his favorites were never truly challenged: if you were eating alone, the best was Broadway Joe on 46th Street; if there was somebody else, the double sirloin at Wally's was the outstanding steak in Manhattan. "Will you have it really rare?" Eric asked. "None of your Irish 'medium' shit."

"Blue we'll have it," Haggerty promised. "My sole purpose of this evening is to cheer you up."

On the way to Wally's, Eric told of his talk with the Captain.

"Lemme see if I've got this right now," Haggerty said when Eric was done. "For no reason other than petulance, you indicated that your boss, your superior, your paterfamilias, was a *schmuck.*"

"That was certainly the clear implication," Eric admitted.

"Genius," Haggerty said. "I'll come visit you when you're walking a beat again. I'll bring you hot coffee from Chock Full o' Nuts to remind you what it was like in the land of the living."

Eric brooded in silence, until they got to the restaurant. It was jammed, as always, but they lucked out, being seated at the table they liked best, the round one in the left rear, where Tony was the waiter. He brought them menus; Haggerty shook his head, he didn't need one, while Eric quickly opened his, studying it to see if anything new had gone in since their last time.

"We're having the double sirloin," Haggerty said, "that much is definite."

"An' how would you like that?"

"Medium," Haggerty said and then as Eric's head jerked up

from the menu, eyes glaring, he quickly put up his big hands in a peacemaking position. "Joke, a joke, Eric, just wanted to see if I had your attention. I'm cheering you up tonight, remember?" Haggerty looked at Tony now. "Rare," he said. "Underlined."

"You want it very rare, right?"

"Wrong, Tony; and we don't want it blue either—we want it *so* red and juicy inside just tell the chef to lean the cow against the radiator."

Eric smiled, closed the menu. "And the cottage fries crisp, the same with the onion rings."

Haggerty nodded. "And bring me a brew."

"What kind, Mr. Haggerty?"

Haggerty shrugged. "Any of 'em, just so it's icy cold." He took the menu from Eric, handed it to Tony. "Hey, let's start with some pasta as an opener; how 'bout the shells?"

"Perfect," Eric said. Then he shut one eye. "Now, my only problem is, since I can't have the same kind of beer with the pasta as with the steak, what do I want with what—?"

"—Tony," Haggerty interrupted. "Would you give us just a minute alone. I'll signal for you, all right?"

Tony bowed, was gone.

Haggerty looked seriously at Eric now. He took a deep breath. "Look, I know you're in a foul mood so this probably isn't the time, and I know I'm supposed to cheer you up and all, and this certainly won't do that—but I've got to say it: Eric, you're getting to be the bore of the world with this beer fetish. You do it every meal we have together and it's not a good habit." He made his voice into a falsetto. "Oh dear, shall I have pale ale with the cottage fries and stout with the onion rings, whatever shall I do?"

Stung, Eric controlled his voice. "Each beer has its own character, Frank—in a very definite way, beer is like wine—and you want to make the most appropriate selection to augment the flavors of your food. And you call it a 'fetish' again, I'll kick your ass."

"I don't want to make too much of this, Eric my boy, but *I know* each beer has its own character, its own special taste. *Everybody* knows that. And anyone with half a brain can tell one from the other. It's the fucking *anguish* you go through that drives me crazy."

"In point of fact, Frank old fart, in a blind tasting they are *very* hard to tell apart—even an expert can be fooled."

"An expert such as yourself, I suppose. Well, I'm not going to get into a beer tasting contest with you, you'd probably throw in some Icelandic lager that's illegal in America and carry the day. I just know I can tell beers apart, hell, I'm Irish, I've been drinking it long enough."

"You think you can tell beers apart?"

"I absolutely can. Not all of them, obviously, but for example, I can tell a local New York beer from a national brand, and I can tell an American from a European. And Japanese beers never gave me any trouble."

"How many drinks did you have earlier?"

Haggerty scowled, took out twenty bucks, slapped it on the table. "Pick four beers—five bucks for me for the ones I get right, if I miss any, each miss is five for you." When Eric covered, they signaled for Tony the waiter.

Five minutes later, Haggerty was staring at four full glasses of beer. "Lemme see I got this right," Tony said. "One of these is a Kirin, one's a Bud, an' there's a Schaefer an' a Löwenbräu." He turned to Eric. "I wrote down which one is which like you said."

"Thank you, Tony," Eric told him.

"Don't mention it; you get all kinds in here." He backed away, went about his business.

Haggerty stared dumbly at the four tall glasses with the bubbles rising inside. "What have I got here again?"

"Kirin, Schaefer, Löwenbräu, and Bud."

"Well, the Bud's a cinch, my old man was big on Bud, I could tell that eyes closed."

"*Don't* close your eyes; listen to me now, I'm trying to be helpful. The color's important. So's the bouquet, so be sure you sniff all four before you taste any. And once you actually do taste, try small sips of each, comparing the nuances and . . ."

Haggerty grabbed the glass on the left, chug-a-lugged half of it, set it down, belched, and said, "Definitely Bud."

Eric just shook his head. "You haven't tasted the others yet."

"Don't need to—that one's the Budweiser, you want to double the bet, I'll double the bet." He slapped another twenty on the table.

Eric matched him, then signaled for Tony. He pointed to the half-empty glass at Haggerty's left. "Which is that?" Eric asked.

Tony consulted a piece of paper. "That's the Budweiser," he

said, then he said "coming," as a customer down the line raised a hand.

"That really pisses me," Eric said.

"Got a very distinctive bouquet, the Budweiser does," Haggerty told him. "Not to mention outstanding nuances."

"I can still win the next three," Eric said.

"Wrong. The best you can do is break even—I'm a whiz when it comes to Japanese beers."

"On account of your old man was Japanese, I suppose."

"You're a really bad loser, aren't you?"

"Not at all, I just hate it when ignorance comes out on top."

"We had a very nice Japanese couple lived down the block and Helen got on very well with this Mrs. Mifune and I got on good with him—we tossed down a lot of suds between us, and it was him explained about oriental beer."

"Explained *what,* for Chrissakes?" Eric said.

"Explained how they put a *sake*-like quality in their brew— *sake*'s very big in Japan."

"I know about *sake*—it's a rice wine, but it's got not a goddam thing to do with beer!"

"Well it wouldn't to you, being an outsider and all—"

"—I don't be*lieve* this," Eric said.

Haggerty tasted the beer on the right of the four. "No *sake* quality there," he said. Then the third from the right. "Same." He pointed to the second beer. "That's gotta be it, that's the Kirin."

"Aren't you even gonna taste it?"

"Don't get so upset, if you want me to taste it, I'll taste it." He did. Then nodded. "Very *sake*-like; definitely Kirin." He handed the glass to Eric—"Drink some of that and you'll get what I mean about the *sake* quality."

"I don't want any goddam Kirin, thank you, and I read every book on beer in print and not one of 'em mentioned something called '*sake* quality.'"

"Were they Japanese books?"

"Of course they weren't Japanese books."

"Well then."

"Tony," Eric signaled, and when the waiter was beside the table Eric said, "Is the glass he's holding the Kirin, I don't think it is."

Tony looked at the beers, then consulted his piece of paper. "I'm sorry, Mr. Lorber," he said, then he held the paper out for Eric to see. "Check me if you want."

Eric shook his head. "Not necessary, thanks." He sat back in silence. "I'll tell you what infuriates me," he said finally. "It's not the money. And it's not that I dislike you personally—you've saved my life any number of times, I tend to take that kind of thing into consideration when I judge a person's character. And it's also not that what you're doing is incredibly hard—these are not good tasting conditions, too much noise makes it hard to concentrate, too much smoke doesn't help either. No. What really ultimately ticks me off is the knowledge that no matter how long we live, *you'll never let me forget this.*"

"I'd like to tell you I wouldn't ever bring it up again, but I haven't got that much character."

Eric put his head in his hands and stared at the last two glasses. "Taste them and tell me, which is the Schaeffer and which is the Löwenbräu?"

"I already did taste them." Haggerty touched the glass on the right. "The Schaefer," he said.

"You sound so positive, you can't be so positive, how can you be so positive?"

"Just lucky," Haggerty said. "Let's say I eeeny-meenied and that's how it came out."

"Did you?"

Haggerty shook his head.

"Tony," Eric said to the waiter who was balancing a plate with a four-pound lobster in one hand, a platter of lamb chops in the other. "Is the one on the right the Schaefer?"

Tony nodded. Eric sagged.

Haggerty pocketed the money. "The lack of saline is the give-away," he told Eric.

"The what of what?"

"Water around here, it's got a much lower saline content than water from Europe. Once you remember that, you won't have any trouble telling them apart."

"Saline content," Eric said. "I'll put that in my Rolodex next to *sake* quality."

Haggerty started to laugh. He could not stop. When he was a kid he used to get the giggles when he went out of control and sometimes ended up peeing in his short pants. He hoped that would not happen now.

"What's so goddam funny?" Eric asked finally.

Haggerty barely got it out: "I snookered you."

Eric looked at him.

"When I booked . . ." Haggerty was trying desperately to get hold of himself . . . "When I booked tonight, I asked for Tony . . . and told him . . . I mean, you're so easy to bait when it comes to beer . . . I just told him that if he got any nutty requests tonight, just to put the beer down in alpha . . . alphabetical order . . ."

"You old fart," Eric said.

"I am, I am."

Now Eric began to lose control. "And I *swallowed* it—who was your Japanese friend?—Mifune—same as the actor?—"

Haggerty nodded. "I went blank on any other Japanese names except for Hirohito and I figured even you wouldn't buy that."

"Mifune," Eric said, roaring now. "Mifune and his saline content—"

"—Mifune was the *sake* quality—"

"—shit—" Eric said, and he sat back and laughed until there were tears. Then they had the shells, and a lot more beer, and the sirloin, perfectly rare, and more beer with that, and the cottage fries and the onion rings were so good they split an extra order, and Eric could not remember food ever having tasted a whole lot better than this, and during coffee he reached over, touched Haggerty on the shoulder saying, "You cheered me, Frank, you cheered me good, I'm on a hot streak now."

A few minutes later he wondered how he could ever be so wrong.

It was after ten and they were walking down Eighth Avenue when Eric stopped dead on the sidewalk. They were heading for *The Best Little Whorehouse in Texas* because Eric had never seen it and Haggerty felt "Hard Candy Christmas" to be the most underrated Broadway song of the decade when Eric froze. Haggerty shut up and stopped too, a half step later, and he followed Eric's stare.

Up ahead, limping around, was the remnants of a Puerto Rican junkie. He was handing out pamphlets for a local massage parlor, moving painfully up to people, trying to push his wares into their hands. Most people avoided him; it wasn't hard, the guy could hardly move.

"What the hell is it?" Haggerty said but then he shut up because he had been with Eric in a lot of strange places, but the look on Eric's face was different now, different from anything Haggerty had seen before, angry but somehow sad.

The junkie kept limping around.

Eric could not take his eyes off him.

Haggerty did what all great cops are good at: he waited.

"Hey!" Eric said then, moving quickly toward the junkie, who instinctively backed up toward the protection of a building.

"It's a clean place," the Puerto Rican said. "I ain't breakin' nothin'."

"Look at me," Eric said.

"I'm lookin', I'm lookin'."

Eric took a while, gave him a good chance. "Well?"

"Lemme alone man, I gotta get rid of these." He held up his massage parlor literature.

"I told you look at me!"

The Puerto Rican stared. Finally he said, "I know you're a cop, you act like a cop, but I ain't done nothin' so how's about a break?"

Eric took a step backward. "You mean . . . you don't remember me?" Haggerty was just behind him now. Eric turned. "He doesn't remember me."

"I ain't done a damn thing—you ask anyone on the street—now lemme just go about my business, all right?"

"You tried to kill me," Eric told him.

Now he looked at Eric a long time. "It's possible, maybe, but I don't think so."

"I'd know your face from the grave," Eric said. He looked at Haggerty again. "It was our first night, Frank." Now back at the junkie. "You and your partner, you robbed a newsguy, late one Saturday night, Harlem, across from Earl's—you robbed him and you stole some magazines and I trailed you, like an idiot, and tried to play hero and make you return the stuff—you tried to kick me to death, you don't remember any of this?"

The Puerto Rican shook his head. "How long ago?"

"Fifteen years, maybe."

"Then you can't run me in—too long—statute of limitations."

"Where's your partner?"

A shrug. "I don't remember, man; everyone I know from those days is dead mostly."

"Dead?" Eric said, and he looked sadder than ever. "Aw shit."

"Am I free or not?"

"How can you not remember a kid you tried to kill?—it's one

of the most important times of my life, and all on account of you,
how can you forget it?"

Another shrug. "I don't know. I been busy."

Haggerty moved close behind Eric now, whispered. "You want
to run him in? Not hard coming up with something."

Eric shook his head. Then he gestured for the Puerto Rican to
go. Eric stood watching as he limped painfully away. "I really
needed that."

"What's with you?"

"Nothing," Eric said. "Not a god damned thing." He slammed
a fist into the side of the building. "But see, I've been looking for
his face all these years. I don't think a week's gone by I haven't
played it out. I'm on duty somewhere and these two guys are doing
something shitty, maybe stomping an old lady."

"And you capture them and turn 'em in."

"No, no, no, Jesus—what I do is I capture them but I *don't* turn
them in. Instead I take them into an alley and I say 'look at my
face' and they're scared shitless—they remember, and I'm armed
and they think I'm going shoot them—but I don't. Very slow, I
take off my gun belt. And toss it away. Did you see the movie
From Here to Eternity?"

"Maybe."

"Well there's this great gesture—Burt Lancaster's about to fight
Ernest Borgnine and he gestures with his left hand for Borgnine
to come for him. I used the same gesture in the alley to the two
guys. And what I didn't know is that they both had been studying karate and were in great shape. But they didn't stand a
chance. I tore them apart. Didn't make a wasted move. I was
a machine. Then when they were both whipped and crying, I
turned them in."

"You're lucky they didn't kick the shit out of you all over
again."

"It's my fantasy, Frank—they didn't stand a chance." And now
he whirled on Haggerty. "And god damn it, don't you mock me."

"It's not that big a deal, Eric."

"It *is*. It is to me." He looked out at Eighth Avenue then. It
was cold but there was action, hookers and cops and theatregoers
and across the street now, the crippled junkie was back at work,
passing out his papers. "It's as if you were in love with a girl when
you were in your teens—nothing's ever as intense as when you're

in love then—and she's beautiful but she pisses on you, and you know, every day of your life you realize there's a tiny part of your mind where she's on hold. Or maybe she didn't piss on you, maybe she was wonderful but she had to move away. I don't care, the point is, there's an unfulfilled pulse inside you. And if you find out she's dead or four hundred pounds, that's not good news, Frank. Like with these two guys—it doesn't matter that one of them's probably dead and the other a burnt-out case—I wanted my second time with them—I wanted to go back into that alley. Son of a goddam bitch, another dream down the tubes." And he stood there, scowling and angry that only a few minutes before, he had *known* he was on a roll, a hot streak, the dice dancing for him, and then this had to happen, and Haggerty was about to say, "Well, we missed 'Hard Candy Christmas,' what'll we do now?" and he got the first part of it said, "Well, we missed," but that was it, because right then Eric realized he'd *been* right, he *was* on a roll, but just sometimes he was dumb and things took awhile to register, and he whirled around Haggerty, shouting for a cab and traffic was heavy coming up Eighth and there was a cab on the far side but nothing like that was going to stop Eric, not now, as he raced into the after-theatre rush, Haggerty hotfooting it as best he could behind him . . .

"My name is Eric Lorber, I'm with the 19th Precinct, and this is Detective Haggerty. We phoned from across the street."

The woman looked out at them from behind the chained door. "I'm a widow," she said. "I'm in mourning. Come back tomorrow. I changed my mind, I don't want to talk now."

"It's about your husband's murder that we're here, Mrs. Herodotos. We won't be more than a few minutes."

"You got a good face," she said to Eric, releasing the chain. "But I don't like detectives. I already talked to detectives. They done shit so far. Nick is dead, the store was robbed, and I don't see no action."

"I understand your feelings," Haggerty told her. "I truly do."

She opened the door. "I don't want to be upset no more. I been through plenty these last couple days. You don't know what it's like, I'm young, but I got no more husband, I'm alone, all I do is mourn."

Eric looked at her. If this was how she appeared in the middle of the night in mourning, she must have been a traffic-stopper on an ordinary day. She was full figured, and even with her robe pulled around her, she threw off sexuality. Her Greek face was probably too long for any claim at genuine beauty. But in any imperfect world, who cared. Now she stood in the doorway, back to the door, chest out, gesturing for them to enter. They brushed by her, both making contact, you had to make contact, there wasn't enough room not to. Her body was soft, but there was muscle tone present.

The apartment was in one of the many new buildings that dotted the Murray Hill area. Six floors down, there was the occasional screech of brakes from Third Avenue. But otherwise, the place was quiet. Mrs. Herodotos sat on the living room sofa, they flanked her in chairs. "Let's start with why this couldn't wait till tomorrow," she said, looking at Eric.

"I ran into an old acquaintance of mine tonight," Eric told her. "Haven't seen the guy in maybe fifteen years and he'd changed, changed a lot. I guess that set me to thinking."

"I think a lot too these days," Mrs. Herodotos said. "I think a lot about my future. You don't think about the future so much when your husband's around as you do when he's gone."

Haggerty sympathized.

"People do change," she said. "So does your life. I'm a young woman, I'm married, he don't drink, he's got a good store, no complaints. Then zap. Mind if I smoke?" They said they didn't. She lit up a Camel. "Now I got plenty of complaints believe me. My Nick, he never smoked, he was always after me to quit. 'You're killing yourself with those Camels,' he used to say." She inhaled deeply. "It's goddam Byronic is what it is." She stared at the ceiling. "I got plenty complaints now, I'm here to tell you . . ."

She went on talking, listing her grievances, but Eric was still back with things being "goddam Byronic." It was such a whopper he was seriously tempted to correct her, except she looked the type that would take it badly so he shut up, let her ramble until he could get around to the subject of her husband's clothes.

"It is ironic," Haggerty put in.

She looked at him sharply. "Like I already said."

"I think perhaps you might have said 'Byronic,' " Haggerty explained, giving her a gentle smile.

"What the fuck is this!" Mrs. Herodotos exploded—"I get bothered in the middle of the night for English lessons?—"

"—I didn't mean—" Haggerty tried.

"—A widow, a widow young and trying to help out, my Nick is dead, I'm alone and you gotta interrupt my mourning with insults!—"

Now a shattering of glass from out of sight in the kitchen. Followed by a muttered "shit." Mrs. Herodotos jumped to her feet, hurried toward the sound. Fierce whispering now: "I told you to stay quiet"—"I got thirsty"—"you're drunk enough now, you can't even hold a bottle"—"it was slippery, you musta had cold cream when you made the last drinks"—"you put cold cream on your face, not your hands"—"—yeah, but you put it *on* your face *with* your hands—"

Then the sound of the whispering dropped so that no words were clear. Then silence. Then Mrs. Herodotos appeared in the hallway, a large, dark-skinned man behind her. He was wearing pajamas. "This is my cousin Constantine," she said. "He's staying here in the second bedroom. He and my Nick were very close and maybe some would say 'appearances, appearances,' but this is the twentieth century and it's good to have a good friend in the second bedroom at a time like this."

"To help you with your mourning," Eric said.

"You got it," Constantine said, waving again, backing out of sight.

"Especially a big man," Eric said to her as she took her position again on the sofa. "So you don't feel afraid."

"I've always favored big men," Mrs. Herodotos said.

"Your husband wasn't that big though, was he?"

She took another cigarette. "Big Nick—his father—he was a moose—I think one of the reasons he opened Hero's was to get decent clothes for himself. My Nick, he was a good-sized man, but not what you might call big."

"Here's what's been bothering me," Eric said. "Your husband was robbed, the store was robbed of cash, but your husband's clothes were also taken. What struck me odd was why rob clothes from a person, why go to that trouble, when there are thousands of dollars of clothes just there, easy to grab off the racks? So the reason I'm here, I suppose, is to ask you this: Was there anything special about your husband's clothes?"

"My Nick was very picky about how he looked—he was in the

clothing business, after all—all his stuff was special. Perfect fit. To a tee."

Eric sighed. "Can we be a little more specific? His jacket, his shirt—what was so special about them?"

"They just fit good is all I meant."

"And his pants just 'fit good' too, right? Not tailor-made or like that?"

"He had his pants fit tight. I've always favored pants that fit that way."

"And his shoes?"

"Boots."

"His boots, then."

"Funny about them. Remember me saying my Nick wasn't big? It bothered him. He worked in a store for big people and he said that's why he did it, but I know the reason he did it was to please me, to turn me on good."

"Did what?"

"Designed those boots. Had them made. Hundreds they cost, but worth it. He was four inches taller with those boots on—"

"—the blond!" Eric said, and now he was out of his chair, looking at Haggerty. "The son of a bitching blond."

Haggerty had seen Eric excited before, but never more than this, and in a few minutes they had said good-bye to Mrs. Herodotos, thanked her, wished her well with her mourning, and then they were headed toward the Bloomingdale's area, Eric explaining how Billy Boy had made himself bigger so no one would notice him, and then while Eric talked Haggerty began to remember the giant who spoke to them as they had walked out of Hero's where the dead Nick had fallen, neck broken, naked.

It wasn't only that he knew what the other guy looked like now, Eric was just as sure where he'd hit next—the same area he'd been lucky in so far, and Haggerty said maybe but you're guessing and Eric said bullshit I'm guessing, I'm on a hot streak, and remember he came right back to Hero's after he'd pulled the job and the Oliver woman had gotten it less than two blocks away.

So what we've got to do, Eric decided—it was after two by now and very cold but Eric insisted on walking around the Upper East Side because it helped him figure things, and what he was trying to figure was how best to blanket the East Side, how many men it would take, and how long, logically, before Billy Boy came into view. It was a big area, Haggerty said, and of course it was, but what it depended on, Eric said, was if he could sell Captain Haig on his notion, and why did he have to pick this day to imply the man was a *putz?* Because if the Captain would free up only a few men, it would take a long time, and a long time meant that Billy Boy would be broke and somebody else would have a neck that angled off strangely. A week at the outside should do it, Eric felt, and Haggerty felt that was possible but optimistic, but Eric said no, he was blazing, and if Haig would really help, they should be able to nail Winslow inside of five days. Maybe three if God was on their side. Eric kept walking, kept narrowing the amount of time down, and yes, he was lucky, sure he was probably running a hot streak, but not even in his wildest imaginings did Eric expect to see Billy Boy less than a city block in front of him, leaving a porno house on First Avenue, walking slowly away . . .

. . . Billy Boy left the porno house feeling cheated. He'd gotten kind of a crush on Marilyn Chambers years ago, when he saw her in *Behind the Green Door,* probably the last time he was legal on the outside. She'd been the Ivory Snow Girl or the Ivory Snow Baby or something, so there wasn't any doubt she had a great face, a face you wanted to touch easy, not one you wanted to hurt. And yesterday, he'd seen *Insatiable* and if she was a great actress when she'd been a kid, now she was better than anything Hollywood had. Maybe Monroe might have been able to do what Chambers could do lying on a pool table, but all the others out there, they stunk. He was so horny after *Insatiable* he went right out and bought a broad and then went back and caught the flick again.

If Marilyn Chambers had one drawback it was she didn't act a lot. Not many pictures. Three. The first one and this one and one in the middle with "Eve" in the title. He couldn't remember any more than that, just the "Eve." He asked the Duchess about it but she wasn't into movies, porno or Hollywood, being blind, but he saw in the paper an ad for a movie over on First that had the word "Eve" in the title. It didn't say any stars, just *The Return of Eve* and the address, so he told the Duchess where he was going and she wished him luck.

But it hadn't been Marilyn Chambers at all. It was a bunch of skinny girls and dumb-looking guys running around in woods that were supposed to be the Garden of Eden. Billy Boy hated how stupid the plot was. And he hated that he couldn't spot his Marilyn. But most of all what he hated was the drunks. There were drunks slopping all over their seats, mumbling and singing and saying "take it all, baby" and Billy Boy said "shut up" out loud a couple times but that didn't work and the last time someone answered "make me" and he thought about going up to the guy and clubbing him except that would draw attention and he didn't want to do that, not now, because he was running low on bread and as soon as the flick was over he figured on going over to the area he'd been lucky in so far and waiting until someone rich came along and then he'd be loaded again. But if he caused trouble in the theatre, that wasn't good; when you were gonna go to work, it was the last thing you wanted.

"Woooo-eeeee" a black guy shouted from the rear and up front another black guy shouted "Maaaah-muhhh." And then they both laughed. At what? Some people were really assholes, Billy Boy thought, trying to get with the stupid story. And now off to the left another plastered guy began to sing: "I did it all, I did the whole fuckin' thing myyyyyyyy waaaaaaaay."

What kind of people do they let in here? Billy Boy wondered. He got up from his seat and moved to the back of the place, looking for an usher but there wasn't one. So he went to the box office door where there was a little slit you could talk through and he said to the fat lady inside when was the Marilyn Chambers part.

"The what, the what?"

Billy Boy repeated his question.

"Ya think we're the Music Hall? We don't sell popcorn either." Then she turned away from him and went back to whatever it was she'd been doing.

Billy Boy could feel his hand just itching to turn into a fist, but no, that would be drawing attention, so he left the lady, stood at the back of the house a few minutes longer, then decided he'd been had, this was the wrong "Eve" and, feeling cheated, he walked out into the night, turned left, started uptown.

Across the way he saw an old couple. He slowed for a better glimpse, then decided against them, they didn't look like they were loaded. Old and poor, who needed them?

Another couple drew his attention now, younger, up ahead, a guy with his arm around the girl. The guy looked flush, his coat new with a fur collar, so maybe he'd take the guy and then rape the girl, not a bad combo, especially if she was pretty or had tits.

Just then she turned to look at the guy, and not only wasn't she pretty, she wasn't young, she could have been his mother, for Chrissakes, and who wanted to rape something like that, a bag.

You're lookin' for the easy way, Billy Boy told himself—just 'cause it was cold and late didn't mean you had to knock off the first ones you see. People were like trains, if you missed one, there was always another coming along. And the dumbest thing to do, the worst thing, the *unluckiest* thing was to rush it, to hurry. No hurry, Billy Boy told himself. No hurry, take it slow.

Then he *sensed* something.

Behind him.

Up ahead in the next block was a new building being built, a fence still around it, but before you reached it there was a shop, a shop with mirrors and old shit in the window and when Billy Boy got there, without moving his head, keeping his head dead front, he could see for a moment before him.

Two of them.

Closing.

He began to move a little faster . . .

. . . Eric said "He spotted us," cutting off Haggerty, who had started to say "I haven't got my gun have you got yours?" but once the interruption happened, Haggerty changed his tack.

"I don't think he has."

"Frank, goddamit listen to me, I read this guy, and I'm telling you he saw us in that antique shop window. And yes I've got mine."

"That's one massive son of a bitch," Haggerty said.

Eric nodded.

"You remember when we brought in that football guy? He was another monster."

Eric stared ahead at the giant blond, maybe a half block ahead now.

"We were great that night," Haggerty went on.

"Forget about the football player, all right?"

"We were some team when we brought him in, I'm here to tell you—he broke my nose and damn near separated your shoulder but we nailed the bastard. Too bad he turned out to be the wrong guy."

"This isn't the wrong guy, goddamit."

"Well if he's who you say he is and he spotted us where you say he spotted us, why is he just walking along?"

"He thinks slow, he doesn't know what to do, he's making up his mind, I'm telling you that's him and I'm right—I'm on a hot streak, never forget that."

"You better be," Haggerty said, and probably he would have said more, a lot more, because God knew Eric was bright, nobody brighter, nobody around with an arrest record to match him, but sometimes he went off on these wild-ass hunches, and sometimes the hunches paid off but other times you busted your nose on the wrong guy's fist, so Haggerty had a lot to get off his chest, except once the blond guy broke into a run none of it seemed to matter . . .

. . . No way he could outrun 'em—he hated to run from people why should he ever have to run from people, people should have to run from him but even when he was a kid he wasn't the running kind, too much of him, he was the power kind, the kind that when he got his hands on you you wished you were someplace else and—

—behind him now they were coming, they were coming, the one ahead of the other and closing—

—and closing—

—the fence—the Cyclone fence around the new building, the fence had a gate and the gate had a lock but shit, flimsy, nothing, nothing to stop him so Billy Boy shouldered his body against it and the fence sagged and the second time the gate was wide enough for him to slip through and inside and run toward the unfinished building, pretty finished, walls and everything done, but no people a long way from people, and now he ripped at the front door and it came open and inside was a sleepy old guy in a blue uniform dozing by two elevators and he said, "You, you can't come in here," which just proved what a creep he was since Billy Boy was *already in* there and now the old guy was getting up out of his chair, but he was slow—

—and now Billy Boy was making a fist of his hand and a club of his arm and the arm went high and started down just as the old

guy stood to meet it and he took it flush and silent and then he
was on the floor, blood from his mouth, and Billy Boy slammed
his fists against the buttons and an elevator door slid open, it was
creaking and flimsy but it was open and he jumped inside and
looked back and they were coming, the two were coming through
the gate now heading toward the building as he mashed his fingers
against the top-floor button and the flimsy door slid slowly shut
but he'd gotten a good enough look to know these were gonna be
tough, these two, these were gonna give him more than a little
trouble, he wasn't gonna just be able to power his way past them,
no, he was gonna have to brain his way past them, well, screw
them, he could do that, he could brain his way past anybody when
he wanted to, and he would, because he was lucky and when he
was lucky he sensed what he needed, and as the elevator slowly
rose he knew one thing sure, there was no way these two were
going to take him, no fucking way in the world . . .

. . . "Leave him!" Eric said as Haggerty knelt briefly by the
unconscious watchman and Haggerty nodded, stood as the second
elevator door slid open, and then they were inside, Eric pushing
fifteen, the top floor.

Haggerty scowled.

Eric checked his pistol as the machine slowly moved upward.
"What's that look mean?"

"We're on a snipe hunt and you know it—we should have called
for reinforcements and waited down below—how the hell can we
guess where he's going?—he probably pushed the fifth floor and
when he got there went back down to the street."

"You finished?" Eric asked. "I sure hope you are because I'm
sick of telling you, *I read this guy.* And he's headed for the top
and then the roof—"

Fifth floor.

Sixth.

"Shit," Haggerty said. "I hate these new buildings."

Eric just waited.

Haggerty pushed his big hands against the walls. "Feel this—
it's nothing—these new buildings, they put them up with card-
board."

Eric concentrated on his gun.

"I wouldn't live in one of these traps—somebody buys a couple brownstones, tears them down, puts up a fifteen story beaut like this—all the goddam builders, *they're* the ones we should be after."

Haggerty rambled on like that and Eric knew what it was about —Frank was a great cop, he's been there, seen it all, but he didn't have a weapon now and that was getting to him. Eric knew that if he gave him his weapon, Haggerty would realize he'd been seen through and get pissed.

Nine.

Now ten.

Risking it, Eric said, "I don't like using guns in the dark, I'm not that good, you're better, take this." He held it out.

Haggerty just froze him with a look.

Twelve.

Thirteen.

"He'll be on the roof by now," Eric said. "If there's another building he can get to, he'll be trying to get to it, if not, he'll be there waiting so be careful—"

"—*you* be careful," Haggerty snapped, still pissed about the gun offer.

Haggerty moved up next to the door.

Fourteen.

Eric took a deep breath, tried to relax, but he could feel the tension of his right hand around his gun and tension never did anybody any good at times like this, except the other guy.

Fifteen.

And before the door was halfway open screaming came Billy Boy charging into the elevator, his fists huge and the first swing spun Haggerty into the wall and the second swing caught Eric on the neck and staggered him and Billy Boy seemed to fill the flimsy area, screaming louder and kicking Haggerty and swiping again at Eric who couldn't get his gun up, couldn't move, couldn't do shit but slam back into the wall and his balance began to go as Billy Boy screamed "cocksuckers, rotten cocksuckers" and he swung his fists and kicked and screamed and Eric thought crazily of *Jaws* when the shark suddenly turns and attacks the boat, and this was like that now, something prehistoric was attacking, something prehistoric and it couldn't think but it knew how to protect itself, it had survived on that instinct and—

—and then the elevator door began slowly to close—

—and Billy Boy was gone—

—and they started down.

Before Eric could ask it Haggerty answered: "I'm okay." His face was cut along the jaw line and the blood flowed, but he'd lost blood before. His body hurt as he made it to his feet.

Eric was getting up too when he saw it. "Look." He pointed. The twelfth-floor button was lit.

"You think he did that?" Haggerty said. "Why the hell would he?" He stared at the lit number. "Must have been like that from the beginning. These goddam flimsy buildings, nothing works."

"It wasn't lit when we went up," Eric said.

"It might have been, you don't know for sure," Haggerty answered, louder.

Louder still Eric told him, "If it had been lit we would have stopped and we didn't stop!"

"I don't want to fight about the twelfth floor, let's drop it, Eric."

The elevator passed thirteen now, moving down.

Eric got his gun ready, stood back from the sliding door, waiting.

"Blast the shit out of him if he's there," Haggerty said.

Now the sliding door was beginning to open.

Slowly. Slowly.

Nothing.

Eric waited a beat, then stepped quickly out into the hallway, pistol in quickshot position. He gestured for Haggerty to follow. The hall was empty and, except for two red Exit signs, dark.

Then came the pounding.

Thunderous rhythmic sounds echoing down. Again. Again. "What's he doing up there for Chrissakes?"

Eric listened as the pounding went on, reverberating down the naked concrete stairwell. "We better find out." He pointed back toward the elevator.

Haggerty shook his head. "I'm not getting back in there."

Together they started toward the Exit sign and the dark stairs. Eric led the way up, up to thirteen with only the pounding for company. For whatever reasons, the sound was frightening, partly because of the distortion of the echo, partially because of their ignorance of what it was. Except that they knew who was causing it, and that was frightening too.

But when the sound stopped, it was worse.

"Shit," Haggerty said.

They were almost to fourteen when it happened.

Then there came a crash, louder than any earlier sound.

"Shit," Haggerty said again.

They waited a moment before Eric led them up again; he had only just started when the thought crossed his mind that perhaps he wasn't the only one around on a hot streak . . .

. . . Billy Boy was in action before the elevator door was fully closed. First thing, the very first thing he did was run to the door that led to the roof and throw it open.

It didn't want to stay.

He was no more than a few steps away from it when it started closing on him. He cursed, went back, opened it fully again, rooted around on the roof, found a brick, pushed it against the door so that it wouldn't shut again.

Then he came back to the hall. No lights but the red Exit signs, one by the stairs up, one by the entrance to the roof. He needed them for now, as he moved to the elevator door. He backed off it as far as he could, then broke into a bull run, slammed his shoulder against it. It made a big sound as the door shook but screw that, that didn't matter—what mattered was that even with that first try, he knew he could beat it.

He backed off again, again threw his body at the door. It didn't give exactly, but it wasn't even as steady as the first time. Again he drove at it and again there was the sound booming out and by the fifth or sixth try, he could begin to sense victory. He backed away, panting heavily now, sweating but he never minded sweat when he was getting somewhere.

And he was getting somewhere now.

He exploded across the hall and the elevator door gave more than before. He backed off and roared into it and now it was close to surrender. Twice more he ran and after that he got on the ground close to it and brought his huge legs up and kicked and kicked and kicked.

Almost there.

He stood and made both his hands into fists and struck at the door's center and if it were alive he would have broken its kidneys by now, would have torn its guts open by now, would have—

—he could hear footsteps from below.

With all his close to three hundred pounds he shouldered the goddam thing and when he did that, nothing could stand up to him.

The door crumpled back into the shaft. The elevator had long since returned to the first floor and that was where the door headed now. Billy Boy leaned way out, watched it slam into the roof of the elevator, tear it apart.

Then he ran to the first red Exit light, shattered it dark. Then he ran to the second, did the same. The only light left now came from the elevator shaft.

Carefully, Billy Boy approached it. To the left of where the door had been there was a ledge. Not much of one, but enough for him. He was good at streets and he was good at heights, nothing bothered him. He moved into the elevator shaft, got secure on the ledge, out of sight. He was in his parlor now with nothing to do but just wait till a fly came calling . . .

Eric moved with silent grace onto the fifteenth floor, gun ready. No movement, nothing. The place was totally empty and totally dark—except for the light rising from the elevator shaft. It was like a glimpse of some other world, some eerie world, a Bergman film. He said that last to Haggerty, who was beside him now.

Haggerty nodded. "Right. Yeah. *Gaslight.* I get what you mean. I loved her in that but she was great in *Casablanca* too."

Eric decided to leave well enough alone.

Haggerty moved toward the elevator shaft, stopped. "My Helen would have had a stroke over something like this. We had a little terrace and she couldn't even bring herself to peek over the edge. Never bothers me—" He stopped.

"What?"

Haggerty pointed. "Roof door's open. Probably went out there."

They headed for the roof. It was a jumble of debris—bricks and wheelbarrows and paint cans. They moved quickly to the edge. The next building was contiguous and perhaps fifteen feet down. "Possible jump," Haggerty said.

"Then why'd he prop the door open with the brick?"

"Maybe he was afraid the door might close and lock him out here—maybe he was just keeping the avenues open. Then maybe he decided to make the jump."

"Maybe," Eric said. He started back to the door, moving fast.

"But you don't think so."

"I don't think so." He gestured for Haggerty to precede him, then closed the roof door hard.

They moved back inside to the corridor. "What do you think then?"

"Not thing one." He turned the knob of the first apartment door he came to. It was unlocked. Eric pushed it carefully open. "Except I'm not leaving without checking these." He entered; Haggerty watched from the doorway. The apartment was small, so were the closets. Eric, gun ready, threw open the first one, then moved to the next.

"You gonna open every closet door on fifteen?"

"What about it?"

"I think it's dumb is what about it."

"Frank," Eric said with some passion. "*We* are what's dumb. There's a brontosaurus on the loose and we can't find it. We get surprised in an elevator, get the crap knocked out of us, and you stand there and tell me opening closet doors isn't the same as nuclear physics." He stormed out of the apartment and went into the next. It was even smaller.

Haggerty stood by the door again. "It's also boring," he said.

"Boring for you perhaps, but for me—pure scintillation. On my deathbed when my grandchildren ask me what was the high point of my life, I will say without doubt it was opening closet doors in a building on First Avenue with Frank Haggerty being a pain in the ass."

"You've had the rag on all day," Haggerty replied, and he wandered out into the corridor, looking at the light rising from the elevator shaft.

Eric left the second apartment, entered the third, searched it, left it, entered the fourth, searched it, left it, entered the fifth when he heard a shout of surprise but by the time he was back in the corridor all he could see was Billy Boy standing where the elevator door had been, his arm around Haggerty's throat. He held Haggerty dead in front of him like a shield.

"Gimme it," Billy Boy said, pointing to Eric's gun.

Eric took his time before shaking his head.

Billy Boy was screaming then—"Gimme the fucking piece or I throw him down the shaft."

Quietly Eric said, "You do I'll shoot your nuts off."

Suddenly Billy Boy moved, shoving Frank out into space, holding him with both hands out in the shaft. *"I'll kill your fucking partner—"*

"—he's not my partner, he's a washed-up old bum they stuck me with, I don't give a shit what happens to him but you kill him, I kill you—"

"—Jesus," Haggerty said, dangling fifteen floors above the street. "Please bring me in."

"I thought you liked heights," Billy Boy said. "I heard you say that. Heights don't bother you." Then he took one of his giant hands away, held Frank out there with just the other.

Haggerty shut his eyes, muttered "please" again.

"Bothers you now, huh?"

Haggerty managed to nod. "Yes. Yes. It bothers me. I don't wanna die like this."

"The gun," Billy Boy said.

Eric aimed it dead at the giant's testicle area. Nothing showed on his face but inside he knew he was good for maybe half a minute more of acting before he turned the gun over.

"My arm's getting a little tired," Billy Boy said.

Eric did his best to keep his hand steady on his pistol.

"Don't," Haggerty said then. "Don't hand over anything, he'll shoot us both."

After that they all froze for a while, the three of them.

Then Billy Boy made a quick move and Haggerty was his shield again.

And then again, the three of them made a tableau.

Haggerty broke it. "Leave us here, Eric," he said.

Eric didn't dignify the suggestion with words, just a quick shake of his head.

"I *mean* it, Eric," Haggerty said, louder; color was coming back, the fear of falling fifteen floors leaving him now.

"Listen to the man, Eric," Billy Boy said.

"That's right," Haggerty said. "We can't stay like this forever, can we? Okay. So you go to the stairs and you start walking slowly down and you call out every so often so he'll know you're not pulling anything. And he can tie me up and when you're a couple floors away and I'm tied he can take off across the roof to the next building. And if we're lucky this time, maybe we won't be able to find him, Slocum's no one I want to mess with any-more."

Eric had no intention of leaving until he heard Frank say "Slo-cum" because that must have meant he had something, some notion of working things out. Still he hesitated till he caught a look from Frank who was in front of Billy Boy and the look meant "Move, friend."

So Eric moved. He went to the top of the stairs, took a step down, waited, listened, took another, another, waited, and when he was halfway down this flight he said it, "Halfway" and he continued moving slowly, wondering what the hell Frank had working—Frank had a way with the dummies of this world, no denying that. In a bar, if there was some big musclehead who had had a couple too many and was looking to lay somebody out, inside five minutes Frank was the best friend he'd ever had. Eric had seen him do it over the years—it was a gift, probably an Irish one—and it worked when they were interrogating prisoners too. The less than brilliant trusted Frank Haggerty. He was big, he had that Irish puss of his, he didn't talk down to anybody. There were times when Eric wished he had it too, that sense of quick trust that—

"—louder!" Billy Boy said from above.

"At fourteen," Eric yelled back.

"I said louder!"

"Fourteen!" Eric shouted. *"And heading down."*

Should he head down though? Eric waited at the fourteenth landing. He was out of sight, he could try screwing around with his voice, make it seem distant, make the giant above think he was disappearing when actually he was waiting there, ready for what-ever.

Risky, Eric decided. Billy Boy wasn't playing with a full deck and if for some reason he decided to drag Frank to the stairwell and glance down and catch a glimpse of Eric waiting, it might not go well for Frank, might indeed go badly for Frank, so maybe he'd head halfway down to thirteen and call out again when he got there and then just rest, just await developments, which seemed a good enough decision and when Eric was halfway down thirteen he really intended to call his position but then the scream began above him, but not above him long, the falling scream of Frank Haggerty was above him and then even and then below and then came the crash that in Eric's mind shook the building, no, more, shook his world, but in reality of course was nothing more than an old man being split open by the roof of an elevator more than a hundred feet below . . .

. . . "You do I'll shoot your nuts off," the pretty cop said. Billy Boy didn't like that a whole lot. It was the way he said it, all quiet and low. As if he meant it. Maybe he did. I'd like to meet you sometime, Billy Boy thought. Just you and no guns against me and my hands. I'd eat that up with a spoon. That would be wonderful. But the look behind the pretty cop's eyes was not the kind of thing that made you happy.

An' it had been so great up till then. Standing in the shaft, waiting, that was great. Because there was no way one of 'em wouldn't come take a peek down. You had to do that. And when the old one did it was all so fast, so easy, just a quick grab and then out of the shaft onto the floor again with the old guy shitting in his pants probably, a perfect shield.

An' gutting it out with the pretty boy, that'd been good, 'cause there was no way Billy Boy could lose, these guys couldn't take him, that was a fact. There was nothing better than playing a game you knew how it would come out, and it had to come out you the winner.

An' now the pretty boy was gone to the staircase and the old one was saying, "You can use my belt to tie me if you want."

"Don't give me no suggestions. If you're so fucking smart how come you're almost dead?" He took the old guy then, framed him in the opening where the elevator door had been, kept a hand on his chest. One push and gone.

"Please," the old guy said. "Let me move a step away."

Billy Boy let him. But he kept his hands ready. It was still one push and over.

"I knew you wouldn't drop me."

"Oh yeah? Well I wasn't sure myself so how could you know?"

"It doesn't fit your record, Slocum—"

"—that's the second time you done that, called me 'Slocum' and I know what you're up to, you're trying to get me to slip and tell who I really am, but that's not gonna happen."

Haggerty shook his head slowly. "Don't bullshit me, son."

Billy Boy made a fist. "Don't call me a liar, down you go."

"We brought the manager of the A&P down to the station. He definitely identified you as the one who robbed the store."

"*Robbed the store?*"

Haggerty went on as he had been, even and soft. "We've got to bring you in, George. It's your bad luck that when you hit the place Captain Haig's mother was doing her shopping. She got all hysterical and now he's eating our asses off. 'Bring me George Slocum *and no excuses.*'"

"When was this?"

"Two weeks ago now. I don't like having my captain on my tail, George; that's why it's all over for you."

"Wait a minute—you guys hassling me over a goddam store someone hit two weeks ago?—I wasn't even in New York two weeks ago."

Haggerty reached a hand out, gently touched the bigger man's shoulder. "George—you've got all the advantages now—don't complicate matters by lying. If you want to lie to the captain, fine. If you want to lie to your lawyer, I couldn't care less. But it's stupid now, agree?"

"I'll kill that fucking A&P guy."

"No, no you won't—it's not your way—your record proves it —you're strictly a grocery store man—what've you hit, over sixty here and in New Haven and Boston?"

Billy Boy looked at the old Irish face. "You bullshitting me?"

"Oh, that would be really smart," Haggerty answered. "Here I am with a guy ten times my size standing by an open elevator shaft. It would really make sense to lie and get you pissed enough to push me." His voice was softer and more even than before.

"Shit son of a bitch goddammit," Billy Boy said, and he slammed one fist into the other. Then he was quiet for a while before shouting, "Louder."

"At fourteen," came the voice from below.

"*I said louder!*"

"*Fourteen! And heading down.*"

"Don't lose your temper, George—no point—like I said, we've got that positive identification—"

"—but it's not me—"

Haggerty shook his head. "Hard for me to believe that, George —after all, how many guys are there wandering around six foot six and blond?—"

"—I'm not blond," Billy Boy said and ripped off his wig. The old guy looked stunned.

"Lots of guys wear wigs," he said finally.

"An' I'm not six foot six—"

"—you sure look it to me—"

"—these are boots—boots I got special—for height—look at them!"

Haggerty knelt down and touched the boots saying, "Well these *are* different" and then he measured the heels and the built-up soles and said, "I've never seen boots quite like this before," and then he was getting up saying, "Could this have been a mistake, this whole thing us after an innocent man, you mean you're really not George Slocum?—"

And he went on and he was shaking his head and talking in that quiet smooth honest way he had but Billy Boy wasn't listening because nothing the guy said mattered anymore, and maybe the greatest thing Billy Boy had ever seen in a movie was when that guy pushed that old crippled bag down the stairs in her wheelchair only this was even better, this was perfect, a straight fall maybe a hundred, a hundred fifty feet, this was a God given chance and there was nothing he could do but take advantage of it . . .

. . . "Well these *are* different," Haggerty said, touching the leather, and a few minutes earlier he doubted he would have been able to sound as convincing. But Winslow was a believer now, so his voice was fine. "I've never seen boots quite like this before." He started to get up, slowly, keeping the sentences flowing, throwing in the "innocent" now, a weighted word, one you had to use carefully when you were into the high point of your sell. That was all this was, really. A sales job. He had to convince Winslow and he'd done it. Not the best work of his career, but nothing to skulk about either. You had to have an honest face and a sincere tone —Haggerty had developed his working with jumpers—he'd lost the first one years before because he'd rushed it, been too pushy, but now he was older and not as dumb as in days of yore.

"Older" definitely, but not a "washed-up old bum" as Eric had so recently termed him. When this was done he was going to have to retaliate for the insult, even though Eric was doing it in a good cause; i.e. his life. Maybe forget the retaliation, he decided as he was almost all the way up. He had zapped Eric good enough with

the beer tasting so even steven is fair enough, nobody needed more
than that, nobody needed—

—then came the push—

—and even as he was flying backward Haggerty knew it was all
a mistake; he understood human nature and Winslow believed
him, believed the George Slocum story, believed—

—Haggerty tried to grab to the edge of where the door had
been—

—and he was successful.

But not for long.

Not for long enough.

His body began to arch out into the air now, and he caught a
glimpse of the thick cables that supported the elevator, and he
tried to grab tight hold of the cables—

—and he was successful.

But not for long enough again.

His scream began then and it surprised him, he had never
thought he would go into the good night that way. But for all his
years on earth, he seemed to have learned nothing, for he went out
as he entered, screaming, helplessly screaming like a baby . . .

. . . Eric had never entered battle knowing he was going to kill
the enemy, but as he took the stairs three at a time it was clear
that that was the situation now, and it bothered him because when
you were blood crazy your brain could take a powder and he had
been in enough violent confrontations over the years to know the
wilder you were the less chance for survival, and Eric was wild
now, as he streaked to the fifteenth floor corridor then out the door
onto the roof and he was halfway across it by the dark shadows
of the elevator housing when he heard Billy Boy move in the
corner ahead of him and he fired, fired again, was about to make
a third attempt before he realized the sound was not Billy Boy but
something metallic, a paint can maybe, thrown from somewhere
and that somewhere was probably behind him and Eric instinctively went into a roll as Billy Boy charged from the elevator
housing and they closed, and as his arms caught Eric, Eric realized
that *Jesus,* he had never felt such power, and he went limp, then
sprung taut, almost breaking the grip, except Billy Boy would not
let go of Eric's gun so they spun around in the darkness both of
them clinging to the weapon and Billy Boy was much the stronger,

Eric the more quick, and their attention was totally on who would control the pistol, until Eric did a stunning thing.

He simply let go.

Billy Boy stood still for a moment, surprised, holding the gun and that moment was enough for Eric to kick him hard in the wrist and the giant hand opened, the gun fell and Billy Boy went for it but Eric tripped him up and then Eric made a move but Billy Boy shouldered him away and finally Eric kicked again, sending the goddam gun across the roof into total darkness.

Now their only weapons were their bodies.

Eric backed away, taking off his topcoat, tossing it aside, ripping his sportcoat the same way, throwing it blindly behind him, the same with his shirt, and it was cold as hell on his skin but if you were a nightfighter what you didn't want was anything someone could grab hold of, you wanted your body free, and yes, he would probably bleed badly when they went to ground as they would, there were bricks on the ground and nails and broken glass too but it didn't matter, nothing mattered if your body was free, not to a nightfighter, and Eric had spent too many hours learning, to lose now.

That was the theory anyway . . .

. . . As the pistol skittered away from them, Billy Boy felt like it was his birthday and the whole world was bringing him cakes. No one had ever come close to him, except when they had guns and all he had was his fist. Even then sometimes it was even.

But with the gun gone, with just him against the pretty boy, it was strictly no contest. The only thing was, he had to be sure to make it last, to really take the pretty boy's face away nice and slow.

Then the striptease started and Billy Boy wondered what the fuck. Off came the coat and then the next coat and then he ripped his shirt away and was that an Apple stunt, did New York cops get taught to fight in the nude in the winter because if they didn't, why was he doing it?

Then the cop stopped with the clothes act and stood facing him. For a minute nothing. Then the cop spun suddenly all the way around and Billy Boy felt the kick hard on the shoulder. Japanese crap, it meant nothing. He'd whipped the shit out of those guys before.

But he'd have to keep watching for it, keep a sharp eye out for it. And the next time it came he'd be ready. The next time he'd grab the foot and twist it till it came off . . .

. . . Eric had no interest in karate, knew only the one move, the spin kick, which he executed with only a fair amount of speed. But he tried to use it at the beginning if he could. It always surprised, and beyond that, once it was in their minds that that was his form of attack, they always were on the alert, waiting for the next spin. You had to divide their brains. You had to win with your intelligence. Sometimes your power could leave you—an arm could be broken, a leg cracked—but as long as you thought, as long as you were in command in the mind, the battlefield was yours.

That was when Billy Boy said, "I'll have you fucking screaming too before I'm done," and for a minute Eric didn't get it. For a minute they just circled. Then Eric realized the giant was mocking Frank Haggerty's death and his mind abdicated leadership, he lost control.

And he charged.

Blindly.

Billy Boy was waiting with open arms. Then the arms closed and began to squeeze and Eric felt himself being lifted off the ground and then he was slammed against the brick wall of the elevator housing and the blow stunned him, and the hard brick ripped into the skin of his back and blood started there and he struggled to get free but again he was slammed against the elevator housing and this time his head took a solid shot and the next time he thought he could feel a rib going and again he was slammed back and this time his hip took the brunt and his right leg felt numb and he was hurting all over now and he was bleeding too, but that had happened before, and he had fought strong men before, brought them down. But what made this different, what made this bad, was his mind was gone, his brain had taken a walk, his body was in charge and it wasn't good enough, not against giants, not against this giant anyway.

Billy Boy went for a knee in the nuts but caught Eric's thigh instead and for an instant lost his balance and in that instant Eric slipped away, slipped free—

—*free*—

—and then he charged again.

And again it was slaughter. Billy Boy grabbed him easily, took him by one arm, spun him across the roof and down. Eric tried to rise but too slow, Billy Boy kicked him in the stomach and it wasn't a solid blow but for an instant the air was out of him and Billy Boy picked him up again, lifted him high, pitched him across the roof and he landed on some paint cans and they jammed into his skin and now it was leaving Eric. He saw Billy Boy lumbering for him and he tried getting up but the paint cans tripped him and he fell again, fell all by himself.

Then Billy Boy brought him to a standing position with his left hand and slowly, as Eric watched, he turned his right hand into a fist and more slowly turned his arm into a club and slower still raised it high and Eric thought, I think he's going to kill me, but that's wrong, that's all wrong, I was going to kill him.

He was thinking again.

The blow started down as Eric jumped into Billy Boy, jumped right inside the blow and when they were very close he brought his head way over to the left and then snapped it up into Billy Boy's face and even before the cry he knew the giant's nose was broken. Billy Boy stepped back, tearing, and while he was still having trouble seeing, Eric grabbed the sleeve of his coat and jerked it forward and kept hold of it while Billy Boy tried to keep balance and then Eric spun the giant around and around, the coat sleeve his weapon, and when he let go, Billy Boy stumbled and fell and as he got up Eric drove his knuckles deep into Billy Boy's neck.

Then when Billy Boy stood up Eric dropped down and drove his heels into the other man's kneecaps and when Billy Boy was down again Eric got up and used his elbow on the damaged nose and this brought a shriek of pain.

Move, move, move, Eric thought, circling, in with a kick, then an elbow into the stomach, then he grabbed the sleeve of the coat as Billy Boy pulled free but that was fine, Eric didn't want the coat anymore, he wanted the nose again and he got it with the palm of his hand, drove the palm dead into the broken tissue and again Billy Boy could not keep silent.

Billy Boy backed away, started to pull his coat off, but Eric would not allow it, jumped in, then away, then in again, again attacking the nose and Billy Boy screamed, "I'll fuckin' kill you," and charged and Eric dropped, lashed out with both feet into the side of the giant's knees, sending him crashing against the elevator housing.

Billy Boy was panting now. He made a fist of his hand and a club of his arm and swung—

—Eric stepped inside the blow, slashed the side of his hand into the side of the giant's nose.

Billy Boy made a fist of his hand and a club of his arm and swung—

—Eric stepped away, and when the force of the missed punch spun the giant past him, Eric brought his knee dead into contact with the base of the other man's spine.

As Billy Boy began again to make a fist and then a club, Eric watched it because it was all the giant used now, all he had faith in, some mystic belief that somehow he would win with that single weapon. Eric watched in the darkness and Haggerty was dead for no good reason far below and on this roof, in this night, Billy Boy seemed to Eric like everything people had been trying to rid themselves of for centuries, he was some throwback to the muck, when if you were a bigger Tyrannosaurus Rex, that carried with it triumph, and Eric realized he was not going to kill this creature, he was going to do something he hoped much worse. *I am going to terrify you, Eric thought. I'm going to make you feel fear.* I'm going to take your mystic weapon and destroy it.

The club blow missed, and Eric slapped Billy Boy with the back of his hand.

Heaving now, enraged now, the next club blow missed and another slap. A dainty slap, almost a feminine thing.

Billy Boy had his hand into a fist—

—and Eric stood there.

He made his fist into a club.

—and Eric stood there.

Billy Boy raised his right hand high.

—and Eric filled his mind with Haggerty, and what a pleasure. Just that day's Haggerty. Haggerty telling the grieving Greek widow that life wasn't necessarily "Byronic." "Definitely Budweiser." "*Sake* quality." "Saline content." "You're lucky they didn't kick the shit out of you all over again." And Eric replying, "it's my fantasy, Frank, they didn't stand a chance."

And now, in the darkness, in Eric's reality, the club blow landed.

Eric just stood there. He felt nothing. The blow dropped away like water.

Billy Boy took a step backward. Eric watched him, thoughtfully. Billy Boy took another step. Eric spoke, voice very soft. "Now you suffer," he said.

Billy Boy screamed and ran. He raced for the edge of the roof where there was a fifteen-foot drop to the next building, but Eric sliced the legs out from under him from behind and Billy Boy crashed into the wall. He got up and tried to run again and this time Eric caught him with a shoulder and Billy Boy crashed into the elevator housing, his head smashing into the bricks. He was making sounds now as he got up and ran again, this way, that way, panic controlling him and when Eric reached him he brought his elbow into contact with the giant's Adam's apple and Billy Boy went down, got up and ran blindly, bumping into things, slipping, falling, running like a waterbug, without direction.

When Eric caught up with him, he finished things quickly, a chop to the nose, an elbow to the stomach and when the giant doubled over, Eric brought his knee up sharp against his chin and Billy Boy fell semiconscious, and Eric took half a minute, got his gun back, then he dragged the giant from roof to the corridor and when the elevator came he threw Billy Boy in and rode down to the lobby where the guard was lying on the ground, moaning and rolling slowly around, and from the lobby Eric pulled Billy Boy out into the street and as they reached the sidewalk, a man in a blue suit came up alongside Eric and hit him a terrible blow to the side of the head and Eric gasped, let go of the giant, turned to his attacker when a second man in a blue suit struck him from behind at the base of the neck and the first one hit him with a pistol barrel across the forehead and Eric went down with his own blood in his eyes, and it was madness, it was all madness, he was going insane, helplessly watching as the two blue-suited men took the giant and placed him in a limousine and then a man who looked like Henry Kissinger was giving curt instructions, and then they were all in the limousine, driving quickly away and Eric on his knees tried for a look at the license plate but he was almost blind now, blind with blood, yes, and sweat, yes, that too, and saddest of all, tears . . .

PART III

CONFRONTATIONS

1

THE CONTACT

Billy Boy lay naked while the two women massaged him with oils. Maybe not totally naked—there was a small cloth covering him, but sometimes when he moved his body a little one way or another on the bed, it would slide away and then they could catch sight of it. When that happened, they didn't make a fuss, just readjusted the small cloth.

In the beginning he figured they were hookers but now considering the white uniforms and all, they had to be nurses. Strong. They both had great fingers. Now one of them was standing above his head, stretching the muscles in his neck while the other gave his calves a going over.

"What's 'at stuff?" he asked after a while. It was hard for him to talk or think good. He was so relaxed. He could never remember being this relaxed before.

"Patchouli," one of the broads said, the one doing his neck. Light brown hair. Probably a little older than the other one but a better shape. If he had to rape one or the other, the one with the light brown hair would get the call.

"Jeannie," Billy Boy whispered then.

"Pardon?"

"You got that light brown hair like in the song." Someone in his family had sung it once. Way back.

"Shhh," the nurse said gently. "You must rest."

Billy Boy closed his eyes and rested.

All he could feel was their fingers. Good and strong and never stopping. The fingers would find a knot and then they'd go to work, smoothing, stretching, till the knot was gone.

"What'sis place?" Billy Boy asked after a while.

"The doctor will explain everything," the nurse at his calves said. "Soon." Now she was working on his feet, rubbing the tired soles. The smell of that patchouli oil was all around him. He really liked it a lot. Next whore I have, he decided, first she's gonna rub me with patchouli oil.

Now the nurse at his neck moved down to one thigh and the nurse at his feet moved up to the other. Ordinarily he'd be hot to trot when that happened. Ram, jam, thank you ma'am. Only now, it was too much effort. Everything was too much effort. The best thing was to lie there and just go with it. He could take off if he wanted. No question, a bust out was his for the asking. But so far, they'd been nice, so far all he'd had to do was rest and eat good hot food done any way he asked for it and lie still while these two made him sleepy.

—*a helluva lot better than being back on that roof*—

"What's wrong?" the one nurse said suddenly.

"Why are you so tense?"

"Relax."

"Yes. Please. Relax."

"Sometimes you remember bad things," Billy Boy said.

"Just don't think," the light brown hair one told him.

Billy Boy gave that a try. Soon he was conscious of the sound of his own breathing. Smooth and even, smooth and slow and maybe he even went out for a while, but he was immediately aware as soon as somebody else came in the room, not because of any noise or like that—

—but the nurses, their fingers dug too deep all of a sudden, they were the tense ones now.

Billy Boy opened his eyes. The guy looking down was tall, thin, brown hair, coat and tie, the face of a guy always smelling something he didn't like a lot; a shitheel. The shitheel said, "My name is Trude, Mr. Winslow."

"Where am I, what'sis place?"

"In the middle of Manhattan, on the top floors of a building."

"Hospital?"

"Partly that, on occasion a research center."

"What's a research center?"

A shitheel smile. "A place where you look for things, Mr. Winslow." A shitheel pause. "That's really much too formal, 'Mr. Winslow.' How would you like to be called?"

William was what he wanted, only no one ever did that—he loved William. William was class. "Billy Boy'll do."

"I don't much like that either."

"Well, it doesn't matter a helluva lot what you like in the long run, does it?"

"I like 'William.' I think I'll call you that."

Billy Boy looked at him closer now. "How long I been here?"

"Eighteen hours perhaps. I trust everything's pleasing to you."

Billy Boy shrugged again. "You can 'trust' that if it isn't, I'm getting the fuck out."

"I would hope it wouldn't come to that."

"What'sat mean?"

"We wouldn't want to detain you forcibly."

Billy Boy had to laugh at that one. "What—these two bimbos would pin me and you'd tie me up?"

"Let's just hope it doesn't come to that," Trude said again. "I make a bad first impression on people, William, I'm afraid I've done that with you. In time I think we may even come to like each other."

"How much time?"

"Let's just take things as they come, shall we?"

"I'm stayin' because I want to—I go when I wanna go—*you remember that.*"

"Of course."

"I'm boss, *I run me!*"

"Of course. The moment you decide to leave, just tell me . . . and we'll bring you immediately back to the gentleman we took you from, no problem at—"

"—*you keep him away from me—*" Billy Boy was sitting now, the nurses backing away as he began to scream. "—you keep that fucker the hell away you know what's good for you, I don't wanna see that fucker, you got me, *you got me?*"

"William, William," the shitheel said. "How can we have begun so badly; the Duchess told me how sensitive you were, and now look what I've gone and done."

"You know the Duchess?"

"For many glorious years." He came close to the bed now, whispered. "How do you think I knew to call you William? You told her, she told me. How do you think I knew what movie you'd be attending? You told her, she told me. We have no secrets, the

Duchess and I—and you and I must be the same." He reached out now, touched Billy Boy's forehead, gently rubbed the temples. "Please lie back down."

Billy Boy did.

Trude gestured for the nurses to return to their labors. In an instant their fingers were on the giant's body. He closed his eyes. Trude's voice went on softly. "What a wonderful creature you are, William. What a misunderstood man. She told me. She told me. As gifted with your brains as with your body. She told me. And the Duchess never lies."

". . . 'at's ri . . ."

"Soon, William, soon." He moved to the door, gestured for the brown-haired nurse to follow him. He opened the door to the hallway, stepped outside, spoke briefly to her when she was beside him. "Alert me the moment he's ready."

"Of course."

"But since I'm sure we'd all prefer that moment come sooner rather than later, may I suggest you immediately alter your style."

"I've been doing massage for many years, Doctor."

"Of course you have but if you're perfect, then you're the first since Jesus to reach that state, so I'm sure you won't mind some suggestions."

She said nothing, waited.

"End the *tapotement* immediately and concentrate solely on *effleurage*. Clear?" When she nodded he said "Excused" and turned his back on her, walked away. He was well aware that she was angry, that he could have simply said, "End the percussion immediately and concentrate solely on stroking." But it was important that all his underlings realize that not only was he more intelligent and knowledgeable than they, he was all of that on their best subjects.

He had been first in every school he ever attended.

Now he stopped by the two men in blue suits who sat alertly at the end of the hall. They had helped him get Winslow into the limousine some hours earlier, and they were both excellent at their profession. Apple, the larger of the two, stood as Trude approached. Berry, the younger and quicker, stayed seated as he was. Berry was bright, too bright perhaps, and might someday require disciplining.

Well, Trude was good at that, too.

"Half an hour or less I should think," he told them.

"Yessir," Apple said.

Trude noted Berry's silence as he continued on past the elevators—he detested waiting—to the stairs, went down the two flights in silence. When he reached his office he unlocked it, turned on the lights, locked the door behind him, made a fresh pot of coffee, and while he waited, took some caffeine pills. He had been up many hours now and it was essential that when Winslow was ready, he, Leo Trude, had to be that and then some. Success, as always, rested solely in his hands.

His office, book lined, was a source of cheer to Trude; his desk, dust free, the same. The entire room was in perfect order—he had been an anal compulsive for so long that he could still remember his parents actually *worrying* about it. "There ought to be *some* mess," his father said often. "Leo, remember, a sweet disorder in the dress kindles in clothes a wantonness."

But then, his father had been a fool. A double FF—Fool and Failure. An unpublished poet, an unread scholar, a professor of excruciating dullness. His mother had been one of his students, unpretty, driven. When she finally realized she had mounted the wrong horse, Leo was the one who was whipped, whipped to run faster, fastest, to win.

Soon, mother, soon.

He opened his central desk drawer, took out a pen. The drawer on the right contained paper, beneath that was a folder already titled "Winslow." Leo glanced at his coffee, perking away. Then he began to print quickly, the letters so small, so perfectly formed, the lines so straight that at first glance it could have passed for typing. He bunched his thoughts toward the center of the page.

First Meeting
11 Feb 1981
10:06 P.M.

What a repellent creature.
Loathsome. Unredeemed.
But, I suspect, useful.

Richard Wagner repelled.
Treacherous. Unredeemed.
But Tristan lurked inside.

It would certainly be nice—
—nice if our heroes were

heroic.

Not the case

Not the case

Oddity

Winslow has *psychotic* fear.
Fear of the policeman—
The one who had control
Until we took control.

I suspect
that fear
may be
useful.

His coffee was ready by now. Trude got up, poured himself a large mug. He took it black and it was blazing hot but he blew on the edge closest to him and sipped. It burned on the way down, as he preferred it. He could finish a cup of coffee before most people could dare to begin.

He finished this cup, poured himself another, carefully took it back to his desk. He reached into the center drawer again, removed a pad, put the mug carefully down on it. He drank a little more of the liquid, blowing always on the nearest edge, sipping, sipping. Then he wrote a few more words.

Hope

The Breakthrough

Fear

Another Rosa Gonzales.

Odd, they were both from the Duchess. Trude didn't much like her, hated her dog. Yet she had a way about her, a touch for sensitives. And if he disliked her, nothing unusual there—he had yet to meet a man he didn't dislike. Or woman.

Beyond that, the Duchess, poor blind thing, didn't matter, not anymore.

The buzz of the phone. The push of a button. The voice of the brown-haired nurse. "Almost asleep."

Trude took a breath, sipped a sip, gave the word: "Take him to the Infinity Room . . ."

The room itself was square, high ceilinged. The walls had been carefully corked, so no unwanted sound could penetrate. Then over the cork came mirrors. The walls, the ceiling, all but the floor. And hanging down every precise ten inches, was a string of delicate lights.

Sounds, when required, came from all angles, surrounding. Winds, tree leaves in autumn, water sounds, dark and steady, sometimes, when needed, the topmost strings of a harp.

In the center of the room was a reclining couch of unsurpassed softness. Behind it, a stiff, straight-backed wooden chair. Beside the chair, a box of toys.

Billy Boy lay on the couch, eyes barely open. Above him the delicate strings of lights twinkled to infinity. From somewhere he heard the soothing sound of wind. Then the wind died and now came water, lapping gently all around.

He blinked.

Twenty seconds later he blinked again.

Those were his only movements.

"William."

". . . huh . . . ?"

"I'm behind you, William, sitting behind you. Doctor Trude, the friend of the Duchess."

"Din't . . . din't hear you . . . come in."

"We're just here together, just you, just me. Now will you do me a sweet favor, William?"

"Sure."

"Look up at the lights. Look up at the lights, will you do that?"

"Shuh . . . shure."

"Are you staring up at the lights, William?"

". . . um-hmm . . ."

"Now I want you to do something else, another sweet favor."

". . . wuh-what . . . ?"

"I want you to take your eyes, the eyes that are looking straight up at the lights, and I want you to try and see me, you can't, but I want you to try, I want you to lie there and breathe and listen to the wind and lift your eyes up into your head."

"Can't see . . . you."

"No, you're not supposed to see me, but you're supposed to try."

"Tryin'."

"Good. Now one final sweet sweet request."

"Yessir."

"Keep your eyes looking up toward your brain, it's as if your eyes were trying to peek at your brain, your eyes are that high, and now slowly . . . slowly drop your wonderful eyelids over your eyes . . . close your eyelids over your eyes . . . gently and slowly bring your eyelids down over your eyes . . ."

"Closin' 'em. Closin' 'em."

"Good."

"Got 'em closed."

"Yes."

Billy Boy said nothing now.

Trude waited.

Billy Boy began breathing deeply.

Trude still waited.

The breathing, still deep, began to slow.

"William."

"Yes."

"You're very strong."

"Yes."

"I want you to lift up your right arm. I want you to make it stiff and straight. And I want you to hold it there even when I try to pull it down. No one can pull it down."

"Still and straight, yessir."

Trude got up from the chair. The arm was aimed at the mirrored ceiling. He was not a great believer in exercise, but Trude walked a great deal and he weighed always one hundred and sixty-one. He pulled on the arm now. He put both of his hands around the wrist and pulled harder.

The arm was immobile.

"Oh that was wonderful, William. You can put it down now, I'm very proud."

"Thank you."

"Could I have your hand, William?" Trude reached over, grasped the limp arm. From his pocket he took out a penknife with a tiny honed blade. "William, I would never hurt you, I think you know that."

"Yessir."

"You can feel no pain, William. There is no such thing as pain for you. Do you understand?"

"Yes."

Trude took the honed blade and placed it just under the fingernail of Billy Boy's index finger. "Now in a few minutes," he said, "I'm going to touch your arm with a knife, but you will not feel it because even now you can feel no pain." Trude began delicately forcing the knife deeper under the index fingernail. "You must promise me, in a few minutes, to tell me if that knife hurts your arm."

Billy Boy breathed very deeply. "I promise."

Trude continued forcing the knife in.

"Because I wouldn't want to hurt you. If it does hurt you, I would feel dreadful." The knife was halfway up the nail now.

Billy Boy took another deep, even breath.

Trude pulled the knife out, put it back in his pocket. "I just touched your arm, did it hurt?"

"Nuthin'."

Trude went back to the stiff-backed chair, closed his own eyes a moment. Winslow was past the dream state and well into coma. Only a few could surpass coma. Only the rare, only the true miracles could enter the realm of the Clinically Insentient.

Ahead of Trude now was a particular part of the mirrored wall that was two-way, and on the other side of the wall was the room where the blue-suited men watched and the nurses watched and where Roget watched, the tiny Frenchman who had helped Trude design this place, and as Trude signaled there immediately came now the glorious poignant sound of the harp.

"Do you hear, William?"

"Yes."

"Do you know what it is?"

"No."

"Could it be angels? If angels made a sound, it would be like that."

"Yes."

"Angel sound for your ears, William, how old are you?"

"Old?"

"Yes."

"Maybe thirty-one."

"Thirty-one; I remember when I was only thirty-one, I'm forty-five now but you know what? All ages are marvelous ages. You'll see when you grow older. What do you like, what are your favorite things, William?"

"Tits and Big Macs and Whoppers."

"Do you like history?"

"Is that like books?"

"Sometimes."

"Don't like that."

"But you know history—I'm sure you know who the President is."

"Reagan."

"There you go. And whom did he beat?"

"Ummmmmm . . . that southern asshole."

"And his name?"

"Ummmmmmm . . . Carter."

"Right again; you see, you do know history, do you like sports?"

"You bet. I like every one but basketball on account of all the niggers."

"Who's your favorite football player?"

"Bradshaw, Bradshaw, Terry Bradshaw."

"And do you have a baseball favorite?"

"Pete Rose is the greatest."

"Do you know what I like, William? Birthdays. I like having birthdays, my birthday is fine now, it's wonderful now, but you know what?"

"No, what."

"It was more fun when I was younger."

"Same here."

"We agree, we agree on so many things, you're such a sensitive person, William, you're sensitive now and I'm sure you were sensitive when you were twenty and when you were fifteen and *now you're ten,* William, do you hear me, you're ten years old and it's your birthday, it's your tenth birthday, your very own wonderful tenth birthday, and now guess what, William, you'll never guess so I'll tell you, I want you to open your sweet eyes because I've got a present for you."

Billy Boy opened his eyes, lay still, blinking.

Trude reached down for the box beside his straight-backed chair, took out two items, put them behind his back, got up and walked about to where the giant lay quietly. "Hello there," Trude said.

"Hi Mister," Billy Boy said. His voice was high now.

"How are you, William?"

"I'm neat, Mister, what's your name?"

"Why don't you call me Leo?"

"Leo? *Leo?* What kind of a name is that?" He put his hands to his lips and called, "Oh Leo. Oh Leo." Then he laughed. "That's what we use instead of butter. Oleo. Oleo. You get it, you get it?" He laughed again. "Can I have my present now, I bet you got my present behind your back, you can't fool me."

"In a moment, all yours. But first, tell me: who is your President?"

"Jayne with a *y* Castelli."

"Jayne Castelli is president?"

"Of the fourth grade, yup, yup, yup, she sure is, and stuck up too, 'Jayne with a *Y*' she calls herself."

"I meant of the country, William."

"Oh. Him. Y'know, old Ike. Only he's getting out soon. The Pope's gonna be in the White House, soon as what's-his-face gets in. I want my present."

Trude brought his left arm from behind his back.

Billy Boy made a face. "A stuffed toy? A dopey stuffed bear? I'm ten, I don't want any dopey old stuffed old bear."

Trude brought his right arm out now.

Billy Boy shrieked—"A baseball glove? For me?"

Trude nodded.

Billy Boy grabbed it, stared. "Omigod, omigod, *it's a Stan Musial.*" He rubbed his fingers over the leather.

"He's your favorite?"

" 'Course."

"More than Pete Rose?"

Billy Boy's face went blank.

"I thought Pete Rose was your favorite in baseball and in football Terry Bradshaw?"

"Bart Starr; I never heard of those other guys."

"Or Jimmy Carter?"

Billy Boy looked blank again.

"Do you know who Ronald Reagan is, William?"

"Bonzo, Bonzo, Bonzo," Billy Boy shrieked, "I loved that pitcher, I loved that little ape."

"What does the word 'orange' mean to you?"

"Orange? A color."

"Wonderful. And do you know what these are?" Trude went into his pocket, held something out.

"A book of matches."

"Do you know how to light one?"

" 'Course."

"Would you like to?"

Billy Boy nodded, took the matches, opened the cover, carefully pulled one match out, closed the cover, struck the match until it flamed.

"Perfect."

"Can I blow it out?"

Trude nodded.

Billy Boy blew.

"I imagine you'll be having your favorite food for your party, William. Big Macs and Whoppers."

"Whaaaaat?"

"Someone told me once you liked them."

"Well they were all wet, Oleo—I'm having hamburgs."

"I hope you have a wonderful party, William. Don't get too tired before it starts. Perhaps you better close your eyes and rest now."

Billy Boy closed his eyes.

Trude took the glove and stuffed animal, went back to his chair. "Rest," he said again, softer, and he gestured toward Roget in the control room.

The wind sounds grew, leaves scattering along the pavement. Billy Boy breathed deeply as before.

"Ten was wonderful," Trude began again. "But nine was better than ten and my seventh birthday was better than my eighth birthday and I'll bet so was yours and five was such fun, I loved being five except that being four was better even, yes it was, yes it was, my fourth birthday was such fun and so is your fourth birthday, today is your fourth birthday, *you are four today,* so why don't you open your eyes, I've got a present for you."

Billy Boy opened his eyes, blinked, blinked.

Trude walked around so he could look down at him; Trude's hands were behind his back. "Happy birthday, sweet William."

"Not my name."

"It isn't?"

"No, no, no."

"Well then, what is?"

Billy Boy put his hands up to his face and squinted shyly out from between two fingers. "Mommy," he whispered. "Mommy, she calls me Keef."

"Why Keith?"

" 'Cause, 'cause, 'cause, 'cause, 'cause."

" 'Cause why?"

Now he closed his fingers over his eyes entirely. " 'Cause Keef is my after name." Then he threw his hands down and said, "I wan' my present, you said, you said."

"I will. Just tell me what 'after name' means."

"After after after is what it means. It means after William comes Keef." His baby talk was more pronounced as he got excited.

"Here's your present," Trude said, and he pulled out the Stan Musial baseball glove.

Billy Boy looked at it and for a moment it seemed he might cry.

"Only teasing," Trude said, and then he held out the stuffed bear.

Billy Boy grabbed it, gave it a hug.

"Keith?"

"Whatty, whatty, whatty?"

"Do you know the word 'orange'?"

" 'Course, 'course, 'course, 'course, 'course."

"What does it mean?"

"Juice. Mommy gives it to me to drink. Orange is juice, orange is juice."

Trude took out the book of matches now. "Do you know what these are?"

"No, no, no, no, no."

"You mean you do know but you're afraid of them."

Billy Boy kissed the stuffed bear. "Yes, yes, Mommy said I might . . ." He kissed the bear again, hugged it with both arms. " 'Hot' Mommy said. 'Could hurt Keef.' "

Trude put the matches back into his pocket. "We would never want to hurt you."

"No."

"And I think it's time for a little nap before your party, don't you?"

"Yes."

"Close those eyes. Gently. And sleep."

Billy Boy began breathing deeply.

Trude took the animal and the baseball glove and went back to the chair. Then he signaled to the control room again and now the water sounds began to swell.

Billy Boy lay motionless except for the deepening breathing.

"You're one year old now, William. One year old and it's your birthday and you're hungry."

Billy Boy sucked his thumb.

"You're so hungry and I know what you want, I know just what you want, I know what you want more than anything else in the whole wide world." He signaled again to the control room and this time a door slid silently open and the brown-haired nurse appeared. She moved silently to Trude, who took the prosthetic breast, felt the temperature making certain the milk inside was warm enough; then he squeezed it, checking the milk flow through the nipple. He nodded finally, the brown-haired nurse turned and moved back into the control room, and the door slid shut.

Trude moved to the sleeping giant. "Oh, such a wonderful baby," he said, "such a wonderful happy baby." He tickled Billy Boy in the stomach. "Ahhhh-*boo*," he said, as he wiggled his fingers. "Ahhhhhh-*boo*."

Billy Boy shrieked with joy and kicked his feet.

"Ahhhhh-*boo*."

He rolled around, laughing and giggling and kicking his feet even higher in the air.

"Such a happy wonderful baby."

Billy Boy sucked his thumb again.

Gently, Trude took the thumb away.

Billy Boy put it back.

The next time Trude took it away he put the breast nipple softly between Billy Boy's lips. Billy Boy hesitated, then lifted his head toward the breast. Trude took the giant's hands and cupped them round the prosthesis. "Good?" he asked.

"Ummmmmmm."

"Is it what you wanted more than anything else in the whole wide world?"

"Ummmmmmm."

"I would never lie to you, not to a glorious wonderful child like you."

Billy Boy sucked at the breast, his jaws working, some dribbles of milk spilling down his chin.

Trude wiped them softly away.

"Ummmmmmm."

"Take your time; it's all yours."

"Ummmmmmm."

Trude watched the giant suck the nipple. He signaled the control room and immediately he could sense the temperature in the room slowly start to rise. Not much. Just so that the environment was comforting, warm, perfect for sleep.

"Ummmmmmm. Ummmmmmm."

Trude waited until there was no more milk. The nipple touched the lips but there was no more sucking. Trude got up, took the breast away, put it with the other toys.

Now deep breathing again, deeper than any before.

Trude touched the tips of his fingers to his eyes, pressing gently, trying to clear his mind of all distractions. He wished momentarily for steaming coffee, a gallon of it, but he knew he was nervous and delaying what he hoped was success but so often had been failure.

Silent prayer. Then he began to talk.

"You're ten months now, ten months, now six, now six, four months old, four months young, four peaceful months of life, now one, one month, now weeks before that, now days before the weeks, now you're there, William, you're in the womb and safe, you're somewhere in the blessed moments between creation and birth, between creation and birth, you're between creation and birth, William, tell me that you fully understand where you are, you're between creation and birth, between creation and . . . and . . . say it."

The breathing ever deeper.

"Say it."

No reply. Nothing. Just the enervating passage of time . . . . . .
. . . .

.
.
.
.
.

.
.
.
.
.

Waiting was always murderous for Trude. Nothing had come slowly for him all his life, nothing had ever taken time, ask a question, the answer came like that. So the waiting now, coupled with expectation, was brutal.

.
.
.
.
.
.
.
.

Trude began to talk again then, setting up more rhythms, sharper cadences in his voice. "Your first words, your first words, your first words, are hard. Your first words, your first words, your first words, bring fear. But no need for fear. No need for fear. You are in the one true safe place. You are in the safest place. Between birth and creation is the safest place. And the best place. The best place. The free place, William. The only free place. The only true free place, William, the freest place on earth, free is what you are, William, safe and free, safe and free, say that, for me William, say free, say free, say it, say it, free, free, free . . ."

.
.
.
.
.
.
.

.
.
.

> "fruh . . .
>   fruh . . .
>   fruh . . ."

Trude had to fight the desire to prompt, to complete the word "free" but he had been at this before and knew he had to wait for the dead sound from the giant body to continue. And it was a dead sound. Slow and deep and there was no hint of emotion. Not yet. But as Trude looked at the other man, he could see, now, the first signs of perspiration beginning to spread across the enormous body.

.
.
.
.
.
.
.
.
.
.

> "free . . ."

"Do you know what you're free to do?
 Do you know what you're free to do?
 Do you know what you're free to do?"

> "no . . ."

"Such a wonderful thing,
 Such a splendid glorious thing,
 A magical thing."

> "mmmuh . . .
>   magic . . ."

"Yes. Magic.
 Yes. Special Magic.
 Magic for you alone."

Trude hesitated now because he knew that there was liable to be a reaction soon, and not a good one.

"Magic for you alone.
Magic only you can do.
Travel."

.
.
.
.
.
.
.
.
.

Billy Boy lay with his eyes closed but now he was perspiring more heavily. And his body was commencing to tremble.

"Travel.
Travel for joy.
Travel anywhere.
Anywhere your dear ones are.
Travel to your dear ones.
To your own and only beloveds."

"huh . . .
huh . . .
hoo . . .?"

"You know who.
Whom do you care for?
Whom do you understand?
Understand completely?"

". . . thuh . . .
. . . thuh . . .
. . . theo . . ."

"Yes, Theo.
Of course, Theo.
Ted, Theo, Theodore.
Theodore Duncan."

.
.
.
.
.
.
.
.
.
.

                              "... theo ...
                                  ... thuh ...
                                      ... theo ...
                                          ... is ...
                                              ... here ... ?"

      "Yes, Theo's here.
       Yes, and waiting.
       On Gramercy.
       Gramercy Park.
       You on Sutton.
       Theo on Gramercy.
       Such a short trip.
       Such a quick trip.
       Such a joyous trip."

                              "... theo ...
                                  ... theo ...
                                      ... close ..."

      "A blink away.
       A quick blink.
       A blink to Theo."

Trude watched, studying. The trembling was worse now, the entire body wet from perspiration, glistening and trembling.

.
.
.
.
.

.
.
.

"... fuh ...
... fuh ..."

.
.
.
.
.
.
.
.
.

*"THEO'S
FUCKING!
FUCKING
CHARLOTTE!"*

"Does he know you're with him?"

"... no ..."

Trude made his voice very gentle now. "Tell Theo ... tell him
not to be afraid. 'Don't be afraid,' tell him."

"... don't ...
... be ...
... afraid ..."

"That's right, but Theo is the one you must give that
information to, dear Theo, let Theo know not to be
afr—"

"HE'S
SCREAMING!"

"What?"

> "SCREAMING
>   SCREAMING 'NOT AFRAID
>   NOT AFRAID!' "

"William—William listen to me—
   you must listen to me—
   he's not afraid of you—
   he doesn't realize yet
   he doesn't know it's you—
   what do you know?—
   what do you know that Theo knows—
   what do only you and Theo know?"

.
.
.
.
.
.
.
.

"... buh ...
      ... bairn ..."

"And what is that?"

"... word ..."

"What does it mean?"

"... buh ...
      ... baby ..."

"And only you and Theo know?"

"... only ..."

"Then let him know you know.
   Say it. 'Bairn.' Say 'Bairn.'

Say 'Bairn' to Theo now."

> "HEARD WRONG.
> HEARD BUREN.
> HEARD *BURN.*"

Trude stared as the giant's body began shaking with pain and terror—the water poured from him now and his giant hands were pressing at his temples—his knuckles were twisting and drilling at his temples.

> ". . . FIGHTING . . .
> . . . HURTING . . .
> . . . CHARLOTTE . . .
> . . . STRONGER . . ."

Trude spoke quickly, brought Billy Boy out, watched him jam his knuckles into his temples, signaled for a sedative, gave the murderous giant enough to make him sleep for a day. Then he went to his office and even before making another pot of coffee, he called Kilgore in Washington to pass on the triumphant news . . .

2

THE PIPERS

Even though it was before dawn, Eric wasn't the least surprised when the phone started ringing. He'd been in his apartment for less than five minutes and he was almost expecting the call. He knew it would be Karen and that probably she'd been dialing for hours.

He hobbled toward the phone. Not in the best of shape. He'd lain bleeding on the sidewalk for he really had no idea how long. But a patrol car had found him and he managed to take them into the building and point out the dread elevator shaft; he had planned on staying right with them but the closer they got the closer he came to light-headedness. Finally he sat on the floor, waved away any help, which made his fellows realize he more than likely needed some. So while one of them stayed in the unfinished building, the other drove Eric down to Bellevue Emergency where they prodded him and X-rayed him, finally bandaged and patched him and suggested he get home and sleep for a week.

"Yeah," Eric said into the receiver.

"Where have you been, Little? I've been phoning and phoning."

Eric sat heavily into a chair and stared out at Lincoln Center and Chagall.

"Little?"

Eric sat staring out, wondering did she wake from a dream or had she been up late when the premonition came. As they'd spent more and more of their lives away from each other, Karen running the Foundation now, their senses of each other had grown even stronger. Once when she'd broken her leg on a winter Vail morning and there was genuine concern that her back was gone too he had known *something*, and that knowledge came in the middle of

a jewel robbery investigation at the New York pied-à-terre of a
Delaware Du Pont. This Mrs. Du Pont, who had lost a considerable number of valuables and was considerably upset, was a little
surprised when in the middle of questioning Eric had said, "Pardon me, may I use your phone." She had expected, apparently,
that he would be calling the precinct house or some such police
business, and when he put in a long-distance call to Colorado, she
became rattled. That led to upset when he called again five minutes later because the line was busy the first time and Eric remembered Haggerty saying, "He has this telephone fixation, Mrs. Du
Pont, but otherwise he's a crackerjack operative, please humor the
lad as best you can—"

"*Little?*"

"It would have been awful if your back had gone."

"The Vail thing?"

Eric stared out at the Chagall.

Karen's voice grew very stern. "You must get hold of yourself
now and talk to me, I'm concerned, I don't like these silences."

She had a point, and Eric was about to explain when he realized,
was quite startled to realize, that he was too full to talk about it.
He could sense the drying in his throat.

"Are you too upset, is that it?"

Eric grunted that that was it.

"Just tell me a few things then—call me later but at least tell
me, are you all right, is it Frank, is he all right too?"

"Not all right too," Eric managed, and then he hung up. He
went to the kitchen, got the Scotch he kept for visitors. There was
maybe a quarter of a bottle left. He took a sip, hated the taste,
chugged the rest, made it across his apartment, fell to bed.

And instantly the phone rang.

And rang.

And rang.

"Whuh?" Eric's mouth felt like some group had been holding
a convention inside.

"Got a few minutes?"

Eric blinked. He knew the voice, knew it well. "Huh?"

"This is Captain Haig, Lorber; have you got a few minutes?
Couple things we might talk about."

"What time is it?"

"Eight thirty."

Eric shook his head. "Still dark out though—that's funny."

"At night, Lorber."

Fifteen hours, Eric thought. Flaked fifteen hours and it went by like a song. Then he remembered Frank. A dirge; it went by like a dirge. His body throbbed.

"Well, what about it?"

"Right," Eric said, not quite sure what they were talking about.

"Should be finished here within an hour—I'll stop by then. Nine thirty."

"Be waiting," Eric assured him, hung up, and immediately was back asleep.

This time the pounding at the door brought him around. "Yeah, yeah, right," he managed as he stumbled to the door, opened it, said "With you in a sec" and retreated to his bedroom, throwing on a pair of wash pants, a cashmere crew neck that was an insane color of purple, the reason, Karen assured him, it was on sale and happy birthday.

"Sure this isn't an inconvenience?" Haig said as Eric came barefooted into the living room.

Eric shook his head, sat.

Captain Haig stared out the window at Lincoln Center. "Some view," he said.

"Reason I'm here," Eric answered, wondering why the hell Haig was here. Haig was really a detestable figure; for a cop. You wouldn't have minded his ruddy good looks and glad-handing if he'd run an ad agency or sold life insurance.

Haig turned from the window then. "The main reason I'm here is that I thought we ought to talk about Frank Haggerty's funeral."

The funeral! Jesus, Eric thought, how could that have not crossed your mind before. And what a thing it would be. You could never wash away the stains of the last hours totally, but if anything could help, it would be the funeral.

Just the size of it alone. Cops have a way when a brother dies brutally. Heroically. Ordinary unknown cops get great turnouts. But this was no ordinary unknown, this was the funeral of Frank thirty-five-years-and-then-some-on-the-force Haggerty; thirty-five years and maybe a couple of enemies, maybe a million friends; thirty-five years of work, not just here but side trips to Philly and Boston—he had cousins on the force in Boston—

—maybe the Pipers would come!

The Boston Pipers. The best bagpipe group bar none counting England, Ireland, Scotland, Wales, *bar none.* And everyone would be dressed in their blues and thousands maybe of lawmen listening to the Pipers, fifty strong, and then after some music a few words, a eulogy from someone close—

—Christ, Eric thought, that's why he's here, he wants me to give the eulogy. I can't do that—my God, give a speech about Frank in front of all the others—I'm too young. It should be a contemporary, one of the old guard, one of—

—it should be a member of the family. Frank Jr., he was the proper choice and as he looked across the room Eric realized that *that* was why Haig was here—to try and soften the blow of his not being allowed to speak at the funeral of his beloved partner. What a jerk Haig was—thinking he'd be upset. Eric shook his head and almost smiled.

"Does that mean you don't want to talk about it?"

"Does what mean?"

"You just shook your head."

"No, nothing like it, just tripping off."

Captain Haig looked at Eric now. "Are you all right, Lorber? We can do this tomorrow."

"Great shape. No need."

The Captain would not look away. Eric could feel his eyes. *"Are you sure you're all right, Lorber?"*

"Like I said, great shape . . ." And now Eric could feel things breaking loose inside him. He tried for a quick smile, missed. "Well . . . great is probably not quite it, maybe okay would sum it up better . . ." And he tried to stop then, tried so hard, but the dam had given and he was helpless. "I . . . I never should have left Frank is the thing . . . See, he had Frank over the shaft but I . . . I had the gun . . . and so it was stalemate . . ." *Stop,* Eric demanded, *don't you dare sully this*—not to Haig—not to a prick like Haig—*control yourself*— ". . . see, if I'd stayed, Frank would still be around . . . and I was gonna stay . . . I had the gun . . . in my hands . . . but Frank, he came up with an idea . . . and he said for me to go . . . he meant it . . . but . . ." *Enough shit Jesus,* Eric shrieked silently into the night, he's gonna tell this story, Haig'll dine out on this, and Frank would cry of shame, if he was here he'd weep and shake his head and say Eric, Eric, didn't I teach you any better than this? ". . . you make your decisions and most . . . most of the time it's all right, you survive with your choice . . . but see . . . but see . . . Frank was no kid . . . he was great but he was no kid . . . and this Winslow . . . this fucking Winslow . . . he's a pig . . . and I left Frank . . . alone with this crazy pig . . . I shouldn't have done that . . . I shouldn't have done that . . . I should have stayed with Frank . . . it was a bad choice, a bad choice . . . I could have stayed, I should have stayed, but I left him all alone and . . . I don't think I'll forget that for a while . . ."

At last then, silence.

Captain Haig got up, went back to the view, stood, hands clasped behind his back. "Terrible accident," he said finally.

Humiliated, Eric stayed seated, immobile.

The blessed silence lingered.

"I'm okay now," Eric said, when he was.

Captain Haig turned away from the window. "I talked to the two men who found you on the sidewalk. At some length. And I talked to the doctors at the emergency ward. You've had some day, was the general consensus."

Eric shrugged.

"Don't come in tomorrow, all right? Get all the rest you can."

"I will rest," Eric said. "Maybe I'll show up for half a day, just to keep my hand in."

Haig shook his head, smiled. "Not tomorrow. I mean this. I'm speaking officially now. I don't want to see you working until I give the word. You're on vacation as of now. Head for the Caribbean why don't you. Grab some sun."

"I don't want to go on vacation. I'm a little rocky, sure, but who isn't in February? It's important for me to work now. I know what Winslow looks like, I've got a bead on how his mind goes. I'll be in tomorrow."

"No," Haig said. "You won't."

Eric looked at him. "Wait a minute," he said. "That's an order, isn't it?"

"You don't come in tomorrow and you don't come in the next day and if I say take a week, you'll take a week, if I say a month, you can consider it gospel. Are we clear?"

"Why?"

"Why do you question everything?"

Eric got up silently, went to the kitchen, took out a Doppelbock, opened it, swigged most of it down. He was about to ask the Captain what he wanted when he decided there was no law that made him be polite to bigots or fools, so he finished the beer, reached inside again blindly, grabbed a Guinness, opened it, returned to the living room.

Haig was staring out the window again. "Because you push yourself too hard," he said. "That's one reason. And because you've been through a dreadful accident, that's another. But most of all, you're on vacation because I say you're on vacation and when the day comes I have to explain my orders I turn in my badge."

Eric could feel a tension beginning in his stomach now.

Haig turned. "Clear?"

The tension was building. "That's the second time you've used the word 'accident.' You mean 'incident.'"

"I don't think so."

"Frank was thrown down an elevator shaft. That's not an accident, that's murder one."

Haig came back to his seat, got comfortable. "Mind if I smoke?"

"No."

"It's a cigar is why I ask."

"Smoke for Chrissakes!"

Haig got out a long cigar, pierced the butt end with his teeth, lit it with a gold lighter. Finally he said, "Did you see?"

"See what?"

"You said Frank was thrown down an elevator shaft. I merely ask if you saw the incident?"

"Of course I didn't—I was two floors away—"

"—then it's all circumstantial, isn't it—?"

"—what the fuck are you talking about—?"

"—you watch your mouth, Mister—"

"—there's something I don't know about—what is it—?"

"—was Haggerty drinking?—"

"—are you serious?—we had beer with dinner and that was earlier—"

"—he did drink—"

"—of course he drank, he was Irish, it's what they do best, but I never saw him drunk and neither did you—"

"—still . . ."

Eric's stomach was knotted now. He stood and shouted across the room at Haig. *"There's something I don't know about. Now tell me what it is."*

"There'll be no funeral," Captain Haig said then.

Eric just gaped.

"No *official* funeral I should say. No police participation. His two children have been notified. They're coming in for it. But it will be private. Just family. Their wishes."

"I don't fucking believe it—" Eric began walking mindlessly around—"You can't stop policemen from coming—a brother was *murdered—murdered in the line of duty*—there'll be thousands there—from up and down the Eastern Seaboard—"

"Wrong. Everyone's been notified."

Eric stopped dead. "You aren't that powerful, Haig—where's it coming from?"

"I'm not here to answer questions.

"Who's ordering this?"

"Do you always lose control this quickly?"

"It's not gonna work—you'll see—they're gonna come—I'm telling you—"

"Highly," Captain Haig said, standing up, "unlikely."

"You never liked Frank, did you?"

Captain Haig considered that. Then he said: "Nothing to like one way or the other. He was probably an adequate cop when he was younger." Now he turned on Eric. "And since you asked, I don't think being with you did him a hell of a lot of good."

Eric tried to put the beer bottle down without trembling, but he couldn't quite. "Captain Haig, please believe me when I tell you this: I'm very strong. And I'm very upset right now. You don't call a great man 'adequate' and then try to fuck up his funeral without my getting upset and so please leave now, please leave very quickly, because if you don't I will break your body into pieces."

Captain Haig left immediately.

"Fucking thousands will be there!" Eric shouted after . . .

It began terribly.

Eric alone on one side of the grave. Elaine and Frank Jr., whom he did not know, close together, standing across.

The coffin began to be lowered.

There was a bitter wind, the sun had lost its battle for the day. And now, in the distance, February thunder.

Eric closed his eyes . . .

Someone was tapping him on the shoulder. He turned, to be confronted by a wonderful-looking gray-haired man in the blue uniform. "You're Eric?" the man said, whispered.

Eric indicated that he was.

The gray-haired man gestured for them to step a few feet away. Eric followed him. "I'm Tim Donovan," he whispered then. "It's a disaster. Our buses got lost, the train was late from Philly."

". . . Philly . . . ?"

"Could they hold up the ceremony till we assemble?" Donovan wanted to know.

"You were Frank's cousin, weren't you?"

Donovan indicated that he was. "We just need some little time to organize. I hate to interrupt Frank Jr. and Elaine, but we've come a long way and it truly wasn't our fault."

". . . a long way . . ." Eric said. Then he said, "Do you want me to ask them, I don't think they'd mind waiting."

"I thought more would come from Newark, I'm sorry about that. But we'll have to do with what we can." He glanced up at the sky. "If we wait just a bit, I think we've got a good chance for some sun."

"That thunder sounded bad, Tim."

Donovan smiled. "My old bones are good for one thing, Eric —I can tell the weather. Trust me." He indicated the Haggerty children. "Ask them, would you mind?"

Cautiously Eric made his way to the brother and sister. Frank Jr. had turned into a fine-looking man, powerful like his father had been. And Elaine seemed a charmer. "Some people have come to pay respects," he began. "But they had all kinds of hell getting here. Could we hold off the casket lowering for a while."

Frank Jr. looked at the sky. "It could get bad soon."

"The weatherman says the sun's going to break through," Eric answered.

"Oh I'd love some sun," Elaine said. "Let's wait by all means."

"Thank you," Eric said. "I know it was your wish that it just be family, but since they made the trip—"

"—where did you get that idea, 'just the family'?" Elaine asked.

"It's what I was told." He looked back to Donovan, excused

himself, hurried to the old cop. "No problem," Eric said; "they were a little worried about getting caught in a storm but I assured them about the sunshine."

"My bones never lie," Donovan nodded. "They ache a good deal, but they're honest to the core." He left Eric then, hurried up the small cemetery hill, was gone. The gravesite was surrounded by hills. There was the open space with the coffin resting above it and Helen's stone beside that. Eric went back to Frank's children.

He was about to say something when Elaine beat him to it: "I know this isn't the proper time, but who told you 'just the family'? Please tell me. It's important that I know."

"Captain Haig."

Frank Jr. said, "He told us father was drinking and it was best to play down the whole thing. So no one would be embarrassed."

"I'll find out," Eric promised. "When this is done, I swear to you I'll find out what's going on. Something is, and when I know, I'll—"

He stopped dead then.

In the distance came a sound:

                    . . . . . may . . . . .
. . . . . uh . . . . .
                    . . . . . may . . . . .
. . . . . ah . . . . .
                    . . . . . maze . . . . .
. . . . . ah . . . . .

"Are those bagpipes tuning up?" Elaine said, and Eric thought, Omigod, they came, they did come, the Pipers, the Boston Pipers are here.

And now, over the crest of a near hill, they came, resplendent, the sound rising high in the brightening day:

> *Amazing Grace*
> *How sweet is the sound*
> *That saves the wretched like me.*
>
> *I once was lost*
> *But now I've been found,*
> *I was blind*
> *But now I see.*

And from another hill adjacent Eric saw Donovan, Donovan and God only knew how many others, all dressed in their blues, all marching in unison, moving straight and solemn down toward the gravesite.

And then over another hill came another blue phalanx; who, Eric wondered, then decided they must be the men from Philadelphia. But it didn't matter where they were from—and it didn't matter where the next group that appeared over another hill came from—Washington, Newark, Baltimore, New York City—what mattered was that they came, they were here, all of them, all of them.

The Pipers massed by the gravesite and for a moment they were silent. The sun was out now—Donovan's bones score again—and a gentle wind was blowing. And Eric wondered how many were bunched around Frank Haggerty's grave. More than he'd hoped. Many, many more. And then the Pipers began again, it was their signature song, and as he listened Eric felt sure they might have once or twice played it as well, but never, not ever better.

> *The Minstrel Boy to the war is gone*
> *In the ranks of death you will find him.*
> *His father's sword he has girded on*
> *And his wild harp slung behind him.*
>
> *"Land of song" said the warrior lad,*
> *"Tho all the world betrays thee*
> *One sword at least thy rights shall guard,*
> *One faithful harp shall praise thee."*
> *The Minstrel fell . . .*

Eric forgot about the words now, just let the music take him where it wanted, and he floated for a while, floated in the sun-splashed day, the music, the sun, the gentle winds, all of them perfect—

—then something made it more perfect. Alone on a far hill now, a single figure appeared, a police officer standing, scowling, a look of total frustration on his face. It was Haig. Captain Haig, staring beaten down at his failure.

Eric could not stop smiling.

"Mr. Lorber?—Mr. Lorber?—"

It ended worse than terribly. Eric alone on the one side of the grave, the two children together on the other; the body lowered all the way now, the movement done, Frank Haggerty in the ground. "Mr. Lorber?" Frank Jr. said again.

Eric opened his eyes, blinked, looked across at the son. The February thunder was above them now. Sleet was starting. "Yes?" Eric said.

Frank Jr. went on talking. "We'd like to be with father for a moment please."

Eric was about to say, "Of course, go right ahead," when he realized that Frank Jr. had left out a word but it was strongly implied, "alone"—"we'd like to be *alone* with father for a moment please."

The sleet was growing harder.

"I'm sorry," Eric managed before spinning away, embarrassed that his presence should cause them embarrassment. He walked quickly up the nearest hill. At the very top he turned back briefly, surveyed the miserable scene. Then he said it out loud: *"I'll get the fucker, Frank."* Then he ran.

When he got back to his apartment he was soaked so he changed into dry clothes, pulled out a New Zealand Leopard, had the bottle almost to his lips before he realized not only did he not want a beer, he didn't want to be in his apartment, so he grabbed his wet raincoat and elevatored down, then outside where the sleet was really slicing. Once he got to the sidewalk he turned around like a clown, not knowing which way to head, except that Winslow liked the Bloomingdale's area and this was a good mugging time what with the streets empty, those out not looking where they were going or what might be coming up to blindside them; Eric spotted a cab with an off-duty sign on which he always figured was how cab drivers got back at all the grief they took from their passengers—when the weather really got shitty they all drove around with their off-duty signs on. Eric stepped in front of the cab, worked his way around to the driver's side and when the driver pointed to the sign Eric simply flashed his detective's badge and got in—that was one of the privileges of the law—you could beat the cabbies at their own game, and he settled back after giving Bloomingdale's as his destination, listening to the driver mutter dark oaths, and after a couple of blocks he realized he was a fool on a fool's errand, because Winslow was long gone now, a killer in a limousine, so Eric told the driver to pull over, got out, walked back where he came from and sat alone in the Lincoln Center plaza, sat on the fountain and stared at the Chagalls until the chill in his bones made him realize that enough was enough so he stood, walked home through the gathering storm.

When he was back inside and again dry he wondered if he wouldn't have been better off by the fountain, risking pneumonia, because the phone began attacking him. First it was a woman wondering did he want *The New York Times* delivered on Sunday and he said no, he got it already, and hung up. The next call was a woman wondering did he want *The New York Times* delivered on Sunday and he said, you just called and asked me that and she said that that wasn't possible, and rather than pursue the argument Eric hung up on her. He hung up on the next caller too, a man who was "genuinely proud" to be representing the "X-L" come-to-your-home rug cleaning service, and as Eric stood drained by the receiver he realized that his punishment was not to be later but rather here on earth because it was clear that the phone company had put his name on some crazy list of theirs, some insane private list reserved for sinners, and he tripped off for a moment, thinking of the charities that would besiege him, the real estate companies asking did he want to get rid of his apartment, the breathers that would wake him in the night, the—

—it rang again. Eric lifted the receiver, heard the words "Duh—duh—Doctor Einbecker spuh—spuh—speaking," before hanging up again.

A stuttering doctor. There was no limit to their cruelty at the phone company. What could a stuttering doctor be selling over the phone except insanity?

Another ring.

This time the doctor explained that he was calling on behalf of Miss Wanamaker and—

"—I don't know any Miss Wanamaker, you've got the wrong number, please get it straight." Eric hung up, but even as he did, he knew his torment was going to continue.

Ring. Ring.

I'll outlast him, Eric decided.

Ring. Ring.

Ring. Ring. Ring.

Ring.

"Thuh—this is Duh—Doctor Einbuh—Einbecker speaking again."

"I thought so."

"And I have the right number, this is Duh-Detective Lorber."

"Yes, but I don't know any Wanamakers—"

"—not a Tillie Wanamaker?"

"No, I'm sorry but I—" Eric said. And then he said, "Does she live in Port Authority?" and when the stammered "yes" came Eric explained that he had known her for many years, known many things about her, but never her last name, no one knew that.

"Miss Wuh-Wanamaker had a struh-struh-stroke and has buh-been critical for days. Then today she impuh-improved enough to tuh—tuh—tell me what I'm calling about."

Eric held the phone very tight.

The message made little sense to the doctor, he said. But as clear as he could make out, Miss Wanamaker had seen the face of a giant, had seen this face going in and coming out of a fortune-telling establishment located behind Port Authority, that this establishment was run by a duchess, a blind duchess who had a dog that could kill.

It took a long long time for the stuttering medic to get all that out, but Eric didn't mind the wait at all . . .

THE TREASURE

Kilgore was perplexed.

He reached his Georgetown home a little after seven—another brutal day, no good news except for Trude, from anywhere, experiments blowing all across the land—to be told by his nine-year-old that Beulah called.

But Kilgore knew no Beulah. He walked inside and headed for the bar, going through the names of all the maids he and his wife had had over the years, all the live-ins, the cleaners, the sitters, the laundresses—but he could remember no black lady named Beulah.

He made himself a not remotely dry martini—half and half, the way God intended—and carried it out to the glassed-in porch and sat down. It was pure masochism that made him select that spot, since his wife had been after him for years to buy the lot just behind theirs before someone else did. He assured her the plot was too small and not to worry. The people who bought it did not find it small in any way, and they were building a garish modern monster that destroyed any privacy Kilgore had once enjoyed. Not only were these savages putting up a turd of a place, they were doing it *slowly.* The noise of construction reduced his wife to tears quite easily now, but in truth, Kilgore had been doing that to her himself quite easily also, so he couldn't blame it all on the construction.

He was physically a small man, Brian Kilgore, but in perfect trim. Handsome, if you thought Thomas Dewey was handsome, quick and precise of speech. He was not scientifically brilliant, but he was sound enough to deal with scientists who were, and he was organized enough to run New Projects remarkably smoothly; he had the gift of seeming interested only in you when you were telling him your troubles, something research scientists excelled at. None of his prima donnas were jealous of any of the others, and if you had asked Kilgore his greatest achievement he would have said that.

He was on toward finishing his first martini when he realized that Beulah was not a name at all, but a code word. He closed his eyes now. Which of the goddam projects was called "BEULAH"? Kilgore hated the weirdo acronyms, and the "operation this's" the military was always coming up with. But BEULAH?

Didn't ring a bell.

He got up, walked through the house to where the twelve-year-old was beating the nine-year-old at Space Invaders. "Mom's at A.A.," the twelve-year-old said as Kilgore entered. "She said just stick in the casserole for twenty minutes if you get hungry."

"I know perfectly well where your mother is, that's not why I'm here." He turned to the nine-year-old. "That phone call. Tell me all about it."

"Nothin' to tell," the nine-year-old reported. "This guy asked for you and when I said you weren't home yet he said he'd call again and that his name was Beulah."

"Holy shit," Kilgore said, before he could stop himself.

He never swore and he could see the stunned look on his sons' faces as he left the room. But he was that surprised to receive a phone call from Mr. R.E.L. (for the inevitable Robert E. Lee) Beulah himself. Obviously, the call meant trouble. But how deep and what kind there was no way of ascertaining.

Kilgore went by the phone to wait.

R.E.L. Beulah had once, in some long ago time, been a congressman from which southern state Kilgore had forgotten or never knew. He was reelected once and probably could have had the seat forever, but he decided not to run and rather to establish a law firm here in D.C. He was immediately successful at that too but then gave that up for what had become a genuinely remarkable if shadowy career. He was a presidential trouble-shooter. As simple as that. His name was never in the papers. No one knew him or who his friends were. But Ike used him and so did JFK and so did LBJ and RN too, Ford naturally. He was out in the cold somewhat during the Carter interregnum, but not too far out. And of course he was back now.

"Have I the honor of addressing Mister Brian Kilgore?" Kilgore had gotten the phone before the first ring was done and before he'd finished "hello" the flowery southern song was coming over the wire.

"Yessir."

"My name is Beulah, sir, and I have heard a very great deal about you."

"That's very flattering, sir."

"I would like very much the chance of addressing you in person."

"Whenever you want."

"I think now would be excellent. If you're free."

"Of course."

"Splendid. We can talk more on the plane."

"Plane?"

"We have to go to New York, sir. Some queries have been raised concerning the Trude Program."

Trude? Kilgore couldn't figure it. Trude was the only ongoing project that was actually ongoing these days. The enlarged children in New Mexico had begun eating each other in the lab. The Dream Stealing trial run had turned into an unalloyed nightmare. The—

"Just some queries that need answering."

"But everything's been going well there."

"Then the answers will be easily forthcoming."

Kilgore was about to press the issue, but he decided one didn't do that sort of thing to R.E.L. Beulah. He sighed, consoling himself that he had never traveled on this level before: private planes, limousines, police escorts. "You want me to arrange a meeting with Doctor Trude?"

"I think for later this evening."

"Fine. I'll do that, sir."

"We'll catch the last shuttle, good-bye, sir."

The shuttle! Kilgore sulked a moment before calling New York, alerting Trude, packing a small case, going to the children, alerting them of his departure.

They nodded their heads, but the truth was they were much more interested in Space Invaders. "Was he here?" they probably asked each other later. "Was that Father? Did he speak? Did he hug us? Your turn."

There was a long line waiting for the final 9:00 P.M. shuttle when Kilgore got there. He assumed there was a V.I.P. hideout somewhere but when he asked was told there was none, which meant either there was none or he didn't look important enough to tell the truth to. Kilgore started studying the line and was surprised to find, almost at the end of it, his round face wreathed in pipe smoke, Beulah.

The man could have been any age starting with sixty. His white hair was magnificent, long, and in disarray, the result of his constantly rumpling his hands through it. His pudgy hands. Everything about R.E.L. Beulah was pudgy, if you were a fan of his.

He stood probably five ten, weighed probably two fifty; strike pudgy, insert fat.

He perspired constantly, and often tied a handkerchief around his neck at the throat, a look he was affecting now. "My name is Brian Kilgore, sir," Kilgore began, moving up next to the older man.

"And I am the disrupter of your house and home, forgive me," Beulah answered, his southern voice very loud indeed. "You may call me Bobby Lee."

The line was beginning to move.

They inched forward, each carrying an under-the-seat bag, an attaché case. "Perhaps when we get on the plane we can talk," Kilgore said then.

"Doubtful, sir," Beulah replied. "My voice tends to boom along the aisles. I have learned through sad experience to avoid crucial conversations in the public halls of this world."

Kilgore wanted to press a bit more again, to find out why they were taking this sudden night flight into what was clearly trouble.

Best not, best not.

They took seats near the rear, Kilgore helped Beulah get his under-the-seat bag under the seat, since the southerner was not skilled at bending. Then they both opened their attaché cases, took out papers, and began to read.

The plane took off. "Tell me about this Trude," Beulah said suddenly, the instant the forward motion began.

"Smart."

"Hell, son, we're all smart, at least that's the theory, otherwise we wouldn't be here. I said tell me about him, I don't know thing one."

He's not a nice man, Kilgore almost began. Trude's a terrible man; cold, humorless, mean. But he's on to something and that makes up for minor blemishes of character. "I find him delightful, personally. He may seen formidable at first, but when you pierce the armor—" He stopped. The old southern eyes were staring at him.

"Never shit a shitter, son," Beulah boomed. The woman in front of them turned, shot him a look. "My dear, forgive me, if my mother were around, I would not be able to sit for days." Mollified, the woman turned away. Beulah turned to Kilgore. "As I said, I don't know thing one, but it doesn't matter, I'll just have to make up my own mind when I meet him." He sat back then and soon was breathing deeply, his face pale now, fatigue showing.

Kilgore looked out the window for a while, then glanced over at what Beulah was reading. Some pages were half out of a folder. He saw a familiar name. With great care, he reached over and flicked the folder slightly open—revealing a dossier on Leo Trude —well thumbed. He knows all about him, Kilgore realized and his next realization followed hard upon: the old eyes were flickering, watching him. Or were they?

Kilgore sat very straight for the rest of the silent flight, doing a great deal of wondering . . .

"Leo Trude, this is Mr. Beulah, from Washington." Kilgore put a slight but he hoped not overly noticeable emphasis on the last word, just to remind Trude that the fat white-haired man was one of import, not to be sniffed at.

Alas. Beulah raised his hand to shake, Trude kept his at his side. This may be a long evening, Kilgore thought. Long and counter-productive.

"I've been very busy," Trude said. "Nights are excellent for serious thought."

Beulah looked around the immaculate office, settled himself in the widest chair, got out his pipe, studied the room again. "Son," he said then to Trude. "I fear we are fated to be deadly enemies —me with my pipe tobacco, you with no ashtrays."

"Here," Kilgore said, scurrying to the coffeepot, taking a mug, handing it to Beulah. "Make all the mess you want."

"That's what he's here to do, isn't it? Make mess." Trude stood rigidly behind his desk, staring at Beulah.

Beulah rumpled his hair, looked at Kilgore. "What was it you said on the plane? 'I find him delightful, personally.' "

"Leo's very sensitive," Kilgore said, knowing now it was his fate in life to see these other two both left the room alive and breathing, when this meeting was all over.

"Leo doesn't like intrusions," Leo Trude said. "From the great unwashed."

"Would Leo like his balls handed to him on a platter?" R.E.L. Beulah asked of Kilgore. "Easily arranged."

"Leo, please," Kilgore said, feeling very Thomas Deweyish as he mollified. "Mr. Beulah is not without clout. Take that as an understatement."

Trude sat, gestured for Beulah to begin.

R.E.L. Beulah settled himself in the chair. Then he got out a pipe. Then he filled it with pipe tobacco. Carefully. Then he lit it. Carefully. Just before he blew the match out, he said one word: "Image."

The other two men waited.

"Believe what I tell you is true. Back when the fifty-two hostages had just been taken, the military came up with a plan. Simply, that plan consisted of dropping in an enormous number of marines and to set up a murderous—an absolutely lethal field of fire surrounding the entire embassy. Instantly destroy anything that moved. And under that cover, to transfer the hostages from the embassy to the contiguous soccer field and helicopter them out.

"I was present when that plan was presented to a number of experts familiar with Teheran. And one of them said, stunned and ashen, I remember his coloring today—'Do you realize how many people *live* in the embassy area? Do you realize how many people you'll *slaughter*?' The Pentagon brass gave their 'you can't make an omelet without breaking eggs' response. But this ashen gentleman was not to be intimidated. He said, 'Instead of shooting everyone, why not cover the area with gas. We have a nerve gas that puts people to sleep for ten hours. Some of them wake up with headaches but that's all. Blanket the embassy with nerve gas instead.' And the Pentagon said, 'Impossible. We can't use gas. It's bad for our *image*.' " He puffed on his pipe, shook his head. "Isn't that a terrible story? Terrible but true."

"I don't see what that has to do with me," Trude said.

"The same thinking is evident now, the proof being that I am here. There is no objection to what you're doing, though you'll have to clarify it for me eventually. But there's a great deal of objection to your test subject. The reason I am here, Doctor Trude, is simply this: There is great resistance to moving forward with William Winslow. If this goes badly, or news gets out, I think you can see it might be bad for our image, using a man like that to spearhead events. With government approval. I'm sure you see the nature and depth of the problem."

"You want me to explain why Winslow is necessary?"

"If you don't convince me one hundred percent *and now,* you'll have to forget Winslow and find others."

"Others?" Trude exploded. *"Others!—"*

"—now Leo," Kilgore said hopefully.

"There are no fucking others as valuable!"

"Leo, please—"

"—get him out of here—I don't have to explain any god damned thing to any god damned body if I don't choose to—"

Kilgore looked imploringly at Beulah. "Everybody's under a lot of tension."

"Of course," Beulah said quietly. "And he's quite right—he doesn't have to explain, God ordained no law—what is this place?"

"Sutton Hospital."

"We own it?"

"Yes," Kilgore said. "The bottom floors are more or less standard. We keep these upper floors private, for whatever uses we see fit."

"Fine. Well, unfit Mr. Trude—I want everything of his out of here—" Beulah looked at his watch. "By dawn. I want it immaculate. I want no trace of Doctor Leo Mark Trude visible to the naked eye. Consider him canceled." He slowly stood, knocked out his pipe into the mug, made his way toward the door.

"Can he do that?" Trude asked.

And now the white head whirled around, the great voice thundered: "He just *did* it. You are *gone.*" He looked at Kilgore now. "I think you overestimate this fellow; I didn't find him very smart at all." He was at the door when Trude hurried to him, took his arm.

"It *is* the tension, I'm sorry, I'm truly sorry, but we're so close and that makes for pressure but I genuinely repent what I said, believe me, please, I'm sorry, if you want me on my knees I'll get on my knees, I'll do anything, but you must not close me down, I'll explain, in detail, as many times as you want, if I've caused you to become angry, I'm sorry, I'm sorry, I'm sorry."

"Apologize then and I'll consider forgiveness," Beulah said.

Trude still clung to the southerner's arm, stared.

"I was being funny," Beulah explained.

"Then you'll let me explain?"

"On the condition that you'll release my arm."

"I'm sorry," Trude said, dropping his hands immediately; "I'm sorry if—"

"Enough 'sorrys.' Just let me sit down and get my pipe lit."

Kilgore watched as Trude went to his desk, Beulah to the chair. So far he had done an absolutely foul job of refereeing things. But at least the combatants were still talking. *Foul* was probably downgrading himself. *Foul plus* was a more accurate grade. Foul plus as a referee, as a father, with two disdainful children, foul plus as a husband with a precariously ex-alcoholic wife, foul plus—cut the shit, he told himself sternly. Attention must be paid.

"A dinner party," Trude began. "In Sweden. Only the great and the famous. Six o'clock. Suddenly one of the guests cries—'A fire. A terrible fire has just broken out. In Stockholm.' Now Stockholm is three hundred miles from the party, and the year is 1759 so communications as we know them do not exist. The party continues. The fire guest becomes increasingly agitated. 'It's spreading. Oh, it's spreading terribly.' None of the other guests know what to do. Nothing to do, really. The fire guest begins to anguish—'it's close to my home now. My home will be destroyed.' This goes on. The fire guest begins to go into the yard, then back to the house, then outside, back in, on and on. Hand-wringing. Despair. Then, at eight o'clock the fire guest says, 'Thank God, the fire has been contained, it's over.' One of the women present asks about his house. 'Quite remarkable—the fire was stopped three houses short of mine.' "

Kilgore looked at the white-haired man. He was lighting his pipe again, the eyes betraying nothing.

Trude went on. "Three days later, by horseback, news from Stockholm. A fire *had* broken out. It had broken out at precisely six o'clock. It was contained at precisely eight. And it stopped three houses from the fire guest's home."

"Fascinating," Beulah said. "Startling and fascinating and if I wanted verification would I find proof in Nostradamus, or the *Star* or the *Enquirer*?"

Trude actually smiled. "I know how much you would like that. Believe me, it would make your life so much simpler if everything could be scoffed away. However, in this case, the man whom I have termed the 'fire guest' was named Emanuel Swedenborg and if you'll call Harvard or Cal Tech or M.I.T. they'll all concur that he is generally accounted to be the greatest scientist in the history of Scandinavia. And the teller of the incident, the witness who wrote it down, was only Immanuel Kant, the most somber and serious of philosophers, I think you'll agree."

"He's certainly not a lot of laughs to read," Beulah said finally. Then he said, "This is all *all* true?"

"Yes it's true and it's nothing! Listen to this—America now, early this century. Kentucky boy, nice enough, God-fearing, all that, normal family—oh, there are hints, premonitions—snakes seem to enjoy his father, they curl around his legs. And this boy, when he's born, he cries for a month, won't stop crying, nothing can be done to make him give up his tears—until an old ex-slave lady takes a needle and boils it in water and pricks a tiny hole in his nipples—*and milk flows from his breasts.*"

"And the crying stopped?" Kilgore asked.

"As the milk flowed. And life became normal. The lad grows up, becomes a salesman, loses his voice—crippling to the success of a salesman. If you can't talk, you don't sell, and he wants to get married and nothing helps so he goes to a man versed in hypnosis and is hypnotized. And he can talk. Normally. But when he comes out, his voice is gone again." Trude paused for a moment. "Please understand one thing in all that follows—we are talking of a genuinely decent man. Not educated well, not aggressive, just a young man with a terrifying problem. For which there seems no solution."

Beulah pulled on his pipe, got it glowing.

"Now it's suggested that he go under again and this time try and tell about what's wrong, give all the symptoms. So under he goes and he's in this second hypnotic trance and suddenly this strange voice says, this new, powerful voice intones 'WE HAVE THE BODY' and gives a lot of medical talk, words the young man had never used in his life."

"Getting a little hard to believe," Beulah said.

"Not too hard for the hypnotist though—he said to this voice, 'I've got a stomach problem, can you help me?' And again, booming 'WE HAVE THE BODY' and another medical talk complete with suggested stomach cures. Well, this time when he comes out he's talking and the hypnotist follows the medical advice and his stomach is cured. Now this is a small southern town and you don't keep news like that quiet. Other people start coming to this guy for help. Only by now he's learned to put himself under and 'WE HAVE THE BODY' and medical advice. And cures."

"For how much money?" Beulah wanted to know.

"Tell you in a second. Word continued to spread. And people would write and say, 'Can I come to see you, I live in New York' or 'I live in Maine' and he would tell them not to come, because he wouldn't know what to look for anyway, he was ignorant of medicine. 'Just tell me your symptoms and where you are.' So they'd write where they were living and what their problems were and he'd go into a trance and 'WE HAVE THE BODY' and he would tell them what to do. And people would come to expose him and he would help them because if it was false he wanted to know about it—but everyone who came to expose him left believing. Because Edgar Cayce did it for forty years and he never took a fucking penny and he had a cure rate of ninety percent, *how high do you think Denton Cooley's cure rate is?*" This last was spoken loudly, almost shouted, at the southerner.

"I'm not the enemy," Beulah said. "I'm an American just like you're an American. And I'm frightened just now, because there's a war stench in the air and we all know it. You don't remember what it was like in the 1930s but that same war stench was there too. Today almost a quarter of Germany looks back on Hitler as the 'good old days.' And that percentage is on the rise. Anti-Semitism is skyrocketing in France, the terrorists are feasting on everyone, there are assassinations and assassination attempts in every civilized country, and during all this the Russians are just sitting there with this big smile—and with damn good reason—they've cornered the market on weaponry, they've got everything from The Doomsday on down, and we don't. Now, I truly enjoyed your little anecdotes—"

"—those 'little anecdotes' were merely to make you aware of a phenomenon—'traveling clairvoyance'—I can give a *dozen* others equally authenticated if you need convincing—"

Now, with surprising speed, Beulah stood and moved to the desk. "I'm not going to say this again, son, so remember it please —*I am not the enemy.* I'm not a nut who won't get out of bed without talking to my astrologer, but *I believe in 'something.'* Most people do. Two-thirds of us think you can communicate with thoughts. When those executives at ABC got caught paying fifty thousand to that seer to predict hits, they got a lot of static —but they only did it because they thought, 'what if she really does know?' They believe in 'something' too, or they never would have done it. I understand 'something' is out there and I hope whatever it is it doesn't get mad at me. But what I *do not* understand, what I am not remotely close to the vicinity of understanding is *why* a man who has spent half his life in jail, who has been a rapist, an animal who apparently lacks the least basic human feelings of decency, who is an escaped criminal that is not only a murderer but now a cop killer, is essential to the enterprise. With that record of his, if we get found out, we are in deep shit, I'm here to tell you."

"You know Winslow made contact with Theo Duncan?"

"You just said there were a dozen more cases of this 'traveling clairvoyance.' Fine. Use one of them."

Trude looked at Kilgore. "He doesn't understand anything, does he?"

Kilgore said quickly, "I think a great deal more than he lets on."

"Assume I don't," Beulah said sharply. "You know the trouble we're in with those mind-expanding jobs we pulled back a ways? You know the story that's building about all the people on that John Wayne movie who got caught in the wind from that bomb experiment and died of cancer? I'm telling you, we've covered for you up to now. We've got the New York police acting just like we want 'em, no one connected with Winslow here is about to tell bad stories. But you better come up with some explanation right now or that's the end of it."

In reply, Leo Trude stood up and began to make a pot of coffee.

"You've got my attention, son; I suggest you don't lose it."

Trude carefully measured spoonfuls of coffee into the paper container, put the container in place. "I'm assuming we could all use a cup," he said.

"Black, when you're ready," Kilgore said.

Trude busied himself with the machine, finally got it perking. "There's a game we all play, as children, in school, often, I think, and it's not a game with any strict set of rules or even a name. But I call it the 'what if' game."

"You better do better than that, son," Beulah said. Kilgore thought Beulah was, for the first time, showing his age. He chomped on his pipe, tapped it out, got a cleaner out and fussed with that—trying to maintain concentration, Kilgore decided.

"Quit playing with that goddam toy and pay attention to me then," Trude said. "Or do you want a nap?"

"It doesn't matter if we like each other," Beulah answered slowly. "Because if it did, you'd be out in the street."

"I have no intention of going there. Just try and stay with me —if I go too fast, raise your hand."

Kilgore watched as Beulah refilled his pipe, spilling more tobacco than seemed necessary on the immaculate office rug. Score one for the old guy, Kilgore decided.

"The 'what if' game is simply when you fantasize. 'What if' Mommy never met Daddy? Or 'what if' I found a thousand-dollar bill or, to put it in historical terms, 'what if' the man who shot the archduke had been delayed, would that have delayed World War One? Or 'what if' Hitler had invaded England in 1939 and Germany had conquered Europe?"

"Spare me any more examples," Beulah said. "I have the concept firmly grasped in my aging cranium." He spilled some more tobacco, ground it into the rug.

Trude studied the rug a moment, then checked on the progress of the coffee. When he spoke, his voice was stronger. "Humor me now. Take the 'what if' seriously for a moment. Use the Hitler example I just gave. If you could somehow arrange for Hitler to cross the Channel, the results might be cataclysmic for America. He might have won the war, he might have lost but damaged us grievously—in any case, the results would be wildly beyond our control. And potentially disastrous."

"Am I done humoring you?" Beulah asked.

"Not quite. Please. All right—altering a major event is a no-no, we've just decided that. On the other hand, altering an inconsequential happening—if we could, for example—change the life of some unimportant person of long ago, that wouldn't do us any good either: because we wouldn't know if we'd truly done anything or not. What we need—what *everything* depends on—is finding something that was important enough for us to monitor the change, but something also in which there would be no undesirable effects. In all history, I've found one event that truly satisfies my needs."

Beulah said nothing.

But Kilgore could sense a rise of energy. Trude turned toward the percolator. Let the coffee the hell alone, Kilgore thought. Get on with it now!

"Have you ever heard of Elisha Gray?" Trude asked then.

Beulah had not.

"Odd," Trude said. "Since he invented the telephone."

"I believe it was Alexander Graham Bell," Beulah replied.

"In point of fact, *both* Bell and Gray did," Trude said then. "In the single greatest scientific coincidence in history, they *both* patented the telephone on precisely the same day. Gray, alas for posterity, did it *two hours* after Bell. Had he been just that much earlier, it would have been the Gray phone we talked of today.

Beulah was sleepy no longer. He put his pipe down as Trude poured three cups of coffee, passed them around.

"Now *what if* Bell were delayed? *What if* Gray got his telephone patent in first on that long ago February day? Mr. Beulah, do you know in one word what we're after here?"

"I await your brevity."

"Control."

"Expand that please."

"We are trying to control the future by controlling the past—Bell was in this city just before his patent was applied for—*and so was Theo Duncan—and that's why William Winslow is everything—he is not just an ordinary traveling clairvoyant, he doesn't just move across space, he moves across time.*"

R.E.L. Beulah closed his eyes.

"When I said Winslow made contact with Duncan, I meant not just down in a Gramercy Park mansion, I meant a mansion in February one hundred and five years ago—Theo Duncan was a poet surviving as a tutor. Nelson Stewart was enormously rich—he was old and single, Charlotte Bridgeman was young and beautiful. Her father was his lawyer. A marriage was arranged—all perfectly standard for the time. The marriage produced two sons but evidently little passion. The children were tutored as rich children were then. Theo arrived. One thing, as I'm sure they said

even in those days, led to another. Theo and Charlotte had inter-
course—Winslow described it clearly to me. *Thoughts were exchanged.* I've never come this far before, it was the breakthrough.
That's why your appearing now from Washington was not greeted
with more cheer."

"Thoughts were exchanged—is there more?"

"Of course—Bell took a walk in Central Park on the thirteenth
of February, one day before the patent application. Winslow will
direct Duncan to the park. And once he meets with Bell, he will
detain him."

"And if Bell chooses not to be detained?"

"By any means possible," Trude said. "And if we're successful,
the world will be unchanged except 'The Gray System' will be
doing a lot of advertising on television."

"Winslow *is* Duncan," Kilgore said quietly. "That's the key to
everything Trude's doing. Everyone has been here before, but
people like Winslow remember it all. Trude is simply trying to put
a use to reincarnation. He's not only our leader in this field, he's
our only practitioner. Our pioneer."

"And if it's successful?" Beulah asked. "The benefits would be
how immediate?"

"No telling," Trude answered. "Depends on who else we find
that can do what Winslow can do. When I said control the future
by controlling the past you could rephrase that to our winning the
future by damaging our enemies in the past. What if we found
someone today who could control someone who was around Stalin? What if Stalin was disposed of as a young man?"

"I've always been a student of Leon Trotsky myself," Beulah
said. "Vastly underrated figure." Then he put his coffee cup down.
"All right, do it."

"I'm free to do what I want then?" Trude said. "There'll be no
interference?" He sounded, Kilgore thought, almost happy.

"I don't mean that at all," Beulah said. "I mean *do it. Show me.
Make contact. Now.*"

R.E.L. Beulah was not overly impressed with the Infinity
Room. For a man who had seen moonshots, who had dined with
presidents and kings, who had been on reviewing stands with
dictators living and dead, the Infinity Room was not such a much.
Oh, the lights strung up and reflecting forever in the mirrored
ceiling and walls were a nice enough decorating touch. And the

wind sounds were first-rate stereo. But the name "Infinity Room" was as pompous as Trude himself. And the rolling in of wave sounds could have made Beluah, had he allowed himself, just the least bit seasick, a disease to which he was prone. So he was, all in all, unimpressed.

He was also bored.

"Where the hell's Trude?" he said to Kilgore. They were standing together by the couch in the center, by the box of toys.

Kilgore, bored himself and also worried, said, "First of all, preparing for a regression is not like throwing together a picnic hamper—and you did spring this on the man—"

"—I suppose."

"And besides, that, Trude is famous for his meticulousness." Was that enough bluster, Kilgore wondered? He hadn't the least idea where Trude was or why it was taking so goddam long to bring the killer in and put him under. "But I wouldn't worry myself. I think we should stay cool and relaxed because I'll guarantee you one thing: Leo Trude is."

In point of fact, Leo Trude was on the verge of panic. For two reasons mainly. First: Ever since the initial contact with Theo, Billy Boy had met with nothing but failure. Hours of waiting in the Infinity Room while the silence and the deep breathing dragged on and on and then the perspiration from the giant as he entered into severe head pain. Followed by: absolutely nothing. No success whatsoever. Boring failure following boring failure. And if that pattern continued now, if another failure transpired in front of Beulah, it might mean the end of everything, all of it over and done. So that was the first reason for Trude's keen sense of unease.

The second reason was a good deal more immediate: Billy Boy refused to do it anymore.

"And you can't make me," Billy Boy shouted.

"William," Trude said—"you've got to understand my position—"

"—fuck you and your position." They were alone in Billy Boy's plain hospital room. A barred window, a bed, a bureau, a mirror, a chair, all standard.

"But very important people are here. *Crucial* to us."

And now Billy Boy was screaming—*"It hurts!—it tears your head apart and I'm done!"*

There was a window in the door, a small square window, and

now the sound of his shouting brought faces there. Billy Boy saw them, the faces in the blue suits. They had guns. You had to be careful when they had guns. Until they weren't looking. There was a speaker outside and now one of their voices came through loud: "Everything okay, Doctor Trude?"

Trude waved the two men away. "Everything's fine here," he said. "Don't worry about William. He'll come through for us."

"I'm done," Billy Boy repeated. "Believe that."

"I need you one last time."

Billy Boy shook his head violently.

Trude glanced at his watch. This had been going on for far too long and God alone knew what kind of fuse Beulah possessed. The last thing helpful in the Infinity Room was anger. "Look," Trude said finally. "I've got this fool down from Washington. We're spending a lot of money and the government wants to see it's getting it's money's worth. I don't think you can object to just that."

"Just what?"

"I'll relax you, put you to sleep—and I'll do the regression. *But that's all.* Once you're a baby, that will be the end of it, I won't take you any further. You know the pain only comes when I take you further."

"I don't know," Billy Boy said.

"It's all for show! The regression is by far the most spectacular part of it. How can you object? He'll be happy, you will have no pain." Trude tried to say this as casually as he could, because if the answer was "no" there wasn't much he could do—drugs were out of the question. You could put someone to sleep with drugs, but you could never segue into a successful regression. It all had to be natural or it was nothing. Trude looked at his watch again. There was simply no time for a decent relaxation. Billy Boy was in hospital whites. "You can go dressed as you are. No massage, no preparation. With any luck at all you can be back here in an hour. And I promise you, I'll never ask anything of you again."

"I'll be free?"

"Absolutely. Get me through this, and we're done. Let's get on with it. I'll put you to sleep here, we can wheel you straight down." He smiled, never his best gesture, but there was no more time for words. And there would be violence later when Billy Boy awoke with his head on fire. But that Trude decided, could be faced in its proper time. The stun pellets had been effective before, never on one of Winslow's power, true, but there was no reason to assume they would fail totally. He smiled again. "Shall we begin?"

"If you're lying, I'll tear your arms off."

Trude managed to hold on to his smile . . .

"Dear Lord, he's a mastodon," Beulah said as the nurses rolled Billy Boy into the Infinity Room, Trude a step ahead of them.

Trude immediately busied himself with the box of toys. "We had a fabulous preparation," he said. "Each time it gets better."

Beulah glanced at his watch. It was already well after midnight. "How long will this take?"

"With the kind of good luck we've been having, we should be finished by dawn."

"*Dawn!*—"

Trude whirled on Beulah—"This is not the Automat in here— you do not put in a quarter and get a piece of pie—I am a surgeon of the brain and this is my operating room—!"

"I'm sorry," R.E.L. Beulah muttered.

Trude continued on the attack. "No, I do not think you are at all sorry. I think you are like everyone in government, you want it yesterday. I cannot work in an atmosphere of hostility. It's damaging to me and mostly to the patient." He looked at the nurses who had transferred Billy Boy to the couch. "I don't want to do this but I must cancel tonight's journey."

"I truly am sorry," Beulah said, his voice soft. "There is no hostility emanating from me, son, I assure you. And I've got to be back in Washington tomorrow so let's get on with it."

Damn, Trude thought, as he said, "Much the best to do it now." He gestured for the nurses to leave the room. He had spent the last minutes carefully planning the regression—a spectacular display was his main hope; if they did not make contact but the regression was in itself of sufficient interest, that might keep things on track for a while, perhaps enough for the next contact to be made. When the nurses were gone Trude turned to Beulah and Kilgore: "Of course you're familiar with regression techniques."

They were not.

"Tedious stuff, but we must get through it, please bear with me." He walked close beside the giant. The breathing was deep and even. Trude gestured to the control room and there was more wind. Then he took his penknife with the honed blade, asked Winslow for his hand. When Winslow lifted it, Trude took it and jammed it deep under the fingernail.

Billy Boy did not move.

But Kilgore did—he jumped backward, said "Holy shit," then "I'm sorry, Leo, forgive me."

R.E.L. Beulah stood where he was, his unlit pipe between his teeth. He looked mightily unimpressed.

Trude began the regression then, first taking Billy Boy to his fifteenth birthday, because at an earlier session he tried fifteen and found that Winslow had raped the neighbor girl in Waukegan and it was very sensual, listening to him describe the way she tried resisting.

Kilgore seemed fascinated.

Not so R.E.L. Beulah.

Trude hurried on, hitting all the best moments, the changing meaning of the word 'orange,' the changing occupation of Ronald Reagan from President to star of *Bedtime for Bonzo* the time his name was, for a period, "Keef," the baseball glove, the teddy bear.

Kilgore was standing next to the couch now, transfixed by what he saw.

Trude concentrated very hard on his labors, but when it was safe, he glanced toward the aged southerner.

No question, he was bombing.

"Ahhhh-*boo*," Trude said, tickling Winslow's stomach. "Ahhh-*boo*." As the giggling began Trude felt a sense of relief because it was *so* strange, *so* remarkable, this Neanderthal murderer kicking and giggling and shrieking with joy that you just *had* to be enthralled with it.

"Ahhhh-*boo*!
Ahhhh-*boo*!!
Ahhhh-*boo*!!!"

"It's incredible," Kilgore said. "Absolutely extraordinary." He turned to Beulah. "Have you ever seen the like?"

"I suspect I would laugh if you tickled me under similar circumstances. Doctor Trude, this seems to be enough preliminaries; I'm here for the main event, if you don't mind."

Trude snapped, "I told you this was tedious!" He signaled for the nurse with the light brown hair and when she entered with the warm prosthetic breast, he took it from her, inserted it immediately between the lips of the giant, waited for the sucking to be done, put the breast down with the other toys.

And a few moments later, Billy Boy was back again, back between creation and birth.

Breathing ever more deeply.

.
.
.
.
.
.
.
.
.
.
.

"How long does this shit go on?" R.E.L. Beulah asked.

"Shhh." Trude put his finger to his lips.

Beulah looked impatiently at his watch. "How much longer do we have to wait before contact?"

"Almost there," Trude said, keeping his desperation behind his eyes.

.
.
.
.
.
.
.
.
.

"Far be it from me to invade the mighty realms of science," Beulah said. "But surely there must be some way to hurry things along."

"This is all still experimental," Kilgore tried helpfully. "Everything Trude does is being done for the first time, more or less."

Beulah scowled, stared at the sleeping giant, stared at his watch, walked around in a circle.

"We know certain things about contact," Trude explained. "At least these are the suppositions we're working on. It's best if the parties are in the same city. It's best if they're the same nationality. It's best if it's the same day, the same time of day. But most important is this: Contact is most easily achieved during a crisis time."

"Explain that."

"When we first reached Duncan he was having a crucial sex act —he was open, he was vulnerable, he was receptive. It was a time of sensitivity, of crisis in his life, if you will. You can't just say, 'skip a week ahead, go back a month!'—you take what contact you can get when you can get it."

And now the giant was trembling, his clothes suddenly soaked with perspiration.

"There, you see?" Trude said excitedly—"we're almost there."

.
.
.
.
.
.
.
.
.

At four in the morning, a surly Beulah began to talk. "When I was a child, we used to have snipe hunts. Some idiot, often me, would be sent out into the woods holding a sack while my so-called friends would supposedly flush a snipe from his hiding place and my job was to catch it in the sack. Night after night I failed and they would say, my friends, 'Okay, Bobby Lee, one more chance but that's it.' " He looked at Trude now. "I am too old to be left holding a snipe sack; *you* have one more chance. And that's it."

The giant began to groan softly.

"I assume that's another wondrous sign for our cause," Beulah said.

"He's in some pain, that's all. Not that he minds it, but for reasons we don't quite understand, it's not altogether without some discomforting moments."

"I am at this time rather discomforted myself," Beulah said. "And don't give me any lecture about spreading hostility, we're past that. I am very hostile and with good reason. I'm an old man in a dry month waiting for rain."

Trude turned away.

Beulah walked after him.

Kilgore began to scream in panic—

—because then, right then, with no warning, William "Billy Boy" Winslow sat suddenly erect. And he spread his arms. And his eyelids parted. But his eyes were high up in his head. So only the whites showed.

And from these whites flowed tears.

> *"CRI-YUNNN!"*

Trude whirled, faced the giant, stunned, because this was a different sound, this was no dead rasp constantly weakening. No. This was *thunder*.

> *"CRIII-YUNNN!*
> *CRII-YUNNN!!*
> *WON' STOP*
> *CRII-YUNNN!"*

Trude moved close to the blind weeping eyes. "Who's crying? Why?"

> *"MUHHH—*
> *—MAMMEEE*
> *CRIII-YUNNN!!"*

"Why is she crying? Why won't she stop?"

> *"DIIIIIIII.*
> *DRAFFFFFF."*

"You'll die because it's so drafty? It's that cold? She's afraid you'll die of the cold?"

"HUNNNNNNN!"

"You'll die of hunger and cold. You're that frail, she . . ." Trude's voice stopped then because an instant before the others he realized it. He turned to Kilgore and said, "He's connected with another life, we've made a terrible mistake—I don't know where he is or when or—"

"—*go on!*" R.E.L. Beulah commanded suddenly.

"Who are you, you're not Theo."

"BOOKER!
BOOKERRR!"

"Last name?"

"JUH—
JACKSON!
AN'—
AN' SHE WON'—
—WON' STOP—
CRIII-YUNNN!"

"Ask him how old he is," Beulah commanded.

Trude took a deep breath, complied.

"TWENNY"

"Now ask him the year!" Beulah's voice was louder.

Trude just stood silently, because it didn't matter, if it wasn't 1876, nothing mattered to him.

"Ask. Ask if this is 1917!" Beulah was relentless.

Trude did as demanded.

"YUH
YUH."

"New York?" Beulah went on. He was all but shouting now.

"New York?" Trude repeated.

"YUH."

Beulah approached the giant, who sat as before, the huge arms outstretched, the sightless eyes continuing to weep. "The answer to our prayers," he said, and then he whirled on Trude and Kilgore. "Don't you see? He's a twenty-year-old Negro. With a mammy. And he isn't cold because of the draft, his mother's afraid he will die when he's *drafted*—and not hunger—it's the *Hun*—the Germans—this was the first half of 1917, right before the war." He stared at them both. "Don't you see *yet?*"

No one seemed to.

"*Trotsky* was in New York the first half of 1917; Leon Trotsky lived *here* before he went back to home—Jesus—once we get back to 1876 and nail Bell, we can go to 1917 and kill Trotsky—we can zap the Russian Revolution before it goes anywhere—we can win it all!" Then he pointed his pipe toward Billy Boy. "This man," he said, and there was no mistaking the emotion in his old eyes; "this man, well, he's a national treasure . . ."

By the time Trude reached his office half an hour later, the celebration was well under way. Beulah and Kilgore had gone straight there once the 1917 revelation had occurred, and Beulah had unpacked the pint of Chivas he felt helped his bones ward off the cold. He poured the liquid into coffee cups and the party had begun.

Trude had to bring Billy Boy slowly to the present and oversee the wheeling back to his plain room. He ordered the two nurses to lock the door behind him, told Apple and Berry to alert him if anything unusual happened. So when he reached his desk, he was already more than a drink behind.

"Jes' in time to settle an argument," Beulah said, his speech already the least bit slurred.

"I say Stalin," Kilgore cut in.

"If you really wanted to cripple Russia once and forever," Beulah went on. "When we get this control business honed down and all the bugs out of it, who would you kill? Mr. Kilgore and I are locked in this intellectual debate. He says Stalin, I say no, Lenin, he was the linchpin figure. Do I mean 'linchpin'? Anyway, if you could kill any Russian you wanted, and thereby destroy Russia forever as our enemy, who would you kill?"

. . . While this question hung in the air, in his hospital room now,

the National Treasure was pulling at his temples to stop the pounding, and screaming wildly . . .

"I've done a great deal of thinking on just that particular problem," Trude answered, the first sips of Scotch warming him. "I'd greatly appreciate it if you would listen to my answer, because, you see, it's very hard because, you see, we didn't travel."

"Don't see the connection," Beulah put in at once.

"Well, if you could control me today and you wanted me to eliminate, say, Mrs. Thatcher, nothing simpler. I'd hop a plane to London, wait outside Number 10, and when she appeared, simply blast away."

. . . While Mrs. Thatcher was being disposed of, Billy Boy managed to get to his feet. He fell back immediately with dizziness, but not for long . . .

"But in the old days," Trude went on happily, "travel was a huge problem. A hundred years ago, it could take weeks to make a trip like that. And whoever you were after might be gone. The point being, people came *to* America—we were the magnet. It would have been much easier for a Chinaman to do it, because there were Chinamen all over the world, and you might find one easily to do your wishes. Even many Russians were here during the Civil War. But very few Americans were overseas."

"So?" Kilgore said.

"Just that thus far, we've found that one controls one's own kind. Americans remember Americans, etcetera. So it would be very hard to get to one of the Russians, but assuming I could, my answer would be neither Lenin nor Stalin, I would do my very best to deal with Karl Marx."

. . . While Beulah and Kilgore considered that answer, Billy Boy staggered to the door, pounded on the little glass window, screamed he wanted the door unlocked. The nurse with the light brown hair used the speaker outside to tell him that was quite impossible and to get some rest immediately. Billy Boy picked up the chair and smashed the glass window on the third swing. Then he started working on the door . . .

* * * * *

"I can't see Marx at all," Beulah said. "Big mistake."

"Don't think so," Trude said. He was proud of his reasoning. It had come to him over many nights. "You'd have to get Marx early is all. The late 1830s say. *Before*—and this is essential—*before* he wrote the 'Communist Manifesto.' You see, his writings didn't just give a platform and foundation to the Russians, it's done the same to every revolutionary group that's come along since. If you destroy Stalin or Lenin, you certainly damage Russia mortally. But some other nation might have grabbed the banner. If you erase Marx, you erase minds, and those are what always cause the most trouble to a democracy."

. . . while democracy was being saved, Billy Boy tried to shoulder the door but it was soon clear to him that it was of some sort of special construction. Outside, the nurses were nervous. Apple and Berry knew about the special construction and told the nurses to relax. This became increasingly hard to do as Billy Boy picked up the entire bureau and began to slam it against the door . . .

Kilgore was exhausted and the second drink hit him hard. "Let's destroy America," he said, "who would you kill?" He couldn't help laughing. "This is more fun than playing Space Invaders any day."

"Washington, he was the father of us all," Beulah replied. "More Scotch?"

. . . while Trude and Kilgore said just a touch please, the specially constructed door showed the first sign of weakening . . .

"I think I've researched every country," Trude said, happily; "I've got a good grasp on just who would be most advantageous for us to get. But there are wrinkles. Example: Bach died neglected and stayed that way for seventy-five years till Mendelssohn revived his reputation. Does that mean if we got to Mendelssohn, there would be no Bach interest? Hardly, because even though he was *neglected,* he was not *unknown*— Mozart and Beethoven both were aware of him, so we can assume someone would have rediscovered Johann Sebastian. In history, there are *manifest* forces— that's what people see at the time—and *latent* forces—things unseen by contemporaries, and . . ."

. . . and while Trude almost emptied the room with his boring chat on forces, Billy Boy continued exerting forces of his own against the offending door. And once she realized there was no question the door would lose, the second nurse began to scream . . .

"Washington was certainly a great man," Trude expounded, smiling into his coffee cup. "But he was also surrounded by others of greatness. Never such talent in America as then. No, I think the man to obliterate is the most hated man in our country's history, Mr. Lincoln of Illinois."

. . . while Kilgore said he hadn't realized Lincoln was a despised figure, the nurse with the light brown hair began to run . . .

"During the war, loathed," Trude said. "Like no one before or since. But he died, you see, in the arms of victory, and the Lincoln myth—he died so our country might survive, might become one again—without that, we would still be fighting the Civil War. Except again, like Marx, you'd have to get to Lincoln early, back in Springfield would be an excellent time, he would have been ripe for the plucking back then."

"Like to propose a toast," R.E.L. Beulah began; it was to have been a brief but flowery speech about the fact that there was no doubt whatsoever in his mind that God Almighty kept a special eye out for this great land of ours—but the brown-haired nurse's arrival canceled all that.

"We can't control him," she said. "He's getting out!"

Trude moved remarkably quickly, considering the hour and the Scotch. He got out a key and unlocked a drawer in the bottom of his desk and took out the stun pellets, was already inserting them into the gun on his way out the door. He ran along the corridor and up the two flights of stairs until he reached Winslow's floor.

The giant was stepping through the wreckage when Trude got there, and he shouted for Apple and Berry to get away but they went for Winslow like the good men they were.

He simply slapped them backhanded across the corridor. Then he saw Trude. "You fuckin' lied to me."

"And I will again if I so desire."

"Not anymore." He started toward Trude now.

Trude raised the gun.

Billy Boy couldn't believe it. "A toy?" he said.

It was small. It held four pellets. One would do the job on an ordinary person. Trude hoped four were enough. Billy Boy was twenty feet away when he fired the first time, hitting the shoulder.

Billy Boy kept on coming.

The second pellet hit the thigh, as did the third.

"I said I'd tear your arms off." He reached toward Trude, five feet from him.

The fourth shot hit the neck and Billy Boy hit the floor like a water buffalo. He got to his knees, got almost to his feet before he fell again. He got almost to his knees a second time, before he made a final growling sound and toppled over sideways.

Trude moved to the wall to avoid fainting.

Beulah and Kilgore came up the stairs then. They stared at the silent behemoth. "I assume he's not dead," Beulah said. "For all our benefits."

Trude shook his head. "Anesthetic mixture."

"How long will he be out for?" Kilgore asked.

Trude muttered, "Many hours."

"Well, we won't waste any time at least," Beulah said. "You put him out when you regress him."

"Not the same at all. It's got to be natural. It's no use trying a regression with any drugs in his system. We'll just have to wait."

"You've got a bigger problem than that, son." Beulah pointed at the crumpled door. "It doesn't appear to me that he's very happy in these surroundings. I don't think you'll have much luck getting him to regress again. You can't use force on him, and you sure as hell can't scare him into doing it."

"Perhaps I can," Trude said.

Beulah shook his head. "Scare *him?* With what?"

"Not 'what,' " Trude said. "Who . . ."

4

THE BLUES

As he crossed the street toward the fortune-telling parlor, Eric knew all was not as it should be. No logical reason: the light was on, the front room empty, neat enough. But Eric knew. Probably one of the many blessed side benefits of dealing with torment all day long; you learned not to let it take you by surprise.

He stopped in the sleet and studied the place. A dump, truly. If you were a real estate salesman and were trying to unload it, *dump* would be the best you could come up with. Eric rang the bell, not really expecting an answer. When none was forthcoming, he reached for the door, not expecting it to be locked. The handle turned. As he pushed his way quietly in, Eric took out his pistol, held it loosely in his right hand.

There was a curtain drawn across the doorway at the rear. Eric moved toward it slowly, reached it, quickly threw it aside.

Chaos.

Even though the room was dark, even though the only illumination came from the front, the fight marks were easily spotted, as were the droplets of blood.

It was then Eric heard the slow breathing.

He turned, studied the bathroom beyond. It too was dark, but as he moved closer, the breathing sound grew. It was coming from behind the shower curtain. The curtain was roughly drawn around the tub below. Eric took a breath, preparing himself. Frank had always had bad times when encountering the results of violence. Eric got through it by being prepared. He had seen more than enough grief in his years on the force, and he summoned old images, just a few, but enough to get him ready for whatever he might face; a butchered Harlem lady his first year up there, her husband sitting beside her as she bled, muttering over and over "she wouldn't lemme watch the Yankee game"—Eric brought her back now and the stoned-out teen-ager who had blown her own heart out with her father's hunting rifle, only she had gotten confused as to which side held her heart, had guessed the right, and Eric had been the one to find her, bloody, weeping with humiliated pain—Eric brought her back too, so he was prepared as he threw back the shower curtain to see the Duchess, blind and dying.

He was not at all prepared, however, to see the dog.

It lay on its side, ripped open, its blood filling the bottom of the tub. It was a huge shepherd and the blood had matted its fur, and probably the Duchess was dead somewhere, but certainly the dog was dying right here.

Eric spun quickly, wondering what the hell he might be able to do to make the animal's final minutes less horrid. He went fast to the back room and the small refrigerator, threw it open, looking for food. There was nothing but in the freezer compartment he found a pint of ice cream, grabbed it, pulled the lid off, took it back to the tub. He wedged out a hunk of vanilla, knelt, put the ice cream close to the dog's tongue. The animal licked the cool vanilla tentatively once, then paused, then licked it again.

Eric knelt there for half a dozen more licks, till the dog was dead.

What was he into and who were these people and where did their power spring from? Dog killers and kidnappers and police force controllers—Eric washed his hands quickly in the sink, then returned to the back room. The place was small and he was skilled at searching, but this was different, because she had been blind. Not too many *National Geographic*s lying around.

He really expected to find nothing, and nothing pretty much summed up the first few minutes. Then, in a closet, in a hat-box, he came across the notebook, filled with the strange practiced writing of the blind. Most of what he skimmed through made no sense to him. Then on a page alone he found the following:

Rosa Gonzales
(1687 Lexington)

Rosa Gonzales was Edith Mazursky

William Winslow
(Address unknown)

William Winslow was Theodore Duncan

Logically speaking, this didn't make any great amount of sense to him either. He was not ready to stand up and deliver a two-hour explication. As he stared at the names, he wasn't really positive what any of it meant.

But he knew it was gold . . .

Forty minutes later, Eric got out of a cab in front of 1687 Lex, near 105th Street. A lone Puerto Rican stood on the steps of the old brownstone, smoking a joint, staring at the sky. "Looking for the super," Eric said.

"You mean the superintendent?"

Eric couldn't believe the way the guy talked. There was not a trace of accent. The voice was at the same time booming but controlled. And the articulation reminded him of Jesse Jackson out of Chicago—the big words were all spoken as if hyphenated. Su-per-in-ten-dent."That's who I mean," Eric said.

"Is this en-quir-y of a pro-fes-sion-al nature or merely for the purposes of fra-ter-ni-za-tion?"

"It's business," Eric said. He looked at the guy closely now. Mid-twenties. Small but quick. Bright-eyed and bushy-tailed.

"The gentleman who fulfills that function here at 1687 is generally regarded as flawless of character. Im-pec-ca-ble." He took another toke of marijuana.

"I assume I'm addressing him now."

"In-du-bi-ta-bly."

"Answer a few questions?"

"Now *I'm* assuming—that you're an officer of the law; the question is, should I seek ver-i-fi-ca-tion?"

"Up to you."

"Since I am innocent of any recent skul-dug-ger-y, you may in-ter-ro-gate at will, Gridley."

"I love listening to you talk," Eric couldn't help saying.

"I doubt you traveled to these hin-ter-lands to tell me that, but thank you. I attend announcer's school. I am awed at the power of the media to ed-u-cate, to el-e-vate, to en-ter-tain. Also, I don't want to work in this shithole for the rest of my natural life." He inhaled on the joint again, offered it to Eric.

Eric shook his head. "Heard of Rosa Gonzales?"

"Alas."

"Tell me about her."

"Major league pain in the ass; at least for me."

"How so?"

"Weird. Crazy. Always having 'visions;' always seeing 'aura's' around people; super 'sensitive.'"

"What's wrong with that?"

"Her mother worked at some donut place near Port Authority. Weekends, she'd take Rosa down with her; that was good. When Rosa went to school, that was good too. But she was sick a whole lot and when her mother worked, she paid me to check in on Rosa, see if she was okay. Usually, when she saw me, Rosa would scream 'cause she could tell I didn't like her from my 'aura.' Throw a hysterical fit if I came near. Sob kick and scream."

"How old a person are we talking about?"

"Ten, maybe. She was small and skinny so she might have been twelve, but I don't think so. Ten."

"Why are you using the past tense?—isn't she here anymore, has she moved?"

"In-du-bi-ta-bly. She's dead."

Eric closed his eyes, took a long pause. "Of what?"

"The pre-va-lent opinion is she died of a truck."

Eric waited for the rest.

"I already in-di-ca-ted Rosa was frail. Her mother used to carry her a lot. Late one night some hit-and-run guy blindsided the two of them. Several witnesses at-tes-ted to that."

"This happen recently?"

"Within the last year."

"Up in this area?"

"No. Downtown more. East 50's I think. At the funeral, our con-sen-sus was you boys in blue didn't work overtime truck hunting."

"I never heard of the incident," Eric said. "And it's crazy that I didn't."

"If they'd been white, you would have."

"There's more to it than that."

"You think so?" the superintendent asked.

"In-du-bi-ta-bly," Eric answered.

The following noon Eric stood in the solarium of Orient Castle watching the Atlantic's anger build. He had just driven the three plus hours from Manhattan to the tip of Long Island. The doctors had believed his need to see Phillip Holtzman—no one ever really questioned the badge. The chief medical man—God alone knew how many worked at the Castle, probably the most expensive "home" in all the East—had said only that Eric could not talk as a detective. Fine, Eric said, tell him I'm an art student doing work on his wife.

Fine, the doctor—named Horn—had agreed, and sent Eric to the solarium to wait.

"Phillip will be down soon," Doctor Horn said, entering now.

"I appreciate this," Eric said. "And I promise it won't take long."

"Please don't mention the death," Doctor Horn said. "It brutalized him, her going that way. I don't think he'll ever come back from it."

"It's not the death I'm here about," Eric assured Horn. "I'm just tracking down some names, and if he can't help me, there's a woman named Sally Levinson I'm going to call."

"I don't think she'll talk to you."

"Why?"

"Just a feeling I have. I know Sally Levinson well enough to tell you she doesn't do much she doesn't want to. The word 'feisty' was invented to fit her."

Eric was about to ask more about her, but then stopped as a tall thin man made his way into the room, aided by a nurse. Eric studied Phillip Holtzman, decided he looked like the husk of Raymond Massey.

"This is Eric Lorber," Doctor Horn said. "The art person who wanted to chat a little about Edith."

Phillip nodded. The nurse helped him into a chair. "Perhaps you're cold," she said, got a blanket, tucked it around him, left the man alone.

"Thank you for taking the time," Eric said gently.

Quick smile from Phillip. "Not too much pressing today. Not a lot on. Not a lot on."

"Why don't I get to it anyway," Eric said. "I was wondering

—this is for some work I'm doing concerning the paintings—what you could tell me about someone named Rosa Gonzales?"

"Again that last name?" The thin head leaned forward.

"Gonzales, sir."

"Superb," Phillip said then. "Absolutely superb."

Eric waited, not understanding.

"Would have beaten Tilden, would have beaten Vines, finest service in the history of the game."

"That was *Pancho* Gonzales, Phillip," Doctor Horn put in quietly.

"Ah," Phillip said and he stared at the water. Then he began to fidget.

Eric watched the fidgeting become more intense. He looked at the doctor.

"I hope the planes are landing," Phillip Holtzman said then.

"Phillip," Doctor Horn said. "I'm sure the planes will be fine."

Phillip looked at his watch. Then he studied the waves through the solarium glass. Again his watch. The waves were starting to pound.

Abruptly Phillip stood—"I'm meeting Edith at the airport, I hope the planes are landing."

"Phillip . . ." Doctor Horn said quietly.

"Well it's getting severe, there's a wind rising, a dreadful damn February wind—nothing good happens in February—bad month, bad month—" A final look at his watch. "I must get to the airport *now,* or Edith will be kept waiting." He tried to take a step unaided.

Gently Doctor Horn had him, brought him back to the chair, covered him with the blanket, all the while speaking evenly and softly—"Edith won't be on the plane, Phillip—this is 1981 and she left us in 1960—that's twenty-one years ago and she won't be on the plane."

Phillip fidgeted, stared at the waves.

Eric thought how much he didn't want to be where he was, watching the remains of what once was probably a wonderful human. Some people hated cancer more than any disease; Eric hated senility. The last two years of his own father's life had been pocked with senility.

"It's in and out," the doctor said.

Eric nodded.

"Try the name again in a moment."

Phillip was off on his own now, drumming his thin fingers on the arm of the chair.

"How long has he been here?" Eric asked.

"Many many years," the doctor said.

"Mexican," Phillip muttered then. "Tempestuous fellow, Gonzales; on the court. Didn't know the man so I can't speak of his private behavior. But in the heat of battle, a firebrand; I always put that off to his cultural heritage."

Eric began wondering if he could take much more, because he was remembering what a dynamo Ike had been, Ike the father, and the genuine anguish his brain's deterioration had meant to those around him, and clearly, he was not going to get much coherent out of Phillip Holtzman. Not today. Not with the winds foaming the water.

So he almost left then, but he didn't, and thank God for that. Because it was less than ten minutes later, when the winds had for a moment quieted, that Phillip softly and with unmistakable clarity, began to talk, so lovingly, about "The Blues". . .

"Miss Levinson?" Eric held a beer in one hand, the phone in the other, stared out at the Chagalls. It was coming up to eight o'clock and the February crowds were scurrying across the great plaza toward the theatres.

"Yes."

"My name is Eric Lorber. I'm a detective, and I'd like very much to talk to you."

"Oh shit, is this about those goddam parking violations again? It's all being handled by my lawyer."

"Miss Levinson—"

"—I resent you bothering me at home. At this hour. And I *really* resent the way you bastards stuck that No Parking sign in front of my gallery—I'll go all the way on this, Detective Lorber —I'm going to park my car where I have a right to park it and these scare tactics aren't going to work. You can tell Ed Koch I said 'screw.' "

Eric had to smile. What was the word the doctor had used about Sally Levinson out at the home? *Feisty*? That was on the right track. "Vesuvian" might be closer, if there was such a word. "This had nothing to do with parking tickets, I promise you."

"What, then?"

Eric knew the terrain was shifting and dangerous, but when he said the words, "Edith Mazursky's death," he was genuinely surprised at the vehemence of the response.

"Hear this now—because our conversation is about to terminate—I have not talked about it, I do not want to talk about it, and there is nothing in this world you could say to make me talk about it—"

Eric could sense she was about to slam the phone down so he cut in with—"you don't know how important this is to me—"

"—and Edith's death—Edith's suicide—was very fucking important to me, Mister—"

"—maybe it wasn't just suicide," Eric said then.

A beat. Then: "Explain yourself."

"I can't. But I think it was more than suicide, and don't ask me what that means, I won't know what it means without talking to you."

And now there came this incredible pause. It went on and on and when it ended, the voice at the other end was washed, the anger gone. Finally Eric heard the words "Come on over."

He reached her Fifth Avenue building a few minutes later, asked the doorman to announce him. That formality done, Eric crossed the lobby, let an elevator man do what he got paid for. When he reached the Levinson floor, there was a small foyer entrance. Eric buzzed. The door opened.

A small woman who must have been June Allyson cute once answered the door. She was wearing a voluminous robe. She ushered Eric into the enormous apartment.

Eric hesitated, then flashed his badge. "These days you should always ask, Miss Levinson. Just because someone says he's a detective doesn't make it so. Don't be so trusting."

Sally burst out laughing.

Eric inquired as to what he said that was so funny.

From the folds of her robe, Sally removed an enormous pistol and pointed it at Eric. "Don't worry, I promise you it's loaded. My father gave me this when I first went to Europe. He thought some Frenchman might try and overpower me. You don't know how funny that is. Detective Lorber, last week I was ripped off slightly by two Caucasian youths who I believe attend Collegiate. I am not a trusting soul, take that on faith."

"You've convinced me."

Sally put on the safety, placed the pistol into a hall table by the door. Then she led Eric into the living room. It was enormous, forty feet long or more, and the view of Fifth Avenue would have been hard to improve on.

But what brought Eric to a halt were the Mazursky Madonnas. They ranged all around the room, each with a small light above. The feel of Edith in the air was overpowering. Eric stared at the famous group of paintings. "I've only seen photographs," he said.

"I'm sick of showing them," Sally said. "For a while they were always off on display. But I thought, 'shit, they can be on display when I'm in the ground, I want 'em here.'"

They sat together on a couch. "I've really got two main questions," Eric began. "Two main areas of discussion."

"I discuss nothing before you make me a promise."

"If I can."

"*If* what you said on the phone turns out to be true, that Edith's death was something more than suicide, if you find whoever or whatever's involved, you must promise to call me and tell me who or what or how."

Eric raised his right hand. "No problem."

"All right; first question."

"Rosa Gonzales."

Blank.

"Take your time. There's a connection between Edith Mazursky Holtzman and someone named Rosa Gonzales."

Sally shook her head. "We were sisters, you know. But loving ones. She knew all my secrets, I knew hers. I swear I never heard that name till now."

Eric waited.

"I'm really sorry. On to the next."

"Tell me about 'The Blues.'"

"Musical form," Sally said quickly. "Black beginnings. South. Plantation origins maybe. I'm just guessing."

Also lying, Eric thought.

"Why are you looking at me?"

"I meant the 'Mazursky Blues.' I'm sorry. I should have been more specific."

"Oh Edith's stuff—sorry—silly of me—long day—" Sally got up and walked to the window, staring out at the park. "Just trying to get it all straight. Edith said she liked having a focus for her work. A central theme, you know; it gave her a foundation." She turned, gestured around the room. "I called these the 'Madonnas.' I showed them at my gallery. Disaster. We're talking 1960 now, right?"

"Go on."

"Now in the next few years, what happened in this country?—the women's movement, right? 'Feminine Mystique,' all the rest. When the movement was casting around for some symbol, they remembered the Madonnas, and how they got pissed on and passed over by the art establishment. So the Madonnas got 'fad' famous. Then people began studying the work, saw how brilliant Edith really was, and the fad part stopped—these are now about the most respected paintings done by any woman in the last quarter century. I can't tell you how many museum hustlers stroke me so I should only leave them these paintings when I'm no longer with us. These are the same assholes, may I add, I fucking *begged* to come see the show when it was on. And no one did."

Eric watched her, thinking he was wrong before when he thought she was lying. This part all was true. She was just being evasive to the nth power.

"Just today I got a call from one of the knotheads in Chicago —since I'm a Chicagoan they thought wouldn't it be nice if I considered leaving the 'Madonnas' to my hometown museum—special room, guarantee twenty years showing—the whole series on display, not just one or two, and I said—"

"—the 'Blues,' " Eric said quietly.

"I was getting there, Mister!"

A rock, Eric smiled, looking at the dynamo. A giant rock rolling down a mountain. Get out of its way if you can. He stared at the paintings, felt Edith in the air.

"I was going to tell you a really hilarious story about human behavior, but obviously you don't want that, you don't give much of a shit about 'why' you only want 'and then.' Okay. 'The Blues' were to be the next series Edith painted. Large portraits of her loved ones. Seven in all. I was to be the last. She did some reading, did some sketches, then she went into the river."

"Phillip told me she painted them, he described them, especially you."

"Phillip, and I hope you're enough of a detective to have noted this on your own, is given to senility."

"He said the two of you were sitting in the living room when Edith came down from her study and said she'd finished the

painting of you and at last 'The Blues' were done. You went up
with her to her study. The portrait of you, he said, somehow
managed to show you as a young girl and you as you were then,
and you were so moved you wept."

"Phillip's fantasy, alas. Whoever sees 'The Blues' will only see
them in fantasy." Sally shook her head then. "Oh, Jesus, but they
would have been great. Edith was on a roll, she was in touch with
whatever's inside us that makes us special, she was—" Sally
stopped short. "Enough. I hate talking about them—that's why
I bullshitted you before. But believe me now when I tell you this:
I'm sorry I let you in here."

"Why?"

" 'Cause you don't know squat—'cause I thought on the phone
you were on to something—after all these fucking years I thought
somebody was on to something—'cause I know that when she
walked into Bloomingdale's that afternoon, she was happy."

"Maybe that's just your fantasy."

"I knew my Edith," Sally said. "And I don't know who or what
or how—but something invaded her brain . . ."

It was the middle of the night when Eric mashed his thumb
against the buzzer of the Lorber Foundation and leaned hard.
Karen was a remarkably sound sleeper—she had trained herself
to be; if you were going to exist on four hours per night, the
minutes spent in thrashing could destroy you.

A foggy voice said, "Whaaa?"

Eric spoke into the mouthpiece. "Me."

"Little?"

"Yup."

Vocal communication ceased then and Eric waited until he
heard her footsteps. Then the standard New York City unlocking,
unlatching, and unchaining. Then Karen's face in the doorway.
"If this isn't of the utmost, you just lost a sister." Eric stepped
inside.

"I'd like some coffee," he said.

"You'd like some coffee?—*you'd* like some coffee—there's no
chance for my survival if *I* don't have some coffee—" and with
that she turned and stomped off toward the kitchen.

Eric traipsed along after her. "Thanks," he said.

She whirled on him then—"I can't handle words now, Little!
—*you must stop throwing words at me*—when I'm on my second

cup, you may speak, not until then." She tied her robe tightly around her and Eric sat at the breakfast table while she got the percolator going. She did it with remarkable speed and precision —even in this unawake state, *almost* everything Karen did was pretty much without flaw.

In her mid-thirties now, Karen Lorber was something of a celebrity. She had her Ph.D. She had her M.D. Both, naturally, from Harvard. She had written four books, two of which sold well enough. Now that their folks were gone, she headed the Lorber Foundation, charged a hundred plus per hour, taught at P. and S.

Her waist, though she had to work at it more than she cared to admit, was the same as when she was a stunning nineteen. Her eyes were the same sea blue, her skin the same Merle Oberon olive. Most men and some women thought she was beautiful; nobody doubted her figure still ought to be declared illegal.

But because He also taketh away, there was always, in Karen's life, the constant lurking *almost:* men. Eric didn't become aware of Karen's idiosyncrasy until her first year in grad school when she got into a screaming match with the super of the building she was staying in; the guy lost his temper, slapped her around badly. Eric, when he heard of the incident, took the shuttle up to Boston intent only on killing the son of a bitch, but when he confronted his adored sister with his plan, she broke down, said he couldn't, he mustn't, please, please, please.

But he beat the shit out of you, Eric said.

But we're dating, Karen whispered, finally.

You're dating the super? I don't believe this—what does he give you, a break on your heating bill?

It's my life, don't mock me.

How did you meet this asshole? I mean, why did he think you'd go out with him?

Pause.

Spiel.

The . . . the janitor introduced us—

—the janitor, shit Karen—

—he's not always going to be a janitor, he's overqualified—

—and he fixed you up with his buddy, the super?

You make it sound so sleazy.

Karen—Karen listen to me—it *is* sleazy.

Pause.

Karen, don't cry.

Long pause.

I hate it when you cry, Karen, I'm sorry if I mocked you, I'm sure he's a very cute super. And overqualified as hell; he'll probably be running the garbage union before you can say Jack Robinson.

Jack Robinson, you bastard, Karen said, drying her tears . . .

Eventually the super was replaced by a cab driver, which didn't sit all that well with Karen's elders, but there was no doubt they were all thrilled when she got engaged to the young genius instructor at M.I.T.

He was handsome, for a chemist at least, and the marriage seemed solid enough at the start—except Eric knew it wasn't; he had noticed something when the chemist met the family: the guy pissed all over Karen. If she tried to say something, he interrupted; if she managed to complete the thought, he corrected her; if she'd gotten it right, he improved on it.

He's just like the super, Eric realized. Beating up on her.

And he was right. The marriage was misery, it lasted as long as Karen could manage. A Cal Tech genius provided her with a second husband; his attitude was more of the same. Karen had not tried for strike three yet; instead she had affairs. With scientists mostly, but that was not a strict rule; Eric figured that as long as they held her in contempt, they qualified. And he wondered, as he watched his sister pour her first cup of coffee now, just who was upstairs at this moment, waiting for her return so he might demean her a bit before dawn.

Karen, for her part, was never crazy about Eric's girl friends; she mocked them—they were all bubbleheads. But every time she fixed him up with someone really worthy, Eric shied away. One night when she was harassing him she realized he realized how young he was going to be when he died, so she found other subjects to razz him about after that.

When she was done with her second cup, she beckoned and they went into her office. It had been their father's. Karen gestured toward the couch. "Begin at the beginning," she said. "How long have you had this compulsion to wake up people?"

Eric smiled and they sat across from each other. He glanced around, got comfortable. His father had sat where Karen was sitting. And probably Frank Haggerty, Jr. had sat where he was, while Haggerty himself, young then, perhaps Eric's age now, waited fretting in the hall.

"Being a feminist, you've heard of Edith Mazursky."

"Sure."

"And you know how she died?"

"Wasn't it kind of horrible? Drowned herself in freezing water?"

Eric nodded. "That was her second try—the first time she desperately slashed her wrists." He paused.

"Drop the shoe, Little."

"I have just spent several hours with a very sane and very tough cookie who was Mazursky's intimate, who swears that the day the attempts began, *minutes* before, she was in a glorious frame of mind. And why I am here, dear one, is to ask you this question: How in the name of sweet Jesus is it possible for a happy person to kill herself?"

"I don't think you want me to say this, Little, but obviously, it's impossible."

"Right!" Eric exploded out of his chair. "Of course it's impossible. It's every which way impossible." Now he leaned across the desk toward Karen. "Except I believe it."

Karen nodded. "Figures, knowing you."

"I also think the government was involved somehow. And since you've been involved with half the scientific community from M.I.T. to Cal Tech, I turn to you for wisdom."

Karen thought awhile. "Would dream research fit?—it's very big now, lots of grants—"

"—how do you mean?"

"Well, there's a story that's going to break soon. This is true, Little. You can call the Federal Center for Disease Control in Atlanta and use my name, they'll tell you. A lot of people from Laos are living in America now. Scattered all across the country. Maybe twenty of them have died lately—all healthy, strong young men—died in their sleep. No violence, no poison, nothing like that. There's a new theory about it that's just making rounds."

Eric sat back down. "What?"

"They died of nightmare. Terror induced by nightmare. Well, little Karen here, when she hears something like that, she suspects the government's involved in some experiments. No proof. Just a hunch, we'll have to wait and see." She looked at her brother then. "Why do *you* think it's the government?"

"Just a hunch, we'll have to wait and see. But a crazy monster comes to town. Frank and I go after him, Frank dies, I grab the guy—then a limousine appears and guys in blue suits—really experts—they club me and kidnap the killer. And not only don't the cops care, they cover it up—they *deny* Frank the funeral he should have had. Only one group I know has that kind of power, and that's Washington. Then I get a tip—the killer used to visit a fortune-teller—"

"—oh-oh," Karen said. "Sounds like the government."

"I go down there, she's gone, I assume dead, because her Seeing Eye dog is sliced up and dying and you would have to be really expert to handle that, because he was no puppy. I find this killer's name on a piece of paper and Mazursky's name. I visit some people, and this brain invasion idea crops up. Which I am dumb enough to believe. Now why did you say 'sounds like the government'? "

" 'Cause a real Moonshot Mentality has taken over down there."

"Meaning?"

"Remember when Kennedy said we were going to go to the moon because it was this glorious challenge? One of my ex-boy-friends was in the room when that decision was made and it was all cosmetic. Kennedy said he was sick and tired of losing and he wanted something he could be guaranteed a victory over the Russkis. Well, they had no interest in going *to* the moon. There was no reason for sending anyone *to* the moon. *Around* the moon, take pictures—just like we did on Saturn. But the Russians had no equipment on the drawing boards for landing there, so we *had* to beat them. The whole moon program, all those billions, was all bullshit. We wanted to beat the Russians then and now it's taken over again—they'll do anything to get ahead. Psychic investiga-tion is this year's fad. I am sure we have plenty of fortune-tellers on our payroll."

"Such as?"

"Well, believe this—we can now take pictures of an empty room and have pretty good success telling who *was* in the room before it was empty. Hell, you and I have been doing thought transfer-ence on each other since the cradle. Think of a number."

Eric thought of six.

"Nine," Karen said. Then she said, "No, not nine, six." She looked at him. "Right?" Eric nodded. "Need I mention they're also doing a lot of experimentation with twins?"

"What about my happy lady painter killing herself?"

"I can ask questions if you'd like. I know a lot of people doing a lot of hush-hush stuff they love talking about. They're into bioenergy and precognition and telepathy and telekinesis and there was one shithead professor when I was at Harvard who claimed the wave of the future was controlling reincarnation."

"Then I'm not necessarily crazy."

"No, Little—you *are* necessarily crazy, you're just not necessarily wrong . . ."

The sun was threatening to rise when Eric left the Foundation, taxied home. He was bone chilled and bleary when he reached his apartment, unlocked it.

The two men in blue suits were seated quietly, waiting while the third man stared out at the view. Lovely Chagalls, he said, his back to Eric, and Eric waited for the man to turn before agreeing. Now, as he studied the man who looked like Kissinger, as he stared into the blue eyes of Leo Trude, Eric was struck with the absolute conviction that death was going to strike before another dawn.

One of us or both, Eric wondered? If both, it didn't matter much; if one, he wondered which . . .

5

THE MURDER

As the nurse with the light brown hair brought him his tray of food, an alarm sounded sharply. Billy Boy watched as the guy in the blue suit standing in the doorway gestured with his gun toward the nurse. "That means move it," he said.

The nurse, anxious not to spill the food, continued toward the bed where Billy Boy lay.

"Move!" from the blue suit and the nurse, stung, put the tray down fast, damn near spilled the whole shebang, and turned, hurrying away, and when she was gone and the alarm louder than ever the blue suit closed the door.

But in the activity, Billy Boy didn't hear it lock.

The nurse ran off, the blue suit ran off, the alarm was pulsing now—something was fucked up somewhere in the hospital—and Billy Boy stared at the door. He almost was afraid to test it, afraid to get up and walk across and put his hand on the knob and turn.

Because if it turned, he could be long gone, and that was the only way he'd ever get out of this room. This place was different from the one he'd wrecked—it was all reenforced and everything was bolted to the ceiling or the walls.

The goddam alarm wouldn't quit.

If he was ever going to make the move, though, it hadda be soon, with all the running outside and the noise, nobody knowing diddledee-shit about what was happening. But if he made the try, if he turned the knob and it was locked, it would mean his bad luck streak was still on. If he just stayed where he was and didn't try, he wouldn't know, and sometimes not knowing was the best.

Still the alarm.

Fuck it. They weren't making a chicken out of him. He shoved the tray aside, got up, dressed fast, went to the door, took a breath, put his hand on the knob, turned it—

—it opened—

—and the alarm stopped.

What'd that mean, what'd that mean, did it mean they knew, did it mean they'd be after him fast, the guys with the blue suits and the guns, he'd get them someday, when he was ready he'd get them but this wasn't a good time for him, not a lucky time, and he didn't want to take them on, not now, not until maybe the Duchess had given him a talk, told him he was back on the track again, the world his apple, the Apple his baby and—

—and where to go, where to go, down the hall was good, down the hall, how could you fuck up by going down the hall—?

—it was a long hall though, and a long hall took time, and what if they started coming back?

He risked it, tried this door, locked, that door, locked, all the goddam doors in the goddam corridor were locked and suddenly he saw the stairs to the roof and that was heaven, this was a top floor, you hit the roof and went across and there had to be a ladder down and heights were no big deal, not for him, he wasn't afraid —*they'd never make a chicken out of him*—

—he turned the knob that opened the door that led to the stairs that led to the roof and threw the door open, stopped dead.

It had started to snow.

But that wasn't what stopped him. Hell, a little snow or a lot of snow, he'd seen blizzards back home where houses disappeared, where there was just a roof slanting and you knew there had to be something beneath it, a house had to be beneath it, you just couldn't see it, couldn't tell a thing because of the snow. So it wasn't the weather that brought him to a halt. It wasn't the weather that made his fingers twitch.

It was going out on a roof again.

Because the last time, *the last time,* was a downer. The last time he'd almost got killed, almost got beat to death by the cop with the blue eyes. He wasn't human was why he could do it, nobody else alive could stand up and take it when he made his hand into a fist and his arm into a club—

—but the blue-eyed cop had taken it, had kept on coming, had almost killed him.

Couldn't be human. Couldn't be real. Must have been something else, a bad dream somehow living, somehow beating him to death on that rooftop.

Billy Boy stared out through the snow. Get rid of those thoughts, bad thoughts can haunt you, can bring you close to crazy, give you nightmares—

—Billy Boy hated it when he got like this, when the heebie-jeebies came, it was all luck, luck would make him fine again, make him brave again—

—not "again"—

—bullshit to "again"—

—he was brave *now*.

He stepped out onto the roof, looked around. The usual crap, the turret where the elevator went; far across, a ladder, a metal ladder curving over the side and down. Billy Boy let the door close behind him and started for the curving ladder, for the steps down, for a run through the snow, for a talk with the Duchess . . .

. . . now he sensed something. Nobody else would have but he did. Nothing moved, no sound, but he knew, all right, he knew. Slowly he turned toward the turret.

The one with the blue eyes was standing there.

Holding a gun.

Billy Boy stared across toward the ladder, back toward the door and the ladder was freedom, but to get to the ladder he had to go close to the turret and the door was behind him, right behind him, just a quick step behind him. Billy Boy went for the quick step, grabbed the knob.

Locked.

He whirled.

It was a nightmare, it was a nightmare, the cop was coming toward him now, silent in the snow, coming step by quiet step.

And there was murder in his eyes.

Billy Boy tried to run, stopped fast—

—because now the gun was raised. Raised and pointing dead at him. And now the blue eyes were narrowing. Billy Boy could see the tension starting in the trigger finger and he screamed *"Shit— shit don't—don't fucking do it shiiitt!!!"* But what good did screaming do when it wasn't human, when what was after you was something else, something different, something that if you made your hand into a fist and your arm into a club, it didn't care—

Just then Trude burst through the door hollering, "You put that goddam thing down!"

"Get away from him. —He's my prisoner—"

"—you get away, he's my patient—"

"—this is police business—"

"—and this is *government* business, now put that down!—"

Pause. Then, slowly, as Billy Boy watched, the arm holding the gun went down.

Trude turned. "Are you all right?"

Billy Boy nodded.

The blue suits were on the roof now and Trude was storming at them— "—one of you must have left his door unlocked—he could have gotten out no other way—I'll deal with that later, now take him back and calm him, give him food, make him warm—" then a wild look of exasperation came over him. "Never mind, I will tend him, no one can do anything correct here but me—" and he took Billy Boy by the arm, turning back to the cop saying, "You go to my office and you stay till I come, you are in a lot of trouble, I promise you." Then he said, "Come along, William," and they went back to the room.

"Why did you try and escape?" Trude asked quietly, when they were alone. "Because you didn't want to go back anymore?"

Billy Boy nodded.

"Well, I'm your friend, William, I always have been, but I would never make you suffer pain. I can only protect you if you are my patient. If you don't want to be my patient, you have done bad things, William, people have died. I can handle the police as long as you are mine, but if you want that ended, consider it ended. I'll send the one from the roof here to take you."

"*You keep him away!*"

"Are you sure? Don't make a hasty decis—"

"*—the fuck away!*"

"Whatever you want, William, I'll go deal with him now. You must rest, you must relax. In a few hours, I will need you."

Trude watched as Billy Boy lay back down. Then he left the room, listened as the door locked, went to his office and said, "It could hardly have gone better, don't you agree?"

"I don't frankly give a shit how it went," Eric said. "You got what you wanted, now it's my turn. I want to know what you did to Edith Mazursky."

"What we *tried* to do would be a more accurate way of putting it. We tried an experiment, but we failed."

"I don't think you failed," Eric said.

"What you think," Leo Trude replied, "is of titanically little consequence to me. Back at your apartment I told you the gist of what I'm doing. William Winslow can reach Theo Duncan. We had hopes of reaching Edith Mazursky."

"With Rosa Gonzales."

Trude nodded. "An insanely difficult little child. Most of the ultrasensitives we find are children, either chronologically or mentally. And they are impossibly difficult to locate. Most are frauds or insane. You have to take what you can get."

"And you took Rosa Gonzales and tried to get her to control Edith Mazursky."

"That was our intention, but, of course, we never made contact."

"You keep indicating that. Personally, I'm kind of titanically sure you're bullshitting me."

Trude whirled away, poured himself some coffee, sipped from the steaming cup. Then he said, "You're a very arrogant young man."

"Oh boy, is that praise from Caesar."

"You want answers—answers you'll get—but you'll get them only once from me so you'd best listen to your elders!"

Eric listened.

"Rosa Gonzales's mother went to a fortune teller. She brought Rosa along. The fortune-teller was a lookout for me. She recognized the child's potential sensitivity. The child was brought here and we tried to make contact with the Mazursky woman. Mazursky was of no special interest to us—we had no notions of having her do anything once we controlled her—she was simply the person the Gonzales child connected with, as Billy Boy connects with Duncan. We were just using her, to see what would happen, to see if we could really do what we thought we could. But as I said, nothing worked, we failed, and there is no point to talking any more about Rosa Gonzales, she was a psychotic, dead now, and of no loss to anyone."

"Like I'm sure the Duchess is dead now, and of no loss to anyone. The Duchess found both Billy Boy and Gonzales for you."

"You've been doing excellent homework—yes, she found them both—I have a number of lookouts, but the Duchess found these two—for which she was well paid."

"She should have been—because you didn't fail—you reached Edith Mazursky and fucked her mind around."

"Believe what you choose—but understand this—if you were right, it wouldn't matter. If I drove Edith Mazursky to take her life, well, of course, that is too bad for her immediate family, but in terms of what I'm doing, it matters not at all. And don't tell me she was one of God's good creatures, generous and kind to small animals—because Humanism was always a dubious concept, one which fortunately is dying day by day. And don't tell me she was a painter, because until recent centuries, artists were treated as little more than lepers, a position I don't find all that flawed. What matters today, all that matters today, is survival. And survival means weaponry. Superior weaponry. Period. End."

"I'm sure glad you're on our side," Eric said. "When you're done here, you might consider running the Red Cross."

Trude was about to reply when a nurse with light brown hair scurried in and Eric couldn't make sense of what she said, something to do with trouble with the sound of the wind, but whatever it was, Trude slammed down his coffee cup and stormed out of the room.

Eric picked up the phone, dialed Sally Levinson, spoke fast. "I promised you I'd call you so I am. The man responsible for the suicide is named Leo Trude, he's a doctor at Sutton Hospital. He looks like Henry Kissinger but not as warm."

"Was that a joke?" Sally asked.

"I don't feel like making jokes," Eric told her. He was about to say "Good luck" or "I'll see you" or something. For whatever reasons, he said "Good-bye."

He paced around after that because he had not slept in a day and a half and he knew he had to keep moving or drop. He felt rotten, reflexes slow, and that was too bad, because back in his apartment the "arrangement" he had struck with Trude involved Eric getting Billy Boy to be more agreeable in exchange for which Trude promised to hand over the giant when he was done with him.

Except Eric knew that was bullshit—Trude gave away ice in only very cold winters, and Billy Boy was obviously a prize to be kept. So Eric was going to have to be ready to use force, and you needed reflexes to do it well.

Trude was in the doorway then. "If you want to watch from the control room, I have no objection."

As they started out of the office, Eric said, "I didn't think you could make someone do, in hypnosis, things they wouldn't do ordinarily."

"In the first place, I can't be bothered with your misconceptions," Trude replied. "And please, don't worry yourself in this case. Theo Duncan is a murderer; at half-past two in a house on Gramercy Park, he killed Nelson Stewart. In very cold blood . . ."

6

THE MURDERER

Two hours before his death, W. Nelson Stewart was in a wonderful mood—except for the manure. The whiff of it was simply numbing, enough to buckle the knees of a Samson, and he was certainly no strongman. Nelson sat trapped in his carriage as traffic came sharply to a halt on Broadway.

Nelson took off his rimless glasses, cleaned them, put them back on, readjusted them carefully.

Traffic had still not moved. Fifteen minutes ago he had left his Wall Street office—he would have done better on foot.

He called up to his driver then: "Can you make out the difficulty, Jordan?"

"It's a frozen horse up at the corner, sir—it's causing all kinds of trouble; hard to get around."

Nelson sat back. He might have known. How many hours of his commuting life had he spent trapped because of frozen horses. Or simply dead ones in the warmer times. Tens of thousands of horses each year were abandoned on the streets of New York. The minute a horse snapped a leg on the unpaved avenues, their owners would desert them.

"I do want to get home soon, Jordan."

"I think conditions are improving up ahead, Mr. Stewart."

How could they fail to improve, Stewart wondered. This was the worst of all days for travel—cold enough at night to freeze animals, but warm enough at the noon hour to allow their perfumed aromas to rise from the streets.

In the old days, when he was rich but no one knew, he used to ride the horsecars to and from work. They were every bit as fast and much more comfortable, being on rails, than a private wheeled carriage. Nelson never minded being with dozens of other people twice each day. But when his wealth became common knowledge, he had to have a carriage—if he hadn't had one, people would have thought his business was in trouble, so there you were.

Uncomfortable in the extreme, he sat in his beaver hat and cashmere coat with the sable collar that his wife had insisted he buy because the Rockefellers had them.

Ahhhhh.

Movement.

The carriage passed Lord & Taylor's, passed Tiffany's, passed the great Broadway hotels where, at five o'clock, the handkerchief ladies would appear, dropping their kerchiefs for young bucks, arranging the financing then and there, before going around the corners to where the handkerchief ladies kept rooms.

They never allowed such behavior where he came from; they frowned on such open tawdriness in Boston. Ahead now, he saw a heavy woman trying to race safely across the street via the hopping stones; she held her skirt with one hand, was doing well enough until a horse reared beside her, reins tangled with the wagon alongside, and the woman lost her balance and sprawled into the muck.

I don't think I would much enjoy riding in a horsecar with that lady, Nelson decided. Perhaps the elevated trains everyone was arguing about were a solution. The El over on Ninth Avenue was already in operation, and it was filthy, and it constantly poured cinders on the citizens below—but at least you were above the problems of animal residue.

"Look out, sir!" Hastings cried, and just in time, for Mr. Stewart was able to brace himself before the sudden halt. He peered out. A barrel had fallen from a beer wagon, had split open up ahead. Now the aroma of beer began to spread.

W. Nelson Stewart sat in his carriage as around him were dray wagons and food carts and conveyances piled high with dry goods and horsecars and taxis and old women pushing pullcarts and old men pulling pushcarts and scavengers and hags and sledges and sleds; all the other vehicles that made up daily Broadway traffic, all of them congealing again, glued there, at least for a time.

I will not miss this commute when I move to Boston, W. Nelson Stewart reminded himself. I will not miss this at all . . .

* * * * *

Ninety minutes before she became a widow, Charlotte was in an absolutely fabulous mood—except for her husband. She lay alone on her bed, thinking about him. Ever since his return from his sudden trip to Boston, Nelson had been, well, just so terribly *nice*. Considerate even. He didn't snipe at the boys and he asked after her days as if he really cared about the answer.

Well, of course, he did love Boston. The city was more than likely responsible for the change. She herself, though she had never voiced her feelings, loathed the place. All the women so snobby, all the men so cold.

This new figure of the past days, this nice Nelson, troubled Charlotte because, well, how could she let her mind drift toward Theo with Nelson being human?

But her mind did drift toward Theo. The pale blue eyes, the brilliance. Fragile he was; almost that sometimes. His body so pale, his pink nipples the only color on his chest.

Charlotte closed her eyes and moved her lips to his words:

> Now folds the lily all her sweetness up,
> And slips into the bosom of the lake:
> So fold thyself, my dearest, thou, and slip
> Into my bosom and be lost in me. . . .

Nelson had said those words were effeminate. But what did Nelson know? About business yes, everything; about money, yes, everything.

About bodies? Charlotte let her mind drift easily toward her genius. He was lying beside her. She had undressed him. He was trembling, he wanted her so desperately. Charlotte moved toward him, undecided as to on which part of his body she should begin to feast . . .

An hour before the murder, Theo could hardly have been more joyous—except for his shoes. He sat in his workroom by the children's gymnasium, tried thinking about the poem he had half finished.

But his eyes kept staring at his shoes.

Not that there was anything wrong with them. Or anything unusual about them. They were the kind of shoes he had used all his life: wear alls. Where he came from in the Midwest, *everybody* wore wear alls. You put whichever foot you wanted into whichever shoe you wanted. Simple, efficient, no fuss over footwear.

Theo had heard of differentiated shoes of course, but they seemed the province of the rich, just another silly way for those with to lord it over those without. Wasteful, it always seemed to him, having a shoe curved so that it would only go over your left foot, another that would only take the right. Ridiculous, really; what if you were harder on the left, say, and it wore out while the right was still in its prime . . . With wear alls, no problem; you just bought a new shoe when you needed one. Of course, wear alls were, in order not to be uncomfortable, enormously large; clumpy in fact.

W. Nelson Stewart's shoes were not clumpy. He had his hand-made, and they made his not particularly small feet seem delicate. Theo envied the stern older man that delicate look.

But more than envy was this: Those differentiated shoes were a symbol. Theo was a poet, he was a tutor, he was an educated incompetent as far as finance was concerned.

And Charlotte was so rich. Even before Stewart, she had been brought up to all the better things, travel and new clothes and shoes that fit your feet.

How was he to match that?

True, Stewart was old, mid-fifties or thereabouts, but even if he dropped over and Charlotte came to him after an acceptable time, he could never receive her with that encumbrance. He was not about to go through life with the sneers of the world forever with him. "He was their *tutor,* didn't you know?" "Of *course* he married her for her money, the question is why did *she* marry *him*?" "She'll come to her senses, she was lonely, he was there, she'll leave him, what woman wouldn't leave a man who couldn't support her?" "Leech." "Bootlicker." "Toady." "Sycophant." "Parasite." "Minion." "Vassal." "Fool."

Theo jerked his mind away from those words, looked at his wear alls, jerked his mind away from them. He looked at the poem he was attempting. "Charlotte" was really an unfortunate name from a poetic point of view—the accent fell on the wrong syllable, *"Char*lotte." If it were the other way, "Char*lotte"* his road would have been ever so much straighter: "Camelot" or "polyglot" or "Aldershot" or "Forget-me-not" or—

—or "tommy rot" Theo decided, scratching out the beginning, starting over. He dipped his pen in the inkwell, closed his eyes, tried ever so hard to come up with a fresh rhyme for "Aphrodite . . ."

Half an hour before it ended for him, Nelson Stewart sat alone in his bedroom, trying to get his speech straight in his mind. He looked at his watch. Two o'clock straight up. No hurry at all.

He had arrived home considerably earlier, totally startling the staff who had not expected him till his usual hour. He told them not to fuss, that all he wanted was tea. Miss O'Connor, the biddy who had been with him for more than twenty years, informed him that Mrs. Stewart was resting in her bedroom. Let her rest, Mr. Stewart replied, I don't mind dining alone. Miss O'Connor fluttered away.

Returning several minutes later, gesturing for the kitchen staff to hurry. Mr. Stewart drank the tea and ate the tiny crustless sandwiches and, much to his surprise, gorged on the chocolate pastries, all of this under the careful eye of the biddy. She rested like a hummingbird in a corner out of his eyeline, but the instant he appeared to want anything, she pounced, fulfilling his desires.

The tea was the favorite thing Mr. Stewart had taken away from his honeymoon. The days in England were bitter damp, but the teas almost made up for the thoughtless weather.

The honeymoon should never have happened, Mr. Stewart told himself again and again, as he decided which pastry to go after now. He had watched Charlotte Bridgeman grow from her earliest squalling days into the rare teen-aged beauty he had decided on, the thirtyish woman who was now resting upstairs, thinking thoughts he had no desire to invade.

Decided on was really the operative phrase. Charlotte had no choice really, but to wed him. If she'd said no, she would have risked losing her father's love not to mention a good part of his income, because although he never said as much, Mr. Stewart would never have kept a lawyer who had been so unable to save him from humiliation.

No, Charlotte was not truly to blame for their present untenable situation. Nor was he. No heroines, heroes only in fables, fact was fact.

"Thank you, Miss O'Connor," Mr. Stewart said as he stood.

"Would you be wanting anything else?" she inquired.

"Confidence I think would be fine," he replied, leaving her

somewhat puzzled, but that was all right, no law against it. He walked to the foyer with the beautiful marble floor, then up the marble staircase to his room. He remembered the night not many nights before when he had crept up these same stairs, had caught them in their games from outside the window, had actually contemplated the violence with his pistol.

Logic was all that was ever truly needed. He went to his room then, sat alone going over and over what he wanted to say.

At ten past two, he decided he knew it as well as he ever would, and with steady step, went to Charlotte's room, knocked. "Nelson," he said.

From inside. "Home?"

"Evidently."

"Come in, come in."

He did. She was seated at her vanity, combing her dark hair. She glanced up at him in her mirror, smiled. "Is everything all right?"

"Quite the reverse, and we both know it."

She turned, faced him now. "Are you ill, Nelson?"

"Physically, no; but I have not slept much of late."

"You fooled me—you've seemed so placid since your return from Boston."

"It comes to this: Our marriage cannot be considered, by any yardstick one might use, a triumph."

"But—"

"—you must not cut me off just now, Charlotte, I'll get all untracked. Please. I promise you time for questions when I'm done."

She nodded.

"Alternatives. Number one: continue as we are. Two: divorce —" She was about to interrupt again, he could see it in her violet eyes, so he said, *"Please!"* with great firmness.

Charlotte held her tongue.

"Three: I could continue to live here, but set up another establishment nearby and perhaps people it with women who were rather fonder of me than I fancy you are." He paused. "I find all these unsuitable, totally, and I will have none of them. There is, however, a fourth, which is what I propose to take up with you now . . ."

* * * * *

It was almost a quarter past two when Charlotte heard her husband speak the word "divorce" and she almost cried out loud in panic.

What could he know, what could he know?

Nothing. They'd been so careful. When he was away in Boston, yes, but other than that, *care had been taken.*

What could he know, what could he know?

A touch here and there, a flick of eye meeting eye, but my dear Lord, Nelson had never raised his voice to her in great anger, had never been tempted to raise a hand, and now he was saying the unspeakable aloud.

Divorce would totally destroy her. She would be marked. Her father would be shattered, her family tainted. And Theo—my dear Lord, what would a creature like Theo do, a sensitive creator; he would take the guilt of the world on his shoulders and flee. Leave. Her. Alone. Without. Him.

I must have my Theo, Charlotte thought to herself. No matter what else, I must salvage that. She tried to pay attention to his words, but it was difficult.

What did he know, what did he know?

"There is, however, a fourth, which is what I propose to take up with you now."

Charlotte waited, trying to concentrate on anything, the tips of her fingers, the powder on the vanity, to help her maintain control.

"I would like us to have an 'understanding' and here it is: I would like to go to Boston to live: to set up a branch of the company there. Everyone knows my love for the city, no one would question my departure. You would remain here in the house with the boys. I would train down, you could bring them up. Holidays, that kind of thing. Then, soon, when they are old enough, I will enroll them at Andover. Twenty-eight miles from Boston, an excellent school, I doubt they are bright enough to gain entrance on their own, but perhaps I can influence that. The 'perhaps' was an attempt at sarcasm; all schools are short of funds. Andover will prepare them for Harvard or Yale, whichever they choose, I don't want to influence the boys unduly."

I don't think he knows anything, Charlotte decided then. It's all too gentle.

"One other point in the 'understanding' would pertain to you. I suggest I have a talk with my lawyer and set up some sort of trust

in your name. Since my lawyer happens to be your father, I'm sure
we can assume your best interests will be protected. This house,
of course, I will put in your name, yours to keep or sell as you
wish, it's probably too big for you, there are lovely places on Fifth
that might be more suitable. And several million dollars, perhaps
five, perhaps ten, we can wrestle with the numbers in the future
if you agree to all this."

"If?" Charlotte wondered. How is it possible not to agree. I
would be well taken care of, I would be alone, I could see the boys.
And I would have my Theo.

"People might talk, I'm sure, but I'm also sure people talk about
us anyway, an old fool such as myself, a young beauty such as you
are. So there it is, that is my version of an 'understanding'—we
would stay together in name, you would live here, I there, the boys
would be in boarding school, which we both agree is where they
can best be outfitted to face the world, you would be wealthy by
any standards with a life to do precisely what you want. Does that
seem fair?"

Careful, Charlotte cautioned. He knows nothing, don't give him
cause. "It's all too sudden a thing, Nelson; I don't know what to
say. You're very generous, but I would be alone."

"I suspect that's more true than you realize."

She looked up at him.

"There's one proviso to it all, Charlotte— One only, but crucial,
essential, the core."

Charlotte didn't much care what it was, but she felt obliged, out
of courtesy to this generous old man, to ask. So she did. "The
proviso being?"

"Give him up," Nelson Stewart said . . .

It was almost two twenty when Nelson Stewart wondered had
he been underestimating this woman all these years. She didn't
pale, she didn't deny, she didn't faint or ask "who?" or use any
other feminine wile. "Why?" was all she said.

"Because," he answered, "he is less than a man and I will not
have him superseding me in your life. I will not be publicly humiliated, it's as simple and as complicated as that."

"Why are you so frightened of him—because of his talent I
think. And because he is more of a man than you can conceive of."

"I admit, he is talented. Do you remember that poem of his you showed me?—I can't quote it but it was about lilies folding up, that sort of image. I was most disparaging about it, never mind my exact words."

"I remember the poem."

"I was wrong. It is not a bad poem."

"No."

"It's rather a good poem, actually."

"Yes."

"Even more than that, I suppose—it is a poem of incredible beauty."

"I agree."

"But alas it was not written by Theo—Alfred Tennyson, if I'm not mistaken, and I'm very much not mistaken. Your Theo may be as much of a man as you claim, my dear, but alas, he is also a plagiarist."

"I repeat: Why are you so frightened of him?—why do you feel compelled to lie?"

"You think I lie?"

"Of course."

"Well, let's get Theo up here and see . . ."

It was close to two twenty-five when Miss O'Connor appeared in his workroom doorway and said that the master requested him urgently. Theo stood, hurried out to the stairs, took them two at a time. He did not get summoned often by Mr. Stewart and he wondered, as he hurried along, if there was trouble.

When he got to the second floor, he could see them both in Charlotte's bedroom, so he knocked tentatively, entered as they requested.

"The lily poem was by Tennyson, yes or no?" Mr. Stewart said.

Theo had been dreading this moment, knowing it would come —he had tried so hard to write a great poem for Charlotte, but nothing matched the Tennyson. He had only done it because his love made him so deathly afraid to fail, and he had planned to tell her when the proper moment came. But this moment was many things, none of them proper. "It is mine," Theo said. "I agonized over it."

Charlotte came to him then, stood by his side.

"It is madness to lie—I can buy a hundred books by Tennyson tomorrow and prove it in every one—"

Theo turned to Charlotte. "He lies." He turned back to Mr. Stewart then, and was more than a little surprised to see him raising his fists as if to strike . . .

W. Nelson Stewart had not engaged in a fight since he was ten in Boston, but rage grabbed him so quickly now that he had no time to reflect on his lack of recent practice. The insanity of the young fool standing there denying what was so evidently true— he hadn't expected it, hadn't expected it remotely, didn't know how to deal with it.

So he struck, crazily.

He had no real intention of hitting Charlotte but she had a half smile on her face and she was moving in front of his tormentor, protecting him, and he hit her more out of instinct than anger, but that didn't make the blow any the softer. She staggered back and down to the floor and her hand went to her reddening face. Nelson was watching the effects of his actions, so he was taken by surprise when Theo attacked.

Attacked was really overstating it—Theo moved in his direction and bumped him with his shoulder and Nelson, unaware, went stumbling back against the wall by the door, which was where Theo joined the battle again, but this time Nelson was ready.

He was overweight and sixty—he had lied to everyone about his age, always had—but he remembered enough to lash out at Theo's face, and he missed, but he struck the shoulder, which took Theo's balance away. Nelson moved forward then, tried another punch, and now there was blood pouring from Theo's nose.

Theo turned, looked toward Charlotte, turned back, just in time for another punch that cut his lip. He fell back against the door, tripped down, tried to rise but Stewart had him then, had him with one hand, began slapping him with the other, till they both lost their balance and went to the floor, but now Theo, when he regained his feet, was outside the room in the second floor corridor and when Mr. Stewart appeared he was ready, butting the old man hard, sending him down, and when he was down Theo kicked but missed and fell against the banister, got his balance, tried to avoid the punch Stewart aimed for his face, couldn't quite. Dazed, Theo stayed upright as Stewart grabbed him by the throat, hit him again, again, was about to land a third blow when he stopped, breathing unevenly.

He felt tremendous swelling in his chest, Nelson Stewart did, and dizziness too, so he grabbed the banister and held tight to it, hoping whatever it was that was happening would pass.

Inside the room, Charlotte, back on her feet, heard the ruckus outside and ran toward it. She saw her husband poised by the banister and she was never sure why she shoved him, was it his accusations or her fear that he might be right; in the long run, it didn't matter, she shoved, and he fell back and over the railing, spinning out of control from the second floor corridor to the foyer floor below, the floor was marble, his skull was bone, no question which was harder . . .

7

THE STORM

"Is Central Park finished?" the bearded man wanted to know.

"Except for the squatters," his landlady said, after a pause.

"Squatters?"

"Yes, 'tis a terrible thing, but they can't seem to get them all out. There were hundreds of families in the beginning; only the hardy survive."

"I've heard so much about it," the bearded man said.

"You should go, especially you."

"Especially?"

"I meant considering your accent and all; they've planted over five million trees and shrubs, so they say, and many of them came from Scotland."

The bearded man nodded. He had been in his twenties before he came to America, and his early years in Edinburgh had formed his speech permanently. "I could walk there by dusk," the bearded man said. "It should be nice then. I like cold weather, the walk itself should prove bracing."

"Dusk on a sunny winter day," the landlady said; "you could hardly plan better."

"I'll go then." He stopped. He was a big man, six feet tall and two hundred pounds. The truth was, he had been six feet tall for many years, but only recently had scaled in at one hundred sixty-five. He was not quick, not anymore, and better safe than sorry. "There's no danger in the park at that hour?"

"Safe as a baby's smile, Mr. Bell," the landlady assured him . . .

Trude took the teat from Billy Boy's mouth, dropped it with the other toys. Then, quickly, he moved the giant back into the period between creation and birth. After that, he signaled to the control room to bring up the breeze and slow lapping waves.

It was two twenty now. There really wasn't much time. It was two twenty, the thirteenth of February 1981, and according to his researching the papers of the period, Theo Duncan killed the older man at half-past two, also on the thirteenth of February.

And according to his research on Bell, the Scot had taken a stroll into Central Park on the thirteenth, entering near dusk. Plenty of time for Theo to get there from Gramercy Park.

If Billy Boy could gain control.

And if that point was reached—*no,* Trude thought, no, not anymore, there were no ifs existing in his universe now, only certainties—so when that point was reached, Trude's main decision was how much information to burden Billy Boy with at the start—should he know, for instance, that there would be murder in Central Park?

Best not, Trude decided. Give the murder command when Duncan was *in* the park, not before, don't make the burden of transmission any greater than need be at the start. Just have Theo go to the place—take a weapon perhaps, no harm in that—just don't tell him what it will be used for.

Trude leaned close to the giant, spoke his "freedom" speech in all but reverential tones, made assurances that magic was Billy's and Billy's alone, spoke in awe of the greatness that was Winslow's alone, promised William he would be immortalized forever for his genius.

.
.
.
.
.
.
.
.
.
.

Fuck, Trude almost screamed. Two thirty had come and two thirty had gone and *nothing.* Trude tried to keep the anxiety from his voice as he preached the greatness of Winslow the traveler.

But in his heart, Trude thought only of Elisha Gray. The great inventor, the great unknown telephone inventor, the man who was forever the pathetic runner-up. Trude knew that feeling. Well. He had done so many brilliant things in his career. But never quite first.

Billy Boy was covered with sweat now. That was something. And he was breathing terribly deeply. And with the perspiration now came pain. Pain was better than "something." Pain was a wonderful sign. Trude picked up the pace of his preaching, deepening his voice, making his rhythms strong. He was like a minister now, and in fact, he was praying. Praying for control and after that, the glorious death of Alexander Graham Bell. I don't ask for much, God, Trude thought. Just a little blood. So much has been spilled in Your name, spill some now in mine . . .

Eric sat watching in the control room. He had no real idea of the actual specifics of what Trude was doing, but he was impressed with the general setup. The sounds were remarkably real and lulling.

He was not alone in the room. There was a nurse, there was a small man who ran the console that made the sounds. And of course, there were The Fruits. As soon as he had been introduced to them back in his apartment, and learned their names were Apple and Berry, he instantly dubbed them The Fruits in Blue Suits. Fruits for short. They were top quality standard government equipment. The kind that guarded the President or started uprisings in Guatemala.

And they were not going to be easy for him. They had guns, were undoubtedly not unacquainted with their use. If he was ever going to make a move on Billy Boy, and he planned very much on doing that, and as soon as the opportunity came, he was going to have to deal with them.

Or try to.

It wouldn't hurt to know where this room was in relation to the rest of the setup. Eric stood, stretched, indicated he wanted to go outside. The Fruits looked at him, then at each other, then nodded. Eric walked out into the corridor. It was two thirty-five. He glanced for a moment out the nearest window. Hours earlier it had started to snow.

Now it was becoming a storm . . .

From his window in Orient Castle, Phillip Holtzman studied the increasingly violent weather. The snow was getting so thick as to sometimes obscure his view of the Atlantic waves entirely.

Phillip fidgeted terribly, fingers drumming on the sill.

"There now, Mr. Holtzman," his nurse said gently. "Nothing to worry about."

The fret lines along Phillip's forehead deepened.

His nurse tried to lead him by his cane hand away from the view, but he shrugged her off, studied the murderous waters.

Phillip's nurse wondered if she should buzz for someone.

"They'll never land," Phillip said then. "They could just circle for hours."

"There now." Soothingly.

"Edith hates the landings," Phillip explained. "Most people, they get bad at the takeoffs. Edith was never like that. The landings, though, they bothered her." He squinted down toward the driveway in the front of the building. "Where's the car? How can I get to the airport if the car's not here?"

His fingers were wild now.

"You yourself said they'd probably circle for hours," his nurse reminded. "So there isn't any hurry."

"But I'd *be* there, don't you see? And she'll feel better knowing I'm down on the ground waiting." He started to make his way toward the door. "Don't try and stop me."

"You're just in a robe, you can't go to the airport dressed like that."

"Don't try and stop me," Phillip said again, and with effort, he lifted his cane above his head.

Doctor Horn appeared then.

"You either," Phillip said, brandishing his cane again.

Doctor Horn stepped away, opening the door wide.

Phillip made it that far, stopped, went outside into the corridor, stopped again, another few paces, slower, another longer pause.

"Let him alone," Doctor Horn said. "He'll be exhausted before he reaches the downstairs. Get him then."

"The weather brings this on," the nurse said.

"Everything brings this on," Doctor Horn said. He was moving slowly forward now, keeping Phillip well in view. Phillip carefully started down the stairs. Halfway down he had to sit. He dropped his cane then, put his head in his hands. "Phillip died when Edith did," Doctor Horn said. He looked at the nurse then. "You know what's sad? He's old, yes, and his mind is feeble, yes to that too. But his body is sound, and I'm afraid he's going to live on like this for years."

As he stared at the corpse of W. Nelson Stewart, Ryan realized he had never been as stunned by a dead body; he had been with the police force for a dozen years, had fought through many bloody battles in the war—Princeton and Gettysburg to name but two—but nothing he had seen before prepared him for the corpse he was staring at now.

He had never seen a rich man murdered before.

And not just any rich man; this was a famous one. W. Nelson Stewart himself, lying very still, blood still draining from his nose, from his half-bitten-off tongue. Rimless glasses, shattered, still clung to the left ear. Look at his clothes, Ryan thought. Look at his beautiful clothes. And the shine on the leather shoes. And the—

—it's a murder, he told himself, do something. He walked around the body, hoping he gave the appearance of efficiency. All he was really trying to do was put the events in order. He'd been walking his usual Gramercy Park beat, a chill but clear afternoon, nothing out of the ordinary when this aged biddy began screaming from the front door of one of the mansions and as Ryan hurried toward her, he knew it was the Stewart estate. He expected the usual: a cat in a tree, a pony misbehaving. But when he reached the old woman, he knew it was something a great deal more. He did not want to go inside—he had never come near the inside of such a place—and he was not sure that this screaming tearstained creature had the authority to let him enter, but her urgency was such he could do nothing but obey. So in he went. And there it was: a murdered millionaire.

Never any doubt of the murder. Before Ryan could as much as ask anything, this little blue-eyed small one was proclaiming his guilt. Over and over: "I did it; I did it; it was me."

The widow, so beautiful, Ryan thought, so pale, said nothing. Simply nodded in agreement.

"I did it."

Nod.

"I did it. It was me."

Nod.

The old biddy was the only one in the room crying. She knelt by the rich man, starting to keen.

Ryan, a big man, big and powerful with thick shoulders, felt glad of his strength. There was something odd about the entire setup, and he knew that if his brain failed him, he could always handle the situation with his might.

The fact was, he wasn't quite sure what to do. He'd been involved every now and then with a murder, but that had been saloon stuff, a burst of rage down in Five Points and a drunk dead on the floor. This was different. Different and strange. Why was the widow just nodding? Why was the little piece of fluff so insistent?

"Why did you kill him?" Ryan asked finally.

"Money."

Ryan nodded. It was beginning to make a little sense—whether it was the poor or the rich, money was usually in there somewhere. "Go on."

"He underpaid. I needed more. I asked. Instead of a raise he told me I was fired. I hated him anyway. I lost control."

Ryan was feeling more in command every moment—until without any warning whatsoever, the little skinny killer cried out and spun around and fell to the floor hard, writhing around.

Ryan was confused; obviously it was the dawning of what had been done that unhinged the little man, but the reaction was so unusual Ryan said, "Get him something," to the biddy, who looked up tearstained and red-faced and said "What?" and Ryan said, "Water, anything, but be quick about it," and the force of his voice got her moving.

When she returned with the glass of liquid, she handed it to Ryan. The murderer was sitting on the floor now, staring at nothing. Ryan gave him the water. It seemed to do the trick.

"Thank you," the killer said. And now he stood, handed the glass back to the biddy. He turned to Ryan now. "I have to go to Central Park," he said then.

Ryan was too stupefied to reply.

"I'm in a hurry now, excuse me."

Ryan stopped him easily, held the waif by the elbow.

"I have to go to Central Park!"

"I'm afraid your traveling days are over, son," Ryan said, firmly enough.

The killer jerked free.

Ryan grabbed him again, harder.

Again the killer jerked free.

Odd, Ryan thought. I had a good grip. That was his last thought for a while, because as he watched, the little man made his hand into a fist, his arm into a club, and struck.

Ryan dropped unconscious; he had little choice in the matter . . .

Sally Levinson sat alone in her Fifth Avenue apartment, watching the storm build. You could sense the power of it, feel its anger. Sally sighed, looked around the room at all the beautiful Mazurskys.

Then she looked down at her lap and the pistol, her father's heavy pistol. Old it was, but deadly too. Loaded and deadly and, when you lifted it, surprisingly heavy.

Sally lifted it now.

She stared at the thing, feeling more helpless than she could remember. If there was one thing she had avoided, or tried to, in her life, it was that quivering feeling of feminine weakness, the inability to accomplish without some man nodding and saying, "You can take a giant step, but *only* if you say 'May I.' "

Sally opened her mouth, put the barrel of the pistol inside, closed her soft lips around the metal, hesitated a long moment. It tasted like hell. She dropped the pistol back into her lap, and studied it, then the Madonnas. The pistol and the paintings. Back and forth, the paintings and the pistol.

Dead weight, both . . .

As he walked up toward Central Park, Aleck Bell could not recall a more beautiful afternoon. True, it was cold, but he hated the heat. When he left Edinburgh, he first lived in Canada and that was like his home, cold. Good and cold.

But his mood did not match the day. So many confusions to sort out. All he really was, all he really wanted to be, was a teacher to the deaf. And here, now, he was involved in the world of invention. Two years before, he had been elected president of the Articulation Teachers of the Deaf and Dumb—a genuine honor and deserved or not, at least he was not some outsider. He cared for the deaf—his fiancée Mabel Hubbard had been totally deaf since she'd been stricken with scarlet fever at the age of five.

He belonged with the deaf, Bell felt; he understood the deaf. He never was perturbed when he was in their presence, but he was perturbed now, worried about his invention, the patenting of it, the odd business with Elisha Gray—

"If you please, sir."

Bell stopped at the corner to let a carriage go by, but stopping was a mistake on Fifth Avenue, because of all the beggars.

"If you please, sir," the beggar said again. This was a surprisingly young man with a scarred face and the left hand gone. In his right, he held a cup. He wore, Bell noted, his war uniform.

Bell dropped a coin into the cup, moved to the hopping stones, hurried on. It was extraordinary, the number of beggars on the streets, so many of them from the war. He had read the figures once: forty thousand dead from New York State, half of those from the city. And untold wounded from the city too. Thousands upon thousands. Many of them had decent jobs. Many more were taken care of by their families.

But the maimed seemed to beg.

And they were so young, many of them; so painfully young and ruined. But then, it had been just ten years plus since Appomattox.

Now a blind one loomed ahead, a small child guiding him.

Bell put another coin in this cup, moved around the two, buoyed because ahead now he could see the treetops of the park. Then he thought of Gray again, and the buoyancy deflated. He had been told of an article in *The New York Times* in which Gray had referred to what he was working on as a "telephone." And had sent the sound of some tune or other hundreds of miles and a Western Union official had said that someday they would be able to transmit vocal sound, voices, over wires.

After all these years, after so many hours, what a torment it would be to come in second. Bell wondered how he would survive such an eventuality.

Perhaps not all that well.

Occasionally, ideas were current. In the air. Others were working on the transmitting of voices. Bell knew that. And back in the gloried days before Jesus was selected, there were many sincere Messiahs. The idea of a Messiah was in the air. And probably there were many, dust now, forgotten dust, who licked their wounds in envy as the carpenter became legendary.

Bell stopped.

For there it was. Just across the street. The gloried park. He was about to enter when the most unsettling vision of all moved beside him: half a man. Half a man, a legless beggar. He had a thick chest and what must have been powerful arms, for he propelled himself along surprisingly quickly. His thickly gloved hands pushed into the ground and he tilted his half body forward at an angle and when it came to rest the arms switched from behind the body to well in front and then the body tilted forward again.

He stared up at Bell, the most appalling look in his bulging eyes. He held his cup in one hand, but did not raise it entreatingly.

Odd, Bell thought.

He turned his attention to crossing the street, which he did quite rapidly, leaving the half-man considerably behind. Now Bell stopped and stared at the beauty. The trees, the walks, the glory of it all. Central Park. Four o'clock. Dusk.

Ahhhh . . .

Theo raced out of the house and turned toward Lexington Avenue. He wore a knit sweater and a scarf and a wool coat and cap and in his pocket he carried the sharpest small knife in the kitchen.

Why the knife, why the knife?

He ran on, knowing one thing only, and that was he had to get to Central Park immediately.

But why the knife?

He hoped he would find a hansom cab to take him straight to the park but when he got to Lexington there were none in sight. Now here came a horsecar. Take it or not? It wouldn't go straight to the park, he would have to get off at 59th and run to Fifth. Take it or not? He looked in vain for an empty cab.

The horsecar stopped, he got in, paid. It was pulled along by a single horse and there were thirty other passengers along with him, but the beast made good time. Theo took out the knife, looked at it closely. The edge was a razor, the point needle-sharp.

A woman across was watching him.

"It's a knife," he told her quietly.

She moved away.

The horsecar continued quickly on. Theo tied his scarf around his throat, pulled his cap down. Cold. It was getting cold. No point in catching cold. Odd—he was a poet but there were no rhymes —only cold, cold, cold—

—the horsecar came to a sudden halt.

Theo jumped up, ran to the driver, asked; in reply the driver pointed up ahead—

—half a dozen pigs were fighting in the middle of Lexington Avenue.

Around them were as many foreigners, all shouting at the animals, at each other, trying to get the situation straightened out without being bitten.

"I must get to the park," Theo said.

The horsecar driver looked at him. He worked seventeen hours a day and his salary for those hours was two dollars and fifty cents. He was in no hurry.

"Central Park," Theo said.

The horsecar driver folded his arms, waited.

Theo gave a cry, jumped from the vehicle, ran to the foreigners, pushed them aside, grabbed the nearest pig, lifted it, threw it across the road. Then he grabbed the second, threw that. The third was an enormous animal and as Theo grabbed it it tried to bite him but he clubbed it and threw it the farthest of all—

—the other pigs ran—

—so did Theo, back to the horsecar. He stared at the driver and said "Central Park!" very distinctly, and the driver, frightened, took out his fear on his beast, which never made better time to 59th Street, Theo's stop. He raced the remaining blocks to the park.

It was dusk when he got there . . .

". . . PARK . . ." Billy Boy said.

Trude stood beside the giant. The perspiration had never been this thick, the pain this evident—but the connection had never been this strong. It was almost like taking part in an ordinary conversation. "The time?"

". . . FOUR . . ."

* * * * *

That was the moment when Bell went wandering. Down in the lower area, near Fifth, near the trees, by the pond. "Kill him," Trude said then. "Now, right now, kill Bell."

". . . *NO!* . . ."

It was the first time he had ever been questioned by a test person. For a moment he was halted by the single negative syllable. Then he moved close and began to whisper at first, gradually building.

"Evil.
  The man is evil.
  The man must die.
  Bell.
  Bell is evil.
  Bell must be taken.
  Taken away."

The breathing was deepening again. Heaving desperate inhales. Trude continued his hymn.

"You
  You are the blessed.
  Taking evil away is blessed.
  You must take evil away.
  Now.
  Bell must be taken.
  Taken and killed.
  Kill Bell!"

Trude waited, watching as the giant's body trembled. Then:

". . . KILL BELL . . ."

The shadows were deepening, the park beginning to empty, but Aleck could not bring himself to return to his boardinghouse quite yet. The tranquillity of the place held him—hundreds of species of trees, all brought here to this magical place in the center of a giant city. Above him, he saw some red-winged blackbirds changing branches.

Tomorrow he would find peace—tomorrow the patent would be in and over and done. No more worry. He had no idea of the future of his telephone but he felt confident there would be uses.

Some, assuredly, would benefit the deaf.

Behind him now, the half-man was studying his sad reflection in the pond. Some departing citizens gave him money, though he did not openly solicit anything. Hard, Bell decided, if you were a veteran, a beggar, to suddenly alert the public that all you wanted was some quiet in the park.

Bell turned for a moment, peered toward the west side of the park. Somewhere, he had heard, ground was already broken for what was to be a splendid building for the wealthy. Enormous apartments with high ceilings and workmen imported from Italy. It was doubted that the rich would want to live in such proximity to each other, much less would they want to live as far away from everything else of interest in the city as 72nd Street.

And then Bell heard his name.

Or thought he did, at any rate. Now it came again, from some distance through the chill twilight air. ". . . Bell . . . Bell . . ."

Aleck peered across the pond and there, although he could not see the face clearly, was a small man calling his name over and over. I must know him, Aleck thought, but it was too far and too dim to see clearly. He had friends in New York, but a few only, and this clearly was not one of them.

Perhaps a fellow Bostonian. More than likely. The calling continued on. ". . . Bell . . . Bell . . ." No one else was answering. There were, in fact, few around to answer. He must mean me, Aleck decided, but what a fool he'd be if such was not the case.

Risking it, Aleck raised his hand, shouted "Over here."

The small figure broke into a run around the pond. Aleck waited where he was. A wild run. The fellow was certainly in a terrible hurry. And when he was halfway round the pond, Aleck was fairly sure he had made a mistake, that in fact, he did not know the fellow at all. When the man was less than twenty yards away, Aleck knew without question it was most definitely a mistake, because no one of his acquaintance had the wild-eyed look of this one running now.

The size of the mistake Aleck realized only when it was too late for him to move, and he saw the knife brandished so tightly in the tiny madman's hand . . .

Theo stood in Central Park and turned around and around and around. It had been so essential that he get to it, and now that he was there, now that the great trees surrounded him, he hadn't the least idea what to do.

So he turned.

Now a departing couple were looking at him, the man so well-dressed, cravat and cashmere coat, the woman lovely, clinging tight, laughing.

I better stop turning, Theo decided. I think she's laughing at me.

So he stopped.

What to do, what to do?

He took out the knife, fingered it.

Why the knife?

It was sharp. Cook kept the kitchen immaculate, and this knife was honed.

But why the knife?

He looked toward the pond, as if to find solutions in the dark waters. None were there. *Pond* was a fair word, if you were a poet. There were some rhymes—*blond*, *bond*, *beyond*—that were useful, but few that were more than that. *Frond* was difficult to make anything but obvious—a frond in a pond, who cared? If you were a poet, a real poet, then that was all you did, you cared, nothing mattered so much to you as words and their grace and their sounds and the pictures they brought forth when they were linked unexpectedly—

—and I am a poet, Theo remembered. A real one.

So why am I here with a knife in my hand?

What use had a poet for a knife?

Not a bad opening line, that: "What use had the poet for a knife? What use had the child for a life?"—no, wrong turn, simpleminded, no echoes, wrong, wrong—

—*Kell* filled his mind then.

Theo could feel his heart. Was that a word? *Kell?* Did it have a meaning? It was in his brain, it was filling his brain, his head was swollen with the constant repetition: *Kell. KELL. KELL!!!*

Theo began to turn again, his hands pressing against his ears to still the nonsense word—

—then the word divided, the last letters going with a name, the first with the word "kill." "Kill Bell. Kill Bell."

Why?

And who was Bell?

The why didn't matter. Bell was evil. Bell was evil and had to be taken away.

Now he understood the knife.

"Bell," Theo shouted. "Bell. Bell. Bell. Bell." He turned toward the pond and went on with his litany. "Bell. BELL."

Now, from across the pond, from a large bearded man, a raised hand, the shouted words "Over here."

Theo began to run. He had never been a runner but he was racing now. He had never been fast but he was flying now. He was not surprised. He had never been strong but the pigs had been sent flying, the policeman had fallen senseless to the floor.

Theo went even faster. Halfway round the pond, halfway more to go. Faster. Now the knife was in his hand. Quarter to go now. He could see the evil ahead of him. He could see fear in the evil eyes. He could see the evil wanting to move, but no time, as Theo leapt with a wild cry into the air and landed on the much larger man, and together they went staggering back as Theo struck with the knife, could feel the blade rip the thick overcoat, slice through it toward the heart . . .

As Billy Boy began to roll from side to side, Trude watched, wondering what it all meant. Now the giant's hands were moving —one moment they made fists, the next the fingers spread and were attacking his own throat.

It must be a reaction to what we've done, Trude decided. He had never had control this long or this closely.

That's it. Yes. It must be simply that. A normal reaction to what we've accomplished. Then Billy Boy began to cry out wildly.

". . . STOY . . . STOY . . . STOY . . ."

What in the world was that supposed to mean? Trude wondered. Now there were other sounds. Pouring out.

". . . UZ-BEET-ZU—UZ-BEET-ZU . . ."

The words were coming so fast they meant nothing—they all were a terrible blend of gibberish at this time when nothing mattered but fact. Now, at this moment of pure scientific truth, insanity seemed to have taken over. Here came more sounds, louder than the ones before.

*"INATCHI-YA UB-EE'-YU-TIBYA—TIBYA—BANDEET—
BANDEET—UZ-BEET-ZU!!!!"*

Madness, Trude thought as the giant was starting to writhe.
It was impossible to ask questions, to find out what it all
meant, there were no questions that could penetrate the
screaming.

". . . TIB-YA . . . TIB-YA—TIB-YA!!!"

Son of a bitch, Trude thought. Goddam rotten fucking son of
a bitch—*what was going on back there . . . ?*

The instant he jumped, knife ready, onto the bearded man,
Theo felt something land on him; the instant he plunged his knife
through the coat toward the heart, Theo saw a hand cover his
own—

—and try to pull it back.

Theo merely shoved harder—this was the hand that had felled
the cop, this was the arm that had lifted the pigs—nothing could
force it back—

—but something was. This hand that was covering his hand,
this hand that was pulling at his hand, pulling the knife away from
flesh, it was, for the moment, stronger.

The three of them fell then, the bearded man, balance gone,
twisting down, Theo slipping off, rolling away, knife held ready,
and in an instant he was on his feet and staring at the one who
had so intruded on the disposing of evil.

Theo stared at a half-man.

Huge chest and shoulders, great bulging eyes. *"Stoy,"* the half-
man said.

Bell was getting to his feet slowly, shaken and terrified.

Theo raised the knife again and ran at him.

The half-man threw his body at Theo's legs and they both went
sprawling. *"Uz-beet-zu."*

Bell was starting to run away now.

Theo scrambled up, gave chase.

But the half-man scuttled into his path, grabbed Theo's scarf,
twisted it around his throat and began to take away Theo's air.
Theo slashed out with the knife.

The half-man released the scarf, ducked away from the blow, muttered more words.

Bell was in full flight now, away from the park. Full speed.

Theo looked at the half-man—more evil. More evil that had to be disposed of. The half-man was making more sounds. Theo ignored them and silently closed for the kill . . .

As Billy Boy became silent, Trude stepped alongside and asked some questions, received some answers. Now Billy Boy was saying the words again, but slower.

"*. . . STOY INATCHI-YA UB-EE'-YU TIBYA . . .*"

"Stop or I'll kill you," Trude translated. He was not a great linguist—four fluent, smatterings of half a dozen more. Not great, but good enough to know Russian when he heard it. Trude wanted to throw his head back and shriek in wild fury.

Trying for the least semblance of control, he left the Infinity Room to call Washington, because there was no doubt about it: The Russians were back there too.

Theo held the knife balanced well in front of him as he advanced on the freak.

The half-man scuttled backward, staying clear.

Theo continued his advance. The pond was coming up behind the enemy now, so the retreat could not last forever. Now the freak noticed the water, glanced to one side, then the other, looking for a place to scurry to. Theo continued his gradual advance—

—and the half-man leapt on him—

—yes, "leapt" was what he did, somehow he thrust his arms hard into the earth and bent them and straightened them and then that horrid body was in the air and then it landed crablike across Theo's chest and clung to the knife arm, trying to force the weapon free—

—but Theo hung on.

Now the half-man pounded a fist into Theo's face and blood spurted from his nose.

Theo cried out and lifted the freak off him—lifted him with his own blood still pouring down, and threw the enemy like he had thrown the pigs—

—the freak rolled over, pushed down with his mighty arms, and was ready for more.

Theo ran at him then, slashed with the knife but it was a fake and when the freak went for it, Theo kicked out with his shoe and caught the enemy on the side of the head, knocking him off balance, stunning him, and then Theo went with the knife again, meaning it this time, and he was thrilled at the scream of pain as his weapon entered the left forearm of the enemy.

But with his right arm, the freak grabbed a rock and threw it, missed, grabbed another, and Theo's mind was gone for a moment as the rock glanced off his forehead and in that moment the freak was behind him and again he had the scarf, pulling it tighter and tighter around Theo's throat, and Theo could not reach the monster, could not make physical contact, and now he was gasping for any air at all, but there wasn't much, and the scarf was tighter than ever and if Theo had not slashed the scarf with his knife and cut it free he would have never survived that.

But he did. Survive. Gasping terribly. Retreating. With the half-man advancing now. It was incredible. He, Theo, had the weapon, but the enemy was doing the attacking.

Theo waited.

Now they began circling each other. Like animals circling some prehistoric fire. Only now, the fire was within them. The half-man's eyes glowed. The park was silent.

Circling . . . Circling . . .

"Tibya."

Circling.

"Tibya."

Circling.

Theo began to growl . . .

Trude threw the door to his office open, stormed to his desk, started to dial Washington, momentarily forgot the area code, told himself to get a grip, dialed 202 and then Kilgore's number. As he waited he thought he saw a shadow outside in the corridor, decided it had to be the policeman shadowing him, but he didn't care. There were no secrets anymore.

"What is it?" Kilgore said.

Trude tried very hard to make his voice seem calm. "The Russians are controlling someone as we are controlling Duncan. They are in violent confrontation now."

"How, for Jesus' sake?"

"I don't know how—I don't care how—we know what they're doing, why shouldn't they know what we're doing, *it doesn't matter how*—what matters is what we do about it. I need your approval to alter plans so completely. Do we continue on? Do we call a halt? Do we forget about Bell and concentrate on Trotsky? That would be my suggestion—Duncan may be dead by now—"

"—I'll have to ask Beulah—you need my approval, I need his —stay right where you are—I'll have him call you directly . . ."

"—there is no time!"

"Are you falling apart on me now?—you sound it—*I'm telling you to wait*—"

Trude took a breath. "I'm perfectly fine. And of course I'll wait. When I said there was no time I meant I left Winslow as he was —I did not want to risk bringing him out, the control was too strong—but that does not mean he can't come out of it by himself —if I leave him too long, that may happen."

(It had already happened, but Trude did not know it yet—Billy Boy was on the loose in the Infinity Room, but that would not become common knowledge for at least another minute, when the nurse with the light brown hair would begin to scream . . .)

At first, staring at the strings of lights above his head, Billy Boy could blink and wonder. He was alone, he realized then. Trude had left him.

He blinked again, made as little movement as possible, got a sense of the room. The control room was the obvious place to go, but he did not want to start until he was ready. He tensed his legs; they felt strong. So did his arms. He took a breath, another. He was fine. There was some pain in his head but nothing like the other times. He was fine, and then he was off the couch and running so fast and the control room door, it was like paper it gave so fast and he was through it and the blue suits were stunned he was on them so quick, and the near one got his gun only into his hand while the far one got his raised, but shit, that was nothing, they weren't about to use their guns on him, he was too valuable for them to do a goddam thing and before any firing he was on them and creaming them and then he had their pistols and the nurse with the light brown hair began to scream and Billy Boy thought what the hell, kill her and shut her up, kill her and kill the blue suits too, except that was dumb, that wasted bullets, and bullets were what he needed now as he broke toward the stairs and freedom . . .

When Trude left Billy Boy alone in the Infinity Room and stormed through the control area, Eric had never seen a look of such blind anger. It drew him, that look, there was nothing doing in the room now but that look must have meant a lot, so when Trude got to his office Eric was outside and he didn't get the whole call, just Trude's part of it, and he didn't really learn that much, and he was set to return to the Infinity Room anyway when the screams of the nurse made him run. He passed The Fruits on the way and they looked some the worse for wear and when he reached the control room the brown-haired nurse made enough sense to point to the stairwell and Eric raced toward it, getting his own gun ready as he moved. He assumed Billy Boy was armed too, he didn't know but it was always best to figure on the worst and the worst would have been Billy Boy had one of The Fruits' guns. What Eric did not know was that he had them both, a piece of information that, before too much longer, would cost him, alas, dearly . . .

By the time they reached Trude's office, Apple and Berry were rearmed and ready. So was Trude—he handed one of them the pistol that stunned Billy Boy unconscious, along with a dozen pellets; he handed the other a walkie-talkie so they could maintain contact. When the phone rang and he heard the southern voice of R.E.L. Beulah, they were already out the door on the fly . . .

—where?—where the fuck was he?— Billy Boy glanced up through the storm and he saw a street sign but it meant shit to him —he was in the 50's, he was near First—who gave a shit?—
    —*where was he?*—
    —he glanced back at the building he'd just left and even though he was only maybe half a block away it was hard getting a decent look at it. The sidewalks were pretty much empty on account of the snow and it was dark and cold and who the hell knew what time or cared—

—what was he gonna do?—

—maybe the Duchess, maybe not a bad idea, he was lucky again, you didn't make escapes on days when you weren't lucky, so maybe she could tell him what to do—

—*but where was she?*—

—near the bus place, she was near that, but what was the name of the bus place, in a town like this there were probably a bunch of them and maybe he'd get the wrong one and freeze to death walking around—

—ahead of him now a bunch of asshole kids sledding—*sledding* for Chrissakes—running along and crying out loud and here came a kid right at him on his sled and Billy Boy lashed out, gave the kid a good kick, caught him on the neck, sent him shrieking into the side of a parked car and that felt like the old days, a good solid shot, you aimed and you hit and that was what it was like when you were lucky and—

—and he glanced back again toward the hospital and here he came running down the stairs, *the nightmare*. Billy Boy stopped, and fired a shot and was about to fire another when he thought, "Asshole, you can't hit shit from here, *run . . .*"

Eric felt terrific when he heard the gunshot. One bullet gone, five more to go. And it was a fool shot, you couldn't hit a thing from that distance in this snow, and you only fired if you were panicked.

Eric felt terrific about that, too.

At last it was back to where it belonged, just the two of them, one gun against the other and it crossed Eric's quirky mind that what a cosmic joke it would all turn out to be if it was just him against Billy Boy and Billy Boy won—

—the face of the boy with the sled made him stop. Blood came from his ear and his neck was tilted all wrong, like the very first moment he knew of the invasion of the monster up ahead, when he'd seen the neck of the dead woman at the terrible angle. Eric dropped beside the kid, shouted to the others around not to move him, gave them the number to phone for an emergency ambulance, threw off his own topcoat, placed it so it guarded the wounded boy from the storm. He did all this quickly and was back on his feet in no time. But no time was too much time.

When he reached the corner, Billy Boy was gone . . .

* * * * *

As his beautiful Mercedes crawled inch by fucking inch down Second Avenue, Hubert J. Hutner could never remember having been as angry at his wife.

She sat beside him now, a silent fireplug. Silent except for cracking her gum. "Almost there; we'll be at the Waldorf any sec," Mrs. Hubert J. Hutner said.

"Is that spearmint or what?" he asked her. "I want to know what flavor's killing me." He took one hand off the wheel, gestured a sign: "Here lies Hubert J. Hutner, dead of Dubble Bubble."

She stared silently out into the storm.

Traffic was murder. *Murder.* Not that many cars but those that were out were crawling. Let me count the reasons I hate her, Hubert J. Hutner decided, to calm himself. I hate her because of the traffic. I hate her because when she married me she was five two, one hundred and five, and curvy in the right places whereas now even her wrists are curvy—she would never tell him her weight anymore but he knew it was over one seventy-five. I hate her because she insisted we go to this goddam heart fund benefit at the Waldorf because her hairdresser insisted he *knew* that Frank Sinatra was going to make an unscheduled appearance.

He tripped on and on, coming up with any number of good and valid reasons, but the chief one was this: He hated her because she insisted he drive from Great Neck to Manhattan in his Mercedes.

He'd told her it was going to snow, so they should take the train but she was having none of it—she would not go from the station to the Waldorf and *ruin* her formal.

So they took the Mercedes. Hubert's Mercedes. His new, *chocolate* Mercedes. He loved it. There was not a Rolls in the world he would trade it for.

But already on this trip he had been bumped twice from the rear by cars unable to stop. Each bump took, he figured, maybe a year off his life.

"And you wanted to take the train," Candy Hutner said.

Candy. What a name. Another reason to hate her.

"I could have wrung this dress a year and it never would have gotten dry if I'd walked from the station to the Waldorf."

"When you crack your gum, that way you don't talk so much; please crack your gum." He peered out into the evening, trying to decide whether he should force his way into the next lane over to the right.

Now a big guy was standing by his window, pounding on the glass.

"Quit that!" Hubert Hutner snapped.

From outside: "Give me your car—"

"Whaat?"

And now the big guy was yanking at the locked door, trying unsuccessfully to open it.

"Quit that!"

"I want your car now get out—"

"—buy your own Mercedes, *asshole!*"

The big guy started away, then turned back and when he turned there was a gun and then there were two shots and shattering glass and the blood actually leapt from where it had been sequestered, in Hubert Hutner's heart . . .

—*run,* that was the message, *run,* don't look back, *run,* something might be gaining on you—so when he got to the corner Billy Boy ran straight into traffic right across the street and he didn't look back to see if the nightmare was following—

—how could he have fired that one shot?—

—he forced his way to the far sidewalk and then he surprised himself even, because instead of going on in a straight line he ducked over, hunched way over and began running with the cars, but you couldn't see him, not if you were where the nightmare was, no, he was invisible, he was gone, safe and gone—

—he ran and ran always hidden by the snow, hidden by the height of the car roofs.

But it was slow going.

Slow and cold.

The cars looked warm—but the traffic was shitty, no point in getting into a car, not when you could make better time on foot —the snow was beginning to swirl around now, the winds picking up, making it even worse for the cars.

He continued his bent-over way uptown, running, passing a side street, running, passing another side street, running—

—hold the fucking phone—

—the side streets weren't so bad—you could almost make time on the side streets, so if you got yourself some wheels and turned off the main drag you could maybe *move*—

—here came this chocolate job, a fat broad chewing gum sitting by a skinny guy at the wheel. Chocolate and foreign, expensive, shit that was great, when he got done moving in the thing he could probably sell it for a ton, so he grabbed the front door by the driver's side—

—locked—

The skinny guy yelled out at him and he yelled in and pulled harder and yelled again and again came the reply, and he felt pretty tough, the skinny guy did, locked and safe, and "—buy your own Mercedes, *asshole!*"

Billy Boy turned away, what the hell, the car was locked, the next one would probably not be, he'd take the next one, he'd—

—no—

—there were some things that just didn't go, and no skinny shitface could call him names, not that name, not "asshole!" with that cruddy rich look on his face and then one of the guns was in his fist and two quick shots and who was the asshole now?

The next car was locked too and the car after that was full of four guys and they were no problem, he'd taken on more than four in his time and come out ahead but what was the point, none, not when the next car had a lady alone in it and she didn't know what hit her as he grabbed the door open with one hand, clubbed hard with the other, shoved her over, got inside, took the wheel in his hands—

—he'd never driven, not in the Apple, close to it, on the trip in, but here he was, behind the wheel, his own boss, ready to roll—

—except the goddam traffic wouldn't move.

Ahead was a cross street. Not a bad one. Half a block ahead and he could gun it good. But Christ, that half block, it was forever. The snow was bad and the wind was bad and people were honking and behind him the fat woman who'd been in the chocolate job was standing in the street screaming her fat rotten lungs out—

—and the traffic still wouldn't move.

Shit! He reached over, took the woman slumped beside him and tossed her in the back on the floor—who needed her staring at him all the time. He kept her purse, opened it, grabbed the billfold. *Eighty bucks!*

His luck was beginning to change.

Eighty bucks and now the traffic was starting to move.

Definitely changing.

Eighty bucks and the cross street coming up and Billy Boy took

it and gunned the motor just for the hell of it, just for the freedom
of it, because there was nothing to stop him now, he owned all the
luck and it was coming up sevens and then he screamed "Jesus"
and held to the wheel—

—because in the rearview mirror now another car was closing,
and the driver of that car was him, the cop, the cop coming to get
him, his nightmare come to get him through the storm . . .

The emotional swings of the last few days had been like nothing
Eric had ever experienced before, but as he stood on the corner
of Second Avenue in the blizzard with his quarry gone, he was
overtaken—it was as if a blanket had been thrown, covering every
inch of him—with despair.

Every instinct told him that tonight was it, Armageddon, tonight there would be blood on the moon—except Billy Boy was
gone.

Eric stood in the snow, scanning the car-clogged street, trying
to see the sidewalk through the white. His clothes were soaked
from the snow now and his hair too, but he felt it not at all and
could have cared less.

Now he began to move—first uptown, then abruptly, for no
reason, down. He began to run, more out of frustration than need,
jogging along the slippery sidewalk, peering into the stores as he
passed, trying to catch a glimpse inside the cars—was anybody
acting funny, were there clues he was missing, was there unusual
behavior he should be able to spot?

He spotted nothing.

Not thing one!

Eric stopped. Uptown was better maybe. He turned, started
that way. Then he decided that he was going too fast. When you
went too fast you missed things.

Eric slowed.

Slowed and paid close attention now to everything, all his senses
ready—a fruit store, the woman behind the counter, did she look
afraid, was there someone out of sight that was scaring her.

He moved suddenly into the store, gun ready—

—that really scared her. The poor bitch gasped and paled and
Eric got the hell out before things got more complicated.

Back in the street he continued to prowl, probably would have
gone on as long as his legs would take him. He would circle around

this area forever if he had to, he would walk the world away if he had to, he would—

—gunshots—

Eric whirled.

—gunshots behind him.

Where though? Below him, yes, but where, which car, he couldn't tell for sure as he ran toward the area. He moved off the sidewalk now, racing between the jammed cars as he headed toward where the sounds had come from more than a block below. It was slow, he couldn't make time, the snow and the jammed cars blew that possibility, but he did what he could wondering where the hell exactly he was headed. But then he knew. Where. Exactly.

Because half a block below him a fat lady stood beside a car in the street and screamed and screamed and—

—and just below her now there was Billy Boy—in a car, his giant shoulders filling the front seat and edging toward the side street that headed toward Third. Eric threw a cab door open, said "Out" to the driver and the customer behind. He flashed his badge and his gun but neither of them wanted to move.

The passenger in the back was a Wall Streeter and he informed Eric getting another cab would be impossible.

"I just put on snow tires," the driver said. "And I had the motor overhauled—I put a bundle in this baby and—"

"I'll blow you both away," Eric said very quietly, and of course it was a lie, he would never have done such a thing, but they had no way of knowing that and evidently they believed him because their evacuation was more than fast enough and Eric made a wild right turn, scraping the hell out of the cab and another car but who cared, not now, nothing mattered now—

—now that he had Billy Boy in his headlights.

As he entered the cross street, Eric thought about the shots— two, it sounded like. Definitely two. That made a total of three. Three bullets gone, three to go.

They were more than halfway to Third Avenue. Up ahead the light had just turned red.

Good.

And there were several cars waiting by the light, blocking the street.

Better and better.

Eric gunned the cab and the snow tires bit and the car moved easily and well and he was closing in now, was getting there when he knew that Billy Boy had spotted him—his car, it was a Chevy, picked up speed suddenly. Or tried to. Its wheels spun, snow flew from the wheels but the car wasn't responding all that well.

Eric picked up his pace even more. The light was still red and the cars still blocked the way so Eric moved his gun from his left hand to his right, ready to fire the instant he had Billy Boy cornered—

—which was when Billy Boy spun his Chevy up onto the sidewalk, managed to get it straightened, and roared toward Third Avenue.

Eric had no choice but to follow and Third was the total reverse of Second, Third was almost empty, the street must have been tied up down below, nothing getting through for now and Eric watched as Billy Boy slid across the street, the car motor roaring, but he was having trouble, no traction, and he was still trying to get it going when Eric blasted broadside into the Chevy and both cars went flying across the avenue, Billy Boy crashing into a parked car, gunning the motor again, starting forward with Eric turning more easily on his tail and for a moment it was like some lethal game of bumper tag, the cab and the Chevy, careening across Third, and Eric got him again at the next corner, except this time, the impact was greater on the cab than he figured and his head took a blow from the wheel, nothing damaging but it smarted, and the Chevy slipped away again and up ahead was another cross street and Eric could see the move the Chevy wanted to make, a sharp left turn, but the wheels didn't dig deep enough, the traction was not there and the Chevy skidded sideways up the avenue and beyond it was a construction site, a large permanent house trailer serving as its office, and Eric gunned the cab now, jammed his foot all the way down and the cab leapt forward and the two cars locked and spun and smashed full tilt into the dark trailer and Eric had initiated the move, he had the power and the momentum, but as they spun, he also took the brunt of the hit and this time his forehead hit the windshield and he knew he was cut as blood splashed down into his right eye and Billy Boy was able to get out of his car first, and he fired, and Eric thought "he must be panicked, what a shitty shot, he didn't even hit a window" and then he realized Billy Boy wasn't trying for a window but his gas tank instead, and Eric fumbled for the fucking door handle, got it, jammed it forward as he caught a glimpse of flame and he rolled out of the car onto the street as Billy Boy fired again and the cab began to blaze. Eric kept moving the hell away because an explosion was going to come and he made good time, was safe enough when the explosion came, and it blew the night apart, but what Eric was thinking at the time was that his right leg hurt like hell and as he looked at it he saw it should hurt like hell, he'd been shot in the thigh, God knew how bad.

Up ahead now, Billy Boy ran into the side street.

The flames from the cab burned into the night behind him as Eric began to move. There were screams from passersby but he ignored them, glancing back only once.

But he wished he hadn't—far across the street but coming his way were The Fruits.

Eric tried to get his brain going as he limped along. Billy Boy was running up ahead still, and that had been two more bullets gone, the one into the gas tank, the other into his leg—

—five down and one to go.

So now it was a three-way chase, he had to get to Billy Boy before The Fruits got to him, so Eric told himself to forget about his leg, he had all day tomorrow to cry like a baby, *just forget the fucking thing and run*—

—his pace picked up.

Billy Boy wasn't that far ahead, visible through the snow.

But The Fruits weren't all that far behind.

And for a moment it all seemed to Eric like that great cartoon where the two mice in the maze are talking and one says to the other, "Do you ever get the feeling this is all part of some crazy experiment?" and was he that too?—was there some person in what to him was the future who was controlling him and Billy Boy ahead and The Fruits behind and was it all to be like that poor poet and the Russian, fighting forever through time?

Billy Boy was running faster now. Eric sometimes lost sight of him when the snow was too thick.

And then it came to Eric where he was; this was the street in the Bloomingdale's area where it all began, where Frank had found that poor Oliver woman with the broken neck and the unused ticket to *A Chorus Line.*

Eric glanced back—The Fruits were still there but no closer. Now he looked forward—and Billy Boy was gone again, but this time Eric didn't bother to sweat it, he knew where he was, he was back in that dark area between the buildings where he'd mugged Sophie the queen of the shoplifters and killed Oliver. Billy Boy did that—returned to places—he was in front of the oversize-men's clothing store and he was up ahead in the darkness now—

—with his one shot left.

Ordinarily the catbird seat, but this was no ordinarily he'd encountered before—not with the two behind him coming closer. Maybe he could handle them, maybe he could handle them *and* Billy Boy, but he was shot and bleeding and not at his best, and if he was going to get to Billy Boy before The Fruits got to him, he was going to have to make Billy Boy come out—

—Eric slowed. The dark area with the stairs leading down was just ahead now—

—and Billy Boy would only come out when he thought he was safe and he would only know he was safe when Eric was dead—

—Eric moved forward into the area just in front of where the giant waited—

—with one shot left—

—not bad odds—one shot and not much light and heavy snow —he had run worse risks before and he was still here, wasn't he?—

—then just to make himself irresistible, Eric faked as if he were looking around confused.

Then he turned his back on Billy Boy.

And waited for the shot.

The barrage that followed kicked him forward into the street, and for a moment the surprise of the number of times he was hit held off the pain the wounds brought with them.

But only for a moment. The pain had him totally then.

Eric closed his eyes and could not not think about dying . . .

He knew his luck was good when he remembered the street and he knew it was better than good when he forced his way back to the dark stairs and waited with his guns ready. If it all went great the cop would come by and maybe slow down enough for a shot.

Billy Boy waited.

Here came the nightmare.

Billy Boy raised his guns.

The nightmare slowed and he was about to fire when it got

better—the guy stopped. Stopped just there in front of him.

Then it got great—the guy turned his back.

And stood there. *And stood there.*

As he fired he remembered all of a sudden some of the great times he'd known, his first fuck, no, not really his first but the first time the girl wanted to, and the first big fight, the one that made him know he was stronger than anybody or anything—

—but they felt nothing like this felt.

The cop was like he'd been jerked by a wire—forward and down and over. Billy Boy didn't know for sure how many bullets hit but he figured most, he was a great shot and he was lucky again.

He took a step forward, then another to the very top of the stairs, looked ahead at his enemy, the blood coming nice and free down his back. Then he looked left and right—

—and shit, here they were coming, the boys in blue, and probably they had guns again and if they didn't then they had that thing that stopped him before because they wouldn't come this far without some kind of protection, so they must have been good and armed—

—and he had nothing, just his fist, and what he wanted was a gun—

—the cop had a gun. What a great thing to have and to keep —Billy Boy liked to travel light, souvenirs were shit, but not this one, this one he'd keep and remember and he moved out to the sidewalk and it wasn't till he took a step into the street that he realized that the dead were coming after him, his nightmare was rising in the darkness . . .

Eric wasn't sure which was harder, pushing himself up with his left hand or raising his gun with his right. Both. Both. Nothing was easy.

And there was no time. He could feel his left hand start to give so he slipped back to his elbow, letting that support him.

Now his gun was becoming too much of a burden. No time. No time. Everything going so fast, but no time. He commanded his index finger to obey him and he hoped his aim was near to true.

Then he tried his very best to blow Billy Boy's eyes out . . .

The Fruits didn't know what the hell to do. There were sirens all around them and it was always hard to tell, but they sure sounded like they were coming closer. Across, in the street, they could see the cop breathing, or it looked like he was breathing.

The giant was not.

He lay sprawled and blind and he wasn't about to do any living anymore. "What now?" the first Fruit said.

"Don't know."

"That working?" He indicated the walkie-talkie.

"I think."

"Give it another whack."

They knelt by the dead one, the siren sound building, trying to get the walkie-talkie going. It seemed to be fine. But if it was, where the hell was Trude . . . ?

Trude had been in a hurry when he left the hospital. He was angry at the slowness of the elevator that brought him down, angry at the wildness of the night. He stepped onto the sidewalk, slipped, and that didn't make him any happier.

Then, of all things, a bag lady blocked him. She stood small and old on the sidewalk, staring at his face. He brushed by her, was several steps past when the most amazing thing happened: she said his name.

"Doctor Trude?"

He stopped, turned, went back. Yes, he was, within limited circles, famous, but not *this* famous. In the scientific community, he was not unknown, but *a bag lady*? Could he have misheard? No. She said it again.

"Doctor Trude?"

He peered at her closely. "Yes?"

"My name is Sally Levinson, I was a friend of Edith Mazursky."

"I have no time—" Trude said sharply, and began to turn.

Sally stood there, more than anything else, bewildered—she had no idea, really, if her father's pistol would actually work but when she tried it now it must have, considering the way Trude crumpled to the snow. Sally stood over him a moment till she was sure, then she hailed a cab to take her to the police station for her sins—the cab was off duty but fifty from Sally and he had a change of heart and she was about to say "the police" to his "Where to, lady?"—

—except she felt simply too wonderful to consider such a destination, so she told him first the East River where she got out and
deposited her father's years-old weapon into the waters, and after
that she headed for the Four Seasons wondering whether she
should have the Taittinger or the Dom Pérignon for this most
glorious of glorious celebrations . . .

Eric could hear the sirens. They were loud so they were close.
He could tell that much.

He could see The Fruits lingering by the giant. Obviously Billy
Boy was dead, you could see it in their eyes. Eric could tell that
much too.

What he could not tell was how much longer he could hold out.
Now there were flashing lights starting to become visible at the
corner, maybe an ambulance, maybe police, maybe fire, none of
them bad news. Not if they hurried. The street was ice but his
wounds were burning and it was not a pleasant place, waiting
between those two extremes. But waiting was all he was capable
of doing . . .

A woman with reddish hair and just the kindest face ap-
proached him from the direction of Bloomingdale's and said,
"You're the young man who was talking with my husband about
'The Blues,' would you like to see them?"

"Oh I would," Eric told her. "I would, very much."

"They're just over here, come along now," and she took him to
where the seven portraits hung. "The two old people are my
parents, the young ones are my children, Phillip and Sally I think
you know, do you like them?"

Eric began to cry. "I do," he managed. "They're so sad."

She smiled then a marvelous smile. Eric would never forget it.
In the days and months ahead, after his wounds had healed, after
his endless hours of rehabilitation had made him Eric again, he
saw that smile and heard her voice. "I'm so glad you feel that
way," she said, "it's what I think sometimes everything's all
about. People you love and sadness."

"Of course," Eric nodded. "People you love and sadness." He
put his tears away, tried a smile. "What else is there . . . ?"